Praise For Roland Cheek's -
"The Phantom Ghost of Harriet Lou"

"Not just a hunting book, this collection of accounts, gleaned from the author's love affair with the elk, is also a family-oriented book; an elk hunter's basic manual but also one of the most entertaining books on the market today."

Brookville (OH) St...

"Few write _____ _ job in expl _____ lso providing _____ ."

C...

"Roland Cheek probably has forgotten more about elk hunting than many of us ever will know. But what the veteran outfitter, guide and outdoor writer remembers and packs into his new book makes it worthwhile for anybody who pursues the elk."

Great Falls Tribune

"In reality, the *Phantom Ghost* is a blueprint for how someone becomes an outdoors expert."

Explore! Magazine

"*The Phantom Ghost of Harriet Lou* is the book for those who want to understand everything from ... grazers and carnivores to mosquitoes and hop toads, but most especially, about the wapiti."

Midwest Book Review

"A heartwarming tale of interaction between the hunter and the hunted."

Independent Record/Helena

"To simply say that Roland Cheek's new book, *The Phantom Ghost of Harriet Lou*, is a deeper read than one expects to find in a work about animals is an understatement."

The Shelby Promoter

"As in his book, *Learning To Talk Bear*, this new book, *The Phantom Ghost of Harriet Lou*, is as much about the human/animal relationship as it is about the animal itself. It is the intangibles of elk hunting that set this book apart from other hunting stories."

Rural Montana

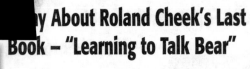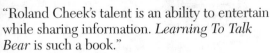

"Roland Cheek's talent is an ability to entertain while sharing information. *Learning To Talk Bear* is such a book."

Beverly Magley, Editor
Montana Magazine

"Provides a treasure trove of information for any wishing to understand the nature and science of the grizzly bear. . ."

The Midwest Book Review

"New book paints perfect picture of grizzlies."

Billings Gazette/Montana

"Cheek is at his best when he's describing bears in action, and at his best he's excellent."

News Tribune/Tacoma, WA

"A major literary contribution in an effort to save the magnificent grizzly."

Marin Independent Journal
San Rafael, CA

"[Roland Cheek] is a born storyteller."

The Register Herald/Eaton, OH

"A compelling read."

Morning Call/Allentown, PA

"...combines research, suspense and good story-telling to help the reader understand Grizzly behavior. It reminded me of two other books, John McPhee's *Coming Into The Country* about Alaska, and Sebastian Junger's *The Perfect Storm*."

Franklin Marchman
(*amazon.com review*)

The Phantom Ghost of Harriet Lou

and Other Elk Stories

The Phantom Ghost of Harriet Lou

and Other Elk Stories

ROLAND CHEEK

A Skyline Publishing Book

Cover design by Laura Donovan
Text design and formatting by Michael Dougherty
Typesetting by Type & Graphics, Bozeman, Montana

Publisher's Cataloging in Publication
        (Prepared by Quality Books Inc.)

Cheek, Roland.
        Phantom Ghost of Harriet Lou : and other elk stories / Roland Cheek. —
1st ed.
        p. cm.
        Preassigned LCCN: 96-71778
        ISBN 0-918981-04-2

        1. Elk. 2. Elk—Anecdotes. 3. Hunting—Anecdotes   I. Title.

QL737.U55C44 1998   599.65'7
                                        QBI98-294

Published by   Skyline Publishing
                    P.O. Box 1118
                    Columbia Falls, Montana 59912

Printed in Canada

TABLE OF CONTENTS

Marc

Cheri

Dedication

It's probable, as a parent, I shall never
again derive such pleasure as in dedicating
this book to our children, Cheri and Marc.
One gives never-failing encouragement.
Without the other, there is no story.

"What is man without the beasts? If all the beasts were gone, men would die from great loneliness of spirit, for whatever happens to the beasts also happens to man. All things are connected.

-Chief Seattle of the Dunwamish Tribe

Acknowledgment

This book is about life amid distant mountains. And it's about the creatures luring me there. Experiences related within these pages happened—make no mistake about that—mostly in the manner related. Though names have sometimes been changed out of respect for privacy, the stories are of real people doing real-people things, and real elk doing real-elk things.

In some cases, circumstances and people have appeared in previous stuff—the story's thread is woven from a large body of my work. For example, bits and pieces of this book, sometimes in different form, have appeared in Outdoor Life, Field & Stream, Sports Afield, Petersen's Hunting, North American Hunter, Game Country, and Montana Magazine. Other bits and pieces first appeared in some of my 900-plus syndicated "Wild Trails and Tall Tales" newspaper columns, produced since 1982.

In addition, the rights to three of these chapters (The Lesson of Avalanche Elk, Trail to Stockade Ridge, and Signals From Telegraph Hill) belong to Petersen's Hunting. I'm grateful to Petersen's for permission to include them here.

I'm grateful, too, to Mark and Janis Moss, who provided access to the setting (along a wilderness river) where my wife and I pulled together the pieces to this book, organizing them in pretty much the manner you'll see.

And let's not forget the biologists—wild creatures need them. So do we. Gary Olson, Montana Department of Fish, Wildlife & Parks, shared both opinion and research. So did Harvey Nyberg, Region I MDFWP Wildlife Manager. Dan Carney, biologist for the Blackfeet, is a man to count on for important info devoid of hyperbole or error. Craig Ely, Oregon's Northeast Region Assistant Wildlife

Supervisor, held nothing back in sharing information. Neither did Larry Green, Glenwood Springs, Colorado Division of Wildlife Manager.

Scott Stouder, Corvallis, Oregon journalist, shared his special Beaver State insights.

And last, this: The writing is mine. Jane and I accept the risk of publishing and burden of promoting to success. But the real story of this book's quality (and the one preceding) lies in the superb team we've gathered to assist in its production: Laura Donovan, cover design; Bob Elman, editor; Michael Dougherty, page design and layout. ∎

Chapter 1

Echoes From the Wrong Gun

Even over the clack of the ancient printer, the door's slam vibrated through the house. I shifted so I could see as the boy skipped through the living room. He saw me and slowed. "Hi, grandpa!"

"Uh-huh. Howdy, boy. You animated over anything special?"

A broad grin swallowed the freckled face of the twelve-year-old, so I added, "Careful your ears don't topple in."

"See!" he said, shoving a paper forward.

"What is it?" I asked, knowing all along what it was.

"Read it, why don't you?"

I smoothed the paper against a window pane and pretended to pore over it. "Hmm. This says you're trained to handle a gun without shooting yourself or somebody else. And it says you can go hunting if some old duffer tramps along."

"Will you?"

"This is just April," I said. "It's still several months until hunting season."

"But will you? Will you take me with you when it comes?"

I handed the boy his Hunter Safety Certificate while settling into my swivel chair. His eyes drifted to the big mule deer head hanging above the clacking printer, then returned. "You will, won't you?"

I stroked my chin, making as if it was a big decision. The boy's lips pursed; he frowned. "Grandpa?"

I'd been funning him long enough, so I nodded and said, "Yep." He near exploded. But an awakening maturity kept him from climbing into my lap like he would have done a few months before.

"Will I get one like that?" he asked, looking up at the huge elk rack dominating the inside office wall.

"Search me."

"But you know how to hunt elk." He started to lay a hand on my arm, but brought it up short. "You'll teach me how to get one like that, won't you, grandpa?"

"Likely not."

"Why not?" He waved his Certificate. "What good is this if you won't teach me how to hunt?"

"Because there's only so much I can teach you. The rest you'll have to learn for yourself. Odds are, a good bull like that comes only after you pay your dues by learning some on your own."

He frowned. I reached for his Hunter Safety Certificate. "All this says is you're ready to begin hunting. This paper opens a door. Same way with a hunting license. A hunting license says you can go hunting—that's all. Neither one of 'em says you'll get anything except the chance to hunt."

"You could teach me how to shoot an elk like that if you wanted, though. You was a guide. You used to take people hunting all the time."

"And I just said I'll take you. But taking somebody elk hunting and teaching him how to elk hunt are two different things. Teaching how takes time, luck, and an interest from the guy wanting to learn."

The boy glanced again at the trophy wall and nodded. "I'll learn. I'll learn everything I need to know if you'll show me."

"No," I murmured. "Nothing's wrong. On the contrary, everything is right."

I expected it, so was watching when Lars, leading our cavalcade, jerked off his hat, turned face to the sun and shouted, "YIPPEEEE!" The boy twisted in his saddle to stare back my way, eyes wide. I grinned and spurred my saddlehorse alongside the normally taciturn man who'd just shouted.

Lars acknowledged my presence with a wide grin and contented sigh. A late afternoon sun threw long shadows from scattered copses of pine and spruce in the valley below. A meandering stream glistened in the distance. We were surrounded by mountains thrusting toward a cerulean sky, toothy peaks jutting bare and gray and sharp above a green forested blanket. I swept the view as always, then eyed my old friend.

He sighed again and started to say something. Just then the boy pushed his horse between us and asked, "What's the matter? Is something wrong?" And the spell was broken.

"No," I murmured. "Nothing's wrong. On the contrary, everything is right."

The boy considered that before shaking his head. "I don't know what you mean."

"You will," Lars said. "Before this trip is over—you will." And the rancher clucked to his saddlehorse, leading his packstring winding down the mountain.

The boy thumped heels to his pony's flanks, following Lars. I brought up the rear with my packponies. It was late when we reached our old camping place. Because it was unseasonably warm, we chose not to set up a tent that first night. Lars and I unpacked and pulled saddles from horses, the boy carried enough wood for a bonfire. While I started supper, the others grained our stock, then belled and hobbled them before turning 'em out to graze.

Lars and I ate in companionable silence, but the boy drooped over his plate. When we finished, I said, "The cook don't do dishes in this camp."

The boy took a hurried bite. Then Lars said, "That's

right. So I'll do 'em tonight and the lad can wash breakfast dishes."

The boy nodded, took another bite, laid his plate of half-eaten food on the ground and drifted to his sleeping bag.

"He's got the makings of a good one," my friend observed as he rinsed a plate. "Give him a few years and he'll be bringing us back here on his off days."

I tossed another limb on the fire. "Being young would be more fun if a body never had so damn much to learn."

As soon as the lantern flared, Lars sat up, shaking frost from his sleeping-bag flap. "God, you always did ruin things—far back as I can remember."

"Get up, you lounge lizard," I growled, poking through the fire's embers and throwing on starter wood. "There's horses to catch, hogs to slop, and elk to slay, and the sun'll be up in an hour or two."

He eyed the stars above. "I believe I'll just wait for it. Besides, unless you and me chucked our rule, there's only one elk to slay and the slayer don't look all that eager to me."

Just inside the lantern's glow, the boy's sleeping bag resembled a cocoon. So far he hadn't wriggled.

"Can you hear that elk bugle?" I said.

The cocoon erupted and the boy's tousled head popped out.

We took a trail up a timbered ridge, tying our horses to saplings halfway to where the hogback bumped against the main mountain crest. Lars dropped off one side while the boy and I hunted down the other toward a spruce bottom. For the umpteenth time, I ran the boy through the mechanics of handling my old lever-action Marlin. He soon made it plain that he'd rather learn how to hunt elk, so I began passing him information about our surroundings:

"This is false huckleberry we're working through. Some folks call it elk brush. It's noisy enough anytime, but especially during dry weather like this. Elk like to lay up in it because they can hear things moving their way. And Lord knows, we're making so much noise they can hear us out on the plains. Pick up your feet, boy."

His face flushed.

"Look now," I told him, "what you don't do is jam your feet down like an elephant stomping egg shells, but kind of set 'em gentle-like and feel what's beneath before you shift your weight on it. If your foot is on something that'll roll, break, or pop, move it someplace else.

The boy's head bobbed like a yo-yo at everything I said, even though he couldn't be retaining it all. Still, in time it would sink in through repetition, if not through common sense.

I pointed. "Look at that elk track. Notice how the dirt was kicked up from the wet spot and hasn't dried out yet. Made last night. Probably within the hour."

He squatted to poke the track with a finger. "Was it a big one? Did it have big horns?"

"Can't tell. At least I can't tell a bull from a cow track—though there's some as would tell you they can."

He frowned—even while his head bobbed. So I added, "There are ways to read whether it's a bull or cow, and maybe we can find some of 'em."

Farther along the narrow game trail, I stopped and pointed to a fresh-looking track. "How long ago you reckon it's been since an elk stepped there?"

The boy stooped and brushed some small plants aside. He studied the track for a couple of minutes before he said, "This morning?"

"Why do you say that?"

"I ... I don't know. The track is damp?"

I thrust my rifle's muzzle against the plants he'd brushed aside. "You've got to learn to see what you're look-ing at, boy. There was a cobweb strung on the ground cover you pushed away. Look sharp and you can still see pieces of it hanging. A spider didn't have time to spin it this morning and he don't work nights. That means yesterday. He built that web yesterday—sometime after an elk stuck his foot there."

The boy studied the track for a long time before asking, "Why does it look damp."

"A seep. There's springs all over this hillside. That's another reason elk like to bed here—there's lots of water."

A short distance farther, I pointed to a track and asked, "Bull or cow?"

The boy looked at it, then at me, puzzled. "Can you tell?"

"Uh-huh. Like I said, you've got to learn to see what you're looking at." I pointed ahead. "See where those tracks lead? That elk ducked under those low hanging limbs. You reckon a bull would do that? With his antlers?"

It was in a tall-grass meadow that we ate our lunch. We sat like lizards in the sun, leaning against a fallen tree, hats and daypacks dangling from broken limbs. I'd just settled back for a short snooze when the boy said, "Grandpa?"

"Mmmm."

"Why did Mr. Glickman yell up there at the top of the pass like he did?"

"'Cause he felt like it."

"But why'd he feel like it?"

"I don't know, son. Has something to do with a man working too hard, keeping his nose to the grindstone, meeting mortgage payments, worrying about beef prices in Omaha or Chicago, grasshoppers in the oat crop, and Lord knows what else. Then once each year he bunches all that for a week or two and trots off with friends into the middle of the prettiest country God ever made. He just naturally has to let the tickle out somewhere. That pass happens to be Lars' 'somewhere.' He's whooped it up at that spot every year since he first came in as a guide for me thirty years ago."

"What did he mean when he said I'll know everything is right before this trip is over?"

"I believe I'll wait and see if you can come up with the answer to that on your own. Besides, I need a little nap."

It was mid-afternoon by the time the boy and I returned to our ponies. Lars' horse was gone, but our tent was up and a decent supply of wood cut and stacked when we rode into camp. "You hunt any today?" I asked.

"Not much. Too dry. Too hot this afternoon. Too much work to be done at camp. Besides, you guys are the ones shooting elk and I thought I'd be a camp-tender so's the lad can hunt more."

Later, as I flipped steaks, I heard the boy ask Lars, "Mr. Glickman ... "

"Lars."

"Mr. Lars, did you say you aren't going to shoot an elk?"

"It's not important to me."

"Are you hunting deer, then?"

The rancher leaned back against a tree, fingers laced behind his head. "No, not deer—that's for certain sure."

"Well, what are you hunting?"

"Same thing as your grandpa."

"He's hunting elk, same as me."

"You sure?"

"Uh-huh. I was with him today and that's what we was hunting."

Lars crossed his legs. "That's what you hunted. I think he hunted hunting."

"Huh?"

"Look lad, your grandpa and me don't care if we shoot another elk. Or deer, for that matter. We both figure we got our share. Maybe we'll never shoot another one, and maybe we will. But it damn sure isn't important. Not near so much as for you to get your first one. What we're hunting is hunting—just being here in the fall, pounding our chests on frosty mornings, watching needles fall from the tamaracks. That's what's important to us."

"But if you get a chance at a really big one, you'd shoot him, wouldn't you?"

Lars' gazed at the meadow, struggling for the right words. I watched the man, but spoke to the boy. "Maybe neither of us knows for sure about that until the time comes."

The next day the boy and I hit for the heavy timber. Frosty mornings and hot sunshiny days makes hunting pleasant but shooting miserable. Elk were scattered, but plenty of sign told us they were there. We started out in the morning bundled in wool coats and by early afternoon, skinned down to T-shirts. To top that, wind currents drifted first one way, then another, swirling so much it was near impossible to have a breeze in our favor. Far as I could tell, we never got close enough to animals to even hear one chase off. I finally gave up and left the lad at a good game-trail crossing, telling him, "You stay here and I'll make a big sashay around and see if I can spook something your way. Okay?"

He nodded, looking about sort of wide-eyed—his first time alone in these big woods.

I was gone an hour and a half, returning to slip up on the youngster. He was alert, standing under a gnarled white-bark pine, staring first one way, then another. It gave him a start when I popped from behind a tree. Before I could ask if he'd seen anything, he blurted, "There was somebody up here on a horse. And they had a dog with them."

"A man on a horse? And a dog? You see 'em?"

He shook his head. "But I heard the horse. I could hear him walking and kicking rocks—especially when they left. And the dog barked. He was close the first time."

"Oh yeah? Just one bark at a time? And did he circle you?"

"No, he went away in that direction. One bark each time, but several times."

"Each time? Like this?" I imitated a cow elk barking in alarm.

"Uh-huh."

"Let's amble over and see if we can find their tracks. What you heard was a cow barking a warning. The hooves clattering on rocks were the rest of 'em getting away as fast as they could. You were close to elk, boy."

Again, Lars was in camp when we returned. The boy told him about the cow barking and how he thought it was a dog. The rancher said, "I'll bet you're a whole lot smarter now, aren't you?"

"Yep. Grandpa said I should have ran after them and hoped to see the rest before they knew why the cow was barking. Is that right?"

Lars chuckled. "You listen to him, lad. Your grandpa knows a bunch about elk hunting."

"Yes, sir, I know he does. But could I go hunting with you someday?"

"Sure. He needs a rest anyway. Why don't we do it tomorrow?"

"Oh boy! We'll shoot us an elk, won't we?"

"We'll try."

The boy crawled into bed with the rise of the evening star. Lars and I sat up sipping bourbon and branch. "We need a good tracking snow to pick up the hunting," he observed.

"I don't see any change coming, do you?"

The rancher shook his head. "Be a damn shame if the lad's first big hunt, he goes home skunked."

"Life," I replied.

"Still be a shame."

> "We need a good tracking snow to pick up the hunting"

The days followed, each one like those previous, without a single cloud to break the monotonous blue of the sky. Elk hunting remained the same—never seeing, seldom hearing. It was discouraging. The boy's spirits drooped like a rooster's in a rainstorm, but he struggled gamely to turn a boy's disappointment into a man's resignation. Despite his best efforts, it looked like he was losing the battle, growing listless and inattentive to my coaching and his hunting.

With only tomorrow's hunt left, he asked me if it would be all right for him to go with Lars one more time.

"Yeah, if it's okay with Lars."

"You should hunt with your grandpa," Lars said when the boy put the question to him that evening. "Tomorrow's our last day in the valley. You should hunt with him on the last day."

"But I'd rather ..." The boy fell silent.

Lars looked at me and I nodded. "Okay," the rancher said, "we'll get him tomorrow."

Sometimes wishes turns real. The change came at last and we awakened to two inches of powder snow. Lars came chortling back into the tent with an armload of wood. "Now we'll get 'em, by golly! C'mon, laddie. Get up. This is the day!"

My watch read 10:17 when the rifle shot shattered the silence. I was outside the tent for an armload of firewood. The sound was muffled and it echoed, but I could tell it came from a nearby canyon. So I made it a point to be outside a couple of hours later, about the time successful hunters would return. They came across the flats, Lars with his swinging ground-eating stride and the boy at a trot just to keep up. I could tell even at a distance that the boy was swelled a bunch and trying to swagger. He hurried to the camp ahead of the man. "We got him! We got him, grandpa! A big one! A six point!"

"Hey! All right!"

He slapped my palms while grinning a Grand Canyon smile, then held his hands out for me to do likewise.

I said to Lars, "The horses are just below Telegraph Hill. I'd have brought them in, but I wasn't sure. One shot only—that's good shooting."

Lars shook his head. "A cup of coffee, then me and the lad will bring the bull in."

I poured coffee for both of us. "Well, tell me the story." The boy looked at Lars, but the rancher merely said, "Later." He swilled down his coffee, then he and the boy hiked away for their horses.

When they returned with the stock and began saddling, I said, "I'll go with you."

"No need," Lars replied. "He's in a good spot and he's already skinned and quartered."

"It's okay, grandpa," the boy added. "I'll help."

They were back in short order—a little over an hour and a half. The bull was a dandy six point—wide spread, heavy and long beams, strong and even points.

"You boys done yourselves well," I said, clapping the boy on the shoulder.

The boy grinned up at me and said, "Thanks for taking me hunting, grandpa."

I ruffled his hair and helped Lars lift down the heavy packs.

Later, with supper cooking and Lars still fiddling with our stock, I said to the boy, "Tell me about it."

He sat cross-legged on his sleeping bag, sipping Kool-Aid. "I can't."

"What's that? You can't?"

He shook his head. "No. Mr. Lars wants to tell you and I promised I'd let him."

I flipped him my most intimidating glare, but the boy's eyes were wide and guileless, and met mine in all innocence.

Finally, supper over, dishes washed, a tired boy fast asleep, and bourbon and branch in hand, Lars settled onto a block of wood while I sprawled on my sleeping bag. He stared into his cup for the longest time as the lantern hissed and the fire in our wood stove spit and popped. "We cut their tracks just across the creek," he began at last. "Two of 'em. Both big tracks. They headed for the low ridge between Jack Creek and here. Saw where one pissed between his tracks, so we knew he was a bull."

"Then both of them were bulls," I cut in. "Bulls don't run with cows this time of year—not this long after the rut."

"Exactly. Anyway, we followed them cautious, figuring they laid up on the ridge to watch their back trail. Wind was right—blowing in our face—and with the snow, everything was quiet. The boy was doing real well, going easy and ready for quick shooting." The rancher's gaze drifted into someplace only he could see. "Damn!" he spat. "I just knew we'd jump one of them bulls and he'd get his shot."

He paused for a long while. The lantern ran low, flaring and waning, flaring and waning, pulsing a wierd light through the tent. "And?"

"We jumped one, all right. He crashed out ahead of us

and we never got to see him." The alternating light bounced from the tent walls.

"What happened to the other one?"

"Never did know. We didn't stop to find where he went because the first one headed around the hill, right for the burn. Well, I knew he'd bust out in the open, so I told the boy to hurry and we'd at least get a shot ..."

The lantern died. Darkness settled on us, broken only by a flickering light from a crack in the stove door that danced upon my friend's face.

"Well, we hurried. But it's farther around than I remembered. And the boy's legs aren't as long as mine." He snaked the coffee pot from the stove, poured a cup, and offered it to me.

> **I was pinned, afraid to move. But where was the boy?**

"And?"

"I got ahead of the lad—waited for him to catch up several times—Lord, he was giving it all he had ..."

He paused, listening to a great horned owl hooting in the distance. It was answered by another, nearer.

"I knew if we didn't move faster, we wouldn't get a look at the bull, and I guess I just got caught up in the chase and kept inching ahead. Anyway, I broke out into a little opening, just before the old burn begins, and ..."

The fire snapped and the lantern hissed on with its lightless pressure. He poured a dash of whiskey into his cup, then stared deep into it as firelight from the stove's crack wavered.

"... there was this big bull pointed my way, not sixty yards off, staring behind—away from me—toward a screen of small firs growing between him and the big open. Branches still shook on them firs, too. See? The bull we chased had just run through. The snow was knocked off 'em and I could see his tracks clear across the little opening. They passed only a few yards from where this big guy was feeding.

"Well, I skidded to a stop. But, hell, I was a good ten feet out in the opening by then and no way to get back without spooking the new bull."

I held up a hand. "Tell me again how it was you got out there in the first place without him seeing you."

Lars shrugged. "I couldn't have done it without he stared after the other bull. By rights, the new bull should have run when the other one passed. But instead, about the time I skidded to a stop, he turned back and went to feeding, facing me."

I reached over and took the whiskey bottle.

"So I was pinned, afraid to move. But where was the boy? I twisted my head so as to see if the lad was close, and the bull caught the motion and stared at me. But he still didn't run."

I laid the empty bottle between us.

"The boy was panting hard a hundred yards away, still in the spruce timber, staring my way. He couldn't see the bull because of the way the ground rolled, and the elk couldn't see him either. I couldn't wave or make any motion without spooking the damned elk. And it wouldn't do any good if I could, because the lad just couldn't give it any more than he already was." The man paused, reliving the scene.

"The boy started my way again, and by gee, the bull put his head down and commenced feeding one more time! Well, I near crapped my pants. Would the boy make it? Seventy yards. Sixty. Fifty. He stopped and leaned against a tree, eyes still only on me. The bull stared at me off and on—he knew something was wrong, but he didn't know what. Forty more yards before the boy got to the clearing's edge. Thirty—close enough I could see sweat trickling down his face.

"Then a sixth sense? The bull turned and started walking toward the screen of trees. Oh no! I thought. The boy won't make it!" Lars paused and sipped from his cup, staring at the stove crack.

"And?"

"Of a sudden a gun boomed and the bull went down."

"What!" I roared, sitting bolt-upright. "Somebody else shot his elk? There's nobody in the country but us!"

The boy stirred in his sleep and Lars peered my way in the shadowy darkness. "It was my gun. I shot the bull. I killed him out from under the kid."

Light from the stove crack played upon one side of his head just enough to tell the face twisted in anguish. One of the owls hooted again, then only the fire's occasional popping cut the stillness of the night.

"Don't you see? He wasn't going to be in time. Wouldn't be in time to even see the bull. His first hunt—skunked. Not even to see an elk! He deserved better than that. He worked hard enough to earn more than that. He's a good kid. I ... I had to shoot it." ∎

Our son Marc at 12. His first elk hunt, with my last elk

Chapter 2

The Tuff & Tandy Show

You ever go after elk," the man said, "you'll never look at hunting the same way again."

Tuff Manning was a big, rawboned man, a logger. By all accounts he was a good one, too, felling the giant Douglas firs that blanketed the southwestern Oregon mountains of my youth. At twenty-eight, Manning was ten years my senior, in the prime of his strength and maturity. Bragging was Tuff's stock-in-trade. More often than not, the man backed up brag with deed.

The four-point buck I'd just carried to the road was on the smallish side, but considering that Columbian blacktail are a smaller breed than Oregon's sagebrush mulies, respectable enough. Truth was I was proud. That's why I didn't immediately drop the buck upon hearing the approaching vehicle; instead, I just stood alongside the road, Marlin 30-30 in hand and buck across my shoulders as Manning rolled his International "crummy" to a stop, swung open the door, and propped a booted foot against it. From his staged-off, suspendered trousers and the dusty fatigue on his face, I knew he was on his way home from work. "Be good eatin'," he said, fumbling for a thermos and coffee cup.

"Yeah, I guess."

"Your first?"

I dropped the buck. "This year, yeah. I'm only allowed one."

He cackled. "And you waited 'til the last day of deer season to get him?"

"What difference does that make?"

That's when Tuff brought up elk hunting. I was aware that the season was to open the following weekend, but it was nothing to me. I'd never hunted elk, knew nothing about hunting elk, didn't even know how to *find* elk. "You wanna go elk hunting?" the big man asked.

"Sure."

"Then be at my house at five Saturday morning." He slammed the door and jammed the "crummy" into gear.

Just like that. I'm going elk hunting.

It was raining Saturday morning, as it had all the previous day, and for three days before that. I sat squeezed between what I considered a beginning elk hunter's dream-team, as Tuff Manning went through the gears of his battered World War II U.S. Army Jeep and Al Tandy peered out the side window into the dark. The Jeep clawed its way up and down winding forest roads, deeper and deeper into mountain country where elk must roam.

Just like that, I'm going elk hunting.

There was no heater in the rusting and drafty sheet-metal cab, but our close-packed, wool-clothed bodies generated enough heat that Tuff or Al constantly wiped fog from inside the windshield while the single driver's-side wiper fought a losing battle with rain on the outside.

"What was that?" Tandy shouted above the Jeep's whine, waking me from a fitful slumber.

"Goddammit," the driver snarled. "How could I miss that?"

Daylight had not yet snuck up from the east and I wondered what they'd seen. As Al climbed from the Jeep, I tumbled after. While he paced back and forth, pondering over animal prints in the roadway, Tuff backed the rig so its headlights played on deep-cloven elk tracks leading up a bank and into the forest.

"What do you think?" Tuff asked as he joined us.

Al said nothing. He trudged back the way the elk came, pushing into dripping roadside ferns, then switching on a flashlight, wallowed for a hundred yards or more. When he rejoined us, he said, "He's alone. Probably a bull. We might get into something better."

Manning turned back to his Jeep. I started to climb in, but Tandy said, "Not yet. Come help me here." And he began pacing up and down beside the elk tracks, obliterating occasional ones. Meanwhile, Manning see-sawed the Jeep back and forth over the tracks.

"I don't understand."

Tandy grinned. "Making it look like these tracks have already been checked out by lots of hunters. That way nobody else'll bother with 'em. If we don't find something better farther down the road, we'll come back here to try for this old bastard."

So I marched back and forth in tandem with Tandy.

Good daylight was just spreading when we found tracks of an entire herd crossing the muddy forest road. Even I couldn't miss the churned ground where they'd bounded up a nearby bank. There was no question this was what we sought. Tuff guided his Jeep off the road and we all piled out. The tracks were still clear and clean as a fresh-plucked peach, amid the pounding rain.

My two companions conferred in whispers. Apparently they figured we'd interrupted the crossing and several elk probably still milled out of sight in the forest to the south, waiting until the coast was clear to brave the road. Tuff followed the elk's backtrail, while Al motioned for me to tuck in behind the herd's path while he made a big, half-circle sweep to try heading them.

I really wanted to impress these men, so I took extra-special care to step on no branches, kick no stones. In the pounding rain, my muffled passage made little sense, and I later discovered it made even less sense to pussyfoot when a herd is hurrying from hunters they already knew were there. Of course, Al Tandy and Tuff Manning knew a lot of things it took me many more years to learn. And they'd planted me where I'd do them the most good.

Me? I only knew that in order to hunt again with these hunter's hunters, I must carry out my assigned task to perfection. Besides, I might just sneak up on the herd bull and ...

Ka-Boom!

The gun's roar startled me. What startled me more was how the forest just ahead erupted in thrashing and crashing as unseen bodies hurtled through the underbrush.

Believing the correct thing to do was to continue my patient stalk, I was more alert than ever, puzzling out the nuances of every track, making not a sound slipping from tree to tree like a Mohican. A half-hour passed. The forest opened, offering perhaps seventy-five yards of visibility. I didn't see him until he spoke.

"You're wasting your time," Al said from behind a fallen tree. "The elk left here a half-hour ago."

"Oh."

"But while you're here, you can help me butcher this critter."

As it turned out, I couldn't help Al butcher the elk. All I had was a pocket knife, and I'd never seen an animal so big. Besides, it lay sprawled on the ground amid dense underbrush. And we didn't have even so much as a block and tackle for lift.

"That little hand tool all you got for a knife, boy? Hell of an elk hunter you are."

I already felt two notches below a loose belt at missing the action. Now a man I was recommending for hero status found my tools wanting. I shoved the knife back into my trouser pocket and hung my head.

"The knife," he said. "Don't put the damned thing back in your pocket—I need it."

"Where's yours?"

"Forgot it. In too big a hurry to go elk hunting. Don't look at me like that!"

I helped turn the six-point onto its back so Al could make the slit for entrails removal. At least my knife was sharp. "Tuff, he'll be along pretty quick, won't he?" I grunted. "He'll have a better knife."

What startled me more was how the forest just ahead erupted in thrashing and crashing as unseen bodies hurtled through the underbrush.

"Won't see him until we're done. Okay, let go the leg and help turn him on his side. More'n likely he's out there somewhere watching us right now. Leastways he's already been here and looked things over. Okay, most of the blood's out, turn him back up. Ol' Tuff knows we've got a big'un down. He knows it'll be one hell of a lot of work to get it to the Jeep. He'll have figured—uh!—how long we'll be. He'll show at the rig just as we th'ow the last quarter in. Here, lay this liver over there on that patch of salal."

Tandy was an absolute craftsman with my little pocket knife. He skinned the elk where it lay. Then, while I ran to the Jeep for the flour sacks he used for game bags, he boned out the rib cage and sliced out the backstraps. He took the hams off by running the knife point around the ball joint, then cutting the ball loose from its socket, and he took off the shoulders by slicing around the blades. Everything else was boned out. He finished by prying the canine teeth out of the jaw—the first elk's teeth I'd ever seen not hanging from some rich guy's watch fob—and cutting out the tongue. *Everything* was done with my little pocketknife—although he used up the edge on all three blades.

Tandy pitched the knife back to me at half-past two. At four o'clock on the nose, we dumped the last sack of boned-out elk meat into the Jeep.

"Was he a big one, boys?" Tuff asked, stepping from the forest gloom. Al held up the heavy six-point antlers, but his friend made little fuss over them. Cedar needles still clung to the back of Manning's wool coat.

Elk hunting with Tuff and Tandy was competitive from the time we stepped out of the Jeep each morning. But I learned. Some things I learned seem peculiar to me today. For instance, I learned to suspect every assignment; learned to worry them over until I understood just how my partners planned to use me to dog for them. I learned to doubt how they *said* they planned to hunt, and even picked up their rhythms until I could listen to what they *said* and figure out what they actually *planned* to do. Until one day I sat on the spine of a spur ridge and pulled the trigger on a four-point bull three miles from where I was supposed to be.

> He raked a thumbnail across a kitchen match. As the match flared, I could see him grinning around his Chesterfield.

"What you doing here, boy?" Tandy asked as I sweated over a half-skinned hindquarter. "You're supposed to be on Sawmill Flat."

I twisted on my haunches to peer up at the rough-stubbled face of my mentor. "I could say the same about you. You told me you were headed down into Coos River."

"I did," he said, fishing in his shirt pocket for a cigarette. "Tracked 'em from Coos River to here."

"Then you saw where the herd went through Sawmill Flat, didn't you?"

He raked a thumbnail across a kitchen match. As the match flared, I could see him grinning around his Chesterfield.

Tuff and Tandy were finely tuned *competition* hunters. They not only used their own home-grown varieties of drivers and beaters—like me—but they figured every angle that would enable them to use anyone else who chanced by. They knew their hunting country like a hallway in their own home; knew the distances between roads, the lay of spur ridges and creek bottoms, the best elk travel routes and hiding places. If they chanced upon a vehicle parked near a likely covert, they'd take stands along escape routes, figuring to ambush elk fleeing from a hunter's passage through their hiding places.

My two companions were excellent trackers, but they spent far more time puzzling out human tracks than elk tracks. "Figure out where your competition is going to be," Tuff said, "and it's easy enough to know exactly where you'll want to be." They could tell within minutes of the time another hunter entered the forest and where he was headed. They worked from intimate knowledge, close observation, and applied logic. As a team, they may have been the best elk hunters I've ever known. They taught me a lot.

Some of their lessons I later discarded, especially if law or ethic was tinged with purple. But what they gave most was a flaming love affair with the creature called elk. And they helped me to see that elk, standing alone without man—or man standing alone, without elk—is incomplete in the world to which I aspired.

Tuff and Tandy's gift, as it turned out, may have had far greater consequences than a mere love affair, because *Cervus canadensis*, the American wapiti, proved to be the

To escape predator detection during their first few days newborn calves depend on their natural camouflage. Since their glands have yet to develop, they give off very little scent. The calf's mother will attempt to lead predators from her young, and will sometimes turn and fight if the calf is directly threatened.

Richard Jackson

lure that attracted me to recognition of, and adventure in, an ever-expanding outdoor wonderland. It was elk that led me to an interest in botany, biology, geology, hydrology. It was elk that spurred me to become an accomplished woodsman, a reasonably proficient survival expert, a spokesperson for things outdoors. In short, it was elk that led to an entire way of life.

After their intense competitiveness finally led to a breakup of the Tuff and Tandy partnership, I, too, drifted from the flawed team. Though I'd lost my teachers, it turned out there was an abundance of infinitely deeper teachers awaiting. I discovered I'd been so absorbed in listening to my instructors that there'd been no time or reason to hear the nuances of the forest itself, and its inhabitants. I explored new places, even new mountain ranges, and discovered new elk herds with different response programs of their own. With new vistas opening, I was forced to utilize my own logic, and the innovative logic of a new group of hunting companions.

Our new group developed into a fine hunting team; one with ideals lofty for its place and time; one without the encumbrances of acute competition with all other hunters. And like my first two mentors, these companions were also driven by an infatuation with elk.

By this point in life, I'd begun hunting elk year 'round: glassing grazing herds during winter, photographing calves in the spring, hiking through summer range in the hope of chance encounters, hunting in the fall.

What was it about the animals that so seized me?

I've often puzzled over this question, and maybe there's no simple answer. The best I've come up with is to take consolation that it's not me alone; thousands of hunters and other wildlife enthusiasts thrill to the sight of a bull elk standing regally in a meadow.

Neither moose nor caribou, fine creatures though they may be, exhibit the obvious pride of a bull elk. One has only to see the same magnificent bull standing, head hang-

Elk are indeed a superb attraction. Each year, thirty thousand adventurous humans take horse-drawn sleigh rides among elk wintering on the National Elk Refuge near Jackson, Wyoming.

ing, after his antlers have fallen free in late winter to see and know that this once proud animal is mortified at being uncrowned.

It's claimed that the bighorn sheep has equally impassioned adherents, and that may indeed be true. Certainly a full-curl ram standing atop a rocky outcrop casts charisma far beyond his shadow. But wild sheep are much more limited in range and number than elk. As a consequence, seasons are limited and bag limits are squeezed until comparatively few people can hunt bighorns.

Nope, it's the elk that dominates the hearts and minds of hordes of America's big-game hunters, more so than perhaps any animal in the world, at least if passion is factored in. And not so surprisingly, it's the elk that thrills millions of non-hunters, too, as witness the teeming crowds viewing wapiti in Yellowstone, and at winter ranges everywhere.

It was just after a night of pouring rain that I hiked to Pine Bench, hoping for a blacktail buck. Found same, too. Also found where, during the rain, a couple of bull elk had plowed the bench's soil in battle. I've since been privileged to watch huge bulls sparring many times. But the morning when I climbed onto Pine Bench after a harem bull and his challenger had gone head-to-head among stately yellow pines was the closest I've ever been to seeing a serious battle between bull elk.

They'd left evidence as clear as a movie script. First one bull would find purchase against a tree root and he'd begin forcing the other bull, all four feet locked and plowing, back. The second bull would find his own starting chocks, and with both elk straining and pawing for traction, at last shoved the first bull back. It appeared as if garden tillers had been at work on at least an acre of the sixty-acre bench, churning the bunchgrass, and ripping pine-needled and pea-graveled soil.

I found no blood, but the rain may have washed that out—if, in fact, injury was done. Neither was there evidence of a clear victor, though I supposed there must be—all elk were gone. It was just as well. Elk season would not open for several weeks.

But they were there again when at last it did open. And we were there, too. ■

Chapter 3

Bucks, Bulls, and Body Language

A canopy of towering Douglas firs blocked the sky. Not that a traveler could have reveled in enriched sunbeams if those trees somehow disappeared, for the ancient forest drip-drip-dripped from a light rain.

I noticed neither rain nor forest—there was the print of an elk's cloven hoof in fresh-turned duff at my feet. Over by the windthrown tree was another. And another. Elk had walked here only minutes before! I pussyfooted to the fallen fir and, standing on tiptoes, peered over. Nothing moved in the forest beyond. But could there not be a better view from atop the six-foot-diameter trunk of the fallen tree? I slid my Marlin up, then shinnied to stand above the surrounding brush. Still no elk.

I cradled my 30-30 and walked along the trunk toward the roots. A flash of movement by the side of the tree caught my eye as, not thirty feet away, a blacktail buck stood from its bed. He stretched, peered over his shoulder, stretched again, then ambled away. I looked down at my rifle, back to the casual buck, and wagged my head in disbelief.

In the Oregon of my youth, elk season opened after deer season closed. But how did the buck know about seasons drafted by biologists and bureaucrats in far-off metropolises? Deer season had ended a scant two weeks before. If

I'd come across that buck then, it would have been Katy-bar-the-door! But now this buck—one on which any hunter would be proud to hang his tag—had just thumbed his nose at a man who was obviously armed and hunting.

How did he know I posed no threat? I thought back to wildlife footage recently aired on television: a cheetah, one of the fastest predators on earth had jogged his way through the middle of a herd of African antelope. The sleek cat occasionally passed within mere yards of feeding gazelles who merely eyed the sleek tabby as he trotted past. The cheetah was not hungry.

But let that same cat appear on the distant horizon while on the hunt and a thousand gazelles galloped a thousand different directions. How did they know? Did the hunter emit something by aura or body language?

Was my encounter with the blacktail buck even more convoluted? After all, I was, indeed, hunting. I just wasn't hunting deer. One would think if, in fact, a human hunter emitted some clue undetectable to our civilization-dulled senses that the clue couldn't be species specific. Isn't it reasonable to assume a hunter's odor warning elk from this same spot only minutes before should at least have caused a modicum of alarm in the buck when I popped atop the log?

Equally strange is how those same elk that bolt for California if I so much as crest a skyline during elk season will often stand alongside the trail and watch me trudge past while hunting deer. This point was never more clearly punctuated than the time I made the loop from Cinder Prairie, over Balm Mountain and back down Boulder Creek, searching for the just-right buck that had rocked me to dreamland the night before opening day of deer season.

The first elk I saw, a respectable five-point bull, sucked on a willow stem along the trail to the lookout building on Cinder Prairie. He seemed so disdainful that I threw a rock at him. But it was in the meadow—a place coincidentally called Elkhorn Springs—where an entire herd relaxed in the midmorning sun. Most were bedded, but a few still milled: cows, calves, three spikes, and a couple of three-

Oregon is second behind Colorado in licensed elk hunters. They're third behind Colorado and Idaho in number of elk taken by hunting.

points. I approached within fifty yards of the nearest; even paused to fill my canteen at the spring. A couple of older cows stood for a better view, but most continued to laze in sunbeams. I rolled my eyes and trudged on.

The final indignity occurred in the Boulder Creek bottom: a huge bull lying atop a low bench, but behind a screen of small firs. He thought he was hidden from the plodding human and, indeed, all I could see was his massive **But now this buck had just thumbed his nose at a man who was obviously armed and hunting.** outline and how the antlers twisted as the bull monitored my passage.

(No, I didn't so much as spot a hind-end flash of a departing blacktail deer—buck or doe.)

Years passed and Montana beckoned. I wanted elk to be part of any new environment. They were.

In Montana, deer and elk seasons coincide. I soon discovered all Treasure State ungulates have no compunctions about heading off to Utah together when I top a ridge and descend toward their valley. But occasionally there've been times when I've already taken a buck and cannot shoot another. That's when, hot on fresh elk tracks, I might round a trail bend and nearly collide with a mule deer buck who seems to view my rudimentary woods-running skills with considerable curiosity.

What secret telepathy is at play here? Why are such instincts unknown or lost to us human predators but readily used by our prey? Where and why have we lost a talent that could serve us well when dealing with our own most dangerous predators: bankers, lawyers, government bureaucrats?

Eventually I turned to guiding hunters pursuing elk. It's an occupation that of necessity makes philosophers out of garage mechanics. But still, I have yet to understand....

A skiff of fresh snow fell during a fruitless day hunting elk in a huge, high, partly timbered basin. Three of our hunters had returned to where we'd tied our horses. One was still out. I checked my watch, then began bridling saddlehorses.

"Chuck is circling the upper end," I told the other guide. "Said he'd be back before dark. You wait for him here while the rest of us go on back to camp."

Kenny nodded. Within minutes the guide hobbled his and Chuck's horses and turned them loose to graze along the edge of the dry lake bed, then gathered sticks for a small fire. With the warming fire blazing cheerily, Kenny leaned back against a pine tree and dozed. When he opened his eyes, a five-point bull elk stood out on the lake bed, not a hundred yards from man and horses.

Kenny eyed the bull, then eyed his rifle in its saddle scabbard. He began crawling toward the horse. The pony snorted and leaped away from his master's unorthodox approach. The elk looked up, then returned to whatever attracted him to the lake bed. Again Kenny crawled after the horse. Again the pony leaped away from the man's belly-down approach. Again the bull looked up. Kenny waited until the elk put its head down, then carefully came to his feet. Moving ever so slowly, he reached his horse and slid out his 30-06. Training the weapon over the pony's saddle, he adjusted the scope.

My guide had no intention of shooting the animal—was not, in fact, permitted to do so, either by law (while guiding) or by his employer, who allowed none of his guides to compete with paying guests. All Kenny wanted to do was view the elk through his scope's magnifying lens.

The elk, for his part, seemed to be pawing and licking minerals from the lake bed. Occasionally the animal raised his head to stare at the two horses and the man hidden beyond, then returned to his pawing and licking.

Long minutes ticked by. Kenny's saddlehorse tired of his role as a stationary blind and wandered away, so the guide hunkered to sit in the meadow. The bull eyed him as he did. More minutes passed as the guide studied the bull, trying to determine what it was the big animal mined on the dry lake's surface.

Of a sudden the elk threw up his head and stared toward the forest fringe where the trail from up-country spilled out to the lakeshore. *Chuck's coming*, Kenny thought.

The elk went back to licking minerals, then threw up his head again. This time the bull took a few steps toward the forest before returning to whatever it was he craved on the lake bed. Again and again the bull gazed up-trail. Each time he did, he drifted nearer the trees from whence he came.

Ten minutes went by. At last, even Kenny heard the hunter, feet crunching in the snow. The final curtain fell at dusk when the bull vanished into the forest just as the hunter stepped from his own tree cover.

Kenny clambered to his feet, brushing snow from his trousers and coat sleeves. "See anything?" he asked Chuck.

The hunter shook his head. "Not even a track. I'm not sure there's any elk in this country."

When they'd mounted, Kenny led the hunter out to where the bull had been and pointed to the tracks. "There's elk in this country, right enough."

"But what gets me," the guide said while recounting the story at camp, "is how that elk looked right at me when I pointed my rifle at him. He just never seemed to care. I even went 'Bang! You're dead!' and he still never spooked. Why?"

I shook my head.

"And the way he heard Chuck coming ten minutes before he actually came out in the open, then sort of faded away just as the man appeared. Sort of makes a body think, don't it?"

Indeed it does. How did the bull know the man he couldn't see would have shot him in a heartbeat? If the animal did know, why was he so casual about the danger that he disappeared only at the last moment? And how did the bull know that Kenny—the man he *could* see—posed no threat even while pointing a rifle his way?

Here's yet another example of an elk's uncanny ability to sense when humans pose no danger:

Ted Modlens first came hunting in the Bob Marshall Wilderness with me back in '74. Ted had just retired as a machinist in a New Jersey factory. He and his wife Sonya had bought a small Pennsylvania farm and settled into a sylvan existence. Naturally curious about my guests, I learned the big man loves good books and all God's creation—not necessarily in that order. He proved to be outstandingly kind, thoughtful, considerate. And he's an accomplished horseman, keeping ponies of his own on the farm. What outfitter wouldn't love to have such a guest in his camp?

Meadow nestled amid the Oregon Cascades. The meadow is one frequented by elk and elk hunters, including this book's author during his youth.

Ted was able to make our White River hunt two different years before the financial limitations of retirement caught up with him. It turned out he wasn't lucky enough to connect with an elk on either of those adventures. But he shrugged off his hunting misfortune, relishing memories and basking in the physical elan, mental restoration, and magnificent beauty of some of the best of all that God hath wrought. Ted's old Maine hunting buddy, Rufus Gehris, came with my Skyline Outfit for seven years in a row, and Rufus and I often talked of how nice it would be if Ted could one day rejoin us; but nothing could be done.

Or could it?

Recalling how many years the friends had hunted together and how Rufus claimed Ted always did their cooking, I phoned the retired machinist. "Say, partner, how would you like to come into camp with Rufus' party and cook for us?"

Ted jumped at the chance. When Ted and Rufus showed up on our doorstep, both men carried Montana hunting licenses. It was fine with me that the cook hunted—as long as he didn't compete with paying guests, and as long as the other hunters in camp agreed. Since they were all amenable, Ted packed in his rifle.

After breakfast on day four of the ten-day trip, hunters and guides had left camp for their day's hunt and Ted was alone. He finished washing dishes, and as he dried his hands he stepped from the cooktent to view the meadow and the towering mountain beyond. A lone bull elk stood in the meadow.

Ted counted to himself. "One, two, three, four, five six ... seven. One, two, three, four, five, *six ... My God! Seven points on that side, too!*"

The man stood transfixed, staring at one of wildlife's most exciting rarities: a bull elk with seven points to each side, a "royal" head.

The bull began feeding. Occasionally, though, he stared in the direction of camp.

"Did he know you were there?" Rufus asked when the cook told of his once-in-a-lifetime experience.

"I don't know, Rufe. But how could he *not* know? I'd been banging pots and pans. When I walked around the tent corner I was drying my hands on a towel."

I walked out in the meadow to where Ted said the bull had stood. There were huge elk tracks in dirt pushed up from a ground squirrel's burrow.

"Why didn't you shoot it?" I asked.

"I couldn't. I hoped one of your regular hunters would come back in time. It wouldn't be right for the cook to shoot the biggest elk in creation." The man was silent for several moments, then added, "Besides, it was right here at camp."

I stared at the mountain. "Besides, Ted, he was beautiful, wasn't he?"

The man's forehead wrinkled as his head swiveled toward the meadow. "He was beautiful," he whispered. ∎

Chapter 4

Bad Elk, Good Horses—Vanished

By my mid-thirties, the thought of a bull elk skylined while crossing a ridge had a stranglehold on me. To justify spending more time in search of the elusive creatures I applied for a state outfitter's license and a U.S. Forest Service campsite permit. The area I chose was near the heart of the famed Bob Marshall Wilderness, amid the wildest reaches of the northern Rockies.

My decision to become a guide for wilderness elk hunters brought a sea change in our family's life. From a weekend-and-holiday hunter regularly employed in a factory, I became a professional outdoorsman, turning casual avocation into full-time occupation. And my career centered entirely on the pursuit of better understanding *Cervus canadensis*, wapiti, the American elk.

With fewer outside distractions, such as the need to punch a time clock, stare down the tax assessor, or "yes, sir"-"no, sir" a highway patrolman, I had time to ponder the practices of elk. Travel routes and bedding places became areas of supreme interest, as did wapiti dining tables.

But the truth is, exploration into habits and habitats of one creature leads to a series of interconnected threads extending to undreamed realms. For instance: Areas of limestone subsurface rock produce more calcium, and the plants growing there help produce more impressive antlers on the deer species. Therefore one wants to know what kinds of geologic processes result in limestone. What, too, is the interrelationship of fire with the succession of preferred plant species and, thus, their overall abundance? How do slope and moisture patterns relate to plant succession?

See how it works? Follow geologic processes far enough to learn that four-hundred-million-year-old lime-

Richard Jackson

stone is created by tiny sea creatures dying and depositing their shells in layer upon layer at the bottom of shallow seas ... and pretty quick one is discovering the fossil imprints of trilobites and brachiopods and pelecypods; follow fire succession far enough and soon one is sprawled on a mountainside admiring God's mosaic across yon valley; follow the effects of moisture on elk ranges and one becomes interested in various cloud formations and can ultimately make reasonably accurate predictions of tomorrow's weather.

Such yearning and learning does not occur in one blinding flash of light on the way to Damascus. At least it didn't with me. My understanding evolved over years—even decades—of methodical observation and even more tedious evaluation. After observation and evaluation, conclusions had to be tested in the field. Some were wrong. Most were not. Some are still being tested. And truth tell, after forty-four years of elk hunting, I now know enough about the creatures to believe I know very little. Still, I'm way ahead of a lot of folks who have yet to discover that single elemental truth about how much they know.

Such yearning and learning does not occur in one blinding flash of light on the way to Damascus.

Evolution is a curious thing, and there came a time when I sought to share my hard-earned knowledge of *Cervus canadensis* with others. Having spent so much time wandering over the mountains and up the creeks, I lacked the social sophistication to understand that *Reader's Digest* had no real interest in K-level writing, no matter how intriguing the subject. Neither did *Outdoor Life, Field & Stream*, or *Sports Afield*. (What's the matter with their idiot editors?)

Finally, in 1982 I sold my first short piece to *Montana Magazine*, and four years later made a breakthrough with one of the big outdoor magazines.

After lo, these many years, from the vantage of hindsight, I see an unusual perspective. Editors really did *want* some of my stuff, else they'd never have created so much work for themselves by purchasing material from an amateurish writer. And in retrospect, I find it fascinating that New York editors of the '90s are susceptible to the same elk magic as an Oregon bushboy of the '50s.

My eyes popped open and I listened for a moment before whispering, "Are you awake?"

My wife's reply was clear, with no dregs of sleep attached: "I've been listening to him for five minutes."

My reaction was probably more grimace than grin. Try as hard as we might, we can't get a bull elk to bugle all day.

Now, here's what sounds like a granddaddy standing above camp in the moonlight, bugling at saddlehorses shuffling in our corral.

"My Lord," Jane gasped, "he's coming closer!"

His next ringing challenge sounded much nearer. "My goodness," Jane whispered, "is he coming into the tents?"

We heard murmuring coming from our hunters' tent. Someone says just loudly enough to carry, "Y'all stay right there, hear? Ah'll be with you first thing in the mornin'."

Still the bull continued to bugle. I sighed. "He's got to be down in the meadow by now."

Incredibly, another bull opened up from the opposite direction—across the creek from camp—and I pounded my pillow in frustration. "Isn't that beautiful?" Jane murmured.

I rolled over in the sleeping bag and nodded into the darkness. *Sure is,* I thought. *They're what's been driving me all these years.* My mind wandered ... five straight days without so much as a cow squeak, let alone these deep-throated, full-scale monster roars from within a hundred yards, and this is going on from two directions right now! I reached over and took my wife's hand. She squeezed, then released as the across-the-creek bull bellowed curses to the meadow bull.

The strange thing is, I thought on, *we've not found all that many tracks.* I sighed again. In all fairness, I reminded myself, the weather had been so hot and dry even fresh tracks aged rapidly.

"My Lord," Jane gasped, "he's coming closer!"

Oh, the irony of it! Elk in camp at night; can't find them during the day. Are they too smart for us? Or are we too dumb for them? Then I remembered how a few days before, our wrangler rode out looking for our loose-grazing horses and returned without them.

"I looked all over for 'em, Roland. Even rode out our Juliet backtrail looking for tracks. They didn't go that way. Don't know where they are." Kenny leaned forward to pat his tan and white paint horse's neck. "Al Joe can't pick out no bells either."

A few minutes later, both guides and the wrangler thundered a-horseback from camp to search for the lost ponies. They returned within the hour. There were no horses to be found in the little valley.

There were ten head of stock out there somewhere. Eight were wearing bells. Two were paints—a brown and white and a black and white—three sorrels, two white horses, two bays, and a black. I swung into the saddle of one of the guide's ponies and led Kenny out in one last search before dark.

Normally our loose-grazing herd fed in the scattered grass and timber east of camp. When at last we found them, that's where they were, holed up in a small thicket, standing so still no bells rang.

"Well I'll be go to hell," Kenny said, staring at the ponies. The old wrangler crossed his wrists on the saddlehorn and leaned forward. "Ain't no wonder we can't find elk."

I grinned.

"Horses are all different colors so as to stand out in any backdrop, most of 'em wear bells so they can be found easy enough, most times they'll graze in the open, and they like people—specially people who give 'em grain." The old man shrugged. "And we can't even find our horses."

My thoughts returned to the bulls surrounding camp. The one nearest quit bugling abruptly. I supposed he had winded us at last.

The next day we found where a couple of saplings had been savaged, one less than a hundred yards from the cooktent. There were surprisingly few tracks, and it was hard to determine which direction the elk took when they waved good-by. Though we guides bugled our guts out, it was to no avail. If it weren't for the fresh rubs and the bugling at camp the night before, we'd not think elk were in the country.

During supper, one hunter asked, "How long you been doing this, Cheek? You shore you know how to hunt elk?"

Later, after we'd headed for our sleeping bags and the camp quieted, the big bull bugled from higher up the mountain that towered above camp. It sounded as though he might be standing on the same ledge where my hunter had sat while I made a morning drive from below.

Jane giggled beside me. "How long you been doing this, Cheek?" she whispered. "You sure you know how to hunt elk?"

The plane—a Mooney—had crashed fifteen years before, killing its occupants who, I'm told, were a woman and two men.

As fascinating as elk are for most hunters, the phenomenon doesn't hold for all hunters—not even all elk hunters. Roger West was a classic example.

Roger hails from a small mountain valley in western North Carolina. He scheduled his first hunt a year in advance. And even with so much lead time, it turned out he was more casual in preparation than most folks. When he showed up two days before the beginning of hunting season, he carried only a brand-new Weatherby Magnum—without sights.

"I'll just go down to Kalispell and have 'em put on a scope," he said. "And while I'm there, I'll pick up a sleeping bag, pair of boots and some spare clothes."

"You might want a raincoat, wool coat, and a couple of changes of long underwear," I murmured.

Roger fired a couple of rounds through his 300 Weatherby and pronounced himself ready to hunt. His guide, Larry, bugled a bull to close range on the first day, but Roger couldn't find the animal in his new scope. Eventually the bull tired of the sport and wandered off.

Later, I guided the man to a different basin. While riding to the day's hunt, Roger spied a morning sun glinting from something shiny on a distant ridge. "What's that, Roland?" he asked.

"An old airplane crash," I replied. "The wreckage is still there."

The plane—a Mooney—had crashed fifteen years before, killing its occupants who, I'm told, were a woman and two men. Apparently they'd filed a flight plan from

Great Falls to Seattle and had flown across the Continental Divide crest into a freak snowstorm. The storm was such that the wings began icing and the pilot radioed Great Falls that he was turning back. They failed to clear the most visible landmark in all the Bob Marshall Wilderness—the famed Chinese Wall—by twenty vertical feet and crashed into the mountainside under full power. Roger was intrigued with the story and kept asking questions as we tied our ponies to saplings in order to begin our day's hunt.

Perhaps an hour later, a bull answered my call. It sounded like the elk was below the game trail we followed, holed up in a patch of second-growth Douglas fir. I chose a spot with a view into the forest and placed Roger where he'd have a decent rest for his rifle. Then I went to work challenging the bull to battle. Each time I did my imitation of a herd bull, the elk below us replied. But he wouldn't come.

Again and again I went through my repertoire of a maddened challenger; again and again the elk replied. I bugled. I grunted. I did my imitation of an elk savaging saplings with his antlers. Finally I even fell silent in the hope that the elusive creature would be lured into range

Remains of airplane scattered near crest of the Chinese Wall.

by curiosity. Nothing worked.

At last, Roger began to fidget. His body language said he expected his guide to do something. But what? Two of us could hardly pussyfoot up on an elk that was already wide awake and watchful. I could stalk the elk, but that would do no good, for Roger carried the rifle. "Roger," I whispered, "it looks to me like you're going to have to try to work in on him."

The man fidgeted again.

"I'll stay here and talk to the bull while you try to come in on him from his right—the breeze seems to be pretty steady from the west. If I can hold him for you and you're especially quiet, there's a good chance we can pull this off."

Roger's reply was not a whisper: "Aw, Roland, I'd druther go on back and look at that airyplane crash." ∎

Chapter 5

The Lesson of Avalanche Elk

Ka-boom!

The spike stood motionless in the middle of a broad avalanche path, unable to locate the source of his danger.

Ka-boom!

The gunner looked for all the world like the frontiersman in a Frederick Remington painting—firing, levering another shell, two steps forward and firing again. Except this frontiersman wore no fringed buckskin, floppy-brimmed hat, or angora chaps. Levi jeans, an imitation-fur cap, and a blaze-orange vest were the order of this frontiersman's day. And his face was freckled, his ears flapped out, and he stood no more than shirt-button high to me, weighing in at an even hundred pounds.

One of the two cows half turned; it, too, was uncertain. A calf pressed tight against its flank. The other cow took a hesitant step forward, but the bull remained rooted.

Ka-boom!

The forward cow wheeled to bunch close to the one with the calf. All three began milling. Incredibly, none of the four elk had thus far identified the source of gunfire.

"Take a rest."

Ka-boom!

"Dammit, I said take a rest!" But he was already turning

away."You got another shell or two in that gun, boy. And he's still there. *Use it!*"

The elk were moving now, their enemies located, their escape route identified. The bull was last to leave in a lunging rush. The boy never even looked after them; if he'd had a tail it would've been tucked tight between his legs like a whipped puppy.

"Where you going?"

"I'm not shooting any more 'til I get this gun fixed."

"What's wrong with the gun? Hey! Come back here."

He returned, not meeting my eyes. His mouth pinched down at the corners, and the lower lip thrust out. "The sights are off."

"That so? Let me see."

He hesitated, then handed over the old Marlin and retreated to lean against a tree. I once-overed the 30-30. It was the rifle I used to take my first elk; first *several* elk. Yep, paid thirty dollars for it second-hand when I was fourteen and, because it shoots so true, I'd been offered more several times since. I rubbed my hand along the barrel, caressing the oiled steel. No carbine this. No sir, a rifle—three-inch-longer barrel. Maybe that's what makes it shoot straight. But it handles like a carbine—light and easy to swing. I put it to my shoulder and glanced through the Williams peep I'd installed myself. As always, the shiny front bead seemed to leap into the peep's center. No, this gun was always accurate in the hands of a man who knew how to use it. Up to 125 yards, that is, and capable to 175 if you knew bullet drop. And it took its share of elk before the big boys came along and convinced me a 30-30 wasn't enough gun for elk. I grinned, remembering that the 30-30 has been around since 1895 and has taken more game animals than will ever be taken with any other caliber.

I laid the rifle across a tree limb, steadied it against the bole, then levered the familiar action.

The boy couldn't help himself—he looked toward the football-sized limestone rock where I aimed.

> I rubbed my hand along the barrel, caressing the oiled steel. No carbine this. No sir, a rifle

Ka-boom!

Rock fragments flew. "It's not the rifle, boy. You reckon it could be the operator?"

The others were still out hunting when we arrived at camp, but that was to be expected. Thad was after a big high-country buck and Lars had tagged along so he could stand atop a wild, far-mountain ridge and drink a full dose of the Almighty's elixir. I didn't expect them until dark.

As soon as we unsaddled and grained our horses, the boy wandered off to be alone. There was work to do, but I let him go, knowing how he felt after missing his first bull elk. At last, with our ponies turned out to graze, wood gathered, kindling split, fire in the stove, and supper fixings laid out, I settled back to bring my journal up to date. When the boy slipped up on me, I don't know, but there he was, standing quiet a few feet to the side, waiting.

"Something?" I asked.

"Yeah, I ..." He paused, began again: "I brought a whole box of bullets and I wonder ..."

"Wonder what?"

"Well, I won't need 'em all. Leastways that's what you said. And I wonder if I could go practice with some of the extras, that's all."

"Mmm-hmm. Take an empty can out of the garbage sack and this time, hit it. Save a magazine load for your gun, though."

I counted the times he fired the old Marlin, and five rounds was all he saved. But it was worth it to see him trudging my way a few minutes later with his rifle in one hand and a shot-up bean can in the other.

"You're right, grandpa," he said. "It wasn't the gun—it was me."

"Do tell? Go put your rifle away, then come on back and let's talk about it."

When he returned, his head was up and he seemed ready to face up to whatever I had to say.

"You got excited, boy. And there's no disgrace in that. I'd be surprised if it happened any other way, seeing as that was the first elk you ever throwed down on. In fact, getting excited is all part of this thing called hunting and, truth be known, I think it's a pretty damned vital part." I trailed off, remembering how it was with me.

"Time was I used to get excited, too. And when it got so's there was no excitement—when my blood stopped pumping every time I spotted a big bull—why that's when it didn't make so much difference whether I went hunting or not. Luckily, I learned about other things—to appreciate the blend of land and plants and animals the good Lord stuck together to make this high country what it is. But let's get back to you. You know what you did wrong?"

He nodded. "I didn't take a rest."

"Yep. A man who doesn't take a rest when he can find one—every time he shoots at something—is a fool. I'd give a bull elk a thirty-yard running start every time if I could get a good steady rest for my rifle. There'll be times when you won't have a chance for anything except an offhand shot. And a man should be able to hit his mark then, too, or he shouldn't pull the trigger. But today wasn't one of those times."

"No, sir."

"You know what else you did wrong?"

"Huh-uh."

"Did you see the elk *behind* the one you shot at?"

The anger was quick. "There was no elk behind ..."

"Good! You did know what was the background. Okay, you missed the bull clean and that's a plus. Better to miss clean than wound one. He deserves better than that. Know where you're shooting, though. That's one of the most important rules in hunting. Know what's another?"

"No."

"Respect the animal you're after. And most hunters do. The animals have earned that respect. That's why hunters are the ones who're paying most to support wildlife programs—because they care enough about all wildlife to put their money where some folks pile only words."

The boy listened and looked, but I don't think he was seeing me at all. Instead, I'd be willing to bet he was seeing only a bunch of elk feeding in an avalanche chute, so I asked, "Did you think the spike was beautiful?"

His head bobbed like a wood chip in choppy water. "Good. Excited but appreciative. You better hope you'll continue to get excited when you bump into an elk. But you better learn to control that excitement and hammer your chance home or you'll never make a hunter."

He nodded again. "I'll sure try." He started away, but turned to say, "Thanks, grandpa."

I patted him on the shoulder as I shuffled past. "You bounce back quick, boy. And that's another plus."

"That's one of the most important rules in hunting. Know what's another?"

Thad and Lars rode in an hour later, and the boy took out grain bags for their ponies. He must have told them what happened because I heard the taciturn Lars say, "Learned something, I'll bet." The boy bounced back all right, but missing his first elk still ate on him. His memory lapses was one way I could tell, as were the occasional times he was inattentive to his surroundings.

"See 'em?" I asked one day. We'd stopped to eat lunch high in alpine country, near a mountaintop. Directly before us, an outcropping of crumpled limestone lay across a small swale. It was a good place to see the tiny round-eared rock rabbits, called pikas or coneys.

"See what?"

"Rock rabbits. Pikas. Three of them out there skittering around." I pointed. "Up by the big boulder, about ten o'clock on the rock pile. See where the boulder casts a shadow? And there's a pile of grass? That's their haymow curing. They don't hibernate, you know. So they store their winter's food supply. They've been running—there goes one now. See it?"

The boy lifted his binoculars and I did the same. "Cute, aren't they?"

"Uh-huh." Soon he again stared into the distance.

"Still brooding over missing the elk?" I asked.

"Uh-huh."

"Spilt milk. Hindsight'll get you nowhere. Fact is, it's making you miss some things going on around you, like them round-eared rabbits. Or those two golden eagles riding the thermals over the ridgetops."

He peered through his binoculars again and asked, "You ever shoot at a bull and miss, grandpa?"

I snorted and he nodded. "That's what I thought."

I realized he'd not understood, so I added, "Lots of times."

He lowered his glasses. "Really? You're kidding me."

This time it was me doing the staring through.

If only he knew the half. It was thirty-five, forty years ago—before I began outfitting—that I missed two bulls in one day....

I'd reined the flighty palomino to a halt on one side of the little clearing and stared in surprise at a raghorn bull elk shuffling nervously near the clearing's far edge. I started to ease out of the saddle, and the palomino settled down as a well-trained saddlehorse should. But the bull, seeing the horse stop, turned to melt into the trees. I settled back into the saddle and let my horse stride on. The bull turned again to look at us.

It'd be quick shooting, so I eased the old Springfield out of its scabbard, and the horse turned skittish once more. Curious about the renewed activity, the bull took a step my way. Rifle in hand, I again shifted in the saddle to slip off. The horse stopped his dancing and the bull again turned toward the forest. I settled back in the saddle one more time and the horse began dancing. The bull stopped. *Fifty yards*, I thought. *I wonder....* The bolt clicked up and slid easily and I thumbed the flop-over safety to half. The sights came easily to my eye, the safety flicked on over, and—well—I hit the ground milliseconds after the gun roared. Both elk and horse were gone when I shook off the cobwebs and clambered to my feet.

After whimpering for a few seconds, I allowed being horseless was more inconvenience than tragedy, and

I inched closer, moving upwind, crawling, my rifle pushed to the front.

decided to go on hunting. Before limping farther into the forest, I lifted my bugle and whistled and grunted my imitation of the challenge of an angry bull elk. Incredibly, even with all the ruckus we'd just made, there was a reply from the distance. The new bull sounded like a dandy. His bugle seemed to be coming from a bench above a much-used natural mineral lick.

I hunkered down with a clear view of the lick and again blew my challenge. The bull replied. But though we talked back and forth for an hour, he never seemed to move. At last, I left the lick and climbed to the bull's bench. Another hour of verbal assaults passed between us, this time at perhaps a couple hundred yards. Again, my patience wore thin. I began creeping on hands and knees through thick sapling shintangle. Soon I crept so close to the elk that I dared make no overt sound. The bull, as it turned out, made enough noise for both of us—bugling, grunting, thrashing saplings with his antlers.

I inched closer, moving upwind, crawling, my rifle pushed to the front. A hundred yards more to him. Fifty. Thirty. At twenty yards, I could make out a sapling's top whipping to and fro as the bull savaged the tree in rage. But I still couldn't get a clear outline of the creature. At fifteen yards, there was a vague shape through the tangle. At ten yards he took on form, but still wasn't clear enough for a shot. Bark and limbs flew from the tree he savaged. Then, from his platform on the forest floor, the beast paused to scream out his challenge. At thirty feet, the bull's roar was deafening; my heart pounded and my knees shook—I'd never been so close to an enraged bull. I quartered right, crawling over damp moss, sliding the old rifle ahead, trying for what looked like a better shooting angle.

Just then the bull decided he'd taken enough insults from whatever upstart dared invade his territory. Leaping from his fortress, he burst through thick spruce and alder brush to land amid the patch of small firs I'd just quit. We couldn't have been more than twenty feet apart!

He skidded to a halt, my scent wafting to him for the first time. He eyed me in my ridiculous quartering-away, bellied-down posture, rifle pushed out front.

Neither of us moved so much as a tail whisker. Then my thumb flipped off the safety and I rolled, whipping the rifle up, jerking the trigger.

There was no way I could miss—not at twenty feet. But I did! Bullet deflection?

Did the whole thing happen at all, or was it a dream? After forty years I hardly remember.

I glanced at the lad. "Anybody tells you he never missed, boy, you can figure he never hunted much."

"Would you tell me about some time when you missed?"

I shook my head as if to clear it of cobwebs. "Let's see, there was the time when your grandmother and I were hunting on Kettle Mountain. Leastways she was along and I was doing what passed for hunting but was really just riding the high country, enjoying the scenery.

> **Did the whole thing happen at all, or was it a dream?**

"It was cold—a lot of snow—and we were bundled pretty good; still enjoying the day, understand? We built a big fire and ate lunch, took a few pictures, then started back to camp. She spotted the bull first. He stood on a little point sticking out from the mountain we rode. It was a long shot for open sights—four hundred yards maybe. I didn't want to take the shot because the mountain we were on is really steep and if the bull didn't drop where he stood he'd roll to the bottom. And that, son, would be hell to pay.

"Well, she urged me on—your grandmother. So I says, 'Okay, but I'll hold high and I'll either take his backbone and drop him right there or miss clean.'"

"What happened?"

I chuckled. "The bull wasn't four hundred yards at all. He was only three hundred and sixty steps when I went to check for blood. I missed. Shot over him. But did he light out when the bullet whistled over his withers!"

We both fell quiet, the silence broken only by the high-pitched whistles of pikas, the hunting shrill of eagles, and the methodical munch of the boy chewing on an apple. Finally he said, "Just what I thought. You didn't miss like me—you didn't blow it because you got excited. I knew you was too smart to do a dumb thing like that."

I should have told the boy about those other misses—I know it now, and knew it then. But who ever said grandfathers aren't proud, too? And what grandfather ever lived who would deliberately cloud the ten-foot-tall image his own grandson holds of him?

The weather soured by mid-afternoon: heavy-bellied clouds rolling in from the southwest, turning gray and dropping below the mountain peaks. We hit for camp earlier than usual but still rode into the compound in a driving rain. Thad and Lars were sharper—back already and with a big fire going in the cookstove.

The rain turned to wet snow by morning and Thad was the only one tough enough—or dumb enough—to try hunting. He was back in three hours, soaking wet and shaking miserably, but with blood on his wool pants and a dandy four-point mulie buck lashed across his saddle. "Should've went with me, boy," he chided. "You'll never get anything rubbing elbows with those two tent rats."

It turned colder still, and flakes the size of quarters began piling up. Visibility fell to zero. "Hunting'll get better when this quits," Lars observed, stooping to peer out the tent flap.

But the snow continued through the next day and into the next. Thad and the boy gave it a go on the third day, but weather drove them back to the tent to enter Lars' and my cribbage sweepstakes. "This keeps up," Lars said, "we'll have to go out and pack more hay for the ponies."

I nodded. "Figure to ride out tomorrow."

"Good. I'll go with you. Double the hands and shorten the work."

"Want me to help?" Thad asked. "Me and the boy?"

"Lars and I can do all that needs doing. More and you'd be in the way. Maybe the weather will break and you two can bag a bull elk or two."

The weather did break and daylight came to a postcard-type snow scene. "Elk'll be moving today," Lars said, surveying our dwindling horse feed. "Maybe you should stay and hunt with the boy and let me pack hay."

"No, we'll get the feed like we planned. Maybe it's time the boy traveled with a dedicated hunter like Thaddeus. God knows, you and me ain't into the messy part of hunting anyway."

Lars and I helped get the other two going for their day afield, then grained, brushed, and saddled our ponies. While stringing packhorses together, Lars asked a question that'd been haunting me for a year or two: "You don't suppose the boy is just a plain unlucky hunter, do you?"

I shrugged. Like most outdoorsmen, I believe luck plays a hefty role in success afield. My years as an outfitter drove it home that fortune smiles on some hunters and frowns on others. One man could work out an area careful as could be and see nothing; another could pass through on his way back to camp and stumble across a monster buck or bull who was not only blind and deaf but stupid as well.

"Not much we can do except try," I said. "Someday it'll all come together for him."

Lars handed me my string's leadrope. "Today just might be the day."

We pulled back into camp with our packhorses loaded with canvas-wrapped bales of hay just as shadows lengthened and an owl started tuning up in the distance. Ours weren't the only laden packhorses to be tied at the hitchrack.

"Come help me with these quarters," Thad grunted from the gloom of one packhorse's far side.

I tied my string and hurried to help. "Who ..." I started to ask just as he staggered away with a heavy elk quarter. Then it was me grunting. And Lars, then me again. Four heavy quarters.

"Who ..." I began again just as Thad called, "Come help me with this buck, will you?"

"Buck?" I muttered.

I slipped the ropes holding a three-point buck and helped Thad lift it from his riding saddle. Then it hit me.

"Hey!" I said. "You already got your buck. This means the boy ..."

A light flared from inside the tent—a lantern just lit. I heard the stove door swing open and wood being thrown onto a fire just a-borning.

"There!" Thad grunted as we dropped the deer under our meat pole.

When he straightened to knead his back, I stepped close enough to see his face in the fading light. Tired lines etched around his eyes and mouth. "The elk—what was it?"

Richard Jackson

He leaned against the hitchrail and fished in his shirt pocket for a cigarette, then thumbed a lighter and squinted my way as he held the flame to his smoke. "He'll be tender. Probably a carbon copy of the one he missed the other ..."

"Where'd you get it?"

Thad's teeth flashed in the gloom. "You don't listen, do you?"

I heard the stove door slam and the two-burner Coleman being pumped. "Huh?"

"I didn't shoot a thing. Hell, the boy dropped the bull

clean with one shot. Then he came back to camp for the packhorses while I butchered it. On the way back with the horses, this buck tried to stare him down."

Lars' quiet chuckle came from somewhere behind. "I guess that answers this morning's question, don't it?"

There was more rummaging in the tent: water splashed into a coffee pot, other pots and pans rattling. Sparks flew from the stovepipe. Dimly I heard Thad as I headed for the tent:

"My God, I didn't think he was ever going to shoot! The elk had started to move by the time he kicked the snow off that log and laid down behind it. Talk about cool!" ■

Chapter 6

All About Elk Trapping

Every elk aficionado has dreamed of "trapping" elk— that is, driving the animals against some impenetrable landform (into a box canyon, to the edge of a precipice, against the shore of a lake). But it's one thing to dream, another to put dream into practice. And in the case of trapping elk, the effort has always led, in my experience, to vertigo, diarrhea, and contusional lesions of the lower cerebrum.

Most attempts to trap elk depends upon successfully "driving" the animals. But if you're an elk-hunting wannabee, my advice is don't waste your time attempting to drive *Cervus canadensis* where they haven't already decided to go—it can't be done.

I've never found an experienced elk hunter who contends that elk can be cornered. Yet there are outfitters, guides, and veteran elk hunters who will argue in favor of driving wapiti. They are wrong. They do not *drive* elk so much as flush them from their coverts. That they can— and do—do.

In certain more arid sections of the mountain west, many of the landforms are high, windswept ridges cut by narrow canyons. Since weather patterns are both harsh and parched, forests exist only within those sheltered canyons, while ridgetop cover is of sagebrush-bunchgrass character. When hunters are about, elk tend to hole up within the forested canyons and shun the open slopes. It's common practice to scatter gunners around the open ridgetops, then send beaters through the forested coverts. In some cases and places, elk have no way to escape except to bolt for the ridgetops.

It's hard to make effective drives in country like this.

That they're taken by using this method cannot be argued. What can be argued is that a drive—in order to be properly considered a drive—must produce a predictable result: elk must be moved from point A to point B within a predetermined timetable.

Yes, elk can be moved from point A, and the timing of their initial movement can usually be accurately predicted. But from that point on, things tend to go to hell in a handbasket. The elk explode from point A, but do they predictably progress to point B? No. Point M, yes, and point X. And—oops—there go some over points F, H, Q, and Z. As for a predetermined timetable? Forget that, too. They may bolt through upon the hour. But most times they come through on the minute. Or even the second. Sometimes all the wapiti in a covert choose to cross one single point on the surrounding ridges at the same time. Usually that point will be undermanned—or not manned at all.

Many folks who are experienced in this type of hunting claim that if one route to safety is left untended, the elk will, with unerring accuracy, choose it. That's why success in this type of hunting depends pretty much on having enough gunners to cover all surrounding ridges.

Vegetative and landform types typical of the country I hunt do not lend themselves to this strategy, though occasionally, when all other reasonable methods had been exhausted, we did resort to flushes which we called drives.

We guides posted our hunter or hunters alongside forest trails that were sometimes traveled by wandering wildlife. Then the guides would simply blunder through wapiti bedding areas in the hope of stirring the pot enough to make the creatures move.

Naturally, the odds were heavily against elk converging upon hunter. With forests covering much of our region, escape cover was everywhere for the animals. It was simply chance—and poor chance, at that—if elk chose, from their thousands of options, the two or three trails our hunters covered.

Another adverse factor was wind. Breezes tends to be erratic in our mountain country. In order for elk to have the misfortune to stumble into one of our hunters, the wind gods had to call the animal's number by remaining consistent. And then that hunter must remain motionless as a Buddha. He must not hack, cough, or spit. He must not unzip a coat, light a cigarette, or lean his rifle against a tree. All the same, when nothing else worked, we tried the technique, and sometimes an ambush worked.

Lacy Sayre and his father Bud were two of the finest elk hunters I've ever led to wilderness adventure, an added incentive for me to try harder. During one of their fall wapiti trips, even these skilled Oregon woodsmen were coming up zeroes. In desperation I outlined a special-effort scheme I'd been concocting to move elk. Bud and Lacy listened to the long discourse and studied my crudely drawn map. "So what do you think?" I asked.

Bud had his head down—I thought studying the map, a half-grin on his face. Lacy glanced at his father—I thought wondering if he admired my plan. Then Lacy glanced at me. His eyes glinted in the lantern light. "I don't think a man can ever drive elk anywhere they don't want to go."

That was more than twenty years ago. What hurt most was that I knew Lacy was right.

Bud lifted his glass and tosssed its dregs down the hatch. "You worry too much, Roland. Nub and I will drift up Table-way tomorrow. If we don't get him then, we'll get him the next day."

The idea that we cannot make an elk go where he hasn't already decided is the right direction is inviolate in the wapiti world. But that's a two-edged law—neither can one prevent an elk from going where he's already made up his mind to go.

I learned this rule early on when hunting a high snow-laden basin during early November with a friend of mine, Don Hall. We'd packed in by horseback and set up our tent, cut a supply of wood, and picketed our stock to graze. The next morning, we left camp a-horseback before good daylight. It was cold. Both of us wore felt-lined boots, wool coats, stocking caps, and mittens.

They're going to circle back to the pass!

We'd not gone far when I whipped off my cap to better hear. Don rode up alongside and I asked, "Did you hear that?"

"What?"

"I thought I heard an elk bugle." It was silly—this was the second weekend of November, the rut had long since ended.

Don shook his head. I pulled the cap back down over my ears and clucked to my saddlehorse, heading for an unusually low and narrow pass between two basins frequented by elk. An hour later, Don and I tied our horses to saplings at the pass, slipped our rifles from their scabbards, and wallowed through thigh-deep snow down into a spruce-filled basin where we hoped to find our quarry.

Tracks were plentiful, but elk standing in them were not. And late afternoon found us slogging wearily back to our horses. Don was in front. Suddenly he seemed to go insane, jerking his rifle from his shoulder and dropping to his knees in the snow. Lens caps flew from his rifle scope as he aimed into the pass.

"The horses!" I said. But the rifle's muzzle swung beyond, and that's when I saw a six-point bull elk and four of his cows milling within yards of the ponies. Don flicked off his safety. His rifle clicked.

"Damn!" he muttered. "It's a dud." My friend jerked the rifle from his shoulder and tried to work the bolt. "What's the matter with this gun?" he cried.

I knew. I'd been there and done that only the year before, hunting in snow all day long, knocking some from tree branches as I wriggled my way along a cold elk trail. Moisture penetrated the rifle's action, then froze with the falling temperatures at higher elevations. Precisely the same thing happened in this case—Don's firing pin and action were frozen.

So was mine. There was only one thing to do. While Don cursed and jerked and yanked at his bolt, I lifted my rifle action to my mouth and began breathing warm air onto it.

But the milling elk had had enough. They broke from the narrow pass they'd intended to traverse, back the way they'd come—from the basin of our camp. Just before they disappeared into trees, my bolt came free and I got off one clear miss. Then I was dashing to my horse.

"Wait for me!" Don called.

Time and elk wait for no man. I vaulted into the saddle and started Old Yeller plowing after the elk. I knew I had no chance to catch them in deep snow—especially in their own living room. But my blood was up and I had to try. Then I saw their tracks veering to the right and a bell clicked inside. *They're going to circle back to the pass!* So I reined Old Yeller right and fed him heels, driving him up the hill.

We broke into a tiny hillside meadow just as the big bull entered from the other side. I slid from Old Yeller's back and, well ... capitalized on their weakness.

Did I trap that bull? No.

Did I drive that bull? No.

I ambushed him. And *that's* a strategy that, even though its dividends are meager, pays at a better rate than trapping or driving.

"All About Elk Trapping" is the title of this chapter, and thus far I've said very little on the subject. So let me tell you about a turning point in my own wapiti enlightenment.

The locale of this episode was the Chinese Wall, the best-known geographic feature in all the Bob Marshall

Wilderness. For much of its length, the Wall forms the spine of the continent, with waters to the east flowing into the Atlantic Ocean, to the west into the Pacific. The Wall, is a fault-block formation, thrust up during tectonic plate collision, then tilted, much as a row of standing dominoes might look after they've been lined up and pushed to fall, one domino partially overlaying another.

The eastern edge of the Chinese Wall constitutes its scarp slope—that is, its sheer-bluff side—while the western side is the dip slope, climbing at about a sixty-degree gradient to the cliff height. I'd often led summer guests below the cliffs to view snow-white mountain goats grazing narrow ledges, five hundred to a thousand feet above our horse trail.

Also pertinent to this story is that most of the eastern quarter of the Bob Marshall Wilderness is a famous game preserve, set aside near the turn of the century as a refuge where wildlife—elk in particular—could not be hunted. The Sun River Game Preserve boundary, along the crest of the Chinese Wall, was about six miles from our early season hunting camp.

We sometimes hunted the gentle sloping side of the Wall to the Preserve boundary. The country had been burned over in a great 1919 forest fire. Due to the harsh climate and relatively shallow soil along the crest of the northern Rockies, the back side of the Wall is semi-open, with terraces of deeper soil where narrow strips of alpine firs, limber pine, and whitebark pine have taken hold.

One day, I'd laid an ambush. Another guide had taken our hunters up from camp and posted them in positions to command an area elk must come through if I could oust any from the tree lines. I'd hiked far down the valley, climbed halfway up the back side of the Wall, and begun methodically working back toward the hunters, shouting and singing as I went.

Imagine my surprise when I topped a rise only a few hundred yards from where the hunters were posted and spotted thirteen elk, two of which were bulls, wending toward their stands.

I shouted: *"Elk! Elk! Coming your way! Two bulls!*

Ten Minutes!"

But the elk turned off at the last second and climbed into a narrow strip of pines that ran up a vertical cleft near the summit of the Wall. No matter, I thought. There's a sheer cliff dropping in front and a two-hundred-foot cliff rising from their right to keep them from doubling back. Their only escape is the open meadow taking them directly to the hunters. They're trapped. I have only to work up through this narrow strip of trees to flush them. What a piece of cake!

The thicket wasn't all that dense. High-altitude forests generally tend to be sparse. This stand was perhaps a hundred feet wide at its broadest—no chance for the elk to elude my one-man drive.

I entered the trees with every sense alert, listening for the telltale shuffle of heavy bodies, like cattle milling in a pen at night; the clatter of hooves on rocks, the breaking of branches as the creatures fled from danger.

"Elk! Elk! Coming your way! Two bulls! Ten minutes!"

Every few steps, I stopped to listen and feel for their movement so I could shout a warning to the hunters. Halfway through the thicket, I got a whiff of them—the musky odor peculiar to elk. But sight and sound and feel for the animals continued to elude me.

On I crept. Only a third of the thicket left. A quarter. *What the hell is going on? Yes, the odor is still here, but isn't it fading, too?* I emerged from the thicket to peer over the top of the cliff. There were no elk! Wait a minute—elk tracks lead out onto that goat ledge! How can that be? Elk won't go onto narrow cliff ledges. Boy, if they were trapped before, they're pinned in a squeeze chute now!

Clinging to a ledge below the Wall's summit, the elk were, of course, just beyond the game-preserve boundary. I knew that we could no longer hunt them. But I was caught up in a chase of the kind that was elemental to our primitive ancestors. I plunged after the elk, intent on reaching the spot where the cliff face curled away from my vision. This was my chance to see our quarry in a place no man had ever before seen elk!

A hundred yards. Two hundred. I began to run.

Elk weren't just beyond the curl of cliff as expected. But I could see their tracks in old snow, rounding yet another bend of cliff. I ran on and on along the goat ledge, around that bend and another, not believing the evidence unfolding before my eyes.

Finally winded, I stopped and took stock. *They really did it! They escaped along a goat ledge!* Then I looked about and had the shock of my life. *My God! I'm out here on a goat ledge!* Just inches beyond the toes of my boots yawned nothing. For a thousand feet to boulder-sized rocks below there was nothing.

Looking down was a mistake. I sat abruptly, swiveled around on the seat of my pants and looked back the way I'd come. It was several hundred yards to where two white-faced hunters and a guide waved anxiously for me to return.

I made it back, obviously, but returning along that ledge wasn't without its lessons in the efficacy of prayer.

My greatest regret is that I was not riding below the Chinese Wall that day; that I did not get to see thirteen head of elk streaming along a narrow goat ledge a thousand feet up one of the most famous cliffs in America. Such a sight, I'm convinced, would have been my all-time high point in a lifetime chock-full of outdoors memories. ■

Chapter 7

Why Some Men Fall for Elk

I used to be a hunter, but a fascination with elk transcends mere hunting. These animals have a way of wriggling into hearts and minds. For much of my life, they were animals of which dreams were made—the last thing seen before drifting away, the first thing upon awakening.

I used the past tense deliberately when saying I used to be a hunter. The last elk I killed was in 1974. Yet there's something inaccurate—untrue to myself—in the implication that I quit hunting after 1974, because I've not missed a hunting season since. I carry a rifle. I hike up hillsides, poke through copses and forest glades, glass distant mountains. I still live to stand on a frosted ridgetop at break of day to pound my chest from sheer joy at being alive. And I can easily snooze on a beargrass-covered hillside after a warming sun burns away that frost. I *was* a hunter? Hell, I *am* a hunter.

Besides, 1974 was also the year I started full-time outfitting and guiding others to elk. It was the year when I became fully convinced it's far more challenging to guide others to the elk of their dreams than to hunt up an elk of my own.

Will I ever again shoot an elk?

Search me. I only know I no longer view my role with the same fervor as before; it's of no consequence in preserving either rite or right of the hunter. But neither am I such a fool as to say either "yea" nor "nay" about some day pulling the trigger. I'm keeping my options open. Because, you see, I may someday cross paths with a huge old bull who's carrying the same mark of destiny as this wrinkling old man. Leastways, the idea is what put me to sleep last night.

One reason why it's impossible for me to abandon the urge to hunt harkens back to the Paleolithic: I enjoy the campfire camaraderie with friends of similar inclination.

The impending innovative hors d'oeuvres were subject to both disbelief and vehemence.

There's no question that camaraderie is an important element of any hunting group, regardless of the species hunted. But the operative words here are "of similar inclination." Elk hunters seem to me a breed apart. They are the halest of the hale and heartiest of the hearty. (A lot of sheep hunters would disagree, and I can only say they're entitled to their opinion.) They usually are more woods-wise, with more advanced outdoors skills. They're adventuresome. They're tough. They're stolid. They are also trustworthy, loyal, helpful, friendly, courteous, kind, obedient, cheerful, thrifty, brave, clean, and reverent. Why wouldn't I aspire to maintain membership among such a lustrous company of outstanding men and women?

Camaraderie comes in many forms: good-natured ribbing, shared experiences, high jinks, and conviviality. Traditions are passed on; the young metamorphose into accomplished adults indelibly connecting with seniors (for whom allowances are made). And over it all lies the tantalizing, mysterious, unpredictable, thrilling information that elk are bugling, or they're down from the high country, or a fresh tracking snow fell during the night.

We tried to give camaraderie a big boost in our hunting camps. One way my wife Jane did this was with a plate of Rocky Mountain oysters. So what's so special about Rocky Mountain oysters? Aren't they on the menu at most fine restaurants from St. Louis to San Francisco?

Ha! Sheep gonads. I'm talking about real Rocky Mountain oysters—testicles of bull elk from the high reaches of the continent, skinned, washed and cleaned, sliced into thin pieces, rolled in flour and salt, then fried to a fair brown. That, my friends, is fare that turns boys into men, puts hair on a glass jar, drives a whipped and beaten executive, upon his return to civilization, to climb his office building with one hand tied behind his back, kiss his secretary hello, and strangle his boss with thumb and forefinger.

Naturally, elk gonads aren't readily available at your neighborhood grocery. So, unless we were really lucky early in a hunt, Jane saved the delicacies until day nine of a ten-day trip. Each guide was, under threat of violence, instructed to bring the gonads back from his hunter's trophy—even if his hunter demurred.

Jane with plate of real Rocky Mountain oysters. To prepare, she soaked them in salt water for 24 hours. Skin off membrane, slice into quarter-inch slices. Season to taste. Roll in flour, fry in hot oil. Then get out of the way!

Almost to a man, our hunters were horrified at the thought of sliced, deep-fried oysters of the Rocky Mountain variety. The impending innovative hors d'oeuvres were subject to both disbelief and vehemence. Most did not believe my petite, attractive wife really capable of cooking them. When the day arrived, many shied from the plate; others only dared when they saw guides, wrangler, outfitter, and cook diving in with relish.

Without exception, any who gathered sufficient intestinal fortitude to sample the delicacy returned for more, all the while berating their weaker-spined comrades.

Dick Read had suffered a near-fatal heart attack a couple of years prior to his first hunt with us. The attack was a wake-up call, and when the forty-five-year-old dentist showed up on our doorstep he was slim and trim and regularly running five miles per day.

I guided Dick and his hunting partner, Tom Blakey, into a high basin surrounded on three sides by cliffs. Tom is a fine, white-haired old gentleman, crusty as cornbread, with a heart the size of a washtub watermelon. Tom had been with us several times, but the World War II paratrooper was afflicted by both glaucoma and a respiratory ailment, so I tried to stay with the man when he was afield.

Dick missed his chance at a bull elk on the first day, and as the afternoon wore on I thought it best to work our way back to camp through the heavily timbered bottoms. It appeared that Dick was a good hunter, confident and careful in the woods. So I placed him on one side of the creek and explained how the country lay and what he could expect to encounter along his route, ending with a detailed description of what trails to look for when he neared the camp area. Then I took Tom, the least physically able, and worked the opposite side of the bottoms.

Tom and I encountered considerable sign, but no elk, and we arrived at camp an hour before dark. Our other hunters wandered in shortly after, leaving only Dick, the newcomer, still afield.

When at last he showed, the Mississippian looked bushed. He drank deeply from the water bucket and happily accepted a beer. "See anything?" I asked.

"Did I ever!" he replied in his deep drawl, wiping forehead sweat with an outsized red bandanna. "I had some of them elk critters all around me. I was plumb into the middle of 'em before I knew it. Sounded like the whole woods was crashing down!"

Dick's ears flapped out beyond his wavy red-brown hair. The eyes were big, brown and lively, and the mouth wide and curled up on each end. His face was etched deep with life—creased laugh lines that accentuated a ready smile, and crow's-feet wrinkles shooting off toward the temples. No doubt about it, Dick's was a happy face—one that made others feel good, no matter if he talked of humorous or serious things.

The drawl was melodious and made you want to relax and listen even if you couldn't see the face, full of lazy words dripping from Mississippi creeks and bayous.

The other hunters and guides crowded around the excited man. A chorus of voices overlaid his:

"Did you get to see them?"

"Were there any bulls?"

"Did you get a shot?"

Dick sat upon a block of wood and took a long pull on his beer. "Hell, yes I seen 'em! They was goin' so many ways, mostly all I could do was look at 'em with my mouth open. I never seen nothin' so big!"

"Where did you jump them?" one hunter asked. He was obviously thinking of tomorrow's hunt.

Dick's eyes widened as he pondered the question. He gazed at the man, then at me, then around the circle of hunters and guides. He shook his head slowly while saying the obvious for a first-time elk hunter just coming off his first hunting day in strange country:

"I don't rightly know where I was, I guess ..." Then he brightened visibly. "... but I can tell you what time I was there."

Excitement is central to humans fascinated with the species *Cervus canadensis*. It's an emotion that grips us at the point of introduction. But it's not an always thing. That truth was hammered home to me the first summer after retiring from outfitting.

Bill and Marie were in their late thirties, nice folks who believed in physical fitness and inquiring minds. Both were college instructors from Reno, Nevada. Bill taught creative writing, and I owed him for his efforts to pass along a few writing tips to a retired guide struggling toward a new career. So Jane and I paid my debt by leading our friends on an early-summer wilderness adventure along the crest of the northern Rockies.

One day we explored a huge, scantily forested basin that

topped out along a portion of the Continental Divide. The subsurface foundation rock for the basin was limestone. Wildfire had swept through this area, sterilizing the shallow soil, and now, after decades, open bunchgrass slopes still predominated over spruce, pine, and fir forest.

The area contained lateral terraces on its dip slope where soil had accumulated more deeply and, in some places, the forest tried taking root, forming what we called "tree lines"—strips or narrow bands of trees of several different alpine species.

It was up this mountainside that our little cavalcade of horses and people toiled, heading for the Continental crest and the spectacular view beyond. Saddle-weary, we'd all dismounted to lead our ponies. But the strenuous climb took its toll, and Jane, Marie, and Bill had remounted.

We struck the first fresh elk tracks while passing across outcroppings of flat limestone mixed with bunchgrass growing amid its cracks. Farther on, out onto more stable soil and meadow, there were more. They looked only hours old. I led my saddlehorse aside and motioned to the tracks.

Then Jane pointed at her nose—an unspoken signal that the smell of elk had wafted in on the breeze.

I wet a forefinger and held it aloft. There was a gentle flow down the mountain, coming from where we headed —just right for us. I hitched my trousers and our party plodded on, expecting to roust elk from first one tree line, then another.

Higher up-slope, the occasional bands of trees thinned, and sometimes the terraces were covered with thick sod and knee-high grasses. We coursed one of those meadow terraces now, moving rapidly along the nearly level bench, hurrying to crest a low knoll and view a huge field beyond. Just above and parallel to our terrace was another, perhaps ten feet higher and a hundred feet distant. The scent of elk was overpowering now. They *had* to be in the field beyond.

Bill and Marie had not yet caught our excitement. But Jane, with her saucer-size eyes and swiveling head, was tuned in. There was movement on the bench above. She described it later as "A sea of horns." Actually it was bedded bull elk clambering to their feet. But because of the curve of the hillside, all the lady could see from her position was antlers waving.

"Horns were weaving and waving everywhere!" she later exclaimed. "All I saw was a sea of horns popping up everywhere! Big horns."

Meanwhile, I'd topped the knoll and spotted the expected elk: cows and calves and raghorn bulls streaming out ahead of us, dashing for the forest edging the huge field's far side. I turned to wave at the others and saw Jane frantically pointing. Then I, too, spotted her sea of horns!

"What's he saying?" Bill asked of Marie, and with more elk than God made bursting all about us, Jane and I both nearly died at Bill's unnecessary noise.

"Elk!" I hissed, then held a forefinger across my lips in the universal sign.

By then, all hell was breaking loose above and beyond, and even Reno college professors could no longer remain oblivious about what was taking place. Probably, though, they didn't realize we were witnessing something few people are ever privileged to see.

What appeared to be an endless procession of huge bull elk burst off the bench above, zeroing in on the safe route of the retreating herd. Aside from the feedlot at the National Elk Refuge near Jackson, Wyoming, I'd never before witnessed such a concentration of elk. I began counting as the leading cows and calves neared the meadow center: "One, two, three, four-five-six, seven ..."

Jane kneed her pony up beside mine. "I can't believe it!"

"... twenty-eight-nine-thirty, thirty one—dammit, woman, count the bulls!"

"They are elk, aren't they?" Bill asked from behind.

"Two, three, four—*Yes!*" Jane said.

"One-oh-two, one-oh-three, one-oh-four ..."

"Fifteen, sixteen, seventeen ..."

"One-twenty-five, one-twenty-six, one-twenty-seven ..."

"Twenty-nine, thirty, thirty-one ..."

We finished our tally with a total of one hundred and

thirty-four elk passing across that lush green mountain hill-side, thirty-six of which were mature bulls. Again, it was a sight we had never before seen. And one that we expect never to view again.

Excited? Yes! Adrenaline rush? You bet! Memories? Ones we'll never forget! Elk is the name of our game. ∎

Chapter 8

Essential Excitement

The man missed his shot.

We'd spotted the bull at a distance—a big one, six points on each side. But the brush was so tangled where he loitered that I laid out a plan to half-circle the animal, then bust through his bedroom hoping to push him into flight along a game trail near where Alex was posted. The plan worked to perfection. The bull broke from cover right on target, crossed the flat amid a screen of saplings, and bolted up the sparsely forested hillside to within seventy-five yards of my hunter.

Alex caught glimpses of the elk as he crashed from the big forest into scattered saplings. It was like movie flicks jerking through a poorly threaded home projector, each flick a reminder for the man that a monster bull elk fled his way, zeroing in on the trail he covered. The lead time to action was long and his suspense nearly unbearable. Alex's face flushed, heart pounded, knees trembled. He heard the elk crashing, caught a closer glimpse, raised his rifle, aimed at a tiny opening where the bull must cross, flicked off the safety.

And missed.

That night, after the sleeping-tent lantern dimmed, then went black; after first one hunter, then another began breathing deeply or snoring softly, one of Alex's companions spoke softly into the night: "Alex ..."

"What, Robert?"

"Tell me, what's the last thing you see when y'all shut your eyes tonight?"

Robert's good-natured ribbing was tastefully done. Alex, who actually was a competition marksman in turkey shoots all over east Texas, got off easy. Even so, disappointment was keen throughout the camp.

Perhaps it goes back to the Paleolithic—I don't know. Perhaps a band of Stone Age hunters peered over a rock ledge and spotted a giant Megaloceros (Irish elk), with antlers spreading upwards of ten feet, feeding below. The best marksman among those hunters would have been selected to cast the first spear. With no cans of pork and beans stocking cave shelves, whether the band ate depended upon the exactness of our hero's cast. A miss not only relegated the marksman to ridicule, but to demotion within the hierarchy of the hunter/gatherer society. If their quarry chanced to be a dangerous creature, such as a cave bear, saber-toothed cat, or giant lion, a miss could be fatal.

Evolution to civilization has considerably reduced the life-threatening aspects of a hunter's poor marksmanship, but it hasn't relieved the poor wretch of the ribald teasing from the fellows in his band.

In most cases, misses occur because of excitement. In most cases where proper preparation by the hunter meets the opportunity to take a trophy, the moment of truth comes in a rush, is over in a flash, and there's scant chance to breathe deeply, consider objectively, and control emotions with a sense of inner peace.

I've watched a few hunters, in their instant of opportunity, jack all the shells from their rifles without once pulling the trigger. I've seen others fire off-hand at a running target when the distance gave them little chance, without a bench rest, to hit even a four-foot bullseye.

But am I ridiculing hunters who miss because of excitement? Not on your life. After forty years hunting and twenty years guiding, I've come to believe near-blood-bursting excitement must be there for anyone to

According to the latest figures available—in 1995 there were 834,402 elk hunters in the United States and Canada who took 166,058 elk—a 19.9% harvest-to-hunter ratio.

—*Status of Elk in North America.* Rocky Mountain Elk Foudation experience the essence of what hunting is all about.

Frankly, I would find an emotionless hunter distasteful; nor would I trust him. Better for that type of guy to take up Mafia work—or golf, a game where he could profit from his lack of normal human feeling. I know this because I no longer have that gut-wrenching, chest-thumping, adrenaline-pumping excitement prevalent during my hunting youth. With the last several elk I took, there was no surge of adrenaline, no shakiness, no blood rush. Instead, I took aim, fired, then began butchering my winter's meat.

And the experience was no longer as exciting.

It was late in the hunt now. Daylight was barely breaking as the riders wended their way up the ridge. A slit of a canyon opened to their right. Beyond, perhaps two hundred and fifty yards distant, was a grass-covered knoll. On the knoll stood a bull elk.

Robert leaped from his saddlehorse, rifle in hand. He sprawled behind a gnarled windthrown whitebark pine, took careful aim—and missed.

Later that night, when the lantern in their sleeping tent flared its last, when the hunters breathed easily and some snored, a voice came from the darkness. "Robert ..."

"What do you want, Alex?"

"What's the last thing you see just before you go to sleep tonight?"

Camaraderie amid failure may have been a luxury that cave clans could ill afford. But my experience has always been that it builds enduring partnerships in hunting camps.

The bull's reply floated eerily along the shadowy spruce bottom. Adrenaline pumped and I flashed an ear-to-ear grin at my hunter. The man stood transfixed by the suddenness and the mystique of the bull's bugle. He never saw me or my grin. I tapped his shoulder and broke the spell, motioning him to follow while holding a forefinger to my lips.

We slipped forward a few yards, oblivious to the wet and boggy ground, oblivious to the teeth-chattering chill of early morning. Then the forest opened a bit and I looked right and left, moving stealthily forward. The hunter hung so close his shadow merged with mine. Satisfied that we'd found the best field of fire available, one with seventy-five yard shooting lanes leading through the trees, I raised a hand. Taking his cue from me, the hunter hunkered down just in front as I performed my idea of the challenge of an enraged bull elk.

His antlers came first. They seemed to loom from nowhere

Our challenges clashed, crossed in the air waves; his more angered and full-throated, mine powered by a considerably smaller chest cavity weakened by fat and easy living. The hunter shifted nervously in anticipation and glanced back, eyes dancing and a toothy grin of his own.

I picked up a dead limb and thrashed a small spruce, rubbing, breaking branches, simulating a bull honing antlers as he prepares for a fight.

The bull bugled again, then again. It sounded like he was barely out of sight, directly before us. I tapped the hunter on the shoulder and pointed, then again thrashed my spruce tree.

His antlers came first. They seemed to loom from nowhere, rising from behind a previously unnoticed swell of ground, followed by the swaggering brawn of an over-sized bully. He came at a shambling run, horns titled before him in ready position, twisting and turning them slowly as he advanced, much the same as with a skilled boxer's searching leads. And he came from the right—not the front, as we expected. I glanced down at the hunter, who still stared intently where I'd pointed. *My God! Can't he see the monster?*

The bull paused to glare angrily about, then began quartering around us, trying to get the scent of his antagonist, narrowing the gap as he came. Still the hunter hadn't seem him. I stealthily tapped the man with my tree limb and pointed. He saw the bull. His gun roared.

The elk continued his stalking advance. The gun roared again, and again. I couldn't believe it—the elk still tromped unflinchingly on! The gun roared again and the bull dropped in his tracks.

"My last shell," the hunter murmured as I leaned weakly on my tree limb. "I got him with my last shell."

It was 36 paces from where we stood to where the bull fell. I turned to peer back at my hunter, clearly hoping he'd explain.

He didn't. But that evening at camp I overheard the man recount his day to his buddies:

"I'll tell you, he was the biggest thing I ever saw! Excited? Why my first four shots, all I saw through the rifle scope was horns!"

No outfitter I know would ever admit to missing a bull elk. You understand I'm talking about steely-eyed "yep, nope" folks who've spent a lifetime striding through elk and deer living rooms. They're people who know every turn a herd bull will make before the animal comes to a trail fork.

They've fondled firearms since they were big enough to keep the barrels from dragging in the dust. They know bullet trajectories, muzzle energies, and bullet expansion. They know distance and how much windage to allow, from a light breeze to a full gale. They can judge the MPH of a speeding antelope and their computer-trap minds spit out the proper lead quicker than a NASA main frame.

They know vital areas for every creature that roams their domain and they can thread a fix on a four-point mule deer bouncing through a quaking aspen thicket. Miss a shot? Never!

So how was it that I once blew a standing shot—at a bull who had his head down feeding? And him not more than seventy-five *feet* away?

I admit it's a heck of a thing to admit. But if it's fess-up time for other macho elk hunters, then a macho guide should fess up missing some himself. You'll not hear about all my misses, understand, because I see little need to call in a clergyman in a black cassock and tie up a confessional—as I would if I told about the time I missed at twenty feet. But the very least I can do is demonstrate that outfitters—like politicians—are fallible. Here's how it happened:

I was but twenty-five in those long-gone days, and elk had filled my mind for six, maybe seven years. It was opening day of elk season. We'd hiked the trail to Pine Bench, where I'd earlier discovered the evidence that a couple of bull elk had been in a shoving match over love-sick cows. Fog lay heavy over the North Umpqua River as I parked the Jeep wagon and locked it. Mist shrouded the trail all the way to the flat bench at top, but showed signs of lifting.

We spread out to move across the bench. I had the steep side, the one where the river canyon yawned. After a couple of hundred yards, a breeze fanned to life, freeing the bench of fog but bringing in tantalizing wisps from below, distressing the hunters with only occasional glimpses through the scattered yellow pine forest.

A wad of fog blew past. When it cleared, the bull elk was feeding only seventy-five feet below. Then the clouds blew in again. I was near to bursting! I knelt, thumbed back the hammer on my Marlin 30-30, fit the stock firmly into my shoulder, and waited. One minute, two. Would the bull still be there when the vapor lifted?

If it lifted.

Fog thinned for an instant and I could see not only his outline, but the outline of another bull who'd fed up the hill toward him! Then they were gone. Three minutes. I suppressed the urge to try closing with them. Indeed, I was afraid to move. Four minutes. I could hear the rustling of a breeze in the treetops. Surely the gods would smile soon! Then in an instant, the fog was gone and my bull was still in place, feeding.

The Marlin roared.

The bull ran off.

The fog closed in so suddenly there was no chance for a

follow-up shot. No need. He was lying out there some-where in the mist.

Five minutes passed and the vapor lifted for good. My bull wasn't in view. No problem. I picked up his tracks—he'd been spinning so hard that great clumps of sod were thrown up behind. No blood—what's this? "It can't be!" I cried.

I had missed. Aiming for his neck, I must have failed to allow for the short range and shot over him.

At least that's the story I tell today. And I'll stick with it, even in a confessional.

"Elk! Elk! Coming your way!"

Earlier, shortly after daylight, I posted one hunter below the rim and returned for the second. Then the second hunter and I spread out and began a pussyfoot stalk up one side of the big basin, hoping to jump elk within range or spook them to the waiting hunter. I tried a couple of bugles. There was no reply....

"Four elk! Bull, cow, cow, bull! Don't answer!

I was out of sight of the left-side hunter most of the time as I worked in and out of the trees, down into ravines and tiny sidepockets, beating my way in a zigzag, pausing now and then to let the slower, quieter-moving man come abreast. Neither could I see the right-side hunter on his far-off stand, though I had an occasional view across the basin and knew approximately where he waited....

"Ten minutes! Bull, cow, cow, Bull! High! Just below the rocks! Ten minutes!

A bead of sweat trickled from beneath my hatband and coursed around an ear. I shifted my daypack and unbut-toned the top three buttons of my wool shirt. The sun barely peeped over an eastern ridge. Then, with a deep breath, I plunged into another ravine and up the other side....

"Five minutes! Cow, bull, cow, bull! Coming your way! Just below rocks! Five minutes!

I popped out of a brush patch and paused, peering left

for my stalking hunter's orange vest. Where could he be? Probably a little behind. Should come through the opening by that big whitebark pine. Yep, there he comes. Okay, he waved. Drop back down the hill, into the bottom, check that little meadow....

"Three minutes! Cow, bull, cow, bull! Still below rocks!"

When I next came out of the bottom, my left-side hunter had wandered my way in a thicket. He saw me fifty yards away and abruptly changed his direction. I waited for him to get a little ahead before continuing my zigzag drive. Meanwhile I studied the basin's far side through my binoculars. That's when I saw the elk....

"Two minutes! Get ready! Cow, bull, cow, bull!"

I wondered how well my voice carried across the canyon and wished I could see exactly where the first hunter waited. If I could see him, I could give better directions.

The four elk trotted single file, also weaving in and out of the brush. They disappeared into a thicket.

Ka-Boom! The big magnum's blast rolled across the basin. The roar startled me, for I didn't think the elk were in an opening. *Ka-Boom! Ka-Boom!*

When the elk again appeared in the open, they were above the rocks and running flat out—all four of them.

The hunter's forked-horn buck was lying right where his third shot dropped him. The small buck, as it turned out, was spooked out by the elk herd and chanced across the opening where my hunter waited.

"I thought you shouted that they were elk?" the man said as I walked up.

"I did."

"So where's the elk? This is a deer."

I smiled at the man and shrugged. "You win some, you lose some."

He frowned. "I don't understand."

"I know." ∎

Chapter 9

Splitters or Lumpers?

Among scientists who deal with species designation, there are splitters and lumpers. In *Elk of North America*, compiled and edited by Jack Ward Thomas and Dale E. Toweill, one finds: "The word 'species' has one significance to the student of taxonomy and another to the student of evolution." Thus the late renowned authority, Dr. Olaus Murie contended in his earlier book of nearly the same title, *The Elk of North America*, that six subspecies of North American wapiti existed until the onslaught of European settlers did away with three of them. But later, Dr. Valerius Geist, writing in *Bugle*, the journal of the Rocky Mountain Elk Foundation, lumped all six of Murie's subspecies into one category and also included a couple of Asiatic wapiti.

Bruce Smith, a successor-biologist to Dr. Murie at the National Elk Refuge near Jackson, Wyoming, goes even farther than Dr. Geist. Also writing for *Bugle*, Smith cites considerable crossmatings resulting in fertile offspring between North American elk and European red deer, when both species were introduced into New Zealand. Smith concludes:

> The lack of reproductive isolation and the extensive harmony of biological traits among red deer and wapiti make designation of more than one species

unwarranted. Molecular analyses of blood serum protein from Eurasian red deer and North American wapiti further support existence of only a single species.

With lumpers ascendant, there is no longer need for a separate scientific name for the animal we North Americans know as elk. Thus, *Cervus canadensis* has been coopted by *Cervus elaphus*, the older latin designation for Asian wapiti and European red deer.

The view from this decidedly unscientific corner is, however, don't get in a hurry to throw away *canadensis*— the splitters may yet rise again. When and if they do, demand will rise for a distinctly American taxonomic name for a distinctly North American animal.

Today's scientific debate over *C. canadensis* versus *C. elaphus* is hardly the first name drain concerning the American wapiti. Right from the outset, the common term "elk' was in trouble. Here again, Thomas' and Toweill's *Elk of North America* is illuminating:

> The problem arose when some explorers, adventurers, and settlers opted for the term "elk." In most if not all European languages, then as now, "elk" refers to the European moose. Subsequent discovery of the North American moose only compounded that problem.

Reference is made to John Lederer, who traveled through Virginia in late 1670 and observed "numerous herds of Red Deer (for their unusual largeness improperly termed Elk by ignorant people)...."

Further reference is made to Catesby who wrote in 1754: "This beast nearest resembles the European red deer ... they are improperly called elks." *Elk of North America* summarizes:

> What resistance still existed to "elk" as the common name for North American *Cervus* came from abroad and certain scientific communities. This resistance appears to have become less an objection to North American "elk" than a concern over the fact that its

interchangeable use (also and first representing the European moose) lent confusion to scientific inquiry, particularly internationally.

However, in America, the common people of the 17th and 18th Centuries were less likely to march in rote with scientific types, particularly scientists of European origin. And "elk" stuck to North American wapiti like hot taffy to cold fingers.

Lewis and Clark—made upwards of six hundred mentions of the word "elk."

The first great comprehensive documentation of plants and animals west of the Mississippi River—the Journals of Lewis and Clark—made upwards of six hundred mentions of the word "elk." North American magazines, newspapers, and diaries all used the term "elk" when mentioning an animal that was slowly wending its way, by dint of toughness, tenacity, and intelligence up the human awareness scale. Ultimately the common people had their way in imposing their lay term for the supposed North American version of the European red deer.

This victory for the voice of the people brings me comfort because during my journalistic career I've written hundreds of magazine stories, newspaper columns, and radio scripts without once agonizing over whether my readers or listeners would misinterpret my word "elk" to mean an ungainly, dew-belled, blackish beast with palmated antlers and a mean disposition.

To their credit, the scientific community long ago floated an alternative name for elk, suggesting the Shawnee Indian term "wapiti" for common usage. But it never really took. Oh, I've used "wapiti" on occasion, even think it more charismatic than "elk." But my use of "wapiti" was always to avoid tiring listeners or readers with too repetitious usage of "elk." I've utilized the scientifically questionable *Cervus canadensis* for the same reason. And I assume it will make little difference to the average reader whether *C. canadensis* or *C. elaphus* is employed to enliven stories about the single North American wild creature that most ensnares hunters' dreams and imaginations. But fail to use "elk" in my articles, and I'd have to get a job as a whistlepunk in a steam laundry in order to meet mortgage payments.

With the great name debate disposed of, what about elk?

They are ruminants. As such, they're equipped with four-chambered stomachs that permit fermentation of cellulose-rich forage, providing much more efficient digestion than the single-chambered stomachs of non-ruminants, such as horses. Bruce Smith points out in his *History of American Wapiti* that ruminant stomachs are more important "in environments with seasonally low-quality forage, such as northern latitudes or high altitudes, because it converts more of the available nutrients into energy."

A regal bull elk is, of course, the stuff of which dreams are made.

According to paleontological evidence, elk are members of the Cervid family, originating a little over fifty million years ago as tiny, reclusive forest dwellers. Through the evolutionary process, Cervids branched and branched again, until some of those branches adapted to grassland habitat, gradually developing large body size and antler growth. One indicator of adaptation from forest to savanna is development from secretive individuals to herd animals dependent upon collective eyes, ears, and noses for detecting enemies. Another is fleetness of foot for avoidance of same.

Which, of course, leads back to the hypothesis that elk, in European man's experience, was a plains animal driven to the mountains in order to survive. Murie puts that idea to rest in *The Elk of North America* (not to be confused with Thomas and Toweill's later treatise of the same name). To dismantle the theory that elk were driven to the mountains, Murie cites diaries and journals of early explorers such as Osborne Russell and Benjamin Bonneville, and also supports his conclusion with archeological and paleontological findings. He writes:

... the fact of migration was often overlooked ... and it was not always clear whether the plains animals were already on winter range or were in transit to and from it.

Murie concludes that there were always elk in the mountains as well as on the plains, but those elk with the plains habit were eventually wiped out.

Splitters and lumpers sometimes haggle over the classification of *sub*species as well as species. According to the splitters (and to the ordinary North American elk aficionado), there are three distinctly different subspecies of *Cervus canadensis*: the Roosevelt, Rocky Mountain, and Tule varieties. Splitters also claim three other subspecies that were present when Europeans arrived in America: eastern elk, Manitoba elk, and Merriam elk. Of the latter three, only the smaller-antlered, dark *manitobensis millais* still exists, its range limited to portions of Manitoba and eastern Saskatchewan.

The extinct Merriam elk formerly inhabited a few isolated mountain ranges of Arizona and New Mexico. Rocky Mountain elk have been transplanted into those former Merriam ranges and, after adapting to habitat differences, appear to thrive there.

Eastern elk disappeared early after European settlement expanded through that part of the country. The bounds of this subspecies' range cannot be fully delineated from fossil and written records, and there is little certainty regarding how far south these elk ranged. Elk bones have been lifted from Maine, Massachusetts, New York, and the Carolinas. How much the eastern elk differed from the widespread Rocky Mountain variety will, it seems, be subject for barroom debate for future millenniums.

Of the three existing subspecies (not counting the Manitoba remnant), only tule elk come in limited range and numbers, existing in a few small preserve enclaves in California. Sometimes called "dwarf elk" the tule animal is lighter-colored than the other subspecies and has smaller antlers.

A regal bull elk is, of course, the stuff of which dreams are made. In most minds, that animal is the Rocky Mountain variety. This isn't only because the wide sweep of the antlers makes one gasp or the contrasty dark mane against the sleek buckskin tan of his sides is so impressive; it's the animal in combination with the stunning mountain and meadow backdrop. And the imagined picture conforms to the truth—a truth that provides a bum rap to the other subspecies.

Richard Jackson

Neither Lewis nor Clark—nor any man of their train—perceived a difference between elk slain in the Rocky Mountains and elk slain in the rain forests of the Pacific Coast. Would they be confused between Roosevelt or Rocky Mountain elk if they were alive today? In a sense, I am.

Common knowledge purports Roosevelt elk to be bigger-bodied but smaller-antlered. Maybe. Boone & Crockett measurements seem to support the contention that Rocky Mountain elk have greater antlers. But most of us will live and die without ever walking up to a record book trophy, and during my early years in Oregon rain forests, I certainly saw a fair share of Roosevelt elk wall-hangers.

Common knowledge purports Roosevelt elk to be bigger-bodied but smaller-antlered. Maybe.

As for body sizes, the largest elk I've ever packed out of the northern Rockies weighed one hundred and thirty-seven pounds per each skinned-out quarter—five hundred and forty-eight pounds of fully dressed meat. I never quartered a Roosevelt elk that approached this particular bull's body size, so that, too, is a suitable subject for barroom debate.

Valerius Geist, in his taxonomic treatise arguing for a single subspecies for all North American elk, claims that differences in body size and antler development is directly attributable to each regional population's habitat. He writes: "Put elk behind a fence and a hay crib year-round and see if anybody can guess where they originally came from. Give Tule elk runts three square meals a day and watch what happens!"

Geist goes on to argue: "Our North American elk, for all their far-flung distribution, have the same hair and color distributions and the same rutting voices. Antler size and shape differ in the wild somewhat, but that disappears with a change in environment."

And he goes on to contend that *all* North American elk will, "given a chance at real feed during antler growth ... grow heavy, long-tined, angled antlers just like those of Rocky Mountain bulls."

What about that antler growth?

With mature bulls in good condition it is, to say the least, luxuriant. I've seen a few large bulls with substantial new antler growth in April, while others still carried the previous year's crown. Growth must begin as soon as old antlers are shed. A modestly large set of elk antlers, when fully grown, rubbed and polished, will weigh four times (or more) than those of even the largest mule deer or whitetail buck. And the elk will grow his in less time. But perhaps what's fair is fair—the elk is four times larger, requires a commensurate amount of food to sustain him, and more than four times as much land upon which to roam.

A bull elk's antlers are usually fully formed by late July or early August. The shedding of velvet begins soon after, usually first undertaken by mature bulls with what is supposed a greater stake in the coming rut. Murie writes:

> The velvet is loosened and scraped away by constant rubbing and threshing by restless elk against bushes and tree limbs, and during the process numerous young evergreens are rubbed bare of limbs and bark and are demolished. As the rut approaches, the bull prods the ground and fights the willow bushes with loud rattling and crashing. This constant rubbing eventually leaves the antlers cleaned, polished and stained and a portion of the landscape more or less disfigured.

Immediately after rubbing, the antlers are bloody, but are soon polished to milk-white. Except for their still-gleaming points, continued rubbing of tree limbs and bark quickly stains them to a ruddy brown.

By the first of September, most mature bulls have shed their velvet and polished and stained their weapons for finding love and fighting wars. The rut begins. Actual battles are few, but sparring and posturing common.

The frenzy of breeding and hustling takes enormous toll on the most dominant bulls, sending them into the rigors of winter gaunt and haggard. Cows, on the other hand, continue feeding throughout the weeks-long gathering-and-breeding processes. One might assume evolution played a cruel joke here were not the bulls left with antlers to knock down tree branches and dig beneath crusted snow during winter's food-gathering forays.

Elk are said to have the least specialized food habits of all the world's deer species—a factor contributing to their wide-ranging dispersal to many habitats. Whereas moose and other deer species are largely dependent on browse, and horses and bison need large quantities of grass, elk are more adaptable as both browsers and grazers.

There's a downside to this omnivorous adaptability, however: elk may well develop harmful competition with other creatures. A few deer feeding on emerging shoots in a farmer's grainfield is one thing, a herd of elk another. Where their ranges overlap, elk often compete with bighorn sheep. And there's no question which wins out— deer or elk—in a shoving match for limited winter forage.

Elk calves weigh in the vicinity of thirty-five pounds at birth. They gain weight rapidly. There is little difference between weights of the two sexes throughout the first year. But thereafter the males grow brawnier and heavier.

Life in the wapiti world is harsh; two-thirds of all calves die before their first birthday. Considering that eighty percent of females in a healthy herd give birth, this means roughly twenty percent of the overall total enter their teen-age years, and ultimately the breeding cycle.

What are the reasons for high infant mortality among elk? Predation is one: cougars, bears, coyotes, wolves, perhaps wolverines. Murie tells of watching golden eagles repeatedly striking a calf until it crawled beneath a bush and died. Death by disease is a little-known or explored factor.

And then there are accidents—like the one my wife and I witnessed.

Jane and I came upon a herd crossing a river swollen with run-off meltwater in the spring. Most of the animals—including several calves—reached the far side safely. But one calf was swept downstream and against a cutbank where he could not clamber ashore. The calf's mother rushed frantically back and forth above the calf as he weakened in his struggles.

Another barroom debate relative to elk is whether newborn calves emit a scent. Murie's research, reported in *The Elk of North America*, reflects that debate. His conclusion is yes, they emit an odor. But that a young calf's scent is extremely weak because their glands have yet to develop to maturity.

A newborn calf may allow itself to be handled (don't!). But after a week, the same calf will resort to flight, usually running with the herd.

The antlers seem formidable, but striking with forefeet is the elk's primary tactic in any serious encounter.

What speeds can a herd in flight attain? Measured top speeds have exceeded twenty-five miles per hour.

Can they outrun a wolf pack? No. But there've been lots of recorded incidents when, given a chance to choose their terrain, individual animals have outfought a pack, even killing or injuring wolves in the fray.

Are bulls better equipped for battle than cows? Likely not. The antlers seem formidable, but striking with forefeet is the elk's primary tactic in any serious encounter. It's possible that a cow's inherent instinct to defend her offspring may contribute to a more determined attitude than that of a bull (outside of the rut).

Perhaps the no-nonsense routine is why cows seem to live longer than males: 15 to 20 years versus 10 to 12 (average among unhunted animals).

Which brings up yet another intriguing question: Why, when birth rates are roughly equal between male and female, are most herds composed of four times more females than males? Some might say it's because hunters seek antlers. But extensive research conducted on unhunted populations arrived at pretty much the same sex ratio. Murie speculates that one reason for the disproportionate sex ratio in adult elk is because females live longer. Other possible reasons might be that the solitary habits of most mature bulls subject them to greater risk from predation. Then there's the fact that bulls enter winter in debilitated condition due to demands of the rut. In addition, bulls winter higher on mountain slopes, on average, than cows. Is it not possible that higher elevation leads to harsher climate, which ultimately takes its toll?

And now this last debate topic: what are the calendar parameters for elk bugling?

I've heard them as early as late May and as late as the second week of November. I can understand that bugling in November might be the vocalization of some horny late-blooming bull. But why would a bull bugle in May?

We were riding up Prairie Reef Mountain in the middle of the Bob Marshall Wilderness. Patches of snow lay round about. Jane twisted in her saddle and asked, "Did you hear that?"

I nodded. "But it can't be!"

Then it came again, this time from farther down the hill. Yet a third elk bugled from farther away.

We tied our horses and approached stealthily on foot. But, though the bugling continued off and on for another hour and though we spotted several cows grazing and milling about mountain meadows, we could spot no bulls. Later, as we gathered our ponies' reins and swung into the saddle, my wife suggested we might have missed the bulls because they'd shed their antlers.

I shook my head. "I glassed every animal I could see, and I paid special attention to their heads. And I didn't see a single bull."

"But they had to be there."

I nodded. "They *had* to be there."

In *The Elk of North America*, Olaus Murie says they didn't have to be there:

> "Each spring during the present study considerable bugling was heard in May and early June, a puzzling circumstance—inasmuch as bugling was considered characteristic of the mating period—until it was discovered that cows were doing much of it. It is possible, of course, that some of the bulls also bugle

in the spring, but they were not seen in the act. Moreover, it should be explained that although this spring call of the cows is termed "bugling," it is by no means so loud and full-chested as the resonant calls given by the old bulls in autumn.

That's just one more piece of the bewildering puzzle called elk—they continually confuse, frustrate, discourage, and overwhelm. Not only do they embarrass ordinary folks who pant after a suitable elk rack to hang over their garage doors; they discombobulate scientists. There is a funny thing about elk scientists. I've known mountain-goat biologists, bear biologists, and bighorn-sheep biologists who wouldn't think of hunting the species they are studying. But almost to a man (or woman) they hunt elk, drool over elk steaks, dream of outwitting a trophy bull.

No, I don't know what it is. Or why! If I had the answers to the questions that add up to the mystique of elk, the animals would not be half so intriguing. ■

Chapter 10

Trail to Stockade Ridge

It'd begun as an adventure to remember, what with Lars' knee blown and scheduled for an operation as soon as this hunting trip ended, and my back taking on airs like it belonged to some Manhattan dilettante instead of a tough old bird who'd spent a lifetime packing ponies and pushing pilgrims into these rugged mountains.

Oh, yeah, we made it to hunting camp, us and the boy. But it was only because of Fred, who did the lion's share of the work saddling horses, and throwing packs. He'd always done more from the day he started as a guide with my old pack outfit more'n thirty years ago. But in those days, Fred worked like he did just to stay even with me; now he's doing it because a couple of his partners are too stove up and the third only comes up to his shirt buttons.

We split the packhorses between us on the ride in, but it was Fred who made all the pack adjustments. Just getting in and out of the saddle was all Lars and I could manage, unable to wrestle loose packs on spooky horses while they stamped along steep hillside trails. Our wives—neither of 'em—could understand why we two old has-beens insisted on going on with this year's hunt, but Lars and I knew.

Sometimes the Gods turn a benign face toward the benighted, and we made good time. In fact, there was an hour and a half of daylight left when we arrived at our campsite.

It was easier for two cripples and a boy to drop packs and pull saddles than it had been to load them onto ponies twelve hours earlier. Camp went up quickly, too, and by the time the others finished graining, belling, and turning our ponies loose to graze, I was banging pots and pans on the way to rib steaks and raw fries.

Lars snored softly from the far side of the sleeping tent as I slid into my down-filled bag. Fred and the boy chattered while washing dishes and putting the cooktent to order, so I eavesdropped for a couple of seconds—until the alarm jangled in my ear. I fumbled in the dark for the clock, knocking it to the ground, finally silencing it.

"Can't be that time yet, can it?" Lars asked.

I yawned and sat up, bag and all, rubbing my eyes. My back bitched a little about the demand, but not nearly so much as could be expected. Soon came a crackling fire in the cookstove, followed by the smell of coffee, flapjacks, and fried ham.

Fred trotted away to bring in saddlehorses from the meadow and Lars limped from the creek with a pail of water and an armload of wood. The boy straggled out to help wrangle ponies just as Fred returned and I hollered, "Breakfast!"

"Turn Buck loose," I told Fred while he wolfed ham and cakes. "Unless my sacroiliac gets more pep, I'll stick close to camp and do chores."

"How about you, Lars?" Fred asked.

The rancher glanced at the boy and raised an eyebrow. The kid surprised me by saying he wanted to tag along with Lars on the first hunting day.

"I'll have to stick close to the horses," Lars murmured, unnecessarily adding, "with this knee."

"I know," the boy said. "But if it's all right, I'd rather go with you."

The rancher nodded. "Can't think of anybody I'd rather partner with—partner."

They chucked saddles to ponies with the aid of flashlights. Fred joined me for a last cup of coffee while daylight wrestled with night for bossin' rights. "I'm thinking of Stockade Ridge," the ex-guide said, "maybe working into that broken country to the east. What do you think?"

I shook my head, muttering, "Tough. Maybe the toughest real estate in this whole country. Hard to get into, even on foot, and harder still to work packhorses into if you get something."

He nodded, sipped from his cup and said, "I looked into it some the last year I guided. I think there's a way down from the saddle below the lookout."

> **Fred joined me for a last cup of coffee while daylight wrestled with night for bossin' rights.**

Seeing into his mind made it easier to understand his real question. Fred didn't want approval, he wanted information; wanted to know what, if anything, I knew about the lay of the land. "You're near right. There's a game trail there, across that pea-gravel scree and down into the first rift. Work to the north, around the rock upthrust, and angle down. Should be elk tracks there and a well-used trail. It'll bring you to the top of some damn steep meadows. Below the middle meadow, and off to your right, is a big natural mineral lick. All trails lead to it if you get close enough."

Bingo! His grin was spontaneous.

"But," I cautioned, "I've never figured a decent way to get a packhorse in there."

He drained his cup and threw it into the dishpan, picked up his saddlebags, and headed for the tent flap. I tried to give him my best sky-is-falling look and said, "Don't expect any help if you get something in that hole, mister. Take a look around and see what you can expect from the handicapped in this camp."

Twelve hours later, Fred was back. He was covered in grime, with blood on his pants, and saying he had the biggest bull ever made lying at near the middle meadow lick. I glared and reminded Fred he was in a camp full of cripples. He chuckled. "Heck, I don't want either of you two old duffers. I'll take the boy."

I glanced where the object of our attention sipped Kool-Aid. "The boy?" I said. "You tell me you've got the biggest bull in the country lying alongside a lick in a place that's near-impossible to take a horse to? And you want to take the boy?"

"You'll help me, won't you, Shaver?" Fred asked.

"Uh-huh."

"Fred, dammit, you can't expect ..."

> "You tell me you've got the biggest bull in the country lying alongside a lick in a place that's near-impossible to take a horse to? And you want to take the boy?"

His smile vanished and he was as serious as I'd ever seen him when there was a big job to do and he was the man to do it. "I need him to hold horses. Look, I tried to work out a trail on the way back to camp and I think I've got it figured. But I'll have to do some clearing, cut a few trees and logs, some brush, that kind of thing. Maybe pioneer in a spot or two. Then when we get to the bull, it's so steep I need the boy to hold the ponies while I load the meat. He can do it. I know he can."

The cracking falsetto of a boy on the way to puberty sliced the stillness: "I can do it, Grandpa. Don't worry."

So they rode out the next morning. Fred was pulling our two best packhorses, carrying only canvas manties, ropes, game bags, a couple of double-bit axes, a can of soda pop for the boy, and a pint of Gatorade for the man. Lars and I watched them from camp. "They'll do just fine," he said. "We're lucky to have a couple of hands like them around."

I nodded without taking my eyes from the spot where our companions were swallowed by the gloom. In a moment I felt the intensity of my friend's eyes. "A long time ago," he said, "I told you he was going to be a good one."

My head bobbed again.

"I said the day will come when he'll be bringing us back here on his off days."

I pointed at the ground. "Can you hand me that rock?" He bent over for the baseball-sized piece of glacier-rounded limestone and handed it to me. I threw it savagely at a tree—and nearly went down from the searing pain. After Lars steadied me, I shook my head. "I want to be with him, Lars. Every time he takes another giant stride toward manhood, I'm hiding in camp or off packing hay, or otherwise twiddling my thumbs."

Lars' short bark was derisive. "He'll turn out to be a man to make you proud. And it won't be because you spent your time hiding out."

Back in the tent, I shoved the cribbage board toward him and said, "It's going to be a long day."

He straddled the bench and dumped the pegs on the table. When I handed him the deck, he cut a ten and I cut a queen. While he shuffled and dealt, I placed the pegs. At last, he said, "Only if we make it long."

It took Lars two hours to beat me best three of five. His reward for winning was to wash our breakfast dishes while I baked a gingerbread cake. Then we spent the rest of the forenoon carrying in wood, Lars picking up blocks and loading my arms as I trudged back and forth from wood-pile to tent.

Come late afternoon, and we both stared into the distance like love-sick cowpokes. "Who'll take the boy now?" I said. "With you and me stove up and Fred already getting his elk, who'll hunt with him?"

Lars hawked and spit into the dust, then scraped dirt over it with his boot toe. "You worry about the damndest things." When the silence grew, he said, "You will. I will. You know Fred will. We'll all do the best we can. You know that."

"Won't be the same, though. Neither of us is mobile enough to really get the kid into elk, and Fred will want to take some time off now that he's got his."

Lars wandered away, not suffering fools gracefully.

Supper was on hold an hour before dusk when the meat packers came in. The boy led the way on his fast-stepping little bay. Fred and the packhorses hove in sight, tramping right behind. I could see in a glance that this really was a big bull. The unusually dark horns were lashed atop the front quarters, ivory tips hanging on each side of the roan's rear knees.

The boy was tuckered, squeezing a moment too long to the horn after swinging from his saddle, steadying his legs before turning loose. But Fred leaped right to work, jerking sling ropes free, lifting down the massive rack and each of the four quarters. While Lars and the boy jerked away the canvas manties, I threw ropes over the meatpole and after we'd pulled them to swing six feet from the ground, tied off each quarter.

Then we unsaddled and grained horses. At last, just as the light began to dim, we gathered to do quick measurements on the antlers.

"Three-thirty," I said. "Maybe thirty-five. Close, Fred. But no cigar."

"Big enough," he replied. "What about you, Shaver? This big enough for you?"

A fleeting smile lit the boy's weary face. "Uh-huh."

"Even one a little smaller?"

"Uh-huh."

The boy and Lars belled the ponies and turned them loose. We watched them run and kick and buck their way out to the meadow to join the others. "I'll bet you thought they were tired," Lars chuckled.

A light snow began falling.

As we headed for the cooktent and an evening bourbon and branch, Fred said, "Now we got to bring in one for the boy. Which packhorses you want us to use come morning?"

"Get washed up," I growled. "Otherwise you can rustle at somebody else's trough."

It was nothing short of a miracle. The pork loin and au gratin potatoes vanished. So did the carrot and raisin salad and most of the gingerbread cake. Fred and the boy arm-wrestled for the last piece.

"Ow!" Fred hollered as his wrist thunked the table. "You win! You win! You can have it."

The boy jumped from the bench where he'd thrown his

entire weight on Fred's arm. "I win, Grandpa! Did you see?"

I dished up the last slice of cake as I asked, "You figure to hunt tomorrow, boy? Or do you want a day to rest?"

He reached for his cake, staring a moment at the ex-guide, and said, "Me and Fred are going to get my elk."

"Maybe he wants to rest."

"That's right, Shaver," Fred butted in. "You tell your grandpa how it is. And while you're talking to him, ask him which packhorses he wants us to use tomorrow."

I snorted. "Even with my back, I could make it up to the little

> The boy was tuckered, squeezing a moment too long to the horn after swinging from his saddle, steadying his legs before turning loose.

meadows and maybe do some bugling. Could be I could even make the big lick. Then ..."

"But, Grandpff"—his mouth was full—"Fred and me want to ..."

"You sure are a stubborn cuss," Fred cut in. "Now, let's try this one more time—the boy and me are going to bring him in an elk tomorrow. For the last time, *which packhorses you want us to use?*"

I stood spraddle-legged in irritation, clenching both fists on hips, the cake spatula still clutched in one. "You think you're goldamned funny, don't you?"

Something cut through my rising ire. It was Lars chuckling. He clambered to his feet and hobbled as quickly as possible from the cooktent while I glared first at Fred, and then the boy. Lars was back in a moment, carrying his private stock of 100-proof liqueur.

As he poured a couple of fingers into my cup and thrust it to me, an amazing thought took root, sprouted, shot up, blossomed and bore fruit, all in an instant. I took the cup and collapsed on the bench—never mind the back! "Where? When?"

The tent erupted. Fred and the boy doubled over in glee, while Lars pummeled the youngster on his back and I stared at the whole lot of them in confusion.

"I'm surprised you never heard the shooting. He got it

going out this morning, right over there in Jack Creek. Did you guys go back to bed the minute we left?"

I shook my head, still confused by the sudden turn of events. "You ... you're not pulling our leg?" It was clear even to a crotchety old outfitter they weren't, so I asked, "The boy shot it on the way to get your elk?"

Both Fred and the boy nodded. "Right along the trail. Well, maybe a few feet above it. Standing there with bunchgrass still sticking out of his mouth. It worked just like you showed me years ago—he had eyes only for the lead horse. I kept moving while I waved back to the boy. But he couldn't see the bull. Then he came around the bend and spotted him. Done just like you said, kept riding while he slid out the rifle, then dropped from his saddle. Wasn't thirty yards from an elk that still watched only me. I about wet my pants!"

"And, Grandpa! When I hit the ground, I was lower than I was on the horse and I couldn't see him no more!"

Lars smiled amiably as I helped myself to more of his 100-proof. "So what did you do?"

"Ran up the trail behind my horse. Then I could see him!"

"Less than thirty yards?"

The boy looked at Fred, who nodded.

"And you got him with one shot?" I asked.

The boy blushed and Fred laughed. "No, he missed him clean on his first shot."

"I don't believe it!" I said. "What then?"

The boy looked at me like a schoolteacher would at a lazy child. "I got him."

"You shot him. Just like that. Was he running?"

"Huh-uh. He never moved. Except to fall over."

I peered at Lars. "I'll be double-dipped. Can you believe this?"

"Just like in a fairy tale," Lars said. "And it couldn't happen to anybody who deserved it more."

"How big?"

Fred looked at the boy and my eyes trailed him. "A five-point," the boy said.

"Not real big," Fred added. "But like we said earlier, he's plenty big enough."

My head finally cleared. "You take care of him?"

"He's all skinned and butchered. We put the quarters under a tree and covered 'em with branches and bear grass. Checked when we came down, too. Nothing has been into him."

I stared at a spot on the tent flap while I lifted Lars' 100-proof. I thought of the boy growing up and how for a while I was afraid his grandmother might turn him into something less than what I reckoned a man ought to be. I recalled his first overnight fishing trip, his first hunt with Lars and me when Lars took his last elk, his first elk and first deer with Thaddeus the year before, both in hip-deep snow. I recalled how he'd missed his first chance at an elk. And I remembered how we'd feared he was just another unlucky hunter. "Cheyenne," I said, "and Tanglefoot."

"Huh?"

I fixed Fred with my most withering glare. "The pack-horses, dammit. Isn't that what you've been hounding me about most all evening?" ∎

Our son Marc at fourteen, with bull taken on way to "Stockade Ridge."

Chapter 11

What Really Works for Elk

Ron Hinchey first saw the light of day and was raised in inner-city London, an honest-to-God Cockney complete with C. S. Forester accent. He was fascinated by mountain men, trappers, hunters, the Wild West. Ron was a well educated, prosperous engineering draftsman living in Calgary, and he wanted me to take him elk hunting so he could learn "how" to hunt.

This is bizarre, I thought. Nobody goes on an expensive outfitted trip in order to learn *how* to hunt. But my second thought was, The hell they don't! It's just that others who do it aren't so up-front about it as is the Cockney. And after reflection, I actually looked forward to guiding a hunter with whom there was no need to learn his strengths and weaknesses, or employ a Talleyrand diplomacy to maximize opportunities limited by distressingly weak knowledge of woods, mountains, firearms, or elk.

Good theory, but challenging in practice.

"Are those the *only* boots you have?" I asked in dismay when he slipped into his leather-soled engineer's boots while preparing for his first day afield.

"Yes. Why?"

"Those are hardly suitable for climbing these mountains."

"You should 'ave told me," he said.

"I did," I replied, handing him a copy of the suggested

clothing list we mailed to each of our hunters. Cleated-sole boots were prominent on the list, as were rubber pacs.

"You should 'ave underlined it, Guv'nor," he said.

I sighed and led Ron from camp. It was apparent the man's gun-handling experience hadn't appreciably advanced beyond that of his 17th-century Roundhead ancestors. But he *was* aware of the muzzle direction. And before the day progressed so far that he might have become lax with fatigue, the man's hunt was over.

Successful elk hunting requires psychological commitment, physical conditioning, and enough time to do basic research.

Ron Hinchey killed his six-point bull elk within an hour of the opening of hunting season. He did so with the sixteenth cartridge he had ever fired in any weapon: eleven rounds through his brand-new 300 magnum at a practice-range target, then five rounds at a muddled bull elk who seemed to stand rooted with a death wish.

Did Ron Hinchey learn to hunt elk? No. Luck intervened. But good luck or bad?

Luck usually plays only a small role in successful elk hunting. More than with any other big-game animal, success can best be described by the adage: *Luck is a circumstance that occurs when proper preparation meets opportunity.*

Today—many years after his opening-day success—Ron Hinchey has yet (as far as I know) to take another elk. Yet some hunters have taken many elk in the same time frame. Why?

There can be but one reason: they are better prepared. Those other hunters know more, and their preparation is a result of that knowledge.

Some ways to prepare are better than others, but the important thing to remember is there are no shortcuts. Successful elk hunting requires psychological commitment, physical conditioning, and enough time to do basic research. If you're not willing or able to spend sufficient time on conditioning and research, this chapter won't be of much help. If you have only a few days to devote to elk, then be sure to schedule with an outfitter because there's simply no way you can effectively do it on your own.

But if you live in elk country and have been outsmarted for years; if you're planning to move to elk country and are wondering how to begin; or if you're willing to devote enough time to learn the ins and outs of elk hunting, read on:

Selecting A Hunting Area

Some places are better to hunt within certain locales. Success potential varies, depending on terrain, vegetative cover, number of other hunters, and that all-important thing called "feel."

I received a kindergarten lesson in "feel" early during my guiding career. Gene was the kind of hunter every guide dreams of: physically strong, and terrain-savvy, with real understanding of the foibles of hunting, a great sense of humor, and an intense feeling for wild places and wild things. In short, only a guide unworthy of the name would give less than one hundred and ten percent for this guy.

The country where I outfitted was half-open, half-forested. Gene had a well-developed tendency to hunt open alpine country. But one particular year came when no elk inhabited his chosen terrain, few even crossed during the dead of night, and we found no tracks close to where Gene wished to hunt.

To make matters worse, I knew where the elk were—down in dank and gloomy bottoms forested with towering Engelmann spruce. Or on benches thick with windthrown lodgepole. Or on brush-filled slopes where nothing moved without crackling a warning. "Gene, dammit, if the mountain won't come to Mohammed, whyn't Mohammed go to the mountain?"

My hunter grunted something indecipherable so, in the days to come, I tried again and again. He met each suggestion with amusement and polite evasion. But one day my persistence grated on a raw nerve because he motioned for me to sit on a table-sized stone and said, pointing first at me, then into the valley below, "Look,

Roland, you want me go down there and hunt, right?"

"I sure do, Gene. I know elk are down there."

"Okay. Here's how it is: If I go down there and kill an elk, I'll enjoy it. If I go down there and don't kill an elk, I'll hate it. If I stay up here and hunt and kill an elk, I'll enjoy it. Or if I stay up here and hunt and *don't* kill an elk, I'll still enjoy it. Now, why don't you tell me again where you want me to hunt?"

To determine where you wish to hunt, you must take advantage of every possible source of information—newspaper outdoor columns, game-department pamphlets, even bragging by local sportsmen. Listen in on lunchroom or barroom gossip; hang around sporting-goods stores, taxidermy shops, or even gas stations if the attendant is a successful elk hunter. Find out where the local folks go, including the drainage or mountain if you can get them to reveal it. Talk elk, think elk, and dream elk.

Eavesdrop on intimate hunting discussions between buddies. If they don't suspect anyone else is listening, it will be the straight scoop. A typical scenario might go something like this:

"I couldn't believe it!" the hunter said. "He came at a run on my second grunt. He was red-eyed, and the hackles on his neck stood straight up. He came right from the meadows, and me out of breath."

Firing-squad stares are all you'll get if you butt in. Simply file what you hear in the memory bank. The day will eventually come when you spot one of those guy's rigs parked in a wide spot in the road and you'll file another bit of information until you, too, have a wild-eyed bull charge into your meadow.

Spotting *dis*information is also an important tool. During my guiding years, I used to instruct our hunters to tell agents at checking stations that each elk we brought through was taken on Sullivan Creek. It was a question which checking-station agents insisted on having answered, and newspaper reporters routinely went through checking-station log books. Thus, the place and time each elk was harvested became public information. Common sense tells you only a fool or a newcomer to hunting would give out that kind of classified information, even if they pulled out his finger-nails with vice grips.

Accumulate, sift, and assimilate your information, then obtain good maps.

Naturally, I wasn't the only one to employ such stratagem—even down to the exact same place. As a consequence, over the years, more elk have been taken on Sullivan Creek than in any other drainage north of the Mason-Dixon Line. And I've even heard the name used as a verb: "We Sullivan Creeked him," or, "He was easy to Sullivan Creek."

I guided a hunter for three years who later moved to my home community and opened a shop. I was recently in his shop and admired a mounted elk rack that Russ took on one of my trips. It chanced that Russ wasn't in that day, so I asked one of his salesladies where he took the bull.

She said she didn't know. I handed her a card and asked if she would ask the owner for me. I was, of course, josh-ing the young lady, but I also wanted Russ to know I was in his store. The girl looked at the card and said, "I'll ask for you. But I don't know if he'll tell."

I grinned.

Russ called the very next day. When I picked up the phone, he drawled, "Sullivan Creek." When I roared, he added, "That's what you taught us to say, isn't it?"

Some excellent information sources are former hunters who have given up the sport for one reason or another. If you find one who has nothing to lose by telling you about the good old days, pull up a chair and listen. If the two of you hit it off, you might be able to ask searching questions. Again, listen—all day and all night if necessary, but listen.

Accumulate, sift, and assimilate your information, then obtain good maps. Most national forests have excellent maps of their lands available, but the best topographic maps are produced by the U.S. Geological Survey. These are sold in many sporting-goods stores and local book-stores. If they're not available locally, write to the

Distribution Section, U.S. Geological Survey, Federal Center, Denver, CO 80225. Ask for a folder describing maps available in your area.

Study your maps carefully. Learn their road grids, trails, forest cover, and terrain contours, then systematically check the maps on the ground. Climb to high points carrying your map and a compass. Pick out ridges, creeks, valleys, and roads. Note each in your mind.

You'll need to determine property boundaries if private land is a factor. In today's world, obtaining permission to hunt from the landowner requires more sophistication and skill than was formerly needed. Once, as a young man, I spotted a small band of elk feeding in a steep sidehill meadow on National Forest land. The catch was that private land lay between the lane from which I glassed and the band of elk. I drove on to the end of the lane, to a small vine-covered cottage with a broken picket fence.

After parking my Jeep station wagon, I swallowed, walked to the cottage and knocked. It was midmorning. I heard shuffling behind the door. A kitchen curtain was thrust aside, then fell back into place. Finally a wizened old man, bent with years and wearing narrow-frame glasses far down on the end of an oversized nose, opened the door. He held a wrinkled newspaper in one hand. "Yes?" he said.

"I, uh ..."

"Oh, spit it out!"

"Sir, I spotted a band of elk in a sidehill meadow behind your home. There's a raghorn bull in the bunch and I wondered if I could go after them?"

The old man tilted his head one way, then tilted it the other, all the while peering up at me. "Do you have a gun?" he said at last.

"Yes, sir. A Marlin 30-30. It's lever-action, but it's really a rifle—three-inch longer barrel. And it shoots ..."

"Do you have a license?"

"Oh, yes, sir. I wouldn't think of hunting without ..."

"Well, son, that's all you need."

No matter how we miss those days, they're long-gone. Now you need your ducks in order before season opens.

Most county courthouses have a land-registration department and will allow you access to property-ownership maps. If you wish to hunt private lands, make your contacts early, then follow up later to build rapport with the rancher, farmer, or corporation.

Gradually, you'll reduce your list of potential hunting spots to a few that "feel" best. Explore them further. Follow each road and trail. Reduce your list. Now, really study your topo maps. Pick out small timbered benches, meadows, or tiny glades not accessed by roads or trails. Find them and explore them. Look for elk sign, but don't bank on these areas until hunting season, even if you find abundant evidence that elk are there. The creatures have a habit of making seasonal moves, depending on vegetation, insects, the rut, fall migration, or winter-range availability.

Jane and I once spotted more than a hundred and thirty head of elk—including thirty-some big bulls—in a huge open basin. When hunting season began some six weeks later, there wasn't a single track to be found.

Choose several areas where you plan to concentrate your hunting. Dig in and learn everything. Search out game trails and other good routes through the area. Time your hike from the ridgetop to the valley floor and back again so you'll get an accurate idea of your ability to cover your area on foot. Poke into every little nook and cranny. Follow elk trails until they peter out, then turn around and follow them back, analyzing the country from the reverse direction.

Congratulations. You've graduated from primary school. Now, on to the next level.

Think Like An Elk

Pay attention when you jump elk. Observe where and how they flee, and where they top out over ridges. Which mountain passes do they use, and to which cover do they retreat? Try to out-think them, then grin and profit from your mistakes. And don't take it too hard when you fail to out-think them, because humans do not have the natural acumen of wild creatures.

Montana ranks fourth in number of elk hunters and number of elk taken by hunting. Success rate for Wyoming hunters is highest of any state allowing over-the-counter elk license sales.

Learn to bugle for elk. It's no longer difficult to learn to use diaphragm calls, reed calls, or grunt tubes. Records and video tapes will coach you through the bugling and grunting process. But you will need to practice, practice,

Richard Jackson

then practice some more. Your landlady will probably call out the police the first week and serve you an eviction notice the second, but it will be worth sleeping on a park bench if you develop your elk-calling skills enough to lure even a raghorn within range.

After you've learned the rudiments of elk bugling, you'll be ready to try your skills in the woods. Don't practice where you plan to hunt. Elk aren't dumb. They quickly learn to identify a bugle, to recognize the rhythm and the notes as telegraphers learn to identify the patterns of those sending messages. If you give away your bugling rhythms and patterns to the elk you plan to hunt, you might as well wait until the rut is over to begin hunting.

You'll be much better off practicing where elk are not hunted. A few years ago, would-be hunters experimented at calling within National Parks, but this is now frowned upon, if not banned.

You need experience, not just the self-satisfaction of

looking at every bull elk in the country. What you should be doing is learning about the creatures. Part of becoming an accomplished elk hunter is learning to estimate a bull's size by the depth of his reply. And you'll learn that herd bulls more often will try to spirit their cows into the next basin than defend them against every testosterone-filled newcomer.

You should also learn that while bulls are vulnerable during the rut, cows are not. They serve as wary, effective sentries surrounding their master.

Smaller bulls normally work the perimeter around a breeding herd, hoping to cut out a lonesome cow while the herd bull is relaxing. Raghorns are prone to mental lapses during the rut—as much as any big bull. And they do not have the cow sentries of the herd bull. Expect to initially encounter a minor bull or a cow if you're attempting to sneak up on grandpa. It's possible to sneak up on a big bull, but the effort takes the patience of Job and the stealth of a coyote tiptoeing through a pen full of snoozing foxhounds. You'll probably not succeed, but it's good field work on your way to a passing grade in "Trophy bulls—101."

Learn to stay downwind of *any* elk or I can guarantee that you will witness the entire herd bolting for the next county. That, of course, is a piece of advice that looks good as it scrolls across my computer screen, but impossible to execute while strolling through Sunlight Basin. The best *practical* advice I can share is *try* your best to keep the wind in your face.

Realize that cold air settles and warm air rises. As night steals across the land, air temperatures fall and cold air settles from above, developing into a steady downhill drift. After sunup, ground air will begin to heat, causing a change in wind direction as it rises, usually beginning sometime around noon—if there's no weather change. Storm fronts can disrupt this pattern. In elk country, most prevailing fronts come from the southwest—except for blizzards. Be advised.

Remember that your eyes are better than those of a wapiti. And although an elk's hearing is sensitive, a herd makes so much noise they pay scant attention to *natural* forest sounds, such as snapping twigs or rolling stones.

Learn about the interrelationships of forest wildlife. To take a trophy bull, you sometimes need to tie unseen movement to an invisible pine squirrel's scolding. You'll grow accustomed to recognizing alarm calls of different birds. Most will be of no consequence. But occasionally....

Learn the habits of elk during the days or weeks between the rut and the migration. Bulls and cows gradually lose interest in one another and wander apart, but bulls often regroup in small bachelor bands for mutual protection.

Learn to differentiate between feeding grounds and bedding grounds, and the travel routes that separate them. Learn the grazing habits of elk and recognize that the onset of autumn (and nasty weather) requires them to spend more time grazing to replenish energy precisely when available forage is in decline.

Whys And Wherefores

Now you've moved up to the school of advanced training. At this level you need to learn *why* elk use particular bedding grounds at certain times of the season and why they feed in particular meadows or on certain forest plants. Elk will usually journey no farther than necessary from bed to breakfast. When you grasp this significant point, you'll understand that if elk are feeding on blue-bunch wheatgrass in a tiny south-facing meadow on one ridge, they'll feed on the same plant, at the same elevation, in a south-facing meadow in another drainage. If they're bedding in false huckleberry thickets on one east-facing sidehill near their seasonal forage, they'll likely be doing the same thing in the next basin.

Along the way, you'll learn that elk are more apt to use natural mineral licks when lots of moisture passes through their bodies, just as cattle use more salt during wet weather. Excessive moisture in foliage moves salt and other minerals through a cow's system, and therefore she needs more salt. It's no different with other herbivorous animals. Conversely, during dry weather or after forage plants have begun to shed their moisture-carrying leaves, elk will merely pass through licks, using the well-developed game trails commonly found nearby.

You'll need to know what makes suitable winter range for elk. South- and west-facing slopes that receive warm winter sun and southwesterly winds called "chinooks" are popular wintering grounds for elk, as are areas of limited snowfall that perhaps lie in the "snow shadow" of a weather-intercepting mountain. With less snowfall, such areas are usually better stocked with suitable forage plants.

You need most to know which types are ice-cream plants to elk and which are the meat and potatoes of their diets, and you need to know where and when elk are likely to feed on those plants.

Learn to recognize plants favored by elk. Browse plants differ from one region to another, but your state's Game & Fish people can help—probably with publications containing drawings and photographs of primary forage types in your locale. You'll need to learn to identify choice forage vegetation where you've chosen to hunt. You need most to know which types are ice-cream plants to elk and which are the meat and potatoes of their diets, and you need to know where and when elk are likely to feed on those plants. For instance, red-stem ceanothus and serviceberry are considered the "ice-cream" winter forage in my part of the country. Deer and elk prefer them when snow blankets the land. However, they are not as prevalent as the mountain maple—the "meat and potatoes" among all the varieties of browse. So where will a hunter be more likely to encounter elk during late-season hunting—amid mountain maple or serviceberry? I'll put my money on the mountain maple.

You should also learn something about why certain migration routes are used. Landforms that lead to natural passes and easily traveled south- and west-facing slopes are favored by elk. On the other hand, there's no use looking for your trophy in a forage desert such as a coniferous tract or on a sheltered ridge, slope, or canyon where snows only build and never thaw.

Eventually you'll learn about the mountain-building process and the interrelationships between rock decomposition, soil types, and food chains. That's where I am today.

Learning about the chain is a much longer process than I originally believed, and pieces of the puzzle still elude me. My only regret is that I'll not live long enough to put them all together. ■

Chapter 12

Phantom Ghost of Harriet Lou

The fence was a dandy—four strands of double-barbed wire stretched taut between well-set six-inch posts. The posts were spaced no more than a rod apart, with at least three brace posts along each quarter. One thing about old Colfax, he knows how to build a fence.

I'd stopped along this isolated forest road for a nature call. Del interrupted my admiration of Colfax's new fence when he said softly from within the pickup, "There's a cow elk."

Sure enough, she stood motionless between a couple of small firs, maybe fifty yards from the road, head up and ears forward as she watched us.

There's little novelty about elk for me, unless one has a spread so big he can scratch his rump patch with a horn tip. I've been around elk all my life; hunted them, guided for them, tried to keep the damned things out of my haystacks. A lone cow is a ho-hum thing for sure.

Del was different, just coming out of guide school, looking forward to his first season as a packer/guide for my little horseback pack outfit. A rattling noise interrupted my thoughts and I looked down the fence. Its two bottom wires were shaking. "I know why the cow's standing there, Delvan. Her calf is hung in the fence."

He'd likely been there most of the night, the poor little

tyke. Both hind legs were scissor-trapped between the first and second strands—apparently he'd fallen as he crawled through the fence his mother had jumped, and his rear legs hung up. He lay on his side all sweated up and the grass mashed flat where he'd thrashed until he became so weak he could barely wiggle. One of the few efforts he had left happened to be while I stood outside the pickup.

All the hide and hair was gone from his hocks to the tiny hoofs, exposing bruised and bleeding flesh and ligaments. It was all we two husky fellows could do to pull the wire apart enough for the legs to fall out. The delicately spotted calf just lay there, too used-up to attempt more than quick, shallow breathing. "He ain't gonna make it," I said matter-of-factly.

Del glanced at the cow. The lad's face said all that needed saying.

We drove on down to Colfax's lower pasture, where we bunched the horses wintering there. Then Del caught and saddled Candy and started 'em for the home place while I drove on into Wise River for a few things for Judy and a glass of beer for myself. Then I took the country road home in order to check the mailbox on the way.

Del brought the ponies in around dusk. We had the gates open, and Judy and I helped haze 'em into the newly greening pasture. "Any trouble?" I asked the lad as he unsaddled.

"No. Everything went fine."

I headed for the house, then turned back. "The elk calf—he was still there, wasn't he?"

I could barely make out Del's face in the gathering gloom as he paused with saddle and bridle in hand. "No. He was gone. The cow was gone, too. At least I couldn't see them. And I looked close."

Summer faded into fall. Fall is a busy time for us, setting up our hunting camp, cutting wood and guiding first for archery season, then, when general season opens for rifle hunts.

It was during Del's fourth year with us that Winton Gardiner scheduled his hunt. You may have heard that name—one of the foremost archers in America. I've guided the man; watched with what grace and skill he moves through the woods; been in his home out by a little lake west of Minneapolis and looked at his trophy room. His reputation is certainly an earned one.

We were hunting up on Demijohn and I paired Winton with Del. It was day four when they got the bull answering on a little bench above a natural mineral lick. The day was breezeless, and Del positioned Winton at one edge of the lick, leaving him where he had a clear view in three directions. Then, as Del related it to me, he began "talking" to the bull.

The bull replied deep and often, but an hour passed and the men figured he'd not moved. Del suggested they work toward the elk, and Winton agreed. But as soon as they crept into the shintangle, their plan appeared less likely. Though the bull sounded as if he remained in place, the dense, head-high young spruce growing amid criss-crossed windthrown lodgepoles was near impenetrable—certainly no place to loose an arrow. And yet they could now hear the bull savaging a sapling with his antlers as the fury of the rut overcame him.

The men conferred in whispers, then squeezed through the dense foliage until they struck a faint game trail that was open along its length for a few yards. Winton crouched there while Del retreated a few paces back into the tangle to go through his bugling routine of tri-level whistle and deep-throated, coughing grunts.

The bull replied—again and again—but still would not come. After another hour, Winton signaled for Del to keep calling while he tried a stalk. The hunter disappeared, and Del continued his periodic bugling, grunting, and simulated "horning" of the dense brush. Though the guide wondered how Winton's stalk was going, he stayed at his task. Another hour passed. Incredibly, the bull seemed to be working into an even greater frenzy. Then he went silent.

Did Winton spook him? the guide wondered. *Shoot him?* He bugled again. Nothing. He vigorously rubbed a tree with a dead limb, and an ear-splitting bugle roared from his immediate left!

The guide knew in an instant what was happening: the bull had at last responded—charged out to defend his territory from an encroaching bull and somehow eluded the hunter in the process, instead closing quickly with the perplexed guide.

The first rumbles of the "Phantom Ghost" began the following winter.

"I did the only thing I could think to do," he said that evening. "I went to ground, hoping to buy Winton enough time to get in position."

"And?"

"I could hear the bull coming closer and closer, snapping limbs, swishing through the brush. But I had my face on the ground and the spruce was so dense I couldn't see him. I thought he was sure to get my scent any minute."

"How close?"

Del shrugged. "He must have walked within fifteen, twenty feet before he got the scent. I ... I could see his legs below the trees' lowest branches. Then he got my wind and took off. Crashed out of there like a runaway locomotive."

Winton sipped a whiskey and water, a bemused smile on his face. "How he got by me the first time without me knowing it, I can't guess. But when he thundered back, I thought he was going to run over me."

"Did you get a look at him?"

"Just the horns." He sipped his drink before continuing. "He passed by not thirty feet away. But it was so dense in there I couldn't see anything but the trees waving as he went through. Except for the horns."

"I don't understand."

"Those trees—they're maybe six feet high. His horns was up above them as he charged through."

I got it at last. "Big horns?"

"*Very* big horns."

I turned to the cookstove and the supper I'd put on hold.

Del cleared his throat. "There's one other thing."

"Yes?"

"His legs. That's all I could see from the ground. But he was close. His back legs had scar tissue all over them—from the knees down. I ... I know it hardly seems possible, but do you suppose ..."

The first rumbles of the "Phantom Ghost" began the following winter. Of course, he wasn't yet famous as the Phantom Ghost of Harriet Lou. But some of Colfax's hands claimed they'd seen a really big bull up near where Harriet Lou Creek runs through a BLM eighty. They claimed he'd go six points on a side and run to sixty inches on his spread. But everybody knew Willard James and Toby Heflin, so they deducted a point to a side and maybe ten inches on the spread.

The boys claimed the bull was raiding Colfax's haystacks, but that winter was a mild one and critters could forage pretty much where they wanted and without much damage to haystacks around the Big Hole. Besides, none of the horn pickers who gathered dropped antlers that spring reported finding any of unusual heft. So most folks kind of passed off Willard's and Toby's eyewitness claim as a ploy to cadge drinks at the Wise River Club.

Nothing more was heard about an unusually large bull that spring or summer, but come fall and opening of hunting season, more rigs than usual were parked along the county roads. McNeill's Diamond Hitch outfit picked up a couple of big bulls in the high country to the south, and one of my hunters took a dandy with a fifty-seven-inch spread. And they say a bowhunter from Butte got a good one on Foolhen Ridge. But none of 'em made Boone & Crockett, and I more or less forgot about the big bull on Harriet Lou Creek until Colfax himself told me he'd spotted the biggest bull he'd ever seen.

It was on New Year's Day and none of his hands were sober enough to feed cows, so Colfax fired up his 820 John Deere with the "farmhand" mounted on the front and busted through a couple of drifts to get to fresh haystacks at the forks of Meadow and Harriet Lou Creeks. Since Colfax had a hangover, too, he didn't make it out until near dusk. He claimed the big bull busted from one of the stacks while the tractor was still a good way off.

Judy and I drove down that way the next evening. Sure enough, five or six elk were feeding on Colfax's hay. None of 'em were bulls. Other vehicles drove by while we were there—Colfax never was long on secrets—but three weeks went by before anyone saw the bull again.

"Saw him goin' and comin'," said Carrot Edmonds, who operates the county's road grader. "Gawd, he was with two other big bulls and put 'em both to shame. Kinda drifted into the trees each time—like a ... a phantom ghost!"

Word spread about the Phantom Ghost of Harriet Lou, and people took to driving out from as far as Dillon and Butte in hopes they'd get a peek at him. Some did, but most didn't. I was one of those who didn't.

Colfax left the Phantom Ghost alone. Normally he's got a short fuse about elk in his haystacks—been known to shoot 'em if they get too pesky—and elk were a nuisance that bad snow year of '73-74. But I suppose he enjoyed the notoriety of having the biggest bull in the country roaming his ranch.

To show you how attached Colfax was to the big bull, he ran his new crewcab pickup into the Jeep of a couple of Butte would-be poachers when they tried to get away. Word was the Butte boys wounded the Phantom, and he didn't show for a couple weeks. Then some kids sledding over on Clayburn Hill saw him.

Spring came again, then summer and fall and another hunting season, and now the mountains and woods west of Wise River crawled with hunters after the Phantom Ghost. Nobody claimed to have spotted him, though. But the next winter, there he was, seven points on each side according to a few lucky folks who actually saw him. And he still buddied with the smaller six-points.

It was a light snow year the next winter, and the following two. Elk pretty much foraged on brush and grass on the windswept ridges—all except those that had grown lazy and relished easy haystack pickings. So sightings of the Phantom were even more rare; but enough to know he was still alive and well.

Funny thing was nobody ever saw the monster bull during hunting season. And that fact stirred lots of barroom speculation throughout the Big Hole country and beyond. Nobody found his shed antlers come spring, either, though many searched. The way I reasoned, his dropped antlers weren't found because the reclusive bull stuck mostly to the timber where looking for horns was akin to looking for a brown thread in a sun-scorched lawn.

Did I have a theory why nobody spotted him during hunting season?

Did I have a theory why nobody spotted him during hunting season? No. And I thought about that one off and on for years.

Then came the bad winter of '77-78. Snow piled up in December, and temperatures plummeted to fifty below in January. Cattle losses mounted on some ranches and Judy and I battled to save our little herd. Haystacks that looked abundant when winter began soon disappeared in the face of the most savage winter I could remember. There simply was no hay to share with pillaging elk and deer—until the Phantom Ghost of Harriet Lou showed up on our place, that is.

The kitchen door slammed behind me as I headed for the barn, figuring to fire up the old crawler International I used to plow feed and bed grounds for the cattle. The thermometer was hanging right at fifteen below—just where it'd stayed for the last week. I pulled the earflaps down on my cap and reached to turn up the coat collar when something lunged to its feet in belly-deep snow, over near the elk-paneled haystack by the corrals.

He was big! Much bigger than any bull I've seen during my thirty years of outfitting and guiding. I eased back into the house and led Judy to a window. While I scraped frost off a pane, she demanded to know what was so important. I shushed her. But when the glass was clear enough for her to press her nose against it, she gasped, "Oh, my Lord!"

"Look at those horns, Jude. You ever see anything like 'em?"

"But he's so skinny. He's starving!"

"He's old. Folks have been seeing the Phantom Ghost of Harriet Lou for four, five years. And he was a grown-up bull then."

She turned to me, her eyes moist. "You've got to take the panels of that stack."

I shook my head. "We're short on hay, Jude."

She placed her hands on my shoulders and stared up with calf-eyes I never learned to resist, even after thirty-four years. "We'll make room for one more at the table, Billy. Take a panel off and let him into the haystack.

I did more than that. I plowed around it with the TD-9, then removed one of the vertical one-by-four-and-wire panels Fish & Game provides for ranchers to help keep game damage down. The Phantom Ghost of Harriet Lou was standing at the haystack when I came back to the house for lunch.

The funny thing is, if I hadn't plowed around the haystack for him, chances are the deep snow would have concealed the fact that the huge bull's hind legs were covered with scar tissue from hock to hoof. ∎

Chapter 13

Elk and Whitetail
The Same Game

You're an experienced whitetail deer hunter from an eastern state and have dreamed of making a western hunt for elk. But you're reluctant to gamble your time and money because you know nothing about the animals. Right? Listen up. You may know more than you think.

Suppose your eastern whitetail buck has undergone just two major physical changes. First, it has grown four to five times its normal body size; second, it's no longer a solitary creature, but a herd animal. What comes to mind when you think of an eight hundred- to thousand-pound herd animal with whitetail instincts?

I think elk.

You know by now that I spent much of my life as an outfitter/guide in one of America's greatest wilderness areas. My specialty was guiding for elk, and our home place is in a mountain valley noted for record-class whitetail bucks. During more than two decades in the outfitting business, I guided many eastern whitetail hunters.

Aside from guiding, I've hunted Rocky Mountain elk in Montana and Roosevelt elk in Oregon. Over the years, I've come to realize there are such marked similarities in the characteristics of whitetails and elk that an experienced whitetail hunter has an edge. Yet all too often I've had eastern hunters apologize for their lack of elk-hunting experience. One such inquiry read:

> ... I have hunted deer all my life, here in Michigan. But an elk hunting trip by horseback is something I have always wanted to do. Is an elk hunt possible for a novice like me?

Is elk hunting *possible* for someone like that? A Michigan deer hunter is *exactly* the kind of hunter an elk guide prizes. Or a deer hunter from Minnesota or Pennsylvania, Ohio or Wisconsin or wherever. Anyone who grew to manhood or womanhood hunting whitetails amid eastern hardwoods *had* to learn to hunt the right way—quietly, in the animal's living room.

No roadhunting for accomplished whitetail hunters, and no copious quantities of magnum artillery rounds in bandoleers crisscrossing their shoulders. Experienced whitetail hunters are woodswise, and they've developed inordinate patience—two important criteria for competent elk hunters.

So they've never before hunted elk—so what? Everybody has to begin somewhere, and it's better to do so after acquiring a modicum of humility instilled by whitetail bucks instead of swallowing story-and-photo spreads in many outdoors magazines. If giant bulls falling in picture-perfect meadows with dynamic mountain backdrops were the norm, would the challenge or the magic be there?

True, eastern whitetail hunters lack familiarity with our wilderness mountains. But I knew automatically how such a hunter would react under a given set of conditions. Most of the time his reactions would be as correct for elk as for his eastern deer. Above all, I knew that with a minimum of training I could modify some of his reactions to make them more applicable to eight-hundred-pound herd animals dwelling in the rugged mountains of northwestern Montana. The whitetail hunters we guided turned into competent elk hunters more easily than broadly traveled hunters with no comparable experience.

Why is it necessary for a hunter to have training or experience if his guide is competent? Because there is only so much a guide can do for any hunter. We guides knew our hunting country well, and we knew elk as well as any guides and most hunters. But at one time or another during the course of a ten-day hunt, we'd likely exhaust our knowledge. We would bugle our guts out during the rutting period, but sometimes bull elk failed to respond. If conditions were right, we could track them with the craftiness of a Kalahari bushman. But sometimes there just wasn't a skiff of fresh snow, or the ground wasn't soft from a soaking rain, or we would lose the trail amid a maze of tracks. We knew where tiny meadows or natural mineral licks or wallows or well-used game trails existed. And we knew where we'd previously spotted and taken elk. But sometimes those places weren't productive during a particular hunt. When that time came and the elk were sticking tight to the thick stuff, I knew that my hunter's best chance for success might well lie in his going into the brush after them alone.

Of course, the trail to success lies in how well the hunter adapts to modification of his whitetail techniques.

When that style of hunting is the only alternative left, a guide is a millstone, for two cannot slip as silently through a forest as can one. In that situation, the best way we could help a hunter was to explain the lay of the land, perhaps take him by horseback to the head of a drainage, then move his horse around to pick him up at another spot some distance away. If that was the way the cards fell, then it was imperative that a sneak-hunting elk hunter know his animal. And that's when an experienced whitetail hunter, with habits modified for elk, had an advantage.

Of course, the trail to success lies in how well the hunter adapts to modification of his whitetail techniques. That's what I mean by training, and it's vital. Any outfitter worthy of the name spends as much time as possible developing his hunters, discussing the country, the animal, and what he believes to be the best hunting methods. Training hunters so they no longer needed me was, I felt, my primary duty, and the duty of my guides.

If it was during the rut, I told my hunters that frenzied bull elk, like whitetail bucks, sometimes do inexplicably stupid things. Aside from coming to an imitation call, I've seen them crash wildly through the brush, drawn to the sounds of a packstring moving through the mountains (horses snapping twigs and clicking rocks with their steel-shod hooves). Is that much different from a whitetail buck drawn to a hunter who is rattling antlers together with his hands? The buck thinks he's coming to the sounds of two rivals sparring; the bull is drawn to what he believes are the sounds of an elk herd on the move.

> A bull that's away from the herd, … will swiftly prove his ears are every bit as sensitive as those of a whitetail buck.

Both whitetail deer and elk make scrapes and rubs to mark their territory. With both species, aggressive territorial defense is the mark of a dominant individual and serves to reduce actual combat during the breeding period.

Of course a bull elk's scrape may be eight or ten feet in diameter, and it may appear to be tilled like a garden where he's ripped the soil with his massive antlers and churning feet. A whitetail's version is seldom more than three feet across—a four-foot scrape is big for a deer. Likewise, whitetail bucks rub small trees, usually two to four feet off the ground, while bull elk always set their goals upward, sometimes rubbing higher than a tall man can reach. Yet with both species, rubs and scrapes serve a territorial purpose, and a fresh one indicates the presence of rutting males. It tells the hunter he'd damned well better get serious with his stalk.

Many times over the years I've watched a big bull elk stand or lie motionless behind a scant screen of brush or small trees, apparently thinking himself hidden, and thus willing to let a hunter wander past. Isn't that trick a favorite whitetail ploy? And doesn't it make you wonder about the many big bucks and bulls that have used it successfully while a hunter trudged wearily past, convinced that the area was stripped clean of all wildlife the week before?

Both species, I believe, depend much more on sound

and smell than on sight. An elk's nose is particularly keen, and (it's worth repeating) if you're elk hunting with the wind gusting at your back, you'd be better off going on back to camp for a cribbage game with the cook. So it is for whitetail deer.

Whitetails have an edge when it comes to hearing, but this is more a result of solitary habits than of more sensitive ears. A bull that's away from the herd, off by himself, will swiftly prove his ears are every bit as sensitive as those of a whitetail buck. Because big bulls are more inclined toward solitude than even the oldest cow, it's safe to say that a careless, noisy elk stalker may also do better at the cribbage board.

It's true, however, that any elk will pay less attention to common forest noises than will whitetail deer. Elk simply cannot move as stealthily as the more delicate deer—nor do they try. It's their size and their herd instinct. An elk will break an occasional dead limb, kick over an occasional stone, swish an occasional branch. No whitetail buck is that careless. But if you let an elk hear an *alien* sound—swish a branch with your vinyl rain pants, unzip your raincoat, curse in a low voice—and you can kiss him goodbye.

What about their eyes? The mountain elk and valley whitetail can't match eyes with mine, and they really are color-blind, just as is commonly believed. I've stood quietly many times, wearing an orange vest or red hat, and had elk or whitetail deer graze around me until they picked up the scent. I do believe their eyes are light-sensitive, however. Blaze orange will stand out as a lighter-colored object against a deep green forest, and it attracts attention if you move. Red, on the other hand, stands out as dark against snow. What about florescents? I don't like them.

Both whitetail deer and elk sometimes tend to disbelieve one sense alone. Often they'll hear your noise but wait until they can see you before leaving Dodge. Or they'll circle to get your wind. Sometimes they've spotted your movement but wait to hear or smell, distrusting their eyes. It's a weakness that's usually academic. Most times, the first glimpse you have of the animal is some seconds after bull or buck has detected you with his second sense and is on the move.

Track a bull elk in snow. Let him know you're back there and it won't matter that he's not a whitetail. It's likely that an eastern whitetail hunter will be surprised to find a bull using every whitetail trick in the book to keep his edge on the hunter. He'll circle, he'll climb, only to drop back again to a creek bottom. He'll lie screened, watching his backtrail. He'll hook, switch back, lose his tracks in a maze of others, follow his own backtrail. And your guts will be twisted into a pretzel before it's over.

Bull elk bed in whitetail-likely spots: on a brush-screened knoll, near the point of a ridge, on a small bench. Two steps and they're gone in any of several directions.

Occasionally, the unusual will work with whitetails or elk. I once jumped a whitetail buck, then whistled sharply when I realized I didn't have a shot. The buck stopped momentarily—long enough for me to aim—then bounded away. When I quit laughing, I filed that trick away in the memory bank. Since then, I've talked to many whitetail hunters who've used a whistle to pause a buck.

Similarly, I've jumped a bull elk and many times used a bugle or a grunt to stop him for a few seconds, despite the fact he was in full flight. A huge bull bursting wildly through a thick stand of saplings at one moment, then stopping on a dime at the next, can be a sight to see. I've several times imagined what was going on in his mind: "What's up? Did I make a mistake?" Then he'll almost shake his head as the wheels grind on: "No ... no, by gosh. That *was* a human!"

Which brings up another point. When elk—any elk—decide to go somewhere, they'll go. It doesn't seem to make any difference how many or what kind of deterrents are in the way. They'll go over a mountain, through a pass, up an open hillside, follow a narrow canyon.

The bumps on a bull elk's head as he begins growing antlers are called "pedicles." It is said the growth of pedicles into antlers is tribbered by increasing daylight. Antler growth, sometimes as much as an inch per day, is nourished richly by blood vessels extended into the calcium and phosphorous formed bones that make up antlers.

A bull must obtain rich and plentiful nutritious food in order to grow impressive antlers. Antlers usually identify bulls that are successful foragers, the ablest of the able. And they're the ones most likely, in a natural environment to do most of the breeding.

Elk are members of the deer family and as such, shed their antlers each year.

Though I've never participated in drives for whitetail deer, many friends have told me that whitetails have this same characteristic, sometimes exiting the woods at a most unhealthy spot and seeming not to care in the least.

Let me share yet another interesting letter:

> Here in Pennsylvania, we hunt deer in bowhunting season by sitting on game trails. Most of our stands are in the trees. I don't have any experience stalking ...

Will the stand-hunting method work on elk? Well, yes, although it isn't used as much out West, even for whitetail deer. We never utilized tree stands in our guiding, but now and again we left a selected hunter sitting at a good elk trail, and a few connected. The main reason we never gravitated to tree stands is because it's appropriate only for certain hunters in certain kinds of places.

Not every hunter is psychologically equipped for sitting all day. I know, because I'm not. My friends call me a nervous hunter. Ask me to sit all day while hunting, and you've just received my notice to quit. Yet there are hunters who are excellent at the method. Most are experienced eastern whitetail hunters.

Not every hunter is psychologically equipped for sitting all day.

Because I like to travel at a high lope when I'm elk hunting, however, doesn't mean everyone should. Is it any more fair that I should drag a whitetail sitter along on my high lopes if there's a more likable alternative for him, than he should try to force me to a stand?

A competent guide tries to discover the method his hunter is best at, and then utilizes that method as much as possible on his hunt. That's a strategy a hunter should and usually does utilize on his own, too.

Another key is to stand-hunt only in areas elk are using. In terms of productive growing land, the Bob Marshall Wilderness is not Lancaster County, Pennsylvania. Growing seasons are short and winters are particularly harsh. In good whitetail habitat, a hunter can justifiably assume that there are deer around; it's simply a matter of seeing them.

Prime eastern farmland will produce, say, three times more foodstuff per acre than our best Montana farmland, and so will the woodlands. Are there three times more deer per acre in the East? Probably. Divide a typical eastern deer population by three and you have a more realistic estimate of ours, out West.

Elk are four times larger than whitetails and require four times more feed. So it's safe to say that you could divide the Potter County, Pennsylvania, deer herd by thirty and have a more realistic idea of mountain elk populations. Are you willing to sit perched on a tree stand and hope to see a creature only one-thirtieth as plentiful as your deer herds back home? And besides all that, whitetail deer are spread throughout their habitat, while elk are herd animals, tending often to concentrate their numbers in a

Elk wintering in Glacier Park

relatively small area. Even solitary elk are generally found in a herd's vicinity.

I suppose that sounds discouraging, yet it's why a tree stand may work—if a hunter can first find an area where the elk are, then locate a stand. Certainly elk have favorite places they use, depending on seasons. Most often, the rut goes on in deep timber and sometimes lasts for many days. It takes tremendous pressure to move elk from that type of secluded refuge. They may move temporarily, but only to drift back at the first opportunity, so this should be a prime place for your stand.

Likewise, maturing food sources are important. Perhaps a meadow sedge turns succulent after a first frost or a browse plant becomes palatable after a soaking rain. Identify those areas, check for sign, then locate a stand.

Staging areas for migration can be important, too, but they're generally utilized more briefly. They can be productive for the hunter who finds them, though.

Having noted the similarities between elk and whitetail deer, let's look at the differences—especially how a whitetail hunter must modify his approach for elk hunting. A big difference, of course, was just mentioned. Unlike whitetail deer, elk simply are *not* everywhere. Some eastern hunters never learn that it does precious little good to pussyfoot for elk if there are no elk on the mountain. That's why most westerners learned to hunt at a high lope—and why we sometimes tend to overrun the elk when we do locate them.

The ideal elk hunter would be mobile enough to cover ground until he located areas occupied by the creatures, then patient enough to hunt as though he were after a trophy whitetail buck.

Perhaps the greatest difference is in habitat. Due to their size and herd instincts, elk, unlike whitetail deer, have never adapted to civilization. No farm lots for them, except when winter snows drive them to raid haystacks. Today, the best elk ranges lie in the most rugged and remote mountains. Many eastern hunters simply can't comprehend the monumental difference our rugged mountains and tremendous distances make. It may be an overworked piece of advice, but good physical conditioning is much more important for elk-hunting success than for hunting deer. Without reasonably good physical conditioning, you may not be mobile enough to find where the elk are.

Whitetail bucks, unlike bull elk, never maintain a harem. At first, one would think it a comparative weakness for the bull to have his attention diverted by sloe-eyed females with a swaggle to their hips. But the contrary is true. A whitetail buck in the rut, like a bull elk, has his mind on sex rather than safety. But unlike the buck, the bull has several sets of eyes and ears and several noses at work for him. A hunter stalking a herd bull is far more likely to spook a cow who'll then spook the herd than to get a shot at the herd bull.

The flagging tail of a whitetail deer is an eye-catcher, but so is the buckskin-colored rump of a retreating elk.

Whitetail bucks and bull elk are canny creatures with many of the same habits and instincts. Both represent the ultimate in American hunting challenge, trophy, and tradition. Learn to hunt one, and you've learned a lot about hunting the other. ■

Chapter 14

The Odyssey of Earl

It was an epic journey. Gary Olson says it was "sort of like a Lewis & Clark Voyage of Discovery—in reverse." Olson has a right to make such comparisons—Earl was his project to begin with.

Whatever accommodations there may have been between Earl and Olson, Earl abrogated the treaty early on. First, like Sitting Bull, Earl fled to Canada. Then, again like Sitting Bull, Earl decided to rejoin folks in the land of the Long Knives. From there, however, any resemblance between the travels of Earl and those of the legendary Hunkpapa Lakota ends.

But, then, Earl is an elk.

Surprisingly Earl, a moniker hung on him by an unknown Associated Press staff writer, but uncharismatically named "964" when first snared during Olson's scientific research, was not the first elk to walk the Missouri wild side. He just traveled farther to get there.

Gary Olson is a biologist with Montana's Department of Fish, Wildlife & Parks. To study the effects of rifle and archery hunting on elk-herd movements, Olson radio-collared ten animals from a herd of three hundred inhabiting an isolated mountain range called the Sweetgrass Hills, along the Montana-Alberta border.

The Sweetgrass Hills were formed by a series of

igneous intrusions leaving volcanic cones. Erosion has worn those intrusions until they're no longer cones but hills rising from the plains. Maps list the components of this scenic "island" range as a series of buttes: East Butte, West Butte, Gold Butte, Grassy Butte, Haystack Butte. To Native Americans inhabiting the region, the Sweetgrass Hills have religious significance.

As you might guess, collaring wild elk is not at all like collaring puppies. Olson's capture method was to fly over a herd in a helicopter, then use a special "net gun" to fire an entangling net over a stampeding wapiti. Such work is not a one-man job, and Olson was ably assisted by pilot Larry Schweitzer and gunner John (Rosie) Rosalind.

Number 964, when captured in mid-February, 1987, was a spike bull approximately twenty months old. There was nothing about the young bull that attracted special attention from the researchers. Olson's plan was to fly the region on a weekly basis, monitoring locations of his collared animals via an airborne receiver. By plotting the combination of animal locations, the scientist hoped to discern overall Sweetgrass Hills herd movement during each season of the year.

As you might guess, collaring wild elk is not at all like collaring puppies.

A "fix" was made on Number 964 on two March occasions, and then the bull who would later be known nationwide as "Earl" seemed to vanish from the face of the earth.

Olson flew ever-widening circles in his attempt to pick up a pulse from 964's collar, until he finally decided the transmitter had failed. Then word trickled down through biologists' circles that an elk wearing a white collar was spotted in the Cypress Hills, another island range spanning the Alberta-Saskatchewan border. The Cypress Hills lie roughly a hundred miles northeast of where Olson had collared his animals. The Montana biologist flew north in an airplane mounting an electronic scanner.

Either 964's collar truly had failed or, on the basis of later evidence, Olson believes Earl kissed off the Cypress Hills in the same manner as he did the Sweetgrass Hills. Maybe cows are prettier down the road. And competing bulls fewer.

In any event, Earl's pages go blank for nearly three years. Until reports of first an antelope, then a moose began popping up in Harry Truman's old home grounds of Independence, Missouri. Here's a brief news item from a local paper, *The Examiner*, February 20, 1990:

> Have you seen any unidentified roaming antelope in your neighborhood lately?
>
> The Missouri Department of Conservation has received numerous reported sightings of an antelope wearing a white collar around the 291 Highway and the Independence Center. Other reports have speculated the animal was a moose or elk....

Apparently the wayward wild creature that had taken up residence near the geographic center of America was spotted frequently, and observers leaned more and more toward elk. Then someone shot video footage of the animal, and that clinched it.

Sometimes you see him, sometimes you don't.

Donna McGuire, writing in the March 22, 1990, *Kansas City Star* offered an illuminating hypothesis of the animal's travels once he reached Missouri:

> Sometimes you see him, sometimes you don't.
>
> Mostly you don't.
>
> But Missouri Conservation officials have received so many calls about an elk in eastern Independence that they are convinced the big fellow exists.
>
> They don't know where he came from or how he wound up in Missouri. They think, however, that he is the elk seen by hunters last fall north of the Missouri River in Ray and Chariton Counties.
>
> How he crossed the river is a mystery. So is the thick, white collar around his neck....

If, in fact, Earl was the will-o'-the-wisp Ray and Chariton Counties elk reported by hunters the previous autumn, that would blow out of the water a later theory that Earl followed the Milk and Missouri River bottoms to Kansas City. While it's true Ray County lies roughly across the wide Missouri from Independence, Chariton County is located almost a hundred miles east.

But what's a hundred miles to Earl?

Montana Dept. of Fish, Wildlife and Parks

Still more intriguing is where had he been? By the fall of 1989, Earl had been gone from the Sweetgrass Hills for two and a half years, and Montana lies *northwest*, not *east* of the Truman Library. Was Earl on his way home from St. Louis?

The Sweetgrass Hills in spring.

No matter where the elk came from, where he headed, or whatever reason there might be, Earl decided a little R&R might be in order amid the bright lights of Kansas City environs. Mary Doyle, writing in *The Examiner*, March 23, reported:

> A lone elk spotted wandering around the area near Missouri 291 and R.D. Mize Road apparently has found all the comforts of home.
>
> Officials from the Missouri Department of Conservation say the elk probably is finding enough in the area to satisfy its diet of buds, berries, twigs, stems and leaves.
>
> Then, too, there's the Little Blue River to quench its thirst.

William Ewing of Independence provided the final evidence that a bull elk roamed his neighborhood when he found a pair of large elk antlers while hunting mushrooms along the Little Blue River. Ewing first found one antler. After having it authenticated by Department of Conservation biologists, he returned to the site and found the other.

Being naturally adventuresome and an experienced globe-trotter, Earl began to lose his fear of humans and their contrivances. Then, in late April, tragedy struck. Donna McGuire reported in the April 28 issue of *The Kansas City Star*:

> "I didn't see the animal at all until this brown thing obstructed my view," Cletus Zumwalt, 71, of Independence said Friday from her hospital room. "I'm just glad my car didn't turn over."
>
> She was driving home from the Independence Center shopping mall about 1 p.m. Thursday when the elk smashed into the driver's side of her car and wrapped around the windshield, which shattered ...
>
> The elk spun into her car after being clipped by a Ford Bronco driven by David Newton, 31, of Kansas City, North....
>
> "I tried to slow down, but I caught its tail end," he said. "My first thought was that it was a big dog because it had this white collar."

Susan Clauder, in *The Examiner*, shed further light:

> Teresa Jacobs, who is employed at the Raytown Animal Hospital, saw the accident. She said she saw the elk in the median and had to come to a sudden stop to avoid hitting it. After it was hit the second time, Jacobs said the elk got up and ran into the woods.

Area residents hoped for the best but feared the worst when their charismatic visitor failed to reappear for several weeks. Conservation officials and a number of other people searched in vain for the animal or his remains. Finally, on June 20, the Missouri Conservation Department issued a press release that ran in *The Kansas City Star*:

> An elk that roamed eastern Independence earlier this year has not been seen since he tangled with two cars on a state highway in late April, and conservation officials fear he has died.
>
> The elk collapsed in a ditch, got up and headed into the woods after being struck by two cars April 26 on Missouri 291, north of 39th Street.

Residents who had grown used to watching the elk graze have searched unsuccessfully since then for fresh tracks.

"I think it is probably time for an obituary," Jim Pyland of the Missouri Department of Conservation said Tuesday. "I wouldn't be surprised if we never saw or heard from him again."

The elk probably died from internal injuries, and coyotes probably have scattered the bones, Pyland said. The only way he expects to receive confirmation of the death is if someone finds the wide, white collar seen around its neck.

Just three days later, Pyland had egg on his face as *The Star* trumpeted: "HE'S ALIVE: ELUSIVE ELK REAPPEARS." The article that followed said, in part:

The reports of his death were exaggerated. Independence's elusive and recently reclusive elk lives. Apparently recovered from his April run-in with two cars, the elk has grown a new set of big antlers and seems content to graze nightly in a field near Selsa Road and 39th Street.

Not bad for a big boy considered dead by Missouri conservation officials, who even had a theory that coyotes had found the body and scattered the bones.

With understandable shyness regarding highways and automobiles, Earl turned to greener pastures. John Buzbee reported in *The Star*:

Tim Graham, a senior at Central Missouri State University in Warrensburg, was driving with a friend Friday night when they saw what they thought was a cow in a softball field next to William Yates Elementary School ...

With Earl's reappearance came superstar status. And as with other superstars, a city set out to ogle the intriguing animal. *The Star* editorialized on September 10:

If you're lucky enough to see the elusive elk of Independence, see him from a distance....

Independence's elk has been living north of the Independence Center shopping mall since early March. He weighs at least 750 pounds and has 4-foot antlers.

"He's become quite a celebrity," [Jim] Pyland [of the Missouri Conservation Department] said. "People all over town are talking about him."

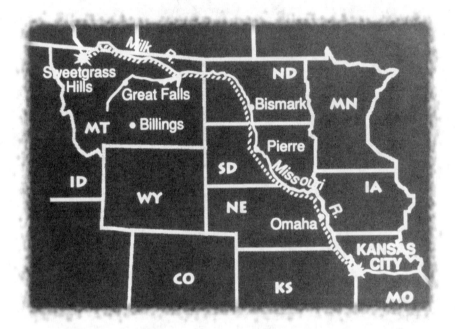

Apparently taking seriously his responsibility as a celebrity, Earl appeared at local events. Here's an item from the September 20 issue of *The Kansas City Star*:

Suggested 1,800 mile route of Earl the Elk.

—Prepared by MT. Dept. of Fish, Wildlife, & Parks

Independence's mysterious elk was trotting north down Adams Street toward a garage sale about 8 a.m. Wednesday when an impatient driver honked his horn.

The startled animal took off in such a hurry that he left foot-long divots in Woodford and Joyce Roberts' yard. He jumped several chain-link fences and vanished behind a chorus of barking dogs....

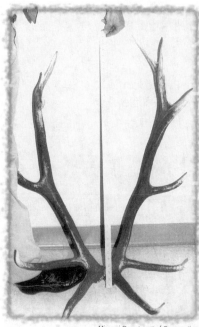

Missouri Department of Conservation

Elk rack found by William Ewing, Independence, measures just over 39-1/4 inches high. (The measuring device is not a yardstick). The right half of the rack was found April 21, 1990 and the left half on April 24, 1990.

A half-hour earlier, about 60 persons gathered around an enclosed retention basin near Phelps Road and 39th Street to watch the elk graze.

"It is a big, I mean big, elk. He had at least a 10-point rack," said Capt. Richard Burton, one of seven firefighters at Station No. 2 who saw the animal.

The sighting represents the deepest the elk has traveled into a residential area ...

With Earl's apparent reluctance to leave Kansas City environs and his increasing penetration into residential areas, the Missouri Department of Conservation decided to trap and move him to an enclosed park near Independence. Dale Brendel told the story in the September 27 issue of *The Examiner*:

The full-grown male elk, weighing an estimated 800 pounds, created a furor among Independence police when it was spotted in the yards of residences near Truman High School Sunday night.

"Up to this time the elk has been no problem," Major Shannon Cravin of the Police Department said. "But now it is getting in residential areas and near major thoroughfares. We're concerned the elk will cause injury to himself or to others. We're working with the Missouri Department of Conservation on this matter. It is a wild animal and it is under their jurisdiction."

Jim Pyland, Kansas City metro services coordinator for the Department of Conservation, says officials are planning to shoot the elk with a tranquilizer dart and move him to Missouri Town in Fleming Park, where other elk are held in an enclosed area....

But Earl had other ideas:

Officials earlier this week had planned to shoot the elk in an Independence pasture, where the elk had developed a pattern of grazing in the evening with some cows. But something spooked the animal Tuesday morning and it led officials on a three-hour chase by Interstate 70 to some land past Missouri 291.

According to an October 4 report in *The Blue Springs Examiner*, officials were still waiting a week later:

Missouri Department of Conservation officials are still trying to capture the wild elk roaming around eastern Independence....

Conservation officials enlisted the help of experienced elk hunters affiliated with the Rocky Mountain Elk Foundation. They tried using elk calls to lure the animal within range of the dart guns but the methods were unsuccessful.

Three days later, *The Kansas City Star* blazoned a headline:

'BIG GUY' THE ELK IS CAPTURED

Apparently "Big Guy" was still growing—putting on weight:

The 900-pound animal that became a celebrity in the last year with his unexpected appearances was captured at dawn Saturday at Drumm Farm, a boys school in a wooded area of Independence.

With Earl's capture came at least a partial answer:

A white collar around the elk's neck had mystified trackers because it did not appear to have any markings. It turned out to be a radio transmitter. Conservation agents this week will attempt to find the owner by tracing the radio frequency through the Federal Communications Commission....

The Star story ended with:

In quarantine now, "Big Guy" eventually will be put in a pen at the park, which has 14 other elk and other animals.

But the real story was just beginning. Unfortunately, tracing the transmitter collar's frequency proved impossible. The news report that the collar contained no markings was not accurate, however. A number—964—-was scratched into its surface, along with the letters G and O.

Jim Pyland conducted a thorough search, calling potential leads, beginning with area game farms, then branching to neighboring states. From twelve states and two Indian reservations, Pyland received the same negative answer every time he asked, "Have you lost a radio-collared elk?"

By then (October, 1990), Olson's Sweetgrass Hills elk research project had ended. It's not really clear how Pyland was finally routed to Olson, but ironically Olson was then summarizing the results of the Sweetgrass research. Here's his recollection of their first phone conversation.

"Jim Pyland, Missouri Department of Conservation, politely introduced himself and then went into a ten-minute narrative about this elk that had Kansas City in an uproar. My first thought was, 'What's this guy really selling?'"

Then Pyland mentioned.the number 964 scratched into the collar, and the letters G and O—and Olson went ballistic!

The Kansas City Star carried this story by staff writer Diane Carroll:

The celebrated elk captured last weekend in Independence came from Montana on what probably was the longest trek ever made by an elk in North America in modern times, wildlife experts said Wednesday.

The 900-pound bull, sighted by area residents for a year, was identified Wednesday through his radio transmitter collar that carried the number 964. Big Guy, as some of his local trackers called him, disappeared three years ago from Sweetgrass Hills, Mont., where he was being tracked as part of an experiment for the Montana Department of Fish, Wildlife and Parks.

"I spent a lot of time looking for that animal," said Gary Olson, a wildlife biologist in charge of the Montana experiment for the Montana Department of Fish, Wildlife and Parks. "It's just so fantastic it's difficult for me to comprehend it."

Olson said he thinks the elk wandered 80 miles north to the Cypress Hills Provincial Park in Canada and then picked up the Milk River, a tributary of the Missouri. The 4-year-old must have traveled 1,800 miles along the Missouri River to Kansas City, he said.

The trek is the longest documented since game-management officials began keeping records in the 1930s....

When the Associated Press picked up the tale, Earl zoomed from local acclaim to overnight national celebrity.

Elk round-up team posing with Elk #964 after successful capture on Saturday, October 6, 1990. From left to right: Ron McNeely, Wildlife Damage Control Agent, MO Dept. of Conservation; Dave Steinhauser, Independence Police Dept.; Dr. Robert Hertzog, veterinarian; L.A. Bartlett, veterinarian's assistant who shot elk; Greg Wilkinson, Bill Trotter, Carl Perry, all Independence Police Dept.; Jim Pyland, Metro Services Coordinator, MO Dept. of Conservation. Photo: Missouri Dept. of Conservation

It seems it was an obscure AP journalist who dubbed the hero "Earl" in an October 11 release. "'EARL THE ELK' ROAMS ALMOST 2,000 MILES" read the headline over a story that captured readers' imaginations in newspapers all across America. And "Earl" became the name most Americans remember today when reminded of the wandering elk.

Newspaper reports claim Earl is the first wild elk to roam Missouri since the 1840s, but evidently that's not true.

Surfacing through the AP story was the potentially thorny question of exactly whose elk Earl was. A thoughtful Gary Olson was quoted as saying:

"The critter might be international. Montana has lots of elk and from a public relations standpoint, Kansas City probably has a vested interest in saying 'This is the elk that traveled from Montana.' Besides, I don't know how our governor would feel about me driving down in a truck to get that elk."

Montana's Governor Stan Stephens answered that question the very next day. His decision was reported in an AP release from Helena, dated October 12:

Earl the elk has become Earl the emissary. Gov. Stan Stephens on Thursday said the wandering elk that somehow found his way from Montana to Missouri will remain in that Midwest state.

The 4-year-old, 900-pound bull elk, nicknamed "Earl" after showing up in the eastern Kansas City suburb of Independence, will be an ambassador for Montana wildlife, Stephens said.

"We're very fond of our wildlife here in Montana, but since Earl apparently has ambitions outside the state, we'll be happy to help him make the best of it," the governor said.

So, how fares Earl the emissary today? Pretty well, I'd say. The first thing Earl did when released in Fleming Park was whip Little Dude, the resident park bull, and take possession of his herd of cows. The next thing Earl accomplished was to sire sixteen calves in three years.

Elk Number 964 has gone through another name change, too. The Kansas City Elks Lodge #26 adopted Earl, contributes to his food and care, and has renamed Earl. He is now Elroy Elk Montana. But most visitors to Fleming Park just call him Montana for short. I recently asked Jim Pyland if Earl/Elroy Elk/Montana/Big Guy/964 is still alive and well? As far as he knew on October 24, 1997, "He's still out there in Fleming Park doing his thing."

But the big questions remain. What made the elk wander in the first place? What kept the animal going for two thousand miles? Newspaper reports claim Earl is the first wild elk to roam Missouri since the 1840s, but evidently that's not true. At one time or another, before and after Earl, elk have appeared in unexpected places.

After Earl's story broke, a B.H. Davidson of Sedona, Arizona, wrote to the editor of *Wapiti*, a publication of the Rocky Mountain Elk Foundation, to recount how he and a friend encountered a five-point bull elk while pheasant hunting in Nebraska, just south of Yankton, South Dakota. Davidson and his friend spotted their elk in 1983, so that bull could not have been Earl.

According to Mark Henckel, Outdoor Editor of the *Billings Gazette*, who put considerable effort into researching the story, Earl is not the first wild elk to show up in Missouri since the creatures were eliminated there. Henckel's story ran shortly after Earl was captured:

> In 1969 ... a deer hunter shot what he must have thought was a huge whitetail. It turned out to be Wyoming Elk No. EE6987 which was trapped in Yellowstone National Park and released near Lusk, Wyo., before heading east and meeting its end in deer season in Osage County.

Interestingly, Osage County lies directly south of the Missouri River, almost in the center of the state. Mark goes on to report that "in the early 1970s, an elk escaped from

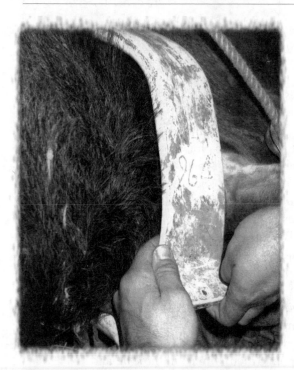

Earl's collar being examined after capture by the Missouri Dept. of Conservation. Note the number 964 scratched onto the collar. Photo: Missouri Dept. of Conservation.

an Iowa game farm and appeared in Atchison County." And, "in March of 1982, another elk was spotted in Cooper County and then disappeared." And Mark concludes his story by noting that collared animals often disappear from research projects:

Terry Lonner, research bureau chief with the Montana Department of Fish, Wildlife & Parks, said that despite the fact they can be tracked by a certain radio frequency, radio-collared animals often are lost.

"There are a pile of animals that are marked that we don't know where they go," he said. "They move out of receiver range. They drop their collars. Sometimes, the collars don't work."

Will other wandering elk show up in Missouri? They already have, according to an October 10, 1991 report in The Kansas City Star, about the dedication of a plaque commemorating the incredible journey of Elk Number 964. It began:

Move over, Montana. There's another elk on the way.

At a ceremony Wednesday honoring Montana's 1,800-mile journey from Montana to Missouri, a conservation official asked Jackson County park officials if there was room for another elk in the 95-acre Native Hoofed Animal Enclosure at Fleming Park.

"We've had some sightings of a wandering elk in Atchison County," said Jim Pyland. ...

The story of Earl the Elk seems incredible. In fact, some of biologist Olson's colleagues scoff at Earl's nomadic travels. Their explanation? "Someone loaded that elk in a horse trailer and hauled him to Missouri as a prank."

Is that explanation plausible? Aw, come on! And leave a collar around his neck? Did they also haul Wyoming elk No. EE6987 to Missouri? The Chariton County elk? Or how about the natural wariness of once-trapped animals? The real explanation seems to be that some elk are much wider-ranging creatures than we've suspected. Earl just happened to range farther than any previously recorded. Our great good fortune was to have a tracking method in place when he began his odyssey. And it was our loss that we either failed to follow up the resultant opportunity, or the bull's radio collar truly did fail.

Earl and harem in Fleming Park, Inde-pen-dence, Missouri

We do know Earl's transmitter was not functioning when the collar was removed by Missouri Conservation Department personnel. But research money is tight and this type of transmitter is of relatively inexpensive design that won't continue to send signals forever. (Actually, most of Olson's collared study animals' transmitters failed by completion of his research.)

Missouri Dept. of Conservation

Olson, the biologist conducting the study, believes

Earl's collar failed within two weeks of first placement. He also believes the bull traveled to the Cypress Hills, then left Canada (or was driven out by older, stronger resident bulls) and simply kept drifting downstream looking for others of his kind.

But did he leave Canada shortly after arrival, or did he tarry for a year? Two years? Maybe he found Iowa corn and Nebraska wheat so delectable that he took his time in transit.

"About two and a half months," is Olson's estimate of how long it would take an elk to walk the eighteen hundred miles from the Sweetgrass Hills to Kansas City. "They can easily travel up to forty miles in a day."

That, of course, presupposes that Earl had clear walking. What about the dogs that must have clamored at his approach? What about the highways and traffic that turned him from his course? The hog farms and feedlots? The fences? The factories? Shopping centers? Subdivisions? Where could an animals so large hide for three years without *somebody* crossing his path?

We'll never know. We had a one-in-a-million chance and missed it because of a faulty transmitter. But, then, as Olson says, "Even if the transmitter had been functioning, no agency could afford the aircraft time for constant monitoring of such an animal."

What will future research bring? What opportunities will satellite tracking provide? Transmitter collars are often slipped when an animal scratches his neck on a tree limb, or a transmitter fails because of faulty transistor components. But improvements in these electronic devices will almost certainly appear in a decade or two. Then is when our understanding of wildlife in general, and the dynamics of elk in particular will take a huge leap forward. We must be prepared to seize the opportunity when it comes. Only by planning strategically can our researchers be ready if lightning strikes the same place again. ■

Chapter 15

Signals From Telegraph Hill

Stars winked out in the east, signaling the coming dawn as the boy brought Baldy to the hitchrack. The big horse's halter was twisted, but I said nothing. If the boy was like most young ones, sleep hadn't come the night before a big hunt. When he turned back to the corral for another pony, I stuck the brush and currycomb in my jacket pockets and untwisted the halter, hung a feedbag half full of oats over Baldy's ears, and began brushing him.

"Joker all done?" Fred called.

I patted Baldy on the rump and nodded. Chances are Fred missed the nod in the dim light, but he knew. That's the way it was with us—the way he'd been trained. If the horse had a feedbag on, he'd been brushed.

The boy brought a palomino from the corral. It shied coming out the gate, full of piss and vinegar and a little fat for the tough trip ahead. The boy jerked him in, cursing softly.

Fred had the saddle on Joker and reaching under his belly to pull up the cinch when the boy hollered, his voice cracking: "You riding Dollar, Fred?"

The man paused and thumbed back his floppy-brimmed hat, white teeth flashing. "I'll ride anything that's too tough for the rest of you." The boy grinned, then snatched up another halter as Fred added, "Dollar'll be fine."

"You'll want Buck, I s'pose," the boy said, glancing my way as he started for the corral.

I hung a nosebag on the palomino and frowned. Ride Buck? Hell, yes, I'll ride Buck. Been riding him for almost twenty years—ever since the fool got it through his brain that he shouldn't stand me on my punkin' noggin' every time I straddled him. The memory brought a fleeting smile.

Buster had finished unloading our gear from "Old Gray," the pickup truck. The portly ex-guide handed a steaming cup of coffee my way. "Coffee, Fred?" he asked, waving the thermos.

I stared at him over the rim of my cup and wondered if the farmer was so easy-going with his own work at harvest time.

"Not now, thanks." Fred had three packhorses saddled now, working like a well-oiled machine. A bead of sweat rolled down his angular, unwrinkled face; another dripped from a lock of sandy-colored hair hanging over an ear. His eyes flicked past mine and he flashed an easy grin. It was a smile that made a man warm when he saw it. Fred knew he was under the eye of the old master; and knew the master liked what he saw.

Buster now, he was something else. He was a good hand, steady, but a little like molasses. It wasn't that he was lazy, but Buster never really cared about time, or whether a job was done today or tomorrow or next week. I stared at him over the rim of my cup and wondered if the farmer was so easy-going with his own work at harvest time. Funny thing about Buster, though, the man was always the first of my guides to roll from bed come morning. And if you looked real sharp, he usually made a turn around camp just before dark, making sure everything was buttoned up the way it was supposed to be when the lanterns flared their last after supper. And there was one other big thing about Buster—he had a clear sense of humor that never once failed him in all the years we'd been together, no matter how bad the weather or how ill-tempered his companions.

down a little, too. But we both knew how to pace ourselves over the long-familiar trail, tickled to merely be here one more time.

The guys let me help drop packs and unsaddle ponies. And to their credit—and my everlasting gratitude—they acted like they didn't see me sitting off to the side, blowing, as they set up the cooktent. But I was perking again soon after, and had coffee ready when they trooped in at full dark. I lit the lantern and splashed a tad of pep-me-up for everybody—including the boy.

They were all tuckered now—even Fred. But they put their heads together to plan tomorrow's hunt while I slapped four rib-eyes on the griddle.

I shrugged when they asked which way I wanted to hunt come daylight. "Just pick your places and leave me what's left." The truth was I planned to stick around camp, put things to order, rest up, maybe bake a pie or cut wood. No use trying to explain it to them, though.

Supper was ready when my partners trooped in the next evening, and they were grateful. I listened good-naturedly to the tales of their hunts. Comparing notes, it sounded like Fred located the best show—where a small band of elk worked the upper basin. They decided it was big enough for everyone to hunt the following day, but I begged off. "Buck and me will head downriver and kind of look the country over, maybe sneak up on Sliver Lake to see if the trout are rising."

The boy raised an eyebrow at that, but Fred and Buster nodded and went back to planning for just the three of them.

The elk outfoxed them, so the next night I regaled the gang about watching a pine squirrel shell lodgepole cones for two hours and another hour watching a Clark's nutcracker waddle from huckleberry bush to huckleberry bush, purple juice dripping from his beak. When I mentioned the huckleberries were especially sweet, the boy said, "Don't sound to me like you hunted much." But he and the others all licked lips over the huckleberry pancakes I set in front of 'em the next morning.

"By the way," Buster asked as he slipped into his day-pack and picked up his rifle, "was the trout rising?"

I shrugged. "Didn't get that far."

"I might have to give it a whirl tomorrow," he said. "All this fresh air and exercise is turning me old." Then he swung around as the boy called impatiently. The two disappeared into the forest just as a pink-tinged false dawn brushed mountains.

Fred bugled a five-point to his gun about ten that morning. His rifle's report echoed from the ridges as I waited patiently by a beaver pond, camera at the ready. A few fresh-cut willow shoots as well as beaver slides in the mud told me a family called this pond home. I figured I owed it to 'em to take a family portrait.

When a second shot echoed a few moments later, I clambered to my feet

When a second shot echoed a few moments later, I clambered to my feet, slung my rifle, and started to look for our loose horses. The ponies were in camp all saddled and the game bags ready when Fred hurried in to gather them.

That was the same day Buster took a mossy-horned mulie. The boy had his chance, too, so he said. But he wasn't fast enough and three other bucks lit out for Yukon Territory.

Since Fred and Buster were tied up packing or taking care of their winter's meat, I figured next day was high time the boy got stuck with me. We hit for a remote basin nobody'd touched, so far as I knew. It was a great day. We watched a bunch of mountain goats gamboling on cliffs high above, spotted a band of far-off bighorn sheep, and several bands of mule deer that contained no good bucks.

"Sure wish I could draw one of them sheep or goat permits," the boy said as we lounged alongside of a freshwater spring for lunch.

"You will, son, you keep at it."

It was after lunch when I took the boy to see a mountain vista that stretched seventy-five miles, clear out to where the plains started. "Buffalo used to roam out there," I told him.

We found a rare fall pasqueflower, watched a colony of rock rabbits curing hay amid talus slopes, and laid on our backs to eye two golden eagles soaring the wind currents. On the way back, the boy asked why we didn't hunt another basin, seeing there were no elk where we'd gone.

I frowned. "The horses sweated plenty just getting us to where we spent the day. Besides, to ride down out of that high lonesome place without looking it over real good would be foolish. No way could we know elk weren't there without checking every pocket."

"None answered your bugle."

"That's true. But it's time you learn that just because there's no bugle doesn't mean there's no elk."

"Why'd we spend so much time watching things we couldn't shoot?"

I sighed and glanced at the lad. He's a good kid, with a well-developed set of values. Healthy, virile. No trouble at all to his mother. "Didn't learn anything?"

"Not about elk hunting."

"There's more than elk out here."

"But elk is what we're hunting."

We rode on with our thoughts. Memory served a bitter fare—how I once thought the same way as the lad. "How long you been hunting with me, boy?"

"This is the fourth year. "Why?"

"Anything else you'd rather be doing now?"

"No, but ..."

"That's worth something, isn't it?"

He fell silent.

The boy hunted with Fred the next day, while Buster went fishing and I stayed in to rest, bathe, and bake a cake. The boy came close to elk. He smelled them, had a raghorn answer Fred's bugle, but failed to cross a hair.

The following day, the boy and Buster headed for the deep timber above camp, planning to work along a mountain shoulder and then, if they found no elk, to search higher on the mountain for the boy a mule deer buck.

"I just gotta get me an elk," the boy said as they left camp.

"Blunder method," Buster told him. "We'll blunder along until we blunder into one. Works when nothing else does."

I figured to wander out and sit on a small knoll rising above the valley floor. We called it "Telegraph Hill," likening it to signal hills from days when semaphores were widely used to send messages. Despite its being a mere hundred feet above the valley floor, the hill provided an excellent view of the surrounding mountains. I planned to watch the mountainside across the way to see if Buster and the boy moved any elk.

"But even if you see any on our mountain, that'll be too far for you to shoot," the boy protested. "What good will that do?"

My reply was a good-natured grin.

It was chilly before sunup, so I built a small fire and pushed enough lodgepole limbs into the blaze to keep my hands warm. Soon, the sun shone on the mountain Buster and the boy worked. But it seemed forever before sunshine kissed my knob. Shortly after, however, grass was wet with dew instead of white with frost. Then, in no time at all, the grass was dry and I grew sleepy in the still warmth.

When my eyes popped open, my watch said nearly forty minutes had passed. I sat up, yawned, stretched, felt *good!* Nothing moved on the mountain, even through binoculars. I dug into my daypack for a cookie and nibbled so as to make it last. Off to one side, an ant hurried to and fro in the sunshine. I laid a crumb in its path and caused an epic struggle. The ant grabbed the crumb and climbed one grass stem, then over another, pushing, shoving, lifting, dragging, never pausing; around a rock here, over a stick there, until it bumped suddenly into the formidable barrel of my old Springfield '06. Unable to lift the crumb and climb over, too far to go around, too steep to drag his fortune, the ant seemed to go berserk. I watched for a while, then moved the rifle to my other side.

Still nothing appeared on the mountain. The ant had his crumb six feet away and moving. I lay back again and studied scudding clouds, then rolled to one side and saw a rounded white rock a couple feet of way. I reached for it. White limestone. No readily identifiable fossils. Hmm, came from the top of this hill. Not rounded by water, but by ice during glaciation. This knob, then, is a kame; a mound of detrital material left by a retreating ice sheet. Other rounded rocks of assorted sizes scattered on the knoll confirmed it. I yawned.

The bull was there when next I opened my eyes. He fed slowly, just below my hill, huge antlers twisting and jerking as he grazed first one clump of bunch-grass, then another.

My first thought was it's ridiculous for an elk to be out in this open valley in broad daylight, especially a bull as big as this one. My second thought was the irony of Buster and the boy clambering over that tough mountain looking for elk when one of the biggest in the country was grazing practically in sight of camp.

The huge antlers waggled on each side of the bush as he nipped shoot ends and leaves from it.

Nice antlers, too. Let's see, one-two-three-four-five-six on that side. One-two-three-four-five-six-seven! Hey, better count the other side again. One-two-three ... nope, six. Seven one side, six the other. Just like the horns hanging over my office desk. About the same size, too. Hmm, royal point more than twelve, maybe fourteen inches. Good spread. Massive beams. Spread'll go fifty-five maybe. Yep, a mate for the biggest I ever took. He's a bull to make any hunter proud.

My head was cradled on my watch arm, so I waited until the bull stuck his head behind a small bush, and then I moved barely enough to read the time. Quarter to eleven. The huge antlers waggled on each side of the bush as he nipped shoot ends and leaves from it. Hmm. Evergreen ceanothus. Fair winter browse, but not a normal food source until snow comes.

The elk jerked his head up and stood motionless, staring behind him. Ceanothus sprigs stuck from his mouth. He sucked them in and began chewing methodically, still looking back. Satisfied at last, he took three or four steps in my direction and dropped his head to feed again. But he looked up immediately. Then I heard horse bells, far off, dinging irregularly. Our grazing herd.

Thinking about the boy and how badly he wanted to get his elk, I twisted my head to squint at the mountain. The bull saw the movement and stood rigid, staring. How far was he? Less than a hundred yards. Eighty, maybe. No, more like seventy. Unsure, the bull moved a few steps nearer, only to drop from view because of the hill's contour. Though his body was out of sight, his antlers were still visible. They soon dipped, indicating the elk again grazed.

I spit on a finger and wiped at the Springfield's front bead to polish it.

I rolled away, dragging my rifle and daypack. When I sat up, it was with a small fir directly behind me to break my outline against a fleecy sky. His antlers were easily visible from the new spot and he still moved my way. I pulled the old Springfield into my lap and thumbed the latch to half-safe, then eased the bolt to chamber a shell. The only noise was a soft shudder and a barely audible click, but the bull's horns jerked higher and remained motionless for several minutes before he resumed feeding.

I studied the mountain through my binoculars. *Where in hell are you, boy?* Laying the glasses aside, I spit on a finger and wiped at the Springfield's front bead to polish it, then held the wet finger aloft to test wind currents. There were none.

It took nearly an hour for the bull to feed his way fully above the hill's contour. I studied each part of him as it appeared; saw the heavy black guard hair of his neck and shoulders, the still-healing scar there, the old wound on his hip. Battle wounds inflicted by rivals fighting over some love-sick cow? The old scar must have occurred during younger days when a more dominant bull drove him to flight. The fresh wound on his shoulder proved he ran no more; but what about the heft and size of the bull that gave it to him? *Does that one still live?*

The bull couldn't be more than thirty yards away now, still grazing unconcernedly. A leg grew numb but I continued to sit like a Buddha, going over in my mind the easy swing of the rifle's muzzle, the last flick of the safety, the squ-e-e-ze of the trigger.

Horses were visible in the distance—the black and white paint we called Domino and the boy's tough little bay. The bull looked occasionally over his shoulder at the approaching horses, but appeared unexcited about them. Then I realized why. He was drifting to top out on my hill, placing it between him and the horses. With the animal so close, I dared smile only with my eyes.

He smelled me at ten yards. His head was down as he moved from one grass clump to another. He paused in midstride. Slowly, he lifted his head and stared, then tilted his nose higher, testing, testing. His lifted hoof came down slowly, as if ratcheted, and he started to turn back the way he'd come. But the horses were behind him and he hesitated, testing the air again, nostrils flaring. At last, he settled on me, lowering his head near ground level, eyes locked, peering. Then, I'll be damned if he didn't take another step my way, still staring and sniffing.

"Hell of a place for you to be, big fellow," I said.

The bull jerked at my voice and turned away, but he stopped, apparently confused by the turn of events.

"Especially out here at mid day."

The bull took several slow-motion strides, angling away. After ten steps he could stand the suspense no more and crashed away, down the little hill, through the scattered small firs and pines, across the dry creek bed below, up the far bank! He was still running pell-mell when he passed through an opening a half-mile away. I grinned, jacked the shell from my rifle's chamber, straightened out the cramped leg, and dug into my daypack for a sandwich.

After a while, I folded my jacket for a pillow and lay down in the shade of the little tree where I'd sat so long, pulling my hat brim over my eyes. *They'll show before long*, I figured.

Their voices came before their bodies. Directly the boy said, "He's asleep!"

I lifted the hat. "Howdy, men. See anything?"

"Yeah. A big bull standing on top of you."

"That so?" I gazed at Buster.

Sweat streaked his face, and the armpits of his flannel shirt were stained dark beyond his orange vest. He wore a pinched smile as he shifted his rifle's sling strap and nodded.

"Big one?"

"A seven-point!" the boy said, his voice dripping with disgust. "I can't believe you didn't see it. He stood right here!" The lad moved until he was at the bull's nearest approach. "Here's his track!"

"Seven both sides?"

"Both sides."

I sat up and put my hat back where it belonged. "Must've been real big if you counted points from up there. Too bad you weren't here instead of me. A man can look for a while before he sees one like that."

The boy shook his head in wonder. "I wish I had been. I would've got him." When I said nothing, he went on: "You was sitting up—asleep sitting up. We thought you'd shoot any minute. I can't believe you was asleep when the biggest elk in the country walked up to smell you."

I smiled.

"Ain't you even gonna look at the tracks?"

Buster laid a hand on the boy's shoulder. "Things sometimes aren't like they seem." He looked at me. "How big was he?"

"Six on one side. You got sharp eyes if you counted seven from that distance, even one side."

"Sun was right. Glinted off his ..."

"You mean you saw him?" the boy exploded. "Why didn't you shoot?"

I held his eyes steady. "Maybe I figure I got my share."

The boy turned away in disgust, trying to act the man. "What about the rest of us?"

"What about you? You weren't here. Tell the truth, I waited for you an easy hour. Maybe two."

"But ... but we need the meat."

"No we don't. Fred's elk and Buster's deer split four ways is all the wild meat any of us need."

The boy looked at Buster and spread his hands in a gesture of helplessness. Buster saw the movement, but the forced smile never left his face and, except for a brief flicker to the lad, he watched me.

"How come you even go on a hunting trip?" the boy demanded.

I leaned back on an elbow. "Who ever said a man's got to shoot something to enjoy hunting?"

"What's the point in going, then?"

My saddlehorse, Buck, waits patiently while I shoot this picture from atop Telegraph Hill

"You mean if you don't kill something, the trip's a failure?"

"To me it is."

I lay back, head to the rolled-up coat, and again placed the hat over my face. "You think about that."

"I have," the boy said. "I'd have killed it."

"Sure you would. And I would, too, in your place. But I'm not in your place." My voice sounded hollow coming from beneath the hat. "And there's more—a whole lot more—to a hunt than merely shooting something." I whipped off the hat and sat up. "You know how long it's been since I killed anything bigger than a spruce grouse?"

The boy shook his head.

"Twenty years. More'n that, really. But I've hunted every year since. And you know what? I quit letting other folks tell me what I should do to enjoy my hunting trips about that long ago, too."

"You ain't me, though," the boy muttered.

"You might listen to your grandpa," Buster said softly. "I've known him longer than you are old. And I've never known him not to get more out of a hunting trip than anyone else who tags along for the ride."

I stared into the distance; saw the bull, and the boy. There were also beaver slides in the mud and mountain goats on cliffs high above. Buster had it at last—the simple truth about the real values of hunting. And I wondered if it would take the boy so long. ∎

Chapter 16

Tackling Tracking Troubles

Western novels of the late Louis L'Amour were always peopled with outstanding, larger than life heroes. Members of the Sackett clan could, without exception, kindle a blaze, boil a pot of coffee, put out the fire, and scatter the ashes before the first tiny wisps of smoke filtered through sheltering juniper bushes. The Sacketts were quick with their fists, steady with a gun, chivalrous toward ladies, and honest to a fault. But the talent I most admired about those peerless western legends was how each could track a piss ant across slab rock.

I am not so talented.

I've spent half a day following tracks of meandering elk through powder snow, only to discover that the creatures were going in the opposite direction; that my trail, instead of heating, was growing cold. I've also followed tracks identified positively as those of a bull—*big* tracks—only to lose them amid a cattle yard-like maze of other tracks left by wapiti who seem to delight in embarrassing a master guide before guests who'd paid thousands of dollars in the belief that I could find tracks with something standing in them.

Along the way, I learned. I learned L'Amour may have exaggerated the aptitude and intelligence of his protagonists. Or I'm hopelessly inferior, impatient, and inattentive to details the Sacketts could easily grasp from the back of a galloping horse.

Beads of perspiration trickled from beneath the man's cap; his shirt was unbuttoned to the waist and sweat-wet underwear showed beneath. A wool coat was tied around his middle by the sleeves, its tail dragging in thigh-deep snow. He paused to wipe his face with a red handkerchief as I reined my saddlehorse to a halt. Other horses, each carrying empty riding saddles, shuffled to a stop behind. The man grinned—grimaced really. It was all he could muster at that moment.

"On to something?" I asked, glancing at a clear animal trail the hunter had followed through the snow.

He nodded, recovering his breath. "Followed him down from the upper bench. He's a big one. I'm going to run him to ground."

The tracks were indeed fresh. But the snow was so powdery I could see no imprint even when I leaned from the saddle to peer. "Want your horse?"

"No. The bull probably won't stick to the trail and a horse would be in my way."

I glanced at my watch. Three hours of daylight left. "Looks like he might be headed up-creek."

The hunter swiped at his face again, then managed a clear smile on his freckled face. "It doesn't matter. Wherever he goes, I'll follow. He's a big one, Roland. And I want him." With no more ado, the man started after the elk of his dreams, wallowing through the deep snow.

"Bud and Lacy are somewhere up there," I called. "You catch up to that bull and get him, they'll help. But remember to get back to the trail by dark."

The hunter acknowledged with a casual wave.

It was early November, and elk season was in full swing. Hunting had been tough, however, what with the weather mild enough to make us pray for tracking snow. Then came a twenty-inch dump overnight. Now just getting around in the heavy, wet stuff took everything we could muster. I'd dropped off our hunters early that morning with the understanding they would hunt their way back to camp on foot.

"Good luck!" I called. The man answered with another casual wave.

Russ gave it his best shot, slogging and wallowing through the deep snow like the tireless animal he followed. Whenever the tracks were clear enough in the powder for him to measure his quarry's mammoth stride, he whistled tonelessly. Though he was an experienced elk hunter, never had Russ been on the trail of such a monster. He redoubled his efforts.

On and on, uphill and down, across trail and creek, he doggedly followed. He peered anxiously at his watch and put even more effort into plowing after tracks that had every appearance of freshening. Until, at the very limit of his endurance, he chanced to bump into Bud and Lacy, two others who were hunting from my camp.

"See any elk?" Bud asked.

Russ could only shake his sweat-streaming head, pointing mutely at the huge tracks that crossed the trail at this point.

"Neither did we," Bud said. "But we did see a heck of a big bull moose only a couple hundred yards up the way you're heading. Reckon you're following his tracks?"

Accomplished trackers must be observant: a broken grass stem, a tiny clump of fresh-turned soil, hoof scuffs on sandstone, a rolled pebble. But no skilled tracker follows his quarry step by step. Instead, he looks ahead, making educated guesses about the routes taken by the animal he pursues. Then he hurries on to cast about for sign. Nine times out of ten, his guesses will be correct, saving time and effort and narrowing the gap between pursuer and pursued. Real tracking talent thus relies heavily on ability to "read" country—to get a sense of travel routes. And it

In 1995, there were 797,445 licensed elk hunters in the United States, 36,957 in Canada.

relies on understanding animal impulses that influence those travel routes.

A classic example of such talent was the skilled tracking performance turned in by one of my guides and his hunter. It all began when another of our hunters downed a bull that erred in choosing where to demonstrate an attitude problem. The single shot echoing across the mountainside brought an explosion of elk bursting from a thicket, surprising Alex and Ed. Alex got off several rounds at a raghorn bull running flat-out at some distance. Though they didn't know it at the time, one round tagged the elk in his *foot*.

Believing he'd missed, the hunter and his guide nevertheless felt an obligation to make certain. It was at the upper reaches of their climb that Ed discovered the first droplet of blood. "Now we have to follow him, Alex," the guide murmured.

A classic example of such talent was the skilled tracking performance turned in by one of my guides and his hunter.

With no air to spare for idle chatter, the hunter nodded. And thus began a methodical day-long journey across a sun-struck mountainside covered mostly with slab rock and corrugated rock outcrops, broken only occasionally by narrow strips of trees and random bunchgrass meadows.

The wounded elk headed straight for shelter in the first tree line. But after reaching safety he crashed on through, then zigzagged across a second rock slab, dropped behind a rocky outcrop, zigged again and climbed to yet a second tree line.

Unraveling the quarry's trail took hours as the animal switched courses in places where he left little telltale sign. "We spread out on the rock slabs and looked for drops of blood," Ed said. "It was all we had."

Tracking went faster when the trail led through the soft soil of meadows or into the tree lines. Noon came and went as the determined hunters plodded on. Twice they lost the trail, only to pick it up by tramping ever-widening circles.

"His wound was drying," Alex said. "We found fewer

and fewer drops."

As the sun sank toward the western horizon, Ed sorted out that the elk was wounded low on his right front leg. "See how he's dragging that foot? No bone broken, though, because he's still putting weight on it."

"What does that mean, then?"

Ed flashed a grin. "It means we have a job cut out for us. It means he's not hurt bad, but he's probably looking for a place to lie down and watch his back trail. It means if we do jump him, he'll be moving and you'll have to be fast. Above all, it means we've got to speed up if we come up on him at all before dark."

"How're we going to speed up when the blood trail is drying?" Alex asked.

Ed shrugged as he panned the country ahead: more slab rock, broken rocky ridges, narrow strips of trees, and scattered meadows. "He seems to have quit climbing. I'm betting he's found the level he wants, and he's working around the side of this mountain. What I'm suggesting we do is I'll stay as much on the tracks as I can, but every time we come to a rock outcrop or a tree line, you take one side and I'll take the other. I'm hoping he blows out on your side. But if he comes out on mine, I'll holler."

Alex nodded. "You're the boss. It's an hour before dark. Let's hit it!"

The bull was lying beneath a limber pine, beside a rock outcrop. He burst from his hiding place on Alex's side.

It was a superb tracking performance turned in by Ed and Alex that day. There was no alternative for them except to employ methodical, careful, step-by-meticulous-step observation to unravel the bull's route. Certainly there are times and places, landforms or weather conditions, that will permit more rapid follow-up. But Alex and Ed did what they had to do at that particular time and in that place. And it took both hunter and guide working as a team to execute a proper approach.

But teamwork cuts both ways as we'll see in another incident. There were two elk. They'd fed slowly through a spruce forest, pausing here to munch frosted groundsel leaves, there to pluck the tops from scattered elk thistle. Their trail wound into a small opening where it looked as though they'd spent an hour or more feeding on blue-bunch wheatgrass.

I scanned the meadow's far side before moving out to study their tracks in the half-inch of powder snow that had fallen through the night. Then I saw it! "One is a bull," I whispered to my companion. "See where his brow tine knocked snow from that beargrass clump as he fed along."

The hunter gazed first at the tracks, then at me as he absorbed the lesson.

We followed the prints to a fallen sapling that had lodged horizontally, about four feet from the ground. The elk I knew was a bull angled around the lodged tree, while the second set of tracks ducked beneath. I was about to tell my companion our second elk was a cow when I bent over to peer at the sapling's bottom side. "The other is a bull, too! See where his points left scratch marks on the bottom of this tree!"

My hunter caught the excitement. "How big?"

I shrugged. "Hard to tell. Not big tracks, but that means nothing. Like people, small elk can have big feet. Or vice versa. The eye guard—brow tine—means one of 'em is more than just a spike. And two bulls working together probably means they've been around a while. I'd bet on 'em being respectable."

"Let's go then."

I caught his arm. "Not that way. They fed to the right. Up the hill."

The man took a bearing on the direction I pointed and plodded after our quarry. I glanced at the eastern skyline just as a tinge of sun peeped above it. The snow was holding now but would melt rapidly under a rising sun, making tracking tough. Where were the bulls heading? More than likely to bed down after daylight. But where would that be?

I caught my hunter and tapped his arm, signaling him to follow me. We headed for a low ridge I knew to be thick with elk brush (menzesia, or false huckleberry) and chock

It is said that an elk wears Hawaiian summer garb and Kremlin winter wear. The summer pelage consists of one thin layer of bright tan hair; the winter coat is darker, thick outerwear and a dense, wool under-coat as heavy as a logger's long-handles.

full of downed trees from a long-ago windstorm. The terrain was tough for us to move through quietly—a perfect early-warning system for elk who've been around for a while.

We circled the ridge until the soft breeze blew in our faces, then began a cautious ascent toward the ridge's high point. My companion—an experienced eastern whitetail hunter—led the way, rifle at the ready. He was quiet, careful, always alert.

So were the bulls.

One lay on one side of the ridge, the other guarded the opposite approach. We saw only a flash of light tan rump patches as they crashed away.

The snow round about was pretty much melted except for their two beds where hair and bodies provided insulation. Both beds were big. They were indeed veterans. They made an experienced, admirable team. They put our team in the shadows.

I looked at my hunter and mustered my best "well, shucks" grin. To his credit, he smiled in return.

An ability to follow tracks is critical, but whether those tracks are the kind you'll want to pursue is another matter altogether. Cow? Bull? Big bull? Raghorn? There are clues, and usually if you follow the route an animal takes for a sufficient period, enough clues will come together to offer some sort of composite picture of the creature.

A bull, for instance, will urinate between his four planted feet. Have you ever watched a horse when it empties its bladder? The male will plant all four feet, while the female spreads her rear legs. Elk do the same thing on a somewhat smaller scale. The bull's stream is more directed; a cow's falls farther and, with minimum directional control, tends to splatter. Find a well-directed pee-hole in the snow, a little back from the center of four slightly spread elk prints, and bingo! You're following a bull.

Wapiti guard hair, under a microscope looks like a honeycomb in a beehive. Each hair traps air—the secret to both their effective insulation against blizzard and their unusual flotation for swimming rivers or lakes.

Another indicator is the animal's way of coping with obstructions. Elk traveling forest country will weave in and out between trees. Cows and calves duck beneath limbs and broken saplings no bull would even try to pass under, and so must detour around. It's heartwarming indeed to follow a herd's tracks between two trees standing four feet apart—and see where one set of prints broke off as one of the animals picked his way around.

Autumn sun never touched the cold and gloomy canyons that lie north and east of the towering Granite Wall. Although the shadowy canyons and jackstrawed hillsides are favored haunts for a large elk herd, hunters seldom have touched there either. Persuade a guest to follow me once into that God-cursed place and no way would he entertain such madness a second time.

> **Persuade a guest to follow me once into that God-cursed place and no way would he entertain such madness a second time.**

In fairness, those canyons are so far from camp that the distance alone is intimidating. Throw in a dark, dank Hansel and Gretel forest choked with impenetrable brush in a confusing, broken landscape, and my inability to match hunter to prey in that hell-hole becomes more comprehensible.

But Dick was different. From the first, it was abundantly clear he was a woodsman *par excellence* as well as a skilled hunter. His dream was to take a respectable bull elk. His dream was also my dream, for Dick was one of the hardest-working, most diligent hunters, and one of the most affable guests we've ever been privileged to serve in our camps. The poor guy was star-crossed unlucky when it came to elk, so finally, late during Dick's second hunt with me, I led a little cavalcade of hunters into the hell-hole canyon, searching for elk tracks.

We found evidence of what looked like a wapiti convention near where the main canyon headed against a two-thousand-foot cliff face. We tied our ponies, and Rob, the other guide and I, began casting about in order to make sense of the cattle-yard maze of tracks.

It appeared the main herd had drifted to the north, toward a series of high basins. Others seemed to fade into the surrounding spruce forest. But a couple of parallel sets of tracks caught my eye. Both were large—not always meaningful, but a reasonable indicator. I followed them a sufficient distance to get a clear grasp of their stride. "They're big," I murmured to Dick. "Do you want ..."

"I'm game," he said.

Rob took two hunters and started after the largest group of tracks. Mike, the least woods-wise of the group, was to patrol the abandoned forest service trail. I knelt to refill a water bottle, shouldered my daypack, picked up the hand axe I carried, grinned at the rest of our party, and said, "Don't wait for us. If we're not back by a half-hour before dark, you get the hell out of this canyon without us. Hear?"

Rob nodded, and I motioned to Dick.

The man was everything I expected, for I set a mean pace and he stayed right with me, stride for stride. Though the skiff of snow wasn't exactly fresh, neither was it deep, and neither was it frozen. I suspected the two elk would skirt the high meadows just below the cliffs, heading for a towering ridge and a different creek drainage beyond. But I'd been in there with a packhorse and I really did think we could catch them before they escaped.

Why not? Chances were good they had no idea we were on their trail. Their tracks showed they were merely meandering, grazing along, as undisturbed animals will. We'd not gone far when I stopped in amazement and motioned Dick forward. Both elk had browsed on groundsel shrubs growing from the dampened face of an embankment. Both had foraged head-on. Both had pressed their antlers—big antlers—into the embankment as they fed.

Dick made the sign of the cross and we sped on up the tiny cutbank. We crossed one, two, three different bedding grounds for the creatures. I guessed they'd stayed an hour here, two hours there. In all cases, the bulls spread out, facing different directions. "This won't be easy," I muttered.

"Nothing worthwhile ever is," Dick whispered, crossing himself again.

Up, down, over, around, and through. I'd like to tell you that after all our effort we caught those bulls. Alas, t'would be untrue. We did hear them crashing away at one point. But it was a point where we were running out of gas and their tank was topped off and ready to roll.

We paused on the ridge between drainages to wet handkerchiefs and sponge our faces. "We're not going to do it, Dick," I said, holding onto a whitebark pine for support.

He sprawled to the ground. "What's below?"

"Another canyon just like we came from. Beyond that ridgeline yonder is the Continental Divide. It marks the game-preserve boundary. That's where they're headed. Even if we were fresh and it was just beginning daylight, we'd still never catch them."

He shook his head. "I sure wanted to see one of those bulls."

I sprawled beside him. "Me, too. But right now we'll be lucky to get out of this trap before full dark."

Dick smiled. "We'd better get going then."

Neither of us moved.

There's another phase of tracking that's often overlooked, sometimes even by experienced outdoors men and women: following your own backtrail back to the point of origin.

Folks who are truly accomplished in wilderness travel—particularly hunters and hikers "bushwhacking" (following no discernible man-made trail)—will spend considerable time studying the lay of the land *behind* them as they make their way crosscountry. Their reason is obvious: a landscape appears quite different when viewed from the opposite direction. Seek out a trout-filled lake in a north-country forest, or hunt through a valley broken by hillocks and ravines. Do so off-trail and don't pay attention to behind-the-back detail. Now try to find your way back—just try it!

Even more important is the ability to find your way back with packhorses to a bull elk you downed at dusk the evening before. Flagging ribbon, you say? Yeah, bits of colored flagging ribbon fluttering from occasional tree limbs is one way. But may the saints strike those idiots who flag their way to or from a location and fail to remove the ribbon when they're finished. Aside from the growing abomination of fluorescent ribbon fluttering from tree limbs through a forest, don't folks realize they're marking the best routes to prime hunting spots where they've taken treasured bucks and bulls? If you have an aversion to encouraging competition amid your own favored rocks and rills, there are more subtle ways to mark the route you must follow on a return journey.

It's not so much the use of flagging ribbon that bothers me as its misuse.

Suppose, for instance, that you found a great mainline elk trail through some spectacularly rich terrain. Say the trail begins on a low bench, skirts the edge of two small meadows, and passes by a series of wallows. Say there are loads of fresh tracks, droppings and rubs. Say you want to return the following morning or the next weekend. But the entry point to this important wapiti travel route is confusing, and so are three or four or half-dozen forks along your preferred route. Hang flagging ribbon along the way and your newly discovered area will be crawling with other hunters before you return. So what do you do?

What I do is mark my trails unobtrusively, in ways only I will recognize. I lean a half-rotted pole against a healthy tree to mark entry to the trail; break a green twig and leave it hanging at a crucial junction; stack a rock atop a larger rock at the second important junction. You get the picture, don't you? Only lack of imagination could keep anyone from adding ways to mark private trails.

If you must mark the critical entry point with flagging ribbon, you can do it in a manner that will obscure your discovery—like tying it to a limb four hundred yards from the real entry point. Only you will know what it means. But you should also know that flagging ribbon is not always a sure thing, either—I know people who believe colored ribbon fluttering in a forest is another manifestation of man's pollution and routinely remove it. Depend too much on flagging ribbon marking your trail's entry point and have someone remove it, then see how much your crutch helped you.

It's not so much the use of flagging ribbon that bothers me as its misuse. We routinely supplied our hunters with a roll of bright orange ribbon, just in case they chanced to be hunting alone when they downed an elk. We simply asked them to flag trees within sight distance of each other along the route from their downed animal to a ridge trail or a creek. Then we could make our way up the trail or creek with packhorses. On our way back, we would remove the ribbon. Unfortunately, not all our hunters readily grasped the purpose of the roll of ribbon. Once when I dropped a hunter off at the head of a drainage so he could hunt back to camp, I handed him a roll of ribbon.

"What's this for?" he asked.

"It's flagging ribbon, John." When he still looked puzzled, I added, "It's to use in case you get something. So we can follow it back to your elk."

I swear to God the man still appeared puzzled, fingering the roll. "Well ... uh ... how do I use it?"

"You tie it to tree limbs."

"You mean tie one end to a limb, then unroll it?"

I stared at him until at last he asked, "Is it long enough?" ■

Chapter 17

When Proper Preparation Meets Opportunity

There's this thing called luck. You don't want to believe it affects your fortune afield, but the bitter truth is most hunters consider the phenomenon vital to success.

Some folks, to put it politely, seem star-crossed in their hunting. I recall two clients from New Jersey. Henry scheduled the hunt; Frank tagged along because it was something to do. Henry was obsessed with a desire to take a six-point bull; Frank barely knew that bull elk grew antlers.

The two men hunted hard for ten days. One took a dandy six-point bull back to New Jersey. Guess who was the lucky one?

Henry, still obsessed with a passion for elk, moved to Montana so he could devote more time to hunting the elusive wapiti. To my knowledge, the man has never realized his life's dream. Frank, by the way, took two barren-ground caribou on a hunt with Henry. And Henry? Guess.

Luck is irrespective of personages. Consider the Brash family. Perhaps no group of hunters ever had a higher Bob Marshall Wilderness profile than did this savvy hunting family from Spangel, Washington. Beginning with Guy and Dolly back in the 1930s and continuing through their sons, Gene and Gary, the clan had a near-unbroken string of fall hunts.

It was only after I began outfitting in 1970, and after becoming acquainted with the family, that I learned the real truth: that luck smiled or frowned even upon members of this famous hunting family. Gene, who later went on to become perhaps the best U.S. Forest Service packer ever to trail up a string of mules, once told me during a hunt with two of his nephews:

"Some are born to be lucky, I guess. Two boys—one can't miss, the other a couple of steps too late, or has a tree between him and the bull." He shook his head. "I wonder if that young pup will ever shoot an elk."

I'd reckon we've all known hunters like that unfortunate youngster—nimrods who seem always to be one step too late or on the wrong side of a ridge or tying a bootlace when a nervous buck bolts its cover. Haven't we all wondered from time to time whether we fit that category? Probably we've even wondered if hunting is pure-D luck?

The answer is no. As an outfitter and guide for over two decades, I've watched hunters come and go. Some seemed to have a constant black cloud over their shoulder. But in my experience, eventual rays of sunlight fell upon those who persevered. Take, for example, the young Brash lad— the one his uncle feared would never shoot an elk. Well, I crossed that boy's path during a subsequent year. It'd be hard to imagine any more button-busting pride than that lad exhibited while showing me the seven-point antlers from a bull he'd taken just the day before.

Luck, of course, comes in two forms: one bad, one good. Most hunters I know ascribe to one but not the other. Pour a cup of coffee just when a massive bull crosses before your stand, and of course it's bad luck. But have an occasion when fortune smiles and there's no luck involved at all— only skill.

Ludwig was as Pennsylvania Dutch as shoo-fly pie, scrapple, and apple pan dowdy, and he had the accent to go with it. He was also the luckiest hunter ever in our camp, despite the fact that he had no prior hunting experience except in the Keystone State for whitetail deer. Ludwig is not the man's real name. But it will have to do. Lud first came with us in 1976. His luck began when he drew one of the few mountain goat permits then being issued. And as fortune would have it, the man took a nine-and-a-half-inch billy with a well-placed two-hundred-yard shot on his first day afield.

The next day, Lud and his guide packed the billy back to camp. A mule deer with massive antlers tried to argue right-of-way with the tired hunter, and the Pennsylvanian nailed him with a seventy-five-yard running shot.

Were the two bulls that chose their beds on the bush-filled ridgetop lucky—or smart?

Ludwig rested on day three. But on day four, he and his guide sallied forth and stumbled across a six-point bull elk still lying in his bed.

With nothing but black bear left to stalk and bears uncooperative in late October, Lud was left pretty much to his own devices, hanging around camp, admiring his trophies, talking to the cook, which was me. Around camp the guy contributed more than his share to both chores and camaraderie. But my principle memory is of Lud after he'd collected his three fine trophies.

"You know, Ludwig," I said as he sipped a cup of coffee, "you have the distinction of being the luckiest hunter we've ever had."

"Vell, yah," he said. "I guess dat's so." Then he leaned over and thumped me on the chest, reared back, cleared his throat and crossed his legs. "But I tink maybe some of dose udder people, dey're not so good hunters, eh? Maybe dey don' know so much how to hunt. Wha'd you tink?"

Perhaps my eyes widened—I don't know. If they did, Ludwig never noticed because he was already nodding complacently to himself. I do know nothing would have been gained by arguing with a man who had three fine trophies hanging from the meatpole—and collected them all in but three hunting days. Perhaps I could have told the man he was destined for a rude awakening.

"Perhaps," I muttered. "Perhaps you're right."

Ludwig was, of course, anxious to return for another hunt. But though he had a clear shot at a massive bull elk, his lucky star seemed to desert him. The Pennsylvanian returned in a subsequent year, saw some elk without horns, and took a buck much smaller than his first. He hunted with us a final time without success of any kind—one of those dry years in more ways than just weather.

He hasn't been back. Luck? Go figure.

When you think on it, however, hunting luck might be compared to luck at the poker table. Perhaps it's not so much what cards you hold as the cards your opponents don't hold. Think for a moment of the equation from the elk's point of view—might not your bad luck be his good luck?

Think of the chapters preceding this; of the hunting vignettes therein. Were the two bulls that chose their beds on the bush-filled ridgetop lucky—or smart? Did the two that eluded Dick and me on that exhausting day have a star shining upon them, or did they employ simple tactics protecting themselves?

Remember, too, that in both cases, the bulls paired for more effective security. It was a shrewd tactic they deliberately employed. We know this because breeding season had already ended and chance encounters between bulls at that time of year are rare. Might we find it odd that in most encounters where we were outfoxed by elk, the lucky bulls appeared to be larger, older bulls? How did they reach that point of advanced adulthood—by being lucky, or by being smart?

Yes, the raghorn with the wounded foot *was* unlucky. But his luck *really* ran out when he failed to watch his backtrail, allowing Ed and Alex to overtake him.

Now let's flip back to the hunter. In the next chapter, let's discover more about the lucky ones. ∎

Chapter 18

Habits and Habitat
Way to the Top 20

Here are numbers to rattle your abacus: twenty percent of all elk hunters take ninety percent of the elk.
Huh?

That's right, they're figures widely accepted by the
knowledgeable among the fuzzy fraternity of elk slayers.
Of course, those top-twenty hunters don't talk much about
their near-monopoly.

To put those figures into perspective, let's say a thousand elk are taken over a five-year period by a thousand
hunters—a twenty percent overall yearly average. Now get
this: Nine hundred of those elk will be taken by just two
hundred hunters—a nine-in-ten chance of success for
those especially blessed wizards *each and every year*!

What about the other eight hundred license-toters?
There's only a one-in-eight chance they'll score throughout
the five-year period.

Such statistics transcend luck. Given the fact that there
are around a million licensed elk hunters in America each
year, there simply cannot be two hundred thousand steely-
eyed throwbacks to Jim Bridger and Kit Carson. Some
must be butchers, bakers, and candlestick makers. But if
the twenty percent who take ninety percent of the elk are
sort of like you and me, they must know something or do

something the rest of us know not and do not. To get to the heart of the conundrum, what?

Here is a compendium of things they know and do:

First, they spend lots of time in the wilds. Their vocation might be slicing bacon, but their avocation is cutting steaks from their own wild game. Outdoor adventure is high on their spare-time priority list. They're the kind of folks who become living-room familiar with a specific block of hunting country. And while they're out there, they pay close attention to the habits of that block's wildlife inhabitants.

Even among the top twenty fraternity, not every hunter has that kind of time. Their lives are like yours and mine, occupied with job, family, community. Perhaps they live in a metropolis, far from hunting territory. Vacation time is limited and fully allocated to the wife and kids. Perhaps there's time for only one hunting trip each year. What, then, do those hunters do to score consistently?

Simple. They find an area with promise and return there year after year. Each season they'll be able to build on what they've learned the year before. Given time, they'll know their hunting country well. Nothing—absolutely nothing—is as vital to hunting success as intimate knowledge of the land one chooses to hunt. You can shortcut the learning process to some degree by acquiring a good set of topographic maps covering the selected hunting area, then studying them to absorption. Don't expect too much, however. Maps can't substitute for being there on the ground. Besides, as strange as it may sound, the topos will benefit a person more *after* a first visit to the land. You'll then be able to grasp what the map tells you, visualize the entire topographic picture. With practice, you'll be able to pick out hidden pockets or isolated benches on the map—pockets and benches you'd not necessarily find on your own.

Is knowledge of the hunting country *really* that important to elk hunting success? Yep. Without it, you'll never

> Migrating honkers have a head only half the size of my fist, but they know that if they hang around a day or two, they learn where to find local cornfields.

move into the elite twenty (unless a guide can help you get there). Without a thorough knowledge of the country you plan to hunt, you'll never learn about bedding areas, travel routes, migration corridors, weather-protected pockets, and refuge thickets. While there's a lot more to elk hunting than intimate knowledge of the land, it's the single most fundamental element. A good working knowledge of the land allows the hunter to cover key areas well. It doesn't guarantee success, but does allow the stalker to make an accurate assessment of target numbers, their recent movement, and sometimes their male-to-female ratios.

I've known many hunters who were proud of the fact they hunted a different area each year. I'm proud for them, too, since their annual objective was to see a new and different chunk of God's handiwork. They make their safaris primarily for beautiful mountain scenery and the physical elan gained by such experiences. But we must remember there are none—not one, zilch, zero—of those people who come close to taking an elk every season. For them, pounds of meat is unimportant. They're content merely to have a chance to take an animal, but are miserable if they never see what's beyond another ridge, and another. It's a poor way to stock your freezer, but a great way to spend time outdoors.

There's another type of hunter; one who flits from place to place, seeking always that valhalla where wildlife trample the unwary. This type never finds what is sought—never becomes familiar enough with any landscape to learn what's there—and they somehow feel shortchanged. Had these hunters taken time to do pre-hunt research, or had they returned a second or third year, utilizing lessons learned in previous visits, they might have discovered they were camped in the middle of America's Serengeti.

Migrating honkers have a head only half the size of my fist, but they know that if they hang around a day or two, they learn where to find local cornfields.

To be more specific about how thorough knowledge of your hunting country can help—let's say you drive around a bend in an old logging road and see fresh-turned dirt in a high-side road cut. You stop and investigate. A band of elk crossed only a short time before. It's a scenario that's repeated hundreds or thousands of times each hunting season. So what happens next?

Most hunters will plunge after the elk. If there's more than a single hunter in the vehicle and no one is intimately familiar with the area, they might choose to spread out and follow the animals' general route. But if someone does know the country, he might remember a low pass a mile away—in the direction these elk seem to be heading. That last hunter fits somewhere among the twenty percent who takes ninety percent of the elk.

Another example: Suppose there's a light skiff of snow. You strike fresh tracks of a small wandering band of elk. You follow for a short distance and note that the animals are browsing frostbitten groundsel leaves. They seem headed for a spruce-filled bottom you know runs heavy to groundsel. A gentle breeze is fitful against the short hairs on your neck. Do you continue tracking them? You do not. You make a big half-circle and tiptoe into the groundsel-rich spruce bottom with the wind drift in your face.

Congratulations, you've just entered the select twenty.

But could you have accomplished either of the foregoing stratagems had you not known your hunting country well?

Still another example: You decide to hunt a big horse-shoe basin on a quiet, windless day. One side of the basin is semi-brush-choked; the other is open, affording a clear view. Your best hunt would be to work through the brushy side, keeping a constant look-out across the tiny creek to open country. With a little luck and a bunch of skill, you might jump a bull in his bed and end your hunt. If not, you could still have a chance for him as he escapes across the open side. Without beforehand knowledge, you had only a fifty-fifty chance of properly hunting that basin. Or you might have clambered up the creek bottom and had scant chance at all.

We've focused on elk, but a working knowledge of your hunting country is also important when pursuing other big

There are just under a million elk estimated to exist in the U.S. and Canada. With over 800,000 hunters pursuing them each year, if everyone scored there'd soon be no elk.

game. Or did you think it accident that some folks enjoy consistent whitetail success? A sound working knowledge of landform-influenced travel routes is vital for successful antelope and mule-deer hunting, too. Similarly, bighorn sheep and mountain goats are creatures of habit, and it's important for the hunter to know and value those sections of their range where a successful stalk is likelier. Most of all, it's essential for sheep or goat hunters to know and avoid the cliff ledges where they might risk their lives to attempt retrieval, even if they do clamber near enough to slay their quarry.

There are other important reasons for knowing your selected country well. Perhaps you'd choose not to hunt there if you'd checked it out first. Perhaps the hills are too steep or the mountains too high for your sea-level heart. (I once had a hunter exclaim, "Damn you, Cheek! I finally figured out why you guides always go first—it's so you can get first crack at the oxygen!")

Mule-deer country, it is true, varies from Colorado mesas and the deep gorges of Idaho's and Oregon's Snake River country to rolling juniper hills of Montana and Wyoming cattle ranges. Similarly, elk can be found in most habitats from the Tetons to tidewater. Perhaps you don't care to hunt an area thick with shintangle. Or maybe there are too many roads. Or not enough roads. Learn your country. Spend the necessary time, be it years, to educate yourself. After you've unearthed its secrets, odds are good you'll find wildlife populations more abundant and the land less intimidating than you first thought.

Also of manifest importance is a good working knowledge of the habits of the animals you seek. Be assured our top-twenty elk hunters know their game's habits well. A thorough understanding of species habits is closely interwoven with habitat. The most successful hunters know both.

I'll lay out a few ideas on habits, and you can see for

Elk have spiritual significance to many American Indian tribes, considered an important spirit animal, valued for their image of strength, speed, cunning, and determination. The animals had material importance to the Indian, too, furnishing hides for clothing and tent covers, antlers into implements, sinews for binding string, and, of course, rich sources of food for the people.

yourself whether they're important:

For elk, the best example is the rutting period. A hunter in pursuit of rutting wapiti should know as much about their habits as possible—their strengths and weaknesses. For instance, in the land I know best, September elk are most always in dense spruce forests where moisture oozes from springs or bogs. We sometimes find them in fringe lodgepole or out in tiny forest meadows, too. But seldom will they be far from wet soil, beneath a dank canopy of towering spruce.

There are several reasons why elk prefer this type of habitat. They seek isolation and the protective cover of the forest for breeding. Wet spots are often turned into wallows—cooling mud baths for overwrought bulls. And the deep basins and spruce-filled bottoms are always cool places to languish.

Bull elk are, of course, vulnerable—uh, make that pre-occupied—during the rut. Cows are not. Cows can be unpredictably scattered, serving as acute warning systems for the herd bull.

You should also know that smaller raghorn bulls are the ones a hunter will most often bump into. They, too, are unwary because they're aroused. And they're frustrated by exclusion from the main body, reduced to working the herd fringe in an attempt to hijack a cow. Raghorns also lack the herd bull's cow-warning system. All the above are reasons why smaller bulls are more vulnerable.

You should learn to make good estimates of a bull's size when you hear him bugle. There are several keys. Chances are, a herd bull will not come to your bugle unless he thinks you're a direct threat to his harem. Interpreted, that means *close*. It's love he wants, not fight. Usually he'll try sneaking his cows away from what he supposes to be competition. On the other hand, a small bull will seldom come to a call he thinks is a larger bull—why should he wind up both frustrated *and* battered? Instead, the small bull will slip away, perhaps bugling courage-builders back your way as he retreats into the sunset.

You should know that the frequency of a bull's bugling

Both cows and bulls come into estrus among elk. A cow's receptive cycle is only for one 24-hour period. If a bull fails to service her during that brief period, she will come in heat again some twenty days later. A cow can have up to four estrus cycles each season.

can be an excellent indicator of his rutting frenzy. Know also that the deeper into the frenzy he succumbs, the more inclined he'll be to do something rash. You should also know when *not* to sound off. If you're bugling your way through fresh tracks without getting so much as a grunt in return, you might as well be accompanied by a band playing "Stars And Stripes Forever."

And don't get enamored of wallows after the rut passes. They may tickle your imagination, but you're wasting your time after your elk moves from boudoir to drawing room.

Natural mineral licks can harbor elk. But you should know that their utilization tails off during cold, dry periods, when little moisture is contained in forage plants. Lick use can pick up again, however, if you run into a week of wet weather. A rule of thumb: More liquids consumed, more salt needed for the system. Works the same for human.

You should know enough about wapiti habits to guess at their bedding areas. A big note of caution here, however. Bedding areas change as elk move to more abundant and succulent food sources. As a result, they tend to have no more loyalty to the one they used yesterday than I do toward Motel 6, despite the best efforts of Tom Bodett. Elk will also change bedrooms because of weather, seasons, and predator pressure (including human predators).

More than likely it's a waste of time, after the rut, to look for bedding areas in the same places as during the rut. After the first deep frosts cut leaves from deciduous plants, elk in my hunting areas favor the cured grasses of south- and southwest-facing slopes. At that time, you'll find their bedding areas in a nearby fringe forest.

Bedding areas will vary from region to region. I read a passage from a recent book on how to hunt elk. By and large, the writer did a good job, but when he said, "Look for bedding elk in alder thickets," he flunked my Montana test. Where I live, alder means tag alder. And in my experience, elk avoid those devilish thickets every bit as assiduously as even the dumbest hunter. In the land where I dwell, favored bedding sites for elk are often found in patches of menzesia (also known as false huckleberry or elk brush). Menzesia grows beneath a forest canopy, and it's stems snap with little more than a touch. As a consequence, it's almost impossible for a hunter to pass through without a clamor. The point? Bedding areas vary from region to region, so it's important for you to discover them wherever you choose to hunt.

After you locate bedding areas, figure out the travel routes elk utilize to and from those places—and you're back in the select twenty.

Knowledge of migration corridors and winter ranges is essential for effective late-season elk hunting. But you need to know enough about wapiti habits to put that bit of habitat knowledge to work. Again, in my country, elk tend to drift with a storm, always toward their winter ranges. Sometimes, if blizzard weather is on the way, they'll drift ahead of the storm.

I've seen them drift as much as *two days* before a blizzard struck. (That's information inexperienced hunters may want to file in their memory banks as a little survival trivia.) When elk drift during inclement weather, they usually follow a broad travel route, most often along south and west exposures where sun and warming winds—where and when they occur—whittle away snow depths.

That's *habitat*, of course. But you should know enough *habits* to know that cows and calves, and sometimes small bulls, tend to migrate earlier than big bulls. Elk on the migration-move are hard animals to catch; intercept maybe, but catch—no. In either case, it's impossible to do so if you don't know your territory, but it darn sure helps to know *when* they're likely to move.

Habits and habitat are inextricably interwoven. If you seek to be the elk-hunting envy of your office, you'd better learn both. ■

Chapter 19

Ironies of the Rut

Flies buzzed around us as a shimmering red ball cleared the eastern horizon, auguring a blistering Labor Day weekend. Late October's hunting season was still weeks away, so we carried no weapon. Four miles up the path, my companion set about to do his thing.

My friend Leroy's thing was bugling for elk. This was before commercial grunt tubes and diaphragm calls. His repertoire, dependent upon his voice alone, included a full range of piercing, multi-toned whistles that ended with deep coughing grunts. The man's only props were a swollen larynx, enormous lung capacity, a bell-shaped high-school cheerleader's megaphone, and an animal belief that if a bull elk existed in the county, the creature would be compelled to reply.

Since Leroy's heyday, of course, elk bugling has taken quantum leaps with professional tourneys and scientifically developed equipment to enhance vocalization. As a result, two-legged creatures have, by and large, taken over sounds of autumn that once were the exclusive domain of the less competitive wapiti.

My friend Leroy was new to northwest Montana. He wanted to prove his brag about being a whiz at calling bull elk to his bugle. I knew the country; we made a deal.

The place was an isolated valley near the Canadian

boundary. The valley had long ago been swept by wildfire and was just coming into its most beautiful successional stage—dotted with random sidehill and creek-bottom meadows, interrupted by fingers of rail-sized lodgepole pine. The trail wound along an open hillside, perhaps three hundred feet above the valley bottom. The valley was wonderful hunting country, and the trail afforded a bird's-eye look at the bottom, as well as excellent views of surrounding hills.

We picked an open section of trail, and my friend slipped from his daypack, pulled out his little megaphone, gathered huge amounts of air to lung, and let loose with a thundering whistle-bugle-grunt that only another elk could replicate.

One did. It was barely discernible—a far-off whistle from up-canyon. We grinned at each other. "He'll never come this far to a bugle," I said.

Leroy agreed.

We'd just shouldered our daypacks to hike toward the bull when something floated downwind to us. "What was that?" I muttered. "It sounded like ..."

"Sonofagun," my friend said. "He's coming." Leroy pitched his pack to the trail and gave his best imitation of an enraged bull elk.

A full-throated reply drifted back. The bull was still upstream and still screened by the lodgepole forest, but undeniably nearer.

A rub sapling skinned by a bull in rut. Note the broken top.

Only a few minutes had gone by when a magnificent six-point bull broke from the forest, perhaps three hundred and fifty yards across the valley bottom. Leroy and I both sat spellbound as the bull stopped to stare up the mountainside in our direction and let out a deep, coughing grunt.

Leroy grunted back, and the bull spun on his heel to

charge a four-inch lodgepole sapling, savaging it with his antlers. Bark and branches flew in shreds, as did shards from the trunk.

My friend bugled again, and the bull paused to glare our way, then attacked the sapling with renewed frenzy. So savage was his attack that the tree bent against the weight and fury. The bull forged on, straddling its trunk, working his way up its length, stripping bark and limbs for its full thirty-foot length. So enraged was the bull that he kept going, even after running out of tree. The sapling sprang back. It was peeled from end to end, a shining flagpole standing stark and white in the middle of a wilderness.

The bull paused in his fury to peer our way, then lifted his nose until his antler tips scratched his butt, and he began the long inhalation whistle and ended in a string of deep, coughing grunts, his nostrils sinking with each until they almost reached the grass at his feet. It was stunning to watch. Then the giant shook his head in anger, spit and sweat flying, and burst into a gallop, bent on combat!

"He won't come uphill to a fight," I muttered to my companion. "No bull will come uphill to a fight—everybody knows that ..."

"I don't know much about these north-country elk," Leroy said, snatching up his daypack.

Yet here came a red-eyed, white-hot bull, with mayhem on his mind, UP a mountainside. Three hundred yards, two hundred, one hundred.

"Jesus!" Leroy shouted, shoving past me down the trail.

Only a wind change and our frenzied, terror-stricken shouting turned the bull. And an isolated fresh-peeled flagpole rocked its mockery at us after the bull paused to take one last swipe on his way out of Dodge.

Short of staring at buck or bull, there's nothing that will inflame a hunter so much as stumbling upon fresh rubs or scrapes. The poor guy can be footsore and weary, slogging toward camp or car or copacabana, dispirited and disgruntled and disillusioned. His mind might be miles away, senses dulled. But put a fresh elk rub on that lodgepole sapling yonder, or a buck scrape in the middle of the game trail he's following, and watch the guy's rifle swing to *present arms* as his eyes turn beady red, shifting from side to side like warning lights at a railroad crossing.

Despite the fact that he's been making as much noise coming down the trail as a switch engine in a marshaling yard, the hunter's ears turn pointy and each will swing like antennas tracking a U.F.O. He'll sniff the scrape, feel the peeled lodgepole, and taste the breeze like a garden snake on full alert.

Scrapes and rubs, you see, *are* that important. Both play an important part in the breeding processes of elk and deer—particularly whitetail deer.

Deer scrapes are generally up to three feet in diameter. They're areas of scratched-up soil, usually beneath overhanging tree limbs or brush. The more these scrapes are freshened by different bucks, the larger they become. Compared to those of deer, elk scrapes (sometimes called wallows because they occur in wet, swampy areas) are monstrous, stretching up to fifteen feet in diameter. Scrapes are marker spots where bucks and bulls announce both their presence and their availability to the opposite sex.

Rubs are for different purposes: territorial rubs, dominance rubs, or sparring rubs. Early during the rut, the most prevalent rub is the sparring variety—where individual animals wipe velvet from their antlers while gradually discovering their heredity. Sparring rubs blend into territorial rubbing. Both types are usually limited to a specific kind of landform within a fixed area—a spruce basin, a river bottom, a series of broken ridges near agricultural land. Territorial rubs are usually the most visible, established for God and everybody to see—like landowners posting blaze orange *No Trespassing* signs. Other rubs will be nearby.

Areas thick with territorial rubs are your best bet for hunting success during the rut. They're boundary marks establishing the area an individual animal considers his own—the area he will defend against encroachment. Unless that encroachment is by a clearly dominant animal. And that's where the dominance rubs come in.

Dominance rubs will be found well within the core area of a bull elk's territory. Dominant bucks or bulls making power statements with rubs can be impressive. How else can one leave a clear message of supreme authority? The bull that Leroy and I watched as he pushed over and stripped the four-inch lodgepole of limbs and bark was a classic example. And when the bull let that thirty-foot tree spring upright to shiver in its nakedness, he left a hell of a message—one that would get any other bull's attention, no matter his size.

> Scrapes and rubs play an important part in the breeding processes of elk and deer

Trail rubs are the most common of all rubs and are, in reality, a blend of sparring rubs and territorial rubs. They're most often found along game trails leading from one landform to another and are likely to be made by younger elk (and deer) not sufficiently powerful to establish and hold their own territories.

Your best bet for hunting trail rubs is to set up your stand along a line where there are several rubs, each within sight of the next. Hunting these rub lines, especially where one is associated with several scrapes, can be effective for whitetail deer, but not nearly so with the less numerous elk.

Sparring rubs are the least promising of all. Most often they can be recognized by the intensity of destruction. Saplings may be broken off or uprooted. What they indicate is that an animal acted out some sort of frustrated sexual frenzy in that spot. Sparring rubs can be scattered randomly across the map.

Realize that scrapes serve as advertisements for trolling bucks and bulls, and are utilized as meeting places for both rutting males and females. Knowing that, the best method a hunter can employ to utilize scrapes is to find one freshened recently by droppings, torn earth, and worn grass, then analyze the surrounding terrain, cover, and travel routes to and from the scrape. Then guess at oncoming weather patterns and choose a stand to your advantage.

Normally, elk rut in late September and early October, while deer rut during the last two or three weeks of November. These are generalities, of course. Whitetails rut later in the south, for instance. And I remember my last season as a guide when elk seemed late and deer seemed early—enough so their ruts overlapped. It was the only year during my entire guiding career when I actually witnessed horny buck deer following cow elk in estrus. Try explaining that one to hunters after telling them all about ungulate rutting at a sport show months before.

Throughout my two-decade guiding career and forty years of elk hunting, I've found outdoor-page reports of a year's rutting season to complain of spotty bugling success. So, join the crowd—it is indeed an annual problem. Were it not so, elk hunting would be a snap and the animal would lose its charismatic hold.

It's funny, though. For the lucky few—archers or back-country rifle hunters who are successful in calling in a big bull—bugling is great. "No luck to it," they'll tell you. "All skill."

Don't listen to them. Bugling is always touch and go. Sometimes the bulls simply don't cooperate. It has nothing to do with your talent or torrent. You see, elk, particularly big mature bull elk, have many things on their minds during the rut. And filling your freezer is not one of them.

Nope, it's that flirty little cow with the nice swaggle to her hips who often holds him willing hostage. Or that motherly type who strokes his ego and bears his children with little fuss and lots of pamper. Could be the bull who fails to answer your call is not so much wary as weary. In order to succeed in calling elk steaks on the hoof, you must catch him before he gives up or gives out. By the time you read this, most bulls will have done both. ■

Chapter 20

Holy-Water Wildlife Viewing

Some have it and some don't, some will get it and some won't. We're talking here about a God-given ability to spot wildlife.

I'll tell you about one who has it. She came into my life as a sagging-stockinged, snot-nosed kid next door, hanging around my parents' empty lot where the neighbor boys played pick-up ball games of a hot summer afternoon. It's still unclear what I saw in her, except at seventeen she had a bunch more to see than she did at twelve. The big problem was that the lass didn't know a damned thing about the outdoors; whereas at eighteen I already knew I was the smartest, toughest outdoor type to trod the West since Kit Carson and Jim Bridger. So how it happened that the lady turned out to have such a refined talent for spotting wild creatures in their own element can only be explained by the Omnipotent taking her under His wing.

She began not knowing what an elk was, then progressed throughout a married lifetime until these days we can be speeding down a highway at ten miles over the speed limit and she's sure to spot an elk's legs when he's standing screened amid doghair lodgepole pines.

Any more when she exclaims, "Stop the car!" I'll automatically slam on the brakes and put it in reverse, knowing full well the next thing she'll say is, "There's a bear feeding on that hillside." Or, "I saw sunlight glint from an elk horn."

Though Jane was our camp cook for most of two decades, savvy hunters soon learned to depend on her for more than that—to stay close to the woman who consistently spotted game their high-paid professional guides would ride past without a clue.

She was more than just lucky. The woman turned uncanny.

There was the time I took the packstring on into camp while Jane rode along with a couple of Oregon hunters who'd been guests many times. It was late afternoon, an hour from camp, when the hunters wanted to stop and photograph a waterfall. Knowing Jane was anxious to get the camp kitchen set up, they told her to go on ahead; they would come along in their own good time.

She was more than just lucky. The woman turned uncanny.

Knowing them to be among our most experienced guests, Jane rode on.

Only a half-mile farther, the trail nudged a steep, grass-filled meadow. Three elk—one of them a bull—fed in that meadow. With astonishing presence of mind, the lady kept her saddlehorse moving until she dropped from sight of the grazing animals. Then she swung from her saddle and held her pony close. Periodically she used the stirrup to swing up and check the still grazing elk. At last, she saw the hunters coming.

Bud and Lacy were still laughing when all three rode into camp. "There she was," Lacy said, "with a foot cocked up like a dog smelling a grouse in a briar patch, waving at us and pointing up the hill."

He paused to chuckle again, then added, "She looked like a pointing dog herself."

Once, after the hunters and guides had all scattered from camp, Jane heard a bull bugling from the mountain above. Then there were two. She carried my spotting scope out to the avalanche path that ended at our horse corral, set it up, and for several hours watched two bulls, each on a separate mountain level (but only yards apart), bugle their hearts out in mock rage.

"You should have seen them," she said when the luckless hunters and guides returned at dusk. "One would walk one way on his bench, and one the other. They would crisscross, slashing at bushes and trees and calling challenges back and forth. I could see them both, but they couldn't see each other!"

I sighed. "And what did they finally do?"

"They seemed to drift into the big spruce timber just before you came in."

"Naturally," I said.

The next morning, our hunters and their guides converged on the levels where the bulls had been the day before. As I expected, there were no bulls—they'd moved on, God knows where. We found their tracks. We even found the bushes and trees they'd torn to pieces while Jane watched. We found a couple of scrapes and a wallow they'd savaged. But elk? No.

My wife met us on our return from scrambling all over that God-cursed mountain. "A bull grunted from across the creek," she said. "I was out looking for grouse when he let loose not a hundred yards away. I came right back to camp, but I heard him running away. Sounded like he crashed out upriver. What do you think?"

To tell the truth, it made no difference what I thought. It made a difference to my hunters what *she* thought, though. Two of 'em hung around camp for the rest of the week, following the woman like puppies, waiting for her to sprinkle holy water on their hunting efforts.

Some folks don't realize it takes considerable knowledge, skill, perseverance, and fortitude to be successful in spotting wildlife, especially when circumstances are less than optimum. Sure, anyone can park a car alongside an alfalfa field in the spring and watch whitetail deer at dusk.

Likewise, you can locate water birds by staking out a swamp, or prairie dogs by spending enough time glassing their towns in midsummer. But even when all vibes are in your favor, some of those times in some of those places are more productive than others.

Time of day is always important, as is location. So is time of year. If your objective is to spot a regal whitetail buck, it'll do little good to watch alfalfa fields in the spring because bucks have shed their antlers and are yet to grow new ones. Spotting prairie dogs during hibernation might rate with the toughest of all wildlife watching, and swamps might be considered more likely to teem with birds when sedge grass and cattails aren't sprouting from a wintertime ice cap.

Spotting prairie dogs during hibernation might rate with the toughest of all wildlife watching

But there's more to comprehensive wildlife viewing than merely understanding a few fundamental givens. Jane somehow learned by osmosis to understand the broad outdoor picture. By casting a quick glance at mountain or meadow, her brain can process exposed colors or vertical and horizontal lines that may well reveal something out of sync. The elk legs the lady spots among doghair lodgepole may indeed have the same vertical lines, but their colors are wrong. The blur behind a serviceberry bush may be out of character with the snow-covered meadow beyond. Or how often does a tree limb glint sunbeams?

Movement, to a trained observer, can be a dead giveaway. Flick an ear here, rub a paw there, scratch a butt at an inopportune moment, and Jane will have the animal on radar in an instant.

It's not so much that my guides and I were klutzes when it comes to spotting wildlife, but that God gave that woman tools to be the best in the world at the kinds of things for which uninitiated easterners paid thousands of dollars—supposedly paying for my expertise. For one thing, she has Irish eyes the size of dinner plates. Those peepers, I swear to God, work independently, covering the countryside like a Dublin pub's twin TV dishes scanning for programming to hold their Sunday-afternoon drinking crowd. For another, the lady has total concentration. With her, proving that she's adept in a world where her male peers delude themselves into believing they're superior has become a way of life.

As diligent as I tried to be while guiding, my mind still wandered. As the owner of thirty head of horses, I might be worried about getting hay and grain to the trailhead. Or I might be weighing the options for next year's advertising.

Jane had no hunters looking down their nose if she goofed a drive or guessed wrong on a cut-off pattern to intercept a herd of elk. No one was there to witness any guiding mistakes when she led only herself. But even without a cheering crowd to help her celebrate victories, she led a world-class, single-person, publicity department that thumped her praises sufficiently to elicit offers of marriage from moneyed hunting clients who believed close association with the woman would lead to field success.

In wildlife viewing, patience is a virtue, trailing only dedication and selection. You have to spend time. Dedication is a measure of how much exposure you will have. Selection has directly to do with the quality of your exposure. After all, it's no more productive to look for elk in unlikely habitat than to search for manatees amid mountains of central Colorado. Your chances accelerate through care in selection. Then comes patience in the doing.

You must be more than a mere mouse in a corner. The essence of the art of wildlife watching requires you to be a *still* and *quiet* mouse in the corner. Even then, there's more to it than knowing a few fundamentals. Advanced wildlife-viewing success can only be achieved by doing. Success comes after failure. Failure is the vehicle driving home the importance of learning fundamentals in order to succeed. Wildlife photography is perhaps the best way for anyone to get a sense of the importance of *still* and *quiet* as fundamentals necessary for successful wildlife viewing.

After mastering patience and allocating the required time, you can tweak selection to spit out higher-quality viewing. Thousands of people drive roads near prime winter ranges, glassing for elk. Most of them see elk. But most fail to spot the really standout bulls sporting huge antlers.

Why? Because those bulls are usually solitary or in small bachelor bands. Most often, the big bulls hang higher, bucking deeper snow than will herds of cows, calves, and younger bulls.

I've heard it said—and believe it to be true—that bull elk tend to gang with bulls that are born during their same birth year. Yes, a spike or raghorn can sometimes be spotted on winter range in company with larger bulls. But if you spend time watching those same animals, you'll see the younger elk drift away with the first bunch of cows and calves to chance along.

If, in fact, bull elk do group with other bulls of their age, it stands to reason that, considering attrition, there would be a larger bachelor band at age four than at age seven. Carrying that logic further, it would explain why the older the bull, the more likely he is to be solitary—none of his contemporaries are left.

As bull elk age, they tend to become lighter in color than cows of the same age. Experienced elk watchers soon learn to locate bulls in a wintering herd without first spotting antlers.

Among elk aficionados, the epitome of viewing satisfaction is to spot a "royal" bull. Of all the thousands of elk I've glassed throughout a lifetime, I've only been privileged to see three elk I knew positively had seven points per side. One, as it chanced, was on winter range in deep snow. He was alone. The bull must have had adequate forage plants at hand because he stayed in the same locale for a week.

With such a rare viewing opportunity, I folded up my spotting scope each evening as daylight waned and returned the next day with a rising sun. During that week, while I served as the huge bull's distant attendant, he lost first one antler, then the other.

Those antler losses must have been a bother to the bull, as I discovered when one morning I bent to my scope's eyepiece and the animal had lost his first antler. And I laughed aloud at the way he carried his head skewed to one side—probably because of unequal weight distribution. Later, as I watched, his muscles adapted and the bull carried his head more or less upright.

Then on the very next day, I was peering at the bull while he pawed and fed on dried bunchgrass growing in the shadow of an evergreen ceanothus bush.

Montana Dept. of Fish, Wildlife & Parks

"Huh!" I muttered, lifting my head to stare over the scope at the distant bull. Then I bent again to the eyepiece. His right-side antler was also gone.

The bull must have snagged the ready-to-shed antler in the brush and it dropped away. As far as I could tell, the event was of no concern to the bull, except that he moved about for the next half-hour with his head cocked to the left. Apparently, muscles that had been compensating for the lopsided weight of his remaining antler now pulled unequally on his neck when both antlers were gone.

Did I mark the spot where the royal bull shed his antlers? Yes. Did I return after snow melt to retrieve the shed royal antlers? No. You see, the bull wintered in Glacier National Park. Picking up shed antlers in the Park is illegal.

And I prefer summering on the sunny side of jailhouse walls. ■

Chapter 21

Help From the Homestead Bull

It was the damned kid's fault that I got old. Leastways it's hell to get old, no matter whose fault. What's worse is to discover that getting old is a state of mind rather than a body failure. I stuck the single-bit hand axe in the splitting block and bent to gather the kindling wood I'd just split. A few years ago, no one could've convinced me I'd ever grow old in the ways I have. I thought growing old would take me from the things I most love: the mountains and wild creatures and wildflowers; the forests and rivers and rivulets; the camaraderie of hunting camps, and fishing adventures in all sorts of weather and with all sorts of people. Nothing prepared me for the idea that I would quit *wanting* to experience them. Like I said, it was the kid's fault.

I straightened and glanced up at twin whiskey jacks fluttering in the tree above, then wheeled and ducked through the tent flap to drop my kindling into the overflowing pile by the cookstove. A couple of pieces fell off and I shoved them so's they lined up with the rest.

Was a time when no one could outdo me at slinging packs, running down elk, or finding the hard-to-get-to holes where lunker trout lurked. The funny thing is I can still do it, too—maybe not as fast as when I was thirty, but not as slow as some of today's thirty-somethings doing most of their adventuring while squatting on a bar stool.

The camp clock's ticking sounded like pistons hammering. Damned annoying, it was. Still a couple of hours before the others could possibly ride in. The thought brought me up short.

Back in the old days I would have rode out with Fred on Friday and come back in with Lars and the boy today. But it turns out plain and simple that I just don't want to make those long rides when I don't have to.

Maybe it wasn't all the boy's fault. Maybe some of it was Lars'.

There was this year-old shadow between me and the kid, ever since I didn't pull the trigger on the wall-hanger bull that wandered within ten feet of me while the boy watched from a nearby mountainside.

"Shucks, I'm ready. You're ready. It's that time of year when bull elk will be singing from the mountaintops."

I thought I was right, of course, to make my own choice over whether to shoot another elk, and he figured the grandfather he adored wasn't half the man he once thought. Sure, if I'd known he was watching, I might've done it different. But maybe I wouldn't, too. And the point was, every hunter has to make up his own mind what's right for him each time opportunity presents itself.

Anyway, there was this shadow between us.

It hurt that the boy didn't jump up and down in excitement when I commenced planning this year's hunt. And when Lars told me he couldn't go right away because he had to finish up a saddle he was building for some fat-butted eastern woman, I threw up my hands and would've called off the whole damned thing if Fred hadn't showed up and said he was ready, and what the hell, we didn't need 'em.

"There was a time when if nobody else went along for the ride, you'd go it alone," the smiley-faced logger said. "Shucks, I'm ready. You're ready. It's that time of year when bull elk will be singing from the mountaintops. If the shaver and Lars can't go, we'll just have to make do without 'em."

That ticked me off, of course. What disgusted me most was that it took Fred to point out what I should've seen without help. "Leave next weekend?" I said.

Then on Thursday Lars phoned. "When do you and Fred figure to come out?"

"Week from tomorrow. We'll be in camp for a week. Why?"

"Look, I'll have this saddle done in another week if I have to work night and day. And I talked to the boy. He says he can get out of school the week following. What say you let Fred bring out the packstring, and me and the boy will come in on Sunday, after the ponies have rested a day."

"You got an attitude problem," I said. "You and the boy both have an attitude problem. You had your chance to go and turned it down."

There was silence from the other end, so I said, "Can't do it, Lars. You know I'd rather be in hunting camp with you and the boy more than anything in the world. But I've got a couple of story deadlines that's staring me in the face."

It would've ended there if it hadn't been for the boy's grandmother. "Don't you think you're being a little pig-headed?" she said. "I looked in your files. One of those story assignments is due in a month, the other in six weeks."

"Damn it. woman, there's the columns, too."

She dropped a packet of papers on my desk. "That's your column rough drafts. They're all done for the next month and you know it."

"Spit it out if you got something to say."

"Then stay in camp and wait for Lars and your grandson. Don't you have any idea what it would mean to them?"

"No groceries. I bought only for Fred and me."

"There's no reason they can't bring in food for the three of you. I'll get it ready for them."

They'd boxed me, right enough—Lars and the boy and the woman. Even Fred, because when he showed up the morning we were to leave for the hunt, he said, "Guess I'll be coming out by myself, huh?"

All I said was, "Not you, too, Brutus."

I picked up the clock and shoved it down into my sleeping bag. The ticking was still audible, even when I walked outside the tent with bread crusts for the whiskey jacks. The clock sounded like the whole damned Swiss Federation mocked me.

So Lars and the boy would be riding in before nightfall. They'd be bushed. But they should make good time, what with only a couple of packhorses because Fred had rode from camp packing no meat. I racked my brain recollecting how it was the first time that wiry-framed hunter's hunter had ever gone skunked on a week-long mountain elk hunt. His own fault, though. I told him there was a bull hanging out in the big spruce timber at the head of the big slide.

The dinging of a bell interrupted my reverie, and when the old fool of a buckskin ambled into camp I had a handful of grain in my fist waiting for him. Other bells tinkled from a distance, but Buck was the only one that came in. He cased the camp as always, saw I was there, ate his grain as he always did, nickered for the other horses as he always did, then trotted out to rejoin them.

I'd discovered the bull the day I decided to climb the mountain towering over camp. I climbed the damned thing to see if it was still there. Turned out to be easier than I expected for an old duffer my age. I went up the right side of the big avalanche chute, crossed the headwall and caught a goat trail along the ledges, finally topping out on the left shoulder. From there it was simply a matter of scrambling across scree, then angling up the mountain's grassy upper slope. I was pleased there was nothing wrong with my legs, even if I did have minor problems with my head.

I stayed on top long enough to add a rock to the cairn our outfit began building thirty years before, then started down before I got to feeling sorry for myself. As always in that high, wild alpine country, I had to shoo mule-deer bucks out of the way. A couple of them were good enough to make any hunter proud. Even felt a twitch in my trigger finger when one of 'em stopped to puzzle out what kind of strange two-legged creature was behind him. Slipped the old Springfield from my shoulder before grinning and re-slinging it.

Coming down, I dropped into the patch of big spruce and came up short at a rub tree just off my game trail. Too big for a deer rub. Had to be an elk. Then I picked up the first fresh prints.

Fred was back and cooking raw fries when I staggered in around dusk. He flashed the patented broad grin that belonged to him alone, and said, "You look like you been drug through a culvert neck first."

"I been hunting," I said, collapsing on a bench. "Isn't that what we're supposed to be doing?"

"That's what I've been doing, all right. But you—I'd be surprised."

When I reached for the whiskey, he said, "Where'd you go?"

"Up the mountain."

"How far'd you get?"

"How far do you think?"

"You didn't go to the top!"

When I wiped my lips and said nothing, my one-time guide said, "I promised the boy and his grandmother that I'd look out for you. She said not to let you do anything foolish." When I never responded, he added, "She didn't say a thing about not letting you do anything stupid, though."

When I still said nothing, he asked, "How'd you go up?"

Holding out a cup while Fred poured coffee, I said, "Same way you and I went the first time you climbed it."

I had most of my wind and some of my color back in a few minutes. That's when I asked, "How goes the hunting?"

"Too dry. Too hot. Too smart the elk. Too dumb the hunter."

"There's a bull has homesteaded the patch of big spruce

on the mountain."

There was a flicker of interest, but he only said, "I'll try the chutes tomorrow. I suppose you'll want to rest?"

I nodded. "I can tell that without even sleeping on it."

It was my turn to cook the next evening. Fred was out until long after dark. "Went clear on through the Wind Funnel, down the 'hell' trail. Still didn't find anything worth writing home about."

"There's a bull working the big spruce, up on the mountain," I said.

He sighed. "I might even have to tackle Stockade Ridge if I don't find something easier."

"There's a bull working the big spruce above camp," I said again.

He laughed. "I'm hunting elk, not mule deer."

I shrugged.

Fred missed a running shot at a bull on Stockade Ridge, then chose the wrong basin to hunt on his last day. When he swung into his saddle for the long ride home, he grinned down and said, "What you figure to do, old-timer, while I'm gone?"

I handed him his short string's lead rope and said, "I believe I'll amble up the mountain to see if my bull is still holding out in the big spruce."

It was Fred's turn to shrug.

I climbed through the trees on the right side of the avalanche path, combing the ground and vegetation for sign that the bull still hung out in the area. Atop the first big terrace, I shook my head in disgust, then pulled a handkerchief from my pocket to wipe sweat. From there, I climbed the big outcrop of limestone in order to get a good look into the open meadow beyond, then sprawled on the cliff edge to glass the slide path clear to the patch of spruce forest. "Where are you, big fellow?" I muttered.

The bull was still there—I could *feel* it. But so far I'd found no fresh sign. I dropped back down from the cliff ledge to the avalanche chute, then worked along the forest fringe to the first wallow. Nothing fresh. Water in that wallow was clear—like it hadn't been used in several days.

What I should have done— what someone less stubborn than an old fool would've done—was

"Gotcha," I muttered.

turn around and head back to camp. Instead, I wet my handkerchief and sponged beneath my collar, then plunged into the big woods.

Though we call the spruce forest a "patch," it's actually a couple of hundred acres of unusually large Engelmann spruce that, for some reason, escaped a 1919 forest fire. These are the most dominant trees in the area, but the patch is merely a portion of a larger forest of much younger mixed conifers that feather into the grove's edges from all sides.

Avalanche paths, including the granddaddy one above our camp, streak down the mountain's flanks, as if some giant bear had swiped it with his claws. And the mountain's upper reaches sprout above the forests, turning to bunch-grass-covered meadows and alpine tundra. Over the years, we've taken a surprising number of bull elk from the rugged slope.

There was no fresh sign at any of the places I searched on this day; no newly turned soil, no still-warm droppings. It was stubbornness that kept me angling up the way I'd worked down to camp a few days before—stubbornness and a burning need to find out if my head still worked like it once did.

Before I knew it, I was on the rub that'd given me the first clue. This time there was a second rubbed sapling only five feet from the first. "Gotcha," I muttered.

I heard them when their ponies splashed through the creek crossing below camp. The boy's fast-stepping little bay led the way, winding through pines to the hitchrail. I was surprised to see him pulling both packhorses. Their loads were lashed tight and riding square.

Lars swung from his speckled appaloosa and held momentarily to the saddlehorn. "A touch of pick-me-up would be highly appreciated, my good man," he said.

I handed him the flask I'd concealed in my hip pocket, then turned to help drop the packs. To my surprise, the boy already had two on the ground and was starting on the final two.

Lars leaned back on the hitchrail with the flask in his fist and drawled, "Maybe if I dawdle long enough, the lad will unsaddle my pony, too."

I carried all four canvas-wrapped packs to the tent while the guys grained the horses and put away their saddles. When Lars and the boy trooped in, they found me busy transferring groceries to the varmint-proof packboxes we used for cupboards. Lars paused to watch while the boy poured coffee for them both.

"If you're wondering what we're going to do with all that food, you'll have to make inquiries elsewhere."

"The whiskey, man," I said. "Didn't you check to see if she put in any whiskey?"

"Grandma wrapped some in my sleeping bag," the boy said.

Lars patted him on the shoulder. "You come from good stock, boy."

The lad's eyes caught and held mine. "I think so, too," he said. Then he dipped a pan of warm water from its pot on the stove and ducked through the tent flap to wash for supper.

It surprised me when the boy decided to hunt alone on his first day afield—he and Lars always seemed to have that "special" relationship. Maybe it was because the rancher was slow into the tent come morning.

"A little stiff this morning, Lars?" the kid asked.

"Yeah, maybe a tiny little hitch in my git-along, lad. But give me a few minutes to limber up and I can waddle away from camp."

"Aww, it's all right. You need the day to rest." He stared at me, so I grabbed the coffee pot and overflowed the cup Lars held out to me. Finally the boy said, "I'll head upriver. That okay?"

I nodded, but he didn't see it because he'd already ducked through the tent flap, into morning twilight.

Lars studied me while he dried scalded fingers on a trouser leg. "Still time to catch up to him, friend. He might need help packing a big one out of the upper basin."

I shrugged. "Maybe so, maybe not. Who can tell?"

"Who's asking?" he said.

I studied on that one until I finished washing the breakfast dishes.

Lars returned to his sleeping bag. It was obvious my friend had been burning the candle at both ends, what with farming and ranching and making fine riding saddles and packsaddles and filing saws better than anyone in the whole country. It occurred to me that maybe a man could be too talented.

The rancher emerged from the tent about midmorning, stretching and yawning. "Thanks, pard. I needed that."

I waved, shifting on my wood block to stare upriver.

"Hear any shooting?" he asked.

I shook my head. "Don't figure to, either. Fred worked that country out pretty well and didn't find a thing. It'll be slender pickings for the boy, I'm a-thinking."

Lars rolled a block over by mine. "You might have told him that before he headed out."

"He don't listen to me no more."

They could've filmed two half-time commercials in the length of time it took for the rancher to reply. Finally, "She said you were being pig-headed."

I twisted around on my block. "What did you say?"

"I said it's about time you and me had a little game of cribbage."

I beat him three games out of three, during which we did no more than count, like: "Fifteen-two, fifteen-four, fifteen-six, and a pair for eight."

After the crib game, Lars made a couple of sandwiches,

poured coffee, and sliced an apple apiece. After we licked our fingers and dotted up the last crumb, he said, "The boy told me about last year."

I stared at a spot on the tent wall that was just beyond the man's head. "I guess I let him down, Lars. I let him find out I'm not the man he thought I was."

When my eyes flicked momentarily to his, my friend said, "Could be you lifted him up, you dumb turd. Maybe he found out you're an even better man than he thought you were."

"You want a cookie?" I asked.

"Maybe he don't know how to tell you."

"Or a candy bar?"

"Then, on the other hand, maybe you really do deserve me telling you what I think you are."

Bells saved us. We ambled from the tent. Buck led the way, followed by the rest of the horse herd. I gave him a handful of grain while Lars scattered a bucketful for the others. I scratched my old pony's ear and asked, "You reckon I'm a dumb turd, Buck?"

"I'll answer for him if you'll let me," the boy said from behind.

"See anything?" I asked.

He shook his head. "Dry and bare. Saw a couple of vibram prints at the lick, and some coming and going at the big wallows. Fred must've been up there, right?"

I smiled. "Fred was everywhere. You know, of course, that he went out with no elk meat."

Lars ambled our way. The boy jacked a shell from his rifle chamber and said, "Fred said you might be able to give me a tip or two on where one might be holed up."

My eyes caught those of Lars, then returned to where the boy wiped a handkerchief along his gunbarrel. "I told him a bull had homesteaded the patch of big spruce up yonder."

The boy followed my gaze to the mountain beyond the avalanche chute. Then he turned to hang his rifle in a tree and wandered off to pet the ponies. When he returned, he said, "Tell me what you saw, Grandpa."

I would've gone with the boy the next morning, but the alarm failed to ring for only the second time ever. Instead it was the whiskey jacks who served to drive away sleep, bringing me tumbling from bed a good half-hour after daylight.

Lars staggered from his sack only moments later. "Did you turn off this clock?" I said, still staring in wonder.

"Nope. Was it off?"

"It was." I turned to the boy's sleeping bag and saw it was empty. "He's gone."

Lars chuckled. "So he is." He ducked through the tent flap, only to return moments later. "His rifle's gone, too."

My underwear was all I had on, but I hitched it before asking, "What does that mean, Lars?"

"It means," he said, opening the stove door, "that you and I better build a fire, boil a pot of coffee, make breakfast, and start a game of cribbage because it looks like we're in for a long day."

The first shot came at 11:23. The second at 11:27. They came from the mountain above camp. Lars stayed to pick up the cards I'd knocked over in my haste to get outside when the first shot echoed down to us. But he stood by my side staring at the mountain when the second rolled out.

"I'll bring in a couple of horses," I told my friend.

The rancher gripped my arm. "Let him do it. Let him show you he can."

The boy poked his head in the tent at 2:28. By then I'd given up on him. "Missed, eh?" I said.

"Nope."

"Was it a big buck?"

"Nope."

"Well, damn it, boy—what?"

"A bull. Raghorn. Five point. He was right where you said he'd be, Grandpa."

I closed my eyes, but a tear trickled out anyway. The thump of Lars' hundred-proof private stock hitting the table brought me back. When he splashed a dash into three cups and handed me mine I raised the cup and said, "To our hunter."

"Our hunter," Lars echoed.

"To my grandpa," the boy said. ∎

Our son Marc at age sixteen, with his "Homestead Bull." Note the cockeyed antlers. The bull tasted good throughout a long, hard winter.

Chapter 22

Hunting is Best When the Bulls Are There

Late-season hunting, when snow comes and temperatures plummet, is often considered meat-hunting time, where a trophy is incidental to the acquisition of a winter's meat supply—which is absurd. Except for places where access is controlled to allow limited hunting, more trophy bulls are taken during the late season than at any other time.

Elk hunting in deep snow and during extreme cold tilt the odds back in favor of the hunter—provided he prepares for his own survival. By late season, elk are in their migration mode, shifting from fall ranges to winter range. And provided a hunter understands the creatures, and understands the lay of the land those creatures must pass through, plans can be made to waylay them.

Aside from hunting on winter ranges that are near plowed roads, or gathering in "firing-lines" alongside limited passages where animals must migrate from a preserve, late-season hunting has the added advantage of fewer hunters afield. Simply said, rotten weather tends to eliminate the casual nimrod.

It is true that a hunter cannot get around in deep snow and bitter cold as well as elk can. How, then, are the odds in his favor? Because he doesn't need to hunt everywhere for elk—only where they're most likely to be during migration.

So how can you know where to find these elk highways? The first thing you must do is stop thinking in human terms. Routes to winter ranges aren't paths on which elk follow one after another like autos on the Santa Ana Freeway. Migration routes vary in width from entire mountainsides to narrow stream bottoms. They pass through dense stands of timber where wapiti can find shelter from blowing, drifting snow. Or they can meander along open hillsides where the same wind blows nutritious bunchgrass snow-free.

But where does one find these *routes?* The most important tool you have is that bump on the end of your neck. Use it. Winter ranges are easy to identify. Your state game and fish department is certain to have information available on elk wintering areas. Or find out from bits and pieces passed on from competent elk hunters in your town.

After you've identified a winter range area, study maps of the lands leading to it. Look for south- and west-facing slopes. Now check out the country in person, on the ground. Pay attention to availability of forage plants. Pay special attention if you find many shrubs that have been "broomed" back—where individual stalks have been eaten into their woody, finger-sized stems. This means, of course, that elk are hungry when they pass through. It means the animals either use the area for winter grazing or use it while en route to winter range.

If, in fact, you check out south- and west-facing slopes stocked with a modicum of palatable plants, and there are occasional stands of trees that can provide shelter from severe storms, then look for lateral ridges, benches, grassy meadows, or strips of forests leading toward the known wintering area. Pay close attention. Don't be surprised to find those places laced by game trails and peppered with droppings. You are looking at a migration route.

Weather conditions play a big role in late-season hunting. Not, as you might expect, by controlling the hours a hunter spends afield, but by influencing the routes elk follow during their migratory movement.

A favorite late-season area for me was a series of south- and west-facing mountainsides near one of our hunting camps. The mountainsides are dissected by several deep canyons. The canyons are timber-covered, but the flanks, though also timbered, are dotted with open sidehill and ridgetop meadows where chinook winds from the Pacific temper winter's harshest onslaughts and bare forage. We've taken our share of elk in that locale, first by glassing from a distance while the creatures fed in those windswept meadows, then stalking to within shooting range.

But twice during the two decades I guided in that country, snow fell heavy and wet, then crusted during below-zero cold snaps. In each case, we would leave our river-bottom camp before daylight to ride those mountainsides, pushing our laboring horses in search of elk on the move. Day after day, we hunted the mountainsides without spotting animal or track, only to return to the river bottom to find that a band had moved through that very day. At last a light blinkered on: the elk we sought were smarter than their human pursuers. They knew the snow on those mountains was too crusted and energy-consuming to make their regular migration route practical. So they moved through the bottoms, feeding on willow shoots and red-osier dogwood branches.

The irony of this scenario is that even after we figured out what was happening, each morning we'd make a quick river-bottom scout for fresh tracks, then head for the high country to search our favorite places for elk that never came. And again we'd return to camp at dusk to find that elk had passed our horse corrals sometime during the day. Which brings us to another essential ingredient for successful late-season hunting: *patience*.

Why didn't we hunt the bottoms? First, we were programmed to expect our quarry to graze across the mountainsides. Then we failed to believe that elk would move through the bottoms after we'd hunted there earlier that day. In other words, we had no patience when it counted.

The fault, of course, was mine. I cut my teeth on run-'em-down elk hunting, and I believed then (and believe now) that if there were no tracks where you were, an elk was busy layin' 'em down on yonder ridge. Besides, my hunters were paying me to be a hard-working guide. And lounging near camp without working up a sweat didn't fit either image or game plan.

It was indeed a mistake. Some of those elk passing near camp were respect-able bulls—we could see where their wide antlers brushed snow from spruce limbs as they pushed beneath. And I'd have served my hunters' interests better if I'd persuaded them to hunt nearer camp.

Pete Ganovsky with bull taken that "big snow" day while Rufus watched from afar.

There are hunters, of course, who have my perspective of elk hunting, and who would've been miserable trying to wait out elk near camp. Others, though, are superb at the waiting game and not only would have reveled in near-camp hunting, but been successful at it. Then there are still others who prefer to stand on some high mountain where a man can look forever and not see enough of God's finest handiwork to quiet the thumping in his heart, even if there are no elk for miles.

Once, I guided two fine elderly gentlemen into a high, open basin. Snow had dumped on us for the two previous days, pinning us to camp. But the third day dawned cold and clear, and we headed out on horseback through eighteen inches of fresh powder.

He just might tumble out of his tent as the storm tails off to find the hills full of migrating elk.

Elk were on the move, too, and we soon spotted a band. I wanted to take both hunters in pursuit, but one said no. Instead, he wished to watch the stalk from a high vantage. The hunter accompanying me took his elk that day and later had a fine taxidermist mount it. I'm reminded of Pete's elk and that great hunting day every time I visit in his Pennsylvania home. But it's the memory the other took home after watching the stalk that I cherish most. The other man said, "It looked like a Christmas card, Roland." Here's an excerpt from Rufus' Christmas letter to us after his hunt:

> The scenery after it snowed was just out of this world. When you saw the elk in the snow, you thought you'd seen Santa and his reindeer. Then Pete goes and shoots Rudolph's grandfather. Oh well, I guess by next year, he would be like I am— too old to reproduce."

Earlier in this chapter I said the odds tilt in favor of the late-season hunter, provided he prepares for his own survival. Let's explain some of those preparations. November weather can be mild and gentle, making it a pleasure to be afield, or it can be raging and brutal. The paradox here is that bitter cold, snow, and wind make unpleasant conditions that move elk. But if a hunter is miles from road's end with a low grub supply and a short woodpile, he just might want to round up the ponies and head for town.

If, however, his grub, wood, horsefeed, and fortitude hold up, and his camp is near one of those aforementioned migration routes, he just might tumble out of his tent as the storm tails off to find the hills full of migrating elk. If good weather follows on a storm's heels, however, the big creatures will soon disappear into lodgepole thickets and brush-covered hillsides to wile away the sunshine until the next storm hits, or at least until the next really big storm approaches.

Approaches?

That's right. After decades of on-site observation, I'm convinced elk can tell, even in bluebird weather, when a severe storm is on its way in. I was surprised twice during my outfitting and guiding years by what seemed inexplicable elk migration during periods of good weather. Both times blizzards struck a day or two later—before we had sense enough to batten down the hatches.

Barometric pressure? Internal sensitivity to shifting wind patterns? Who knows? Whatever it is that gives wild creatures an edge in predicting weather, mankind no longer has it. Because of that fact, it's best we drag along a second pair of socks for our November hunts.

Depending on the remoteness of the area you plan to hunt, you may wish to prepare in advance. Perhaps you'll pack in supplemental horse feed, or cache food or stove fuel, or set up a small tent. You may not need to do so, of course. But if you're late-season hunting, the best rule to follow is to prepare for the worst and hope for the best.

Late autumn in the high country is not a season with which to trifle. I've spent a couple of weeks in a stocked tent twenty miles from road's end when the temperature hovered at twenty-five below and two feet of snow lay across the hushed land. We had a big wood supply cut and enough hay to carry our stock through. And it was still damned tough! Our eggs and potatoes froze. So did the apples. Even our whiskey clouded. Despite the healthy wood supply, we ran out of fuel two days before time to head home and wound up wallowing through snow to cut more in order to survive.

But elk were moving. Oh, how they were moving!

Think, though, what our chances would have been if we'd not prepared for the worst.

One doesn't always buck deep snow and bitter cold for late-season hunts, however. There were at least three years out of twenty when there was no appreciable snow on Thanksgiving Day. And that's bad—sort of.

You see, wapiti won't drift toward their winter ranges in mild weather. Instead, they'll keg up wherever there's a good food source along their migration route. Remember, they're expecting a bad winter just like you and me. As a result, they'll instinctively want to stay away from a winter range that will inevitably dwindle through the months ahead. Because they'll feed where forage is best, look for them in the same meadows or palatable brush fields where you'd expect to look if they were on the move. But pay more attention to early morning and late evening. And if they are yet to arrive where you're waiting, look for them back upcountry.

During the rough weather of late season, elk need more energy to sustain themselves. They *must* spend more time taking on nourishment just when many of their forage plants have lost their leaves or gone dormant. Elk feeding time is up. Elk forage sources are down. Simple arithmetic. Elk must eat during daytime, even though there's less daylight in late fall and early winter.

Both horses and people should be prepared for late season hunting. Incidentally, I'm man-tying elk quarters

Snow and cold, warm and balmy, late-season hunting is the best. We had a veteran elk hunter who said all that needed to be said about why this is so.

The man was having a tough time of it, wallowing fruitlessly through knee-deep snow for the previous week. He was after the big one and it seemed he was always a few seconds late, on the wrong ridge, or suffered a momentary lapse at the wrong time. Others in his party had already scored on this late-season hunt, but my man's luck just seemed to fade away each time he needed it. He was wearing out, I could see.

I shouldn't have worried.

It was after a long, arduous stalk down into a deep canyon, then up the other side to a tiny meadow where we'd spotted a band of elk an hour before. They were gone, of course—cut and run for a distant ridge. And us too far gone to follow.

I sighed, but the hunter fished in his pocket for a cigarette paper and a sack of Bull Durham. His eyes caught mine as he trickled tobacco onto the paper, then licked its edge. "The bulls are here," he murmured. "The bulls are here." A match flared.

That's it, you see. The bulls are most apt to be there in late season. ∎

Chapter 23

Angel Basinitis

It's a disease that sooner or later afflicts all hunters. And future success may well depend on your coming up with the proper antidote before it's too late.

Thus far we've talked about how essential it is for an elk hunter to become familiar with the area he chooses to hunt; to discover its nooks and crannies; the plants and springs and wallows and licks. He needs to learn travel routes and escape hatches and shelter belts. He needs to ferret out hidden benches and isolated meadows and fringe areas between habitat zones.

Yes, indeed, there are dozens of reasons why a serious hunter should make a serious effort to learn his hunting country in detail. But he still needs to be versatile enough to play the field. In short, he does not need to marry a specific place.

There was a huge open basin accessible from one of our hunting camps. The name I'm giving it for purposes of this chapter is not real because I may someday wish to hunt there again. We'll call it Angel Basin.

Angel Basin is a beautiful place, burned over by a long-ago wildfire but laced now with meadows and second-growth fir thriving on the fertile soils of natural terraces. Grass-covered meadows spread like

> Future success may well depend on your coming up with the proper antidote before it's too late.

fingers up the coulees. It's a pastoral setting: big, quiet, promising—among the finest of God's works.

Angel
Basin Elk
Country

Every one of our hunters who saw the place fell in love with Angel Basin. And over the years we took many trophy elk and deer from its meadows and forests. More often than not, however, the basin proved fruitless—deerless and elkless. In fact, several areas near our hunting camp produced more trophies than did Angel Basin.

Without exception, though, the more fruitful places had not nearly the scenic charisma of Angel Basin, and once our hunters were introduced to the basin's spell-binding charm they often opted to hunt nowhere else. My guides and I even coined a name for the affliction: we called it Angel Basinitis.

Most experienced hunters have their own Angel Basin-type afflictions, though they're called by other names. Why wouldn't a hunter fondly recall the place where he took a fine trophy in another year? It makes no difference if it's a tiny glade in the middle of a thicket of lodgepole blowdown, the location is mesmerizing even though its latest elk track might have been laid down on the Fourth of July.

Maybe in your neck of the woods its a matter of waiting long enough for a bull elk to wander through the same notch where you took the trophy in '83, but in my experience, elk and mule deer are where you find them, not where they find you. And if there are no tracks in Angel Basin, one must overcome his infatuation with that place or do without.

Sometimes I would set one of my afflicted hunters down on a log and talk to him like a Dutch uncle: "Wally, it just doesn't look like elk have moved into Angel Basin yet. We can hunt here if you want. Or we can go where there's elk. What do you think?"

After working on the guy for a couple more days, I could often convince him to follow me into Whitehorse Canyon or up Flatiron Ridge. But unless the antidote dosage was heavy enough to include more than merely loads of fresh elk tracks, the worst afflicted of my hunters would often relapse.

"Roland," a victim might say. "Is it possible elk may have drifted into Angel Basin since we were there?"

"Not likely," I'd growl.

"But possible?"

"Yeah. Lightning might strike yonder tree, too."

"Then let's take a chance and go back to Angel Basin tomorrow. What do you say?"

Angel Basinitis can wound more deeply than just mis-guided infatuation with a single preferred place within an entire landscape. For instance, a too-monogamous embrace of landscapes with limited access can cause some otherwise rational men and women to sink into a blue funk, sometimes even abandoning the urge to go afield in the fall.

Earlier in this book, I told how my own hunting group discovered that elk inhabited a portion of the central Oregon Cascades, and how we were on hand when the first limited permits were issued. We applied the following year and were drawn. But the third year we were crushed to discover our luck in the draw had played out.

Our only recourse was to return to the Coast Range mountains we'd formerly hunted—an option none of us four wanted to pursue because of that landscape's dense rain forest, plethora of roads, and competitive hunting environment. So we descended into a funk, only getting our heads screwed on in time to go ahead with our second choice. The truth is we had a fabulous hunt. But because of mental blocks against *where* we hunted, we failed to enjoy the experience.

That's asinine. There will always be disappointments. Many first choices are simply unreachable. Lots of folks would like to hunt the Vermejo Ranch, but few will ever do so. Some might like to follow the safari circuit into deepest Africa, but how many have either the money or time?

In the state where I dwell, the Charles M. Russell Wildlife Refuge is noted for a dynamic elk herd inhabiting the Missouri River Breaks. This is semi-arid country of rolling grasslands and timber-filled canyons—fabulous habitat for wildlife, from prairie chickens to bighorn sheep.

Wapiti inhabiting the Missouri Breaks, however, are not sufficiently abundant to allow everyone wishing to hunt the CMR an opportunity to do so. As a consequence, drawings are held. It's not uncommon for unsuccessful applicants infected by the charisma of Missouri Breaks wapiti to give up elk hunting until they again succeed in drawing the rare CMR permit. Again, that's asinine.

This carries over to selecting *states* where one plans an elk hunt. During my outfitting and guiding years, I had occasion to serve clients who would rather hunt Wyoming, but failed in that state's draw. Without exception, guests who would rather be elsewhere were tough to please. And I know several individuals who'd previously hunted with my Skyline Outfit who were pains in another outfitter's derriere when they were forced to hunt elsewhere.

Still, being a pain in the rear somewhere is better than abandoning the idea of pursuing elk just because one's first hunting choice is denied. To give up elk hunting is to disregard the annual opportunity to stand on distant ridgetops, thump one's chest in exhilaration, and listen for far-off bugling of bull elk. Folks who give up the greatest of outdoor adventures because of a minor disappointment have become too attached to place. It's Angel Basinitis in its most virulent form; a form that has overcome the majesty and mystique of the greatest animal on earth. Men and women—get your acts together. Elk took you to adventure and it's elk that will keep you there. Be careful you don't sever the artery while manipulating the heart.

I'm treading a fine line here—and know it. I've spent entire chapters telling how important it is for elk hunters to learn the territory they plan to hunt. Now I'm saying an individual can become too infatuated with place. How can the two admonitions be reconciled? Simple. There can be no interest in territory if there is no hunt. Think about it sequentially: I'm going elk hunting—period. After that, I'll choose where. After that, I'll try to learn as much as possible about the habits and habitat of animals using the area I choose. Keep your priorities in order and you'll keep your sense of adventure foremost.

A fine example of everything we've discussed thus far is the Brash family of Spangle, Washington.

Their story began, so my old outfitter friend Russ Baeth told me, back in the 1930s when a couple of young wheat farmers from Washington's Palouse country decided to travel to what later became the Bob Marshall Wilderness to go elk hunting.

Such a journey was no small decision during those Depression times; roads were graveled and winding, trucks but poor antecedents to today's sleek transports. The 400-mile journey from the couple's Spangle farm, in those long-ago times, took days.

The Brash's—Guy and Dolly—had but two horses during their first year. The ponies were packed with flour, beans, coffee, and a slab of bacon. Guy and Dolly Brash walked everywhere they went. That first year, the couple spent a month amid some of the wildest lands in the northern Rockies and loved every minute of it. They came again the following year. And again. When they had children, they brought the kids along. When Gene and Gary reached school age, Guy and Dolly took them from school for a month on what had by then turned into an annual family odyssey. When the boys grew up and married, they brought along the boys' wives. When the young couples had children, the hunting clan grew to include the grandchildren.

The Brashes were, by the time I arrived in Montana in 1964, legends in their own time. Guy and Dolly both passed over the Great Divide shortly thereafter. It was my loss that I never met them.

The legend continued, however, through their sons Gary and Gene. Gene later become the head packer for the Spotted Bear Ranger District, retiring in 1997. Brett, Gary's son, worked as a guide for me. Over the years, I learned much of the family's legendary exploits.

Once, I met Gene and his packstring at a creek crossing. I led my own thirsty packstring into the stream. While our stock drank and switched tails at flies, Gene pulled a cup with an extension handle from his saddlebags. "You know, when we first started coming back here, we walked everywhere we went. Now," the man said, pulling out the handle to full length, "I don't even get off my horse to get a drink." And he illustrated by dipping a cup of water while still sitting astride his saddlehorse.

Local newspapers from the Rockies to eastern Washington carried stories and photos of the Brash bunch upon their return from their annual month-long hunts. Trucks were festooned with elk and deer racks, goat hides, bear hides. They were the most colorful characters imaginable, and they worked at projecting the image.

Larry Gleason, a friend of three decades and also a guide, told of an adventure that took place while he was working for the Forest Service at Spotted Bear. The late November weather turned brutal, accompanied by deep snow and bitter cold, and people at Spotted Bear became concerned about the Brash family, known to be somewhere up the Spotted Bear River. Finally, on Thanksgiving Day, straws were drawn to see who would ride that direction in an attempt to find the family and see if they needed help.

"Monty Montgomery drew the short straw. He started out and hadn't gone far when he met the Brash 'advance party,' consisting of two or three hardy men." Larry said those men of the advance party were torching off big stumps along the route so the rest, mostly women and children, could warm themselves before continuing on to safety.

I talked to Gary Brash about that epic journey:

"It got down to forty-two below on that trip," he said. "We didn't pull saddles from our horses for four days, figuring we couldn't get them back on if we did."

"The Brashes were the awfullest lookin' outfit you ever saw when they pulled in late on Thanksgiving afternoon," Larry Gleason said. "They jerked a whole deer from the back of a horse and set it upright in the deep snow. It was a big buck and it'd frozen stiff as a board, so it just stood there like it was alive. And they had a whole mountain goat they did the same."

"Dude" horse Blondie in "Angel Basin."

Larry said everybody from the Spotted Bear lodges and the Forest Service headquarters gathered to watch the family unsaddle horses and try to get the engines on their trucks started. "Talk about characters," Larry added.

I once ran into the family at Brushy Park, near the heart of the Bob Marshall. Gary invited me to have a cup of coffee. While I was talking to the man, their loose grazing horses wandered through camp. Gary pointed at one buckskin and said his name was Brushy. I asked how it happened they gave the pony that particular name.

"Because he was born in Brushy Park," the stubble-faced wheat farmer said.

"They took a pregnant mare with them!" I later told my friend Russ Baeth. "A pregnant mare, for God's sake!"

Russ, who knew them well, laughed. "You've got to understand them, Roland. When they got ready to go hunting, they caught whatever horses was closest to the house."

When I later repeated this story to Gene, he said it was true. "Lots of time we got to the trailhead with horses that never had a saddle or shoes on 'em before. But by the time we turned 'em upside down and nailed shoes on, then th'owed a pack on and dragged 'em forty miles into the wilderness, they was broke enough for us to use for the next twenty years."

Gary once stopped at our cooktent for a cup of coffee. When I mentioned their nonchalance regarding whether they brought trained horses on their adventures, he turned sour.

"That's right." he said. "We got one of them ponies Gene started that way up at camp right now. Had him in the Forest Service corral yesterday and he jumped it with a foot to spare. Now the boys are chasin' him through the lodgepole. We catch him again, I'm gonna put four hundred pounds on him on the way out!"

The Brash party left the next day with their wild one in tow. It didn't look to me like he carried four hundred pounds, but it did look like he knew what his role was supposed to be.

The point here is that maybe the Brash family *was* infected with a sense of place, but it's probable they were more infected with a sense of *adventure*. They spent time most hunters cannot spare. But they had a family standard that held their hunters to six-point bulls only. For the most part, they stuck to that standard. Because time was not a factor for the Brash bunch, and because they could, like grizzly bears, go anywhere they chose, they were never infected by Angel Basinitis (though they often hunted the place I call Angel Basin).

Theirs was a plethora of adventures most folks only dream about. And theirs were adventures everybody damn sure wants to read about. ∎

Chapter 24

It's All Quite Logical, Don't You See?

Bob paused in the middle of his backcast to cock an ear, then whirled to stare behind him as a ten-inch rainbow shot from the depths to pluck his Royal Wulff from the coils of tippet and leader. His friend, fishing nearby, laughed.

"Didn't you hear that?" Bob asked.

"Hear what? Only thing I heard was the plop of your tangle hitting the water."

Bob stripped line while playing the scrappy trout to the shallows at his feet, where he released it. "I thought I heard an elk bugle."

The orthodontist and his companion had horsepacked into picturesque Elizabeth Lake, located in Glacier National Park's Belly River backcountry. The date was in late August, over twenty years ago.

Bob perched on a log to untangle the rat's nest the fish had made of his line. Again he heard the long, eerie whistle of a distant bull elk. This time his companion heard it, too.

"Sounded like it came from the Ptarmigan Trail side," John said.

Bob, an experienced elk hunter, laid his fly rod aside,

cupped hands to mouth, took a deep breath, and gave a fair rendition of an angry bull grunting a response. The Ptarmigan bull replied. So did two others, one from the hillside behind their perch, the other from up-lake.

Bob told me of that Elizabeth Lake adventure shortly after it happened. "Those elk bugled around our camp all night. We got to see two of them—one down by the shore, and the other came right up to our tent before he shied away."

"Did you help 'em along, Bob?"

"What do you think—of course I did. It's a great place to practice bugling, and someday I'm taking the boys in there to teach them how to call elk."

At the time, I still operated an elk-hunting guide service in the Bob Marshall Wilderness and had no time during the rut to sample the pleasures of bugling elk in a national park. But the opportunity to practice calling the reclusive creatures in an unhunted environment intrigued me, and it was something I planned to do upon retirement. The flaw in my plan was that I failed to take into account civilization's inexorable march.

It was early September, 1992. Jane and I had recently sold our outfitting and guiding service and we were hiking the Highline Trail in Glacier National Park. A lady ranger caught up with us and paused to exchange pleasantries. My wife mentioned that we hoped to hear the whistling challenge of rutting elk. That's when I first learned it's a no-no for visitors to practice bugling in Glacier. "Ma'am," I said, "when did that regulation go into effect?"

"I don't know for sure. A couple of years ago." Then she was gone.

We walked on down the trail, me absorbing the rupture of a dream, Jane wondering why I was despondent. I recollected that some of yesteryear's great elk images were taken by photographers vocalizing to bring bulls into camera range. At last I asked Jane, "Did she mention *why* the regulation was imposed?"

"No, I don't think so."

As chance would have it, we encountered the same ranger later in the day, so I asked the reason for the prohibition.

The lady said it was because of growing numbers of humans visiting the Park.

"But," I said, "aren't most of the people gone by September—when elk go into the rut?"

So she said perhaps it was for fear of harassing wildlife.

That's when I first learned it's a no-no for visitors to practice bugling in Glacier.

"You mean like chasing wildlife on snowmobiles during the deep snows of winter? Does photographing elk in September constitute harassment?"

She was silent for a long time. Finally she said, "What about poaching—someone using bugling methods to poach elk?"

"Well," I said, "it takes more than a grunt tube to kill an elk. Would you let them in with a rifle or bow and arrows as long as they promised not to call elk? Don't you think you're going after the wrong tool to stop poaching?"

She said someone might use the method to call elk out of the Park.

I pointed out that it's hardly illegal to bugle for elk outside the Park boundary.

She nodded, but said, "What if someone went into the Park and lured the animal across the river in order to legally or illegally kill it?"

I really cackled at that one! A vision of the Pied Piper of Hamelin immediately came to mind, with me tootling my way down a mountainside, leading a whole raft of bull elk into camp so my hunters could select the bull of their choice without having to rise from their sleeping bags. Why didn't I think of that while I was still outfitting?

What I said, though, was: "You're stretching my credulity, ma'am, if you think that's a possible scenario. To sneak into Glacier is one thing. To cajole a wary bull elk away from his kind, through a forest and across river, takes far more technique than, to my knowledge, any human has *ever* possessed.

The ranger flashed a pinched smile, then hurried on her way. Again I was alone with my thoughts....

Why, really, is elk calling no longer permitted in Glacier? Is it because of poaching? If some creep decides to poach an elk in Glacier, do you think he'll obey a rule prohibiting bugling one to his gun?

Are hunters sneaking into the Park and luring elk to their destruction outside the Park? Come on now! We've spent an entire chapter in this book discussing the fact that you can't drive wapiti or trap wapiti. Does anyone think we can pipe them from their refuge to the butcher shop? Good God!

> Are hunters sneaking into the Park and luring elk to their destruction outside the Park?

Is it fair to ask for case histories of such examples? More to the point would be to ask about management research and the discussions that led to this prohibition. What documentation exists showing that the regulation was needed to protect wildlife in the first place?

The lady ranger did say that banning elk bugling in National Parks is within the discretion of individual superintendents—or even rangers on site. So now we get to the crux of this issue: is it the insidious and unfailing manifestation of a bureaucrat's inner urge to regulate?

Or is it that other insidious thing: that there really are too many of us scrabbling for the same finite resources? That there really are poachers plying the backcountries and frontcountries of our National Parks?

Can we all take comfort that this prohibition on a visitor letting out a surreptitious animal-like grunt in a likely looking elk covert will enable managers to apprehend the nefarious evildoers?

Is it fat chance?

Or a slim chance?

"The real question is whether you want a one-week elk season or a five-week elk season," said the Montana Department of Fish, Wildlife & Parks biologist.

I glanced up from my notepad. The man was trying to explain the controversial management question of escalating road closures on forest lands in cogent terms that every Montana elk hunter should understand. I, for one, didn't.

"Please explain."

"That's already proven down on the Targhee Forest in Idaho," he continued. "They once had a five-week elk season. But they've so cut and roaded that forest, they're down to a one-week season."

The biologist was talking about habitat, of course; specifically, escape habitat. We all need it—someplace where we can retreat to escape harassment. For humans, it can be golf courses, beaches, theaters, libraries, or wilderness. For elk, it's sanctuaries, refuges, thickets, and roadless areas. Without some sort of inviolate home, hiding place or haven

Richard Jackson

where we can relax and replenish, neither individual nor society can grow spiritually or physically.

Too many roads mean too much access; too many hunters plus too much access mean too little sanctuary—which means so many elk are harvested every year that the herd can't replenish itself. What is the result? A shortened hunting season.

Perhaps a longer hunting season isn't important to God's overall scheme of things, but I suspect it is to most hunters, no matter where they call home. And so it always should be to any state's wildlife agency. At least, that's been one of the primary objectives of my state's wildlife management for the four decades I've monitored it—to provide maximum opportunity for folks to hunt and fish.

No, I didn't say—nor do they—that their objective is to provide maximum opportunity to kill and catch. *Hunt* and *fish* are the operable words here. In my state, it's fisheries

Richard Jackson

and wildlife management *policy* to provide license holders with the maximum chance to be on lake or stream, in field or forest.

Unfortunately, the Department of Fish, Wildlife & Parks, or the citizens' Fish & Game Commission that controls it, is not the sole arbiter of wildlife fate. They aren't the only ones who control wildlife living rooms, food supplies, or hiding places. Fish & wildlife people have scant control over subdivisions and condominiums on private lands, and strip mines and road construction on federal lands. All they can do is manage species based on an available supply of wildlife that is, in turn, controlled by overall quality of its habitat.

Perhaps, in the long run, answers will lie in determining acceptable trade-offs. Will maximum roads for maximum access by maximum numbers—whether huckleberriers, the handicapped, weekend sightseers, or anyone else—mean fewer elk, fewer deer, fewer hunting and fishing opportunities?

Life is a series of trade-offs, everyone knows that. But in order to weigh those trade-offs, we need to know what they might be—all of them. Are we talking quality or quantity? Is it better to pump more gas or to retain the view from our living-room windows? Can we eat our cake and still have it, too? Should we trade outdoor heritage for values decided for us in corporate boardrooms, sometimes located in foreign countries?

In Idaho's Targhee, forest management has been so intensive that elk are vulnerable, their refuge limited. Hunting opportunity has been pared from five weeks to one. Thus, elk aficionados from that region must go elsewhere to hunt for more than a paltry few days. That's a fact worth considering when plans are being developed for management of forests elsewhere.

In the Oregon of my youth, elk seasons were usually set for two weeks in the western part of the state and four weeks over east. A hunter merely went into a sporting-goods store and purchased a license across the counter, then decided where he wished to hunt. In those halcyon days of the 1950s and early '60s, I could hunt for Roosevelt elk in the Coast Range Mountains near my home, and then join friends headed for Rocky Mountain elk inhabiting the Wallowas in the northeast corner of the Beaver State.

That's all changed. Today, an Oregon hunter must decide *where* he plans to hunt *before* buying a license: Roosevelt or Rocky Mountain elk? Say he chooses to pursue the Roosevelt variety. Then he must decide whether to hunt in the Cascade

> **Should we trade outdoor heritage for values decided for us in corporate boardrooms, sometimes located in foreign countries?**

Mountains or the Coast Range. Let's say he goes for Roosevelts in the Coast Range. But wait a minute! The Coast Range season is split into a five-day early November hunt and a seven-day late November hunt.

Aw, to hell with it, he figures—I'll head for the Wallowas and pack up the Minam River for Rocky Mountain elk. That'll solve the problem, won't it?

Except for one small detail: he must first decide whether to hunt the five-day late October season or the nine-day early November season.

What's the reason for Oregon's convoluted season hodgepodge? Is it because more hunters are after fewer elk? Or, as with Idaho's Targhee country, are more restrictions placed on hunters because of other land-management policies? Have Oregon's forests been so laced with roads and timber sales that today's wapiti have too few places where they can find refuge—a place to relax and recharge?

Are elk numbers really down in Oregon? How about throughout the West? Colorado? Utah? Arizona? Idaho? Washington? We'll take a look in the next chapter. ∎

Chapter 25

Tough Decisions

According to statistics compiled by the Rocky Mountain Elk Foundation and published in a booklet, *Status of Elk In North America*, the number of Oregon elk hunters has increased 27 percent since 1975. During those same years, elk numbers increased 35 percent, and the total elk actually harvested zoomed 46 percent. Though harder to quantify, hunting opportunity for Oregon hunters appears to have declined markedly during the same period. Why?

Scott Stouder, a respected Oregon journalist, says he's not sure hunter opportunity really has declined.

"But Scott," I said, "when I hunted elk in Oregon, the seasons were much longer than today."

"Rifle season," he replied. "But did they have archery seasons then? And let's see, we have blackpowder hunts today, and depredation hunts, and special antlerless hunts. It may be that more hunter days are available now than when you hunted in Oregon."

"Then why all the convoluted regulations: choosing between Roosevelt and Rocky Mountain species, the split seasons, split mountain ranges?"

"Don't forget the 'choose-your-weapon' split."

Why the need to make things complicated if elk numbers are up?

Craig Ely says it's because bull-to-cow ratios were so low that breeding was becoming impaired. Ely, Northeast Region Assistant Wildlife Supervisor for Oregon's Department of Fish and Wildlife, said, "At one point in the mid-'70s, bull ratios in some areas were at 0.5 to 100 cows. We *had* to do something."

"Did you say less than one bull to a hundred cows?" I blurted.

"That's right. So we began adopting a series of regulations to help us improve that ratio."

"Rather than limited entry, you mean?"

"That will be next if we can't get bull ratios where we need them to maintain healthy herds."

Thus far, Ely said, the mixed bag of regulations seem to be working. "We're up to eight bulls per hundred cows in some units. If we could reach ten, we'd probably consider that reasonable."

"Did you say less than one bull to a hundred cows?"

The Wildlife Supervisor is talking about *mature* bulls. "We have studies that show one-and-a-half- and two-and-a-half-year-old bulls will breed cows, all right, but they breed two to three weeks later than older, mature bulls. That delayed impregnation means calves born later in the spring, and that means calves going into winter two or three weeks younger. Those two or three weeks can make a critical difference to survival during a severe winter."

"What was the reason for your region's bull-ratio crash in the mid-'70s?"

"Because management decisions were made on U.S. Forest Service land—accelerated timber harvests and massive road construction associated with those harvests. That's what led to our bulls being hammered."

According to the U.S. Forest Service's Baker City office, there are 2,521,280 acres on the Wallowa-Whitman National Forest. It's a big forest.

But Scott Stouder says there are ten thousand miles of roads on the Wallowa-Whitman, "and that's just roads on the books. Nor does it include roads on private land in the region."

So I asked Craig Ely the really crucial question: "Would it be possible to achieve your bull-ratio management goals without all this split-season, choose-your-weapon, limited-entry garbage if there were more road closures limiting motorized access?"

"Yes."

"Might that mean a two-day elk season?" I asked.

"You don't even have to think about that question?"

"Not at all. That's the reason our bulls were so hammered to begin with. With proper road restrictions, our herds would all prosper."

Stouder said it more colorfully:

"If we want hunter opportunity *and* healthy elk herds, we've gotta give 'em room."

Montana's Region I Wildlife Manager for the Department of Fish, Wildlife & Parks, Harvey Nyberg, says state and national-forest road closures can help poor bull-to-cow ratios, but he's not aware of any conclusive research demonstrating that road closures are essential to overall elk populations. "We can have a lot of elk in areas that are heavily roaded, but we won't have many bulls."

Nyberg agreed, however, that security is the key to quality elk hunting opportunity. "If we want to provide opportunity for anyone to buy a license and hunt elk, then we have to provide security for the animals."

"Might that mean a two-day elk season?" I asked.

"Well, yes, that might be one way of providing security. Closing roads to provide the necessary security could be another."

Perhaps there is no conclusive research demonstrating that closing a few roads can be essential to overall elk populations, but new research spilling out of Idaho demonstrates clearly that high road densities are indeed detrimental to both hunting opportunity and bull elk quality.

Two different areas in Idaho were targeted for the study on forest-road density's effect on elk, one on the Coeur d'Alene River elk herd in Idaho's Panhandle, the other in the Clearwater River drainage. The research considered different levels of road densities. Here are some in-a-nutshell results:

Nearly two out of every three bulls were killed *each and every* hunting season in the highly roaded areas. On units of low road density, only half as many bulls were taken yearly! Using those harvest ratios, Idaho did some computer modeling. In the areas of high road densities, no bulls lived past age five, only 5 percent lived to age four, and 9 of every 10 bulls remaining for herd breeding were immature (less than three years old).

Elk are discovering unique refuges in some sectors— Subdivisions up the Roaring Fork, for instance.

In contrast, in the areas of low road density, 2 percent of the bulls lived until age ten and 30 percent lived past four years old.

The significance of those figures lies in this sentence from a report on the study contained in *Idaho Wildlife* (Winter 1993):

> Bull elk continue to add body mass until 4.5 years of age and antlers do not reach maximum development potential until bulls are 5 to 7 years old.

What the report says, then, is this: In highly roaded environments, bull elk do not live long enough to reach maximum antler growth. It also means, according to an article in the Fall 1989 issue of the same publication:

A fully roaded area open to all motorized vehicles is well suited to hunting from a pickup. But easy access and high vulnerability must be offset by relatively short seasons, or too many elk will be killed.

Here's yet another passage from *Idaho Wildlife* that covers the flip side of the coin:

> ... the potential reduction in elk vulnerability to hunt-
> ing mortality that results from road closures holds
> out the possibility of liberalized seasons and an
> increase in hunter opportunity.

Hunters aren't the only stakeholders in road restrictions resulting in bull elk growing to maturity. According to the report:

> This will give the non-consumptive user an
> increased opportunity to view mature elk and the
> hunter a better chance to harvest a trophy animal.

If it sounds as though the Idaho study of road density and elk came down on the side of reduced timber harvests, consider this:

> ... access management does not preclude timber
> harvest. Management of elk security and the supply
> of timber that is important for jobs and industry in
> Idaho can be compatible.

Lessons from the Idaho study seem clear: Drive wherever we wish and we're certain to get more restrictive hunting and wildlife-viewing opportunities. Drive wherever we wish and we're sure to see the quality of the creatures we treasure decline.

Colorado, which traditionally maintains 20 percent of America's elk, experienced a 93 percent increase in elk numbers between 1975 and 1995. During the same period, Centennial State hunters increased by 57 percent and elk actually taken increased by 60 percent.

Larry Green, Colorado Division of Wildlife Manager stationed at Glenwood Springs, said habitat changes beneficial to the animals are one reason for an increase in elk numbers. Another reason is that the animals are popular with the Colorado public, influencing his agency's management.

A third reason suggested by Green was that elk are discovering unique refuges in some sectors: "Subdivisions up the Roaring Fork, for instance, where the animals seem to have learned they can get in between the houses and be safe from hunters."

Boulder Creek, with Illahee Rock in the distance— typical elk country in the Oregon Cascades.

Despite an increase in elk numbers exceeding the increase in hunters, Colorado has gone to a plethora of seasons and restrictions, including not one but three splits in the rifle hunting seasons. A Colorado hunter must choose a five-day, twelve-day, or nine-day season. In addition, a hunter has to choose his weapon: rifle, archery, muzzleloader. Green said this compares with an early-1970s rifle season that was two weeks long.

I asked if the reason for the reduced opportunity for Colorado rifle hunters was to increase the bull-to-cow ratios, as in other states.

"No, in our case it's to spread out hunters. Maybe you can have a hundred-thousand hunters in the field and be comfortable. But when you reach two hundred-thousand, you no longer wish to hunt. The decision to split the season was actually a request hunters themselves made to our governor; they told him they were seeing too many orange vests crawling all over the countryside. So the governor came to us and ..."

"So, what about bull/cow ratios. Do you feel they're adequate in Colorado?"

"We think they're okay. We were concerned when they declined down as low as five bulls per hundred cows. Then we went to our four-points-or-better regulation, and we're up to twenty per hundred in many areas."

"As I recall," I said, "you went to the four-point [Western count] minimum in the late '80s. The regulation seems to have improved the quality of bulls taken by Colorado hunters. Are you happy with the four-point standard?"

"I think so. We still have the option of opening limited cow hunting during the last (nine-day) season. That's always a decision we make when analyzing our post-season bull-to-cow counts. Or we can issue special antlerless hunts to go beyond the mature-bull harvest. The important thing is, it leads to more mature bulls and the public likes that."

> **Hunters consider high-quality elk hunting to mean an opportunity to take a mature bull.**

I asked Green if more restricted motorized access would improve the quality of elk hunting in his district.

"Perhaps. But it isn't going to happen. The average age of hunters is rising. They're growing older. They insist on riding their ATV's and Jeeps everywhere. Politically, we won't see roads closed. It's not a question worth bothering with, because it just won't happen."

One lesson to be learned from the foregoing pages is that we can't draw broad conclusions applicable to all states and all elk herds. A thread that seems to run through my discussions with wildlife managers in every state, however, is that their hunters consider high-quality elk hunting to mean an opportunity to take a mature bull.

Without exception, mature bulls can exist only where they have at least some modicum of security. Different states have different methods of striving for that security. Several limit the number of hunters by licensing only through permits. Others limit individual hunter-days afield through split seasons, or assign designated geographic areas, or restrict opportunity through weapons choice. Still others pare season lengths, or limit harvests by sex or age classification.

With very few exceptions, hunters seek mature bull elk that are branch-antlered and heavy-bodied. But thus far—again with few exceptions—hunters seem unable to make the connection that they cannot drive wherever they wish in their four-wheelers and still have the quality bulls of their dreams—not without cutting down drastically on their opportunities to hunt. It's the experience of the Targhee over and over again: a five-week season with motorized access reduced or a one-week season with unfettered mechanized travel.

Mature bulls can exist only where they have at least some modicum of security.

Oregon's Craig Ely says his state has pretty much exhausted the options for improving bull/cow ratios. He says that if what they're doing now won't maintain adequate ratios, then the only option left for game managers would be to allow elk hunting by permit only—unless the federal land agencies elect to close some of their roads for the benefit of wildlife.

And therein lie the trade-offs that every hunter and wildlife watcher must make, either voluntarily or involuntarily. The choices are: drive wherever you wish on public land and ultimately wind up with reduced hunting opportunity through limited seasons and bag limits; or accept limits to access in order to have more opportunity to hunt or view mature bull elk.

According to the Rocky Mountain Elk Foundation's summary, *Status of Elk in North America*, Colorado has more elk than any other state (203,000 in 1995). But they also have more hunters (219,000) and more elk harvested (36,761). Oregon is second in elk numbers with 120,000, followed by Idaho (116,000), Wyoming (102,000), and Montana (93,000).

Other states with over-the-counter license sales are Washington (61,000 elk) and Utah (60,000). Arizona, with 51,000 elk, and New Mexico, with 50,000, provides only "limited-entry" hunting.

Surprisingly, hunter-to-elk ratios run close to one-to-one in states without limited-entry regulations: Oregon hunters totaled 140,000 in 1995; Idaho sold 101,000 licenses; Wyoming, 53,000; Montana, 110,000; Washington, 85,000; and Utah, 37,000.

Harvest rates followed a pattern: Colorado, 36,171; Oregon, 22,395; Idaho, 22,437; Wyoming, 17,695;

Montana, 21,961; Washington, 6,429; Utah, 9,470; Arizona, 10,139; New Mexico, 12,204.

Four Canadian provinces showed substantial elk popu-

lations: Alberta (21,000), British Columbia (49,000), Manitoba (9,000), and Saskatchewan (11,000). Nineteen thousand Albertans pursued elk in 1995, There were 13,000 British Columbia hunters, 2,900 in Manitoba, and 2,500 in Saskatchewan. Their harvests were: Alberta, 2,241; British Columbia, 2,800; Manitoba, 850. (No harvest figures are available from Saskatchewan for 1995.)

This Utah landscape was once winter range for elk. Who knows? Perhaps, someday, it will be again

Other states with small introduced or remnant herds of elk are Alaska, Arkansas, California, Kansas, Michigan, Minnesota, Nebraska, Nevada, North Dakota, Oklahoma, Pennsylvania, South Dakota, Texas, and Wisconsin. Other Canadian provinces or territories with elk are Ontario, the Yukon, and the Northwest Territories.

Today, as we enter the 21st century, overall elk numbers in Canada and the United States nudge a cool million. That compares with a beginning-of-the-20th-century level of less than a hundred thousand. The ten fold increase is due to a number of factors, including the banning of market hunting, improved wildlife management, and rising wapiti popularity with humans.

The Rocky Mountain Elk Foundation's analysis of the future for North American wapiti concludes: "Overall, states that are aiming to reduce or stabilize populations will offset the minor expansion of elk herds into remaining western habitats and elk herd restoration efforts by midwestern and eastern states."

The upshot is that "elk populations should remain fairly stable into the new millennium."

But I'm not sure the RMEF study considered *all* the trends taking place today, especially in the private sector. Many are trends that embrace the American principles of free enterprise, landowner rights, tribal treaties, and metropolitan escapees' "piece of heaven."

If I'm reading the situation correctly, those trends will enhance overall elk numbers a great deal—but only peripherally for the average hunter.

Especially for a hunter who remembers how it was in "the old days." ∎

Chapter 26

Another Jackson Hole Elk Herd?

The gaunt, sunburned man pulled the brim of his hat down to shade his eyes. Then he stared up and down the line of grim-faced riders, raised an arm, and let it fall. As he did, dozens of horsemen, some with repeating rifles balanced across saddle pommels, began chousing hundreds of cattle across forbidden ground.

The year wasn't 1866. And the riders weren't Nelson Story's hardbitten pioneer cowhands destined for far reaches of Montana Territory. The year was 1943. The forbidden ground was the newly created-by-proclamation Jackson Hole National Monument.

Those dozens of armed riders were northwestern Wyoming cowboys and cattlemen spoiling for a fight with federal agents who presumed to tell them they must now have a permit to trail cattle across what became a key component of Grand Teton National Park.

The fiercely independent ranchers of Teton County, Wyoming, sought to maintain their way of life. But according to historian Robert Righter:

> Jackson Hole seemed destined for the ubiquitous uglification coincidental with unplanned tourist development.

From the vantage of history, it seems ludicrous that

nearby property owners threatened armed insurrection in opposition to a Grand Teton National Park that guaranteed preservation of the natural character of their region, especially since that was the very thing for which they professed a willingness to fight.

Today, of course, views of Grand Teton and her sister peaks are still unmarred by the tawdry commercialism surrounding many of America's national treasures. To add another dimension to Jackson's rough-and-tumble history, today's northwest Wyoming economy is firmly rooted in tourists who come from afar to sniff of the beauty and majesty that local folks enjoy year-round—something that people of the region no longer take for granted.

The creatures were so desperate that ranchers slept on their haystacks, rifles in hand, to fend off starving elk.

Elk are no small part of the Jackson Hole mystique.

That elk are mainstay attractants to the area did not occur by happenstance—the land round about is home to our nation's greatest elk herd—and residents are justifiably proud. Just north of the town of Jackson spreads the 24,700-acre National Elk Refuge.

Concern over the welfare of the Jackson Hole elk herd began soon after settlement. As migration routes between the animals' summer and winter ranges were constricted by fences and homes, and their traditional ranges were decimated by domestic livestock grazing, periodic wapiti die-offs occurred—enough to bring cries of alarm from the very people contributing to the dilemma.

Twenty-five hundred elk were reported to have died during the severe winter of 1911, finally focusing national attention on the animals' plight. It is said the creatures were so desperate that ranchers slept on their haystacks, rifles in hand, to fend off starving elk.

Congress appropriated modest funds for emergency feeding, and additional money was appropriated in subsequent years to continue feeding and to fund the first purchases of private lands, resulting in the nucleus of the National Elk Refuge. Additional lands were acquired during the 1920s and 1930s. Then came the adjacent Jackson Hole National Monument and its subsequent inclusion in what became Grand Teton National Park.

Today, it's estimated that the National Elk Refuge contains some 25 percent of all Jackson Hole's historic winter elk range.

With additional winter ranges in Grand Teton National Park and acquired by the state of Wyoming in the nearby Gros Ventre River Valley, it's a good bet that today the Jackson Hole elk herd approximates its former numbers.

What were those numbers?

Try rolling twenty-five thousand around on the tip of your tongue. Then discover that, at one time, America's entire elk population was estimated to be no more than fifty thousand, most of which were concentrated around Yellowstone National Park and Jackson Hole. Surplus elk from the region were trapped and transported for release to a number of states and Canadian provinces. Without timely preservation of the Jackson Hole elk herd, it's easy enough to see that today's amazing recovery of the mighty wapiti might have been a different story.

According to a treatise called *Jackson Hole Elk*, written by National Elk Refuge biologist Bruce Smith and published by the Rocky Mountain Elk Foundation:

> The Jackson elk herd ranges across some 2,100 square miles, about 98 percent of which is federally administered land. This vast domain encompasses all the Snake River drainage north of Jackson, including the National Elk Refuge, Grand Teton National Park, southern Yellowstone National Park and portions of the Bridger-Teton National Forest.

The RMEF pamphlet goes on to estimate that 30 percent of the Jackson herd summers in Grand Teton, thirty percent in the Gros Ventre drainage, 25 percent in Yellowstone, and 15 percent in the National Forest's Teton Wilderness.

Smith, a biologist responsible for managing the National Elk Refuge, is a fine writer who packed his treatise with much helpful information. One particular sentence captured my attention:

> ... it is far more difficult to reduce than to produce animals in the Jackson elk herd.

Smith was responding to a dilemma all managers have faced since the critical refuge's inception: how to keep the animals from loving the place to death. As a consequence, ambitious—and expensive—winter feeding programs were instituted, and have continued.

Visitors are charmed by the animals, and the feeding programs are popular with folks in Wyoming and throughout America. In addition to the high-quality hunting that exists on surrounding public and private lands, each year thirty thousand Americans take horse-drawn sleigh rides among the wintering elk.

The Jackson Hole elk herd is one of a kind. No other place in the world can match either the productiveness or loveliness of Jackson Hole's elk environment—a fact that cannot be refuted. Or can it?

Gary Olson believes otherwise.

Olson is with Montana's Department of Fish, Wildlife and Parks. As the area wildlife biologist for north-central Montana, he is intimately familiar with the Rocky Mountain Front from the Canadian Line, two hundred miles south, to the Dearborn River. This is a landscape photographer's paradise where range after range of fault-block mountains abruptly meet the northern plains.

It, too, is a land inhabited by fiercely independent ranchers dedicated to the proposition that their way of life is worth fighting for. And it, too, is high country regularly impacted by harsh climates, high winds, and short growing seasons.

But the front has the habitat for a vast panoply of wildlife, from bighorn sheep and mountain goats to two species of bears, two kinds of deer, moose, mountain lions, wolves ... and elk. And according to Olson, it has even more important advantages. Like the Jackson region, Montana's Rocky Mountain Front has many—or most—of the components that made Jackson Hole the dynamic elk center that exists today. Olson says there's potential here for another Jackson Hole elk herd.

Winter range is, of course, the key. It's a rough rule of thumb that, amid much of the mountainous northern Rockies, ten times more summer-range forage exists for grazers than the limited winter ranges will support. One needn't have matriculated from Oxford to understand there'll be no more animals dispersing to summer range than can live through the previous winter.

But the front has the habitat for a vast panoply of wildlife ... there's potential here for another Jackson Hole elk herd.

The vast area, anchored on the west by the huge, sprawling Bob Marshall and Great Bear Wildernesses and by Glacier National Park, has a long conservation tradition among its residents. That concern first manifested itself in the 1912 legislative establishment of the Sun River Game Preserve. The 200,000-acre area was an outgrowth of early concern for the preservation of elk. Unfortunately, wildlife science was then in its infancy and very little winter range was included within the set-aside.

Bob Cooney, pioneer Montana wildlife biologist, wrote in the book, *Montana's Bob Marshall Country*:

> The future for the Sun River elk herd looked very bleak by the mid-'40s. It seemed inevitable that elk numbers would have to be drastically reduced, probably to a point where they would lose identity as a nationally recognized herd.
>
> A break came in 1948. Two large adjoining ranches became available for purchase. It was the very grass and rolling timberlands the elk had been trying to reach.

Cooney goes on to tell how the renowned biologist from the National Elk Refuge in Wyoming—Olaus Murie—visited the newly acquired Sun River Game Range and called the 20,000-acre management block "one of the very finest winter elk ranges on the Continent."

Additional private lands were acquired for winter range

along the Front, becoming the Blackleaf (11,000 acres) and Ear Mountain (3,080 acres) Wildlife Management Areas.

Private organizations contributed enormously, with Nature Conservancy's acquisition of the key Pine Butte Swamp (13,000 acres) and the Boone & Crockett Club's purchase of what is now their Theodore Roosevelt Memorial Ranch (5,400 acres), where research is done on how to ameliorate conflicts between domestic livestock and wildlife.

Elk counts have zoomed from virtually nil to a herd two thousand strong—and growing.

But it is north of all of this sprinkling of component winter ranges where the *real* potential for producing elk exists—the Blackfeet Indian Reservation. "Some of the best wildlife country in Montana is on the Blackfeet Reservation," Olson says. "I'm convinced they could produce ten thousand elk at a minimum—there's that much potential."

Perhaps the Fish, Wildlife and Parks biologist is right. Since the Blackfeet Tribal Council imposed a series of rules and regulations governing hunting by tribal members on the million-and-a-half-acre reservation, elk counts have zoomed from virtually nil to a herd two thousand strong—and growing.

Today, any Blackfeet tribal member can buy an elk license for reservation hunting. The cost is five dollars. According to tribal biologist Dan Carney, bowhunting season runs for the first two weeks of September, then rifle season opens and runs until the end of November. Twelve hundred of the Tribe's fifteen thousand members purchased elk licenses in 1997.

Couple mushrooming elk numbers with generous season length, sprinkle with unfettered opportunity and add a pinch of unusually low license cost, then mix in some of the most splendid vistas in the world, and presto! You have what may be the best elk hunting on the continent.

Olson is excited about the possibilities. "It's like the Berlin wall coming down—it's that significant for wildlife. We could be looking at another Jackson Hole elk herd. And it wouldn't take that long—ten years."

I asked Olson if similar potential for an increase in elk numbers exists south of the Blackfeet Reserve. The biologist thought not. "It's up in Blackfeet country where the real potential exists. It's up among the foothills coming out of Glacier Park where they have the mixed aspen and grasslands habitat that's so attractive to elk."

"But that's the same sort of country to the south," I protested, "the Badger-Two Medicine, Boone and Crockett, Pine Butte Swamp, Sun River."

"It's like the Berlin wall coming down—it's that significant for wildlife."

"Yes, but to the south it just doesn't have the same rich potential as the land on the reservation."

As a trained biologist, Gary Olson has my respect. But I've hiked and trailed horses over much of the land along the Rocky Mountain Front and I'm not fully convinced the man is correct in his analysis of the composite lands south of the reservation. True, the country to the south runs more to cliffs and rocky soils; it's dryer and the climate is as harsh as on the Blackfeet Reservation. But that southern portion has more than a quarter-million acres of protected habitat that is set aside to benefit wildlife—and that's a bunch.

I don't know, perhaps Olson is counting on the Tribe's recent commitment to produce elk to benefit their members, expecting that commitment to lead to his predicted wapiti yield. But it seems to me that tremendous possibilities exist for expanding wildlife numbers all along the southern half of the Front, too. Especially might that become true if those fiercely independent ranchers in the area turn more tolerant of wildlife. After all, they own the bulk of the key wintering areas in tracts intermingled with wildlife refuges.

And that's a trend already under way.

Ranching as a way of life is never easy. If it's not snow from the frozen north sweeping level with the barb wire fences, it's hail turning the oat fields to mush. There's scours in the cows and drought shriveling their grass. A hot wind blows steady from the east while dry lightning pummels ridges to the west. A blizzard blows in at calving time and prices plummet at sale time. What little hay there was got wet from a cloudburst while still in windrows. The barn needs painting and the well is near dry. There's no end to the work during the days and little sleep at night because of the next damned mortgage payment.

So why is it those who live the life are so adamant about continuing in it?

Cows are down and hogs are up. But cows are what he's got and the only hog he's interested in comes on his plate first thing in the morning. He needs salt for his stock and a night out for the little woman; but the storekeep says he's out of credit and his wallet is flat as a shingle. Then the phone rings at four a.m. and when he wakes enough to fumble for it, some damn fool from Missoula wants to hunt on his ranch at first light.

"Kee-rist!" he yells into the mouthpiece. "You wake me up from the first good night's sleep I've had in a month of Sundays to ask me will I do a favor for somebody I don't even ..."

Grande Ronde River near Troy. The surrounding hills are some of Northeastern Oregon's best winter elk range.

But wait! This dodo-head is offering to *pay*!

All across the West, landowners are turning wildlife they once considered pests into profit. It's the American way. More to the point, it may be the only way to help them stay on the land, in a way of life only they could love. Give up a $500 cow and let three wild elk eat the grass and see how many city dudes trample momma's petunias in a stampede to the front door.

Considering that half of Montana is in private hands—and most of that is the productive valley bottoms and low-elevation hillsides elk most need to survive brutal winters—the potential is enormous.

But wait! This dodo-head is offering to *pay*!

Kelly Flynn, a third-generation Montana rancher, explains—for my benefit—how much so:

> We've diversified ranch operations in order to meet our financial obligations. We raise cattle and sheep, produce hay and grain, offer summer ranch vacations, take a few hunters each fall. We've cut livestock in order for more elk to use our ranch. But there must be a way to turn a profit raising elk that wander on and off our ranch. Without an economic return, we'll no longer tolerate four hundred and fifty head of elk.

Jackson Hole is a one-of-a-kind place, world-famous for its elk herd. But other areas have the potential to at least approximate Jackson's production. A good case has been made for Montana's Rocky Mountain Front. An equally good case could be made for Oregon's northeastern corner: the Grande Ronde-Blue Mountains-Eagle Cap country. There, substantial numbers of wapiti already exist, as well as protected enclaves of public land for spring-to-fall security. As elsewhere, winter range is the key—and most of it is in private hands.

The good news is that human development has been light in Oregon's sparsely populated Baker, Union, and Wallowa Counties. As in Wyoming's Teton County and along Montana's Rocky Mountain Front, Oregon's premier elk country is peopled with folks who don't spend Sunday afternoons waxing the family sedan. Their faces are lined like roadmaps of an Indiana countryside and they spit snoose, swear some, and drape their boot heels along the polished brass rail of the nearest bar. But if you get stuck in a boghole, they're the ones likely to happen along in a mud-splattered pickup to help you out.

Most of 'em care about elk, too, just as they care about most things wild. Can there be a *third* Jackson Hole elk herd? You bet! All it takes is a little more refinement of components: a little more security, a little more winter range, a little more public commitment.

It's hard to believe Colorado, with 20 percent of America's elk, doesn't have its own Jackson Hole elk-herd potential. Perhaps it's already in place and canny Coloradans are keeping the news to themselves.

Montana Dept. of Fish, Parks, and Wildlife

And Idaho—my goodness! With as much wilderness security as already exists in the Gem State, tweaking the winter range perimeters to enhance elk numbers must be a hell of a viable option.

Those are the *easy* ones. Beyond those lie countless opportunities, depending merely on the amount of tweaking we're willing to do. It's my gut feeling that America's affection for the wild wapiti, combined with that great symbol of the free enterprise system, the profit motive, will accomplish much toward future elk enhancement.

Can there be a *third* Jackson Hole elk herd?

The animals' *real* future, however, depends upon our commitment. I know my commitment, but what's yours? ■

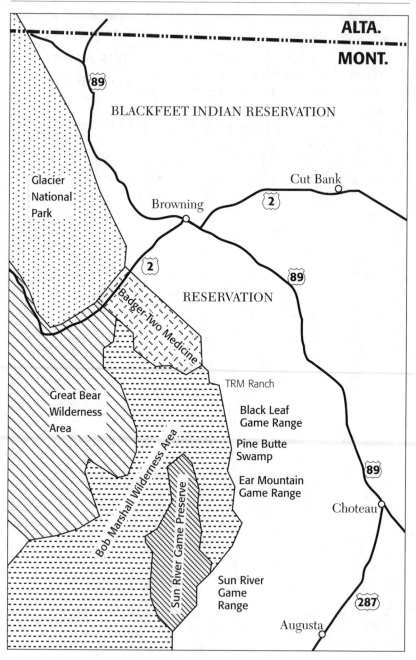

ALTA.
MONT.

BLACKFEET INDIAN RESERVATION

Glacier
National
Park

89

Cut Bank

Browning

2

Badger-Two Medicine

2

RESERVATION

89

TRM Ranch

Great Bear
Wilderness
Area

Black Leaf
Game Range

Pine Butte
Swamp

Ear Mountain
Game Range

89

Bob Marshall Wilderness Area

Sun River Game Preserve

Choteau

Sun River
Game
Range

287

Augusta

Rocky Mountain Front

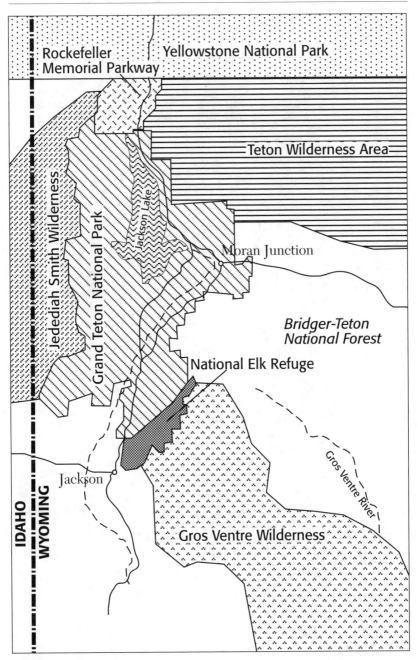

Jackson Hole Country

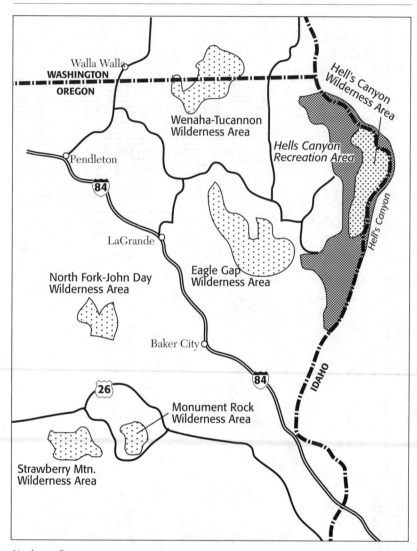

Northeast Oregon

Chapter 27

The Last Laugh

I don't know how the old fool knew to stop, but he did; paused right alongside a ten-foot spruce hanging heavy with last night's snow. First thing I looked at was the set of his ears. They weren't locked straight ahead as if the horse had spotted something up-trail. Instead, his black-tipped listeners flared like they did when he dozed without a care in the world. His head was up, though, and I could see him peeking back at me from an eye corner.

Was a time, twenty years before, when I'd have kicked him in the ribs and growled to get a move on. But that was before we'd covered upwards of twenty thousand miles over some of the toughest trails in the northern Rocky Mountains; before the big buckskin and I developed a mutual respect for each other's instincts. So I twisted in the saddle to glance behind at my three packhorses. Sure enough, the saddle on the tail animal was skewed off to one side, and so were the two bales of hay lashed to it.

Lars was already off his saddlehorse, swinging the halter rope around a ten-inch pine. "I was going to say something pretty soon," he called, "but I guess old Buck beat me to it."

I leaned forward to pat my pony-buddy on the neck. It beat all how the old veteran kept an eye on whatever packhorses he led, moving 'em at just the right pace to get maximum speed for the trail we followed. "You're quite a cayuse," I murmured.

Be nice to know how the horses communicated between themselves. How did Jughead get across to Buck that his packs were turning uncomfortable? However it was, the old leadhorse was one in a million. Most pack-strings would have plodded on until packs and packsaddle rolled beneath Jughead's belly, and there'd have been hell to pay.

"Maybe they already got their elk."

Lars had the packsaddle jerked upright and was tightening Jughead's cinch. But I swung down anyway and tramped back to him, giving each horse a reassuring pat while passing down the line. "Making good time," I said as Lars gave the bales a satisfied jerk and stepped back to run a professional eye along each of our packhorses.

He broke a twig from the tree his saddlehorse was lashed to, dug for his pocketknife, and whittled it into a toothpick. Finally he said, "Damned seldom we didn't make good time during the last thirty years—'specially when old Buck took over ramroddin' the outfit."

I unbuttoned my fly and stepped to the side of the trail. *Praise a man's horse,* I thought, *and make a friend for life.*

"Half-hour to camp," Lars said. "You don't suppose they'll have coffee on, do you?"

I shook my head. "With this fresh snow, Thad and the boy'll be looking for tracks. You can make book on that. Stove'll be out, tents cold, and only left-over grounds in the pot."

Lars flashed his I-don't-give-a-damn-it's-great-to-be-alive grin. "Maybe they already got their elk."

"Could be. Weather's been right for it."

We swung into our saddles and I said, "Okay, you old fool. Let's go to camp."

Buck stepped out. Like a giant double-jointed caterpillar, our two strings plodded behind.

We were late for this year's hunt, Lars and me. Somehow or other, we'd let the boy and Thad talk us into passing up bugling season and going for a late hunt instead. Then came mid-October, and the man Lars had lined up to pitch hay to his cows got into a bar fight and wound up in the hospital. Losing the hired hand for a month happened about the same time the cyst started growing on the inside of my left arm. I hid it long enough to go in and help set up camp and cut a little wood. But when it turned sore to touch, I came out of the mountains to let Doc McFarland drain it with a scalpel. Naturally, that was a mistake, because then it was X-rays and CAT scan and he wanted me to give up the one cigar a day I'd fought a guerrilla war to keep ever since me and the woman I love got hitched more'n four decades ago.

Well, the tests were inconclusive, but McFarland decided to cut. And when he got a chance to dig around deep, he took tissue samples. That was a week ago and he was still waiting to hear back on the samples. Meanwhile, the arm was near healed from the surgeon's axe, Lars' hired man was back at work, and we decided there wasn't nothing keeping us from joining up with Thad and the boy for a few days. The boy's grandmother kicked at the idea, but McFarland, he's a hunter, and he allowed it would be better to let us go than to see me turn cranky.

Buck angled from the main trail and headed toward camp without me touching a rein. He hadn't traveled fifty yards until we hit a little glade and I put a whoa on him. The place was cut up with elk tracks.

Lars rode alongside to say, "You're right. The boys won't be in camp."

I leaned down to make sure my old .06 slipped easily in its scabbard — though I don't know why. If the biggest bull elk in the country stepped out into that glade right now, me'n Lars would have a knock-down fight over which one *had* to shoot it.

It was only a couple of hundred yards into camp and like we figured, no smoke climbed into the still air. The boy's horse nickered at us from the corral as we pulled to the hitchracks, but Thad's was gone. I wondered at that.

As we lashed the ponies to the rails, Lars said, "Must be the lad's trailing on foot and Thad rode out to try and get ahead of 'em."

I nodded, looking around. "Can you beat that. Those elk grazed right through camp."

"This is exciting," my friend murmured. "Elk comin' to dinner!"

"This is exciting," my friend murmured. "Elk comin' to dinner!"

"You guys are in early."

Lars and I both jumped at the unexpected voice. The boy peeked from the sleeping tent.

"What are you doing here?" I said.

"Everybody's got to be somewhere, grandpa."

"Why aren't you out after elk?" I swung around to where I could see the meat pole. "None hanging. You can't have one down or you'd be out packing it in. Why aren't you after 'em, boy?"

He shrugged, stepping from the tent, rubbing his eyes, hair tousled. "Just felt like sleeping in today, I guess."

"Sleeping in? *Sleeping in!* Elk tracks in camp and you're sleeping in?"

The boy frowned, then he smiled at Lars and walked over to thrust out a hand. "Long time no see, Mr. Glickman."

Lars flashed two rows of white teeth. "The name is Lars. You do know elk has been through camp, don't you, son?"

"Huh? When?" His eyes fell to his feet where the snow was cut by our horses' tracks but still showed an occasional clear elk print. He looked beyond horse tracks to the hay tent and around the corral. The snow was filled with elk tracks. To his credit, the boy grinned and ran his fingers through his unkempt hair. "They weren't here this morning."

My eyes and Lars' met over the boy's head. "When did it quit snowing?" I asked.

"Search me. It was still coming down when I went back to bed." Then he added, "And that was right after Thad rode out."

"Which was when?"

"Dunno. About when it was beginning to lighten up."

"After daylight," I said. "They came through camp in broad day, after it quit snowing—while you was asleep and with your horse in the corral. That's a once-in-a-lifetime thing, boy. Likely they're not far ahead. Grab your rifle and get after 'em."

Instead, he walked over to a packhorse and began loosening packs. "Naw," he said. "I made up my mind yesterday that I wouldn't hunt today. Let's get these packs off, then make a pot of coffee. You guys had lunch?"

Later, as the boy stoked the stove, he said, "You and Lars can go after the elk if you want. I'll grain the stock and put 'em in the corral."

"I already got enough elk to do me two lifetimes," I growled. "What I don't understand is why you aren't hotfooting it on their trail?"

Lars cleared his throat to get our attention. His elbows were propped on the cooktent table, chin resting on palms. "Tell us about yesterday," he said. "What happened that makes you not want to hunt today?"

I almost jumped when he said, "All of a sudden, there he was!"

"I missed."

I stood spraddle-legged, listening, mad at myself for not being as perceptive as Lars.

"Well?"

"I got into 'em," the boy said, lip curling at the memory. "Up on Rainy Point. Bunch of bulls. I could tell because when they grazed, I could see tine marks in the snow."

I nodded while rocking on my heels. Rainy Point is a good place to catch elk—especially with tracking snow.

"Well, I done everything right—just like you showed me, Grandpa. Snow was soft and quiet. I came in on them with the wind in my face. Could smell 'em, knew they was close. Tracks drifted into the trees, so I half-circled to keep the wind and came in again."

"Coffee's boiling over," Lars said, and the boy whirled to cut down the burner.

When he straightened, he was looking at me, but staring at something else. I almost jumped when he said, "All of a sudden, there he was!"

The boy shifted his gaze to the coffee pot while we waited for him to sort out his tale.

"Broadside. Not over seventy-five, maybe eighty yards."

"You missed?" I said.

"I missed."

"How?"

He shrugged.

"Well, where were you aiming?"

"The neck."

"The neck! Boy, if I never told you anything else, I told you to *always* anchor an elk. Didn't I tell you always to take him in the shoulders?"

He spread his hands, then offered the pot. After he'd poured, I said, "You're sure you missed?"

"Uh huh. I couldn't believe it either. So I spent plenty of time makin' sure. Little hair and that's it. Even followed the tracks until I lost them amongst all the others. No blood. Not one drop. No. I just plain missed."

"Everybody does one time or another," Lars said. "Was he a big one?"

"Yup. Not as big as the last one you got. But big enough to take home."

"Where'd they go?" I asked.

He shrugged. "I don't know. I was so mad at myself for missing that I came on back to camp. Made up my mind I didn't deserve to get to hunt today, either."

Chock-full of pride at how the kid was developing, I smiled at Lars. Then my head snapped around and I glared. "Did you take a rest?"

He grinned. "What do you think?"

I sighed. "You'll go for the shoulder next time, right?"

His grin never wavered. "What do you think?"

Thad rode in after the shadows lengthened, but before they blended with a darkening sky. "Where'd they go?" he demanded as he swung from his horse.

"Nobody here knows," I said, slipping off the pony's bridle in order to hang a bag of oats on his head.

"You mean nobody followed them? Why not? When did

they come through?"

"We thought maybe you could tell us?"

Thad slipped his rifle from its scabbard and slung saddlebags over his shoulder while Lars stepped in to pull the saddle from the tired and sweaty horse. Thad's eyes fastened first on the boy, then mine. "They weren't there when I rode out this morning. Hell, it was still snowing. Didn't quit until probably an hour after daylight. They came through after that. Say eight o'clock." He eyed the boy again. "Where were you?"

"Sleeping."

Thad glared at the boy, Lars, and me, then he turned back to the boy, smiled, and asked, "Will it be all right if I hover around you tomorrow? That's where all the elk seem to be hanging out. Maybe you should go on back to school and see how many follow you into the classroom."

Later, Thad told how he'd gone to where the boy missed his bull and unraveled that the elk had fled into the hole of the Big Dry. He'd gone back to his horse and rode back down the mountain from Rainy Point, then around to the mouth of the Big Dry and beat his way through tag alders up that dense canyon without cutting any tracks. "They're holed up in that brush somewhere. But it's too tough for me."

If it was too tough for Thad, it was way too tough for anybody else. He was a guy who always hunted like a starving dog. Funny that such a tough-minded bachelor had a soft spot in his heart for kids—Thad may have taught the boy more about hunting even than me, the lad's own grandfather. How long ago was it when Thad was afield with the kid when he took his first elk *and* his first deer? I snapped back to the present with Thad still talking:

"The elk that came through camp will still be in these spruce bottoms tomorrow. Without anyone spooking them, they're probably still close to camp. How about if we post the boy below, where the canyon narrows along that open gravel bar? Then the rest of us can make a drive through the spruce."

The drive worked just like Thad planned—almost. Five

cows and three calves trotted across the gravel bar, right under the boy's gun. But the lone bull, a respectable five-point, doubled back through the drivers. Where he made his mistake was doubling back past Thad, who, unlike me and Lars, never paused to consider whether he wanted to shoot another elk.

Apparently Thad had also been chiding the boy for trying to shoot for the neck, because the ex-guide was quick to point out how he'd anchored the running five-point from sixty yards with one bullet through a front shoulder. Again the boy was big enough to grin and take the ribbing.

The bulls beat us to the canyon mouth, probably drifting out during the night.

A couple more days slipped by—fine sun-shiny days and crisp clear nights where the temperature sank into the teens. Still, those days were warm enough and chest-pounding enough so Lars and I tagged along while Thad and the boy pummeled the high country for a crack at the big bucks that hang out there.

The bucks eluded them, but Lars and I could care less, spending most of our time hiking through alpine country, drinking in the kind of mountain views that make a man seem small but feel big.

Most of the snow had fled from the sunny sides of the ridges and I even found a spring buttercup struggling against impossible odds to bloom one more time before winter's onslaught.

Then the weather changed. It began with rain and changed to a blowing, drifting snow. We tucked in at camp, chucking wood to the stove and gulping coffee sometimes fortified with something stouter.

The storm passed quickly, however, and when I came in at dusk with an armload of wood, I told the boy his Big Dry bulls might be on the move tomorrow and he'd ought to check.

Thad was determined to find a high-peaks buck. So the next morning Lars and I rode with the boy just in case we could help with a drive. The bulls beat us to the canyon mouth, probably drifting out during the night. But they'd also doubled back after daylight, along the more open south exposure.

We figured out what they'd done, then caucused. I suggested the boy work his way into the canyon of the Big Dry to see if he could find a bull still feeding on one of the south-facing meadows. Meanwhile, Lars and I would hike the trail up Triangle Creek, climb the ridge between our creek and the Big Dry, and work back toward where the boy hunted.

It was agreed. We left our horses tied back in the timber near where the two canyons came

That damned ridge growed a lot and turned steeper since the last time I was on it.

together. I patted the boy on the shoulder and wished him good luck. "We'll see you back at the horses around three. You got to remember, though, Lars and me aren't as young as we used to be, so hang around where you can see the second and third openings until at least two-thirty. Okay?"

He nodded. "Luck, Grandpa."

I swung away. Lars whispered, "Get him, laddie," then followed.

That damned ridge growed a lot and turned steeper since the last time I was on it. And seemed like the brush turned meaner than a bulldog with an overbite, grabbing at a man's coat and shirttail, snagging at his hands and face, tripping his feet. To top that off, halfway to the top a cold rain began falling.

Lars and I got together on the ridgetop to compare notes. Neither of us had spied any fresh elk sign. "Looks like the lad will have to do it all himself," my friend said.

I shrugged. It'd always been my strong point—the ability to make the best plan possible with the available information, then accept whatever occurred. If ours was an elkless mountain, so be it. I snuggled a little closer to the bole of our sheltering spruce and dug for a sandwich.

Lars said, "He's sure growing, ain't he?"

"What? Did you say something?"

"The boy. I remember when he wasn't much more than a wart full of questions. Now he's near got his growth. And a head on his shoulders to go with it."

I gnawed on both the sandwich and his question. It's true. The boy is turning out so as to make his grandpa proud. I said, "Remember when you wondered if he was doomed to be an unlucky hunter?"

Lars chuckled. "And do you remember when you wondered if he'd ever amount to anything?"

I chuckled with him.

By the time we started moving again, the drizzle turned to mixed rain and snow. The previous day's dry snow became saturated and so did my woolens. Every tree and bush we brushed against unloaded its wet, sagging snow load. Miserable? It'd been a while since I'd allowed myself to get caught out in this kind of weather.

We had our collars turned up and hats pulled down, plodding along, when the shot came.

The boy's tracks were there in the soggy snow when I hit the bottom of the Big Dry. Looked like he was maybe ten minutes ahead, judging by the way the chain-link soles of his rubber pacs stood out crisp and clear despite the wet. I glanced at my watch. Three-thirty. It was an hour after I told him we'd be out, so he'd waited long enough. Probably harder on him than us, sitting wet as a drowned rat on a stand, waiting. Easier to be the driver in this kind of weather.

I took off my hat and shook wet snow from it, then hunkered down to wait for Lars. That's one thing about wool—a man can be wet and still be warm. I jammed the hat in place and glanced impatiently up the canyon, expecting Lars to loom from the mist and snow at any minute.

The minutes ran to fifteen before he ambled up, and I was beginning to second-guess my wool's ability to ward off the chilling damp. "Worked my way up to the openings, just in case," he said, "but I couldn't tell whether the elk had been in there today or not."

I pointed to the boy's tracks. "I see 'em," he said. "He's not far ahead, is he?"

I shook my head, then rose and followed the rancher on down the canyon. We had our collars turned up and hats pulled down, plodding along, when the shot came. Lars whipped off his hat, cocked an ear, then turned to me with an eyebrow raised.

"I don't know," I said. "I thought I heard it, too."

The buck was lying in the snow when we walked up. Back in the trees, horses stamped at their tethers. A smoky fire licked fitfully at dead spruce branches piled high on it. The boy crouched over the buck, already finishing removal of its entrails.

He came to his feet as we neared, wiping the knife blade with a fistful of snow. The buck was a respectable four-point.

"Never figured a deer down here," I said. "Strange place for a mule deer—in this heavy timber."

The boy shook his head.

Lars poked the buck's neck with his rifle's muzzle. The neck was twice its normal size. "Sure enough in the rut," he said.

I ambled to the smoky fire, saw where the boy had crouched in the snow just beyond the flames, back against the bole of an outsized spruce. The forest was dense here, with an understory of young spruce. Visibility was limited as all hell. The deer dropped less than fifteen *feet* from where the boy had crouched. I took it all in again, not believing that a big buck, even during the rut, would let himself get so close to a human being. Near where the boy had hunkered was the imprint of his rifle's butt plate in the snow. It'd leaned against the same spruce as its owner. I shook my head and went back to the deer. The animal's tracks showed he came down the narrow trail from our horses.

Lars took a perch atop the deer carcass. He watched my tracking analysis with tolerant amusement. "Wasn't what you'd call a taxing shot, was it?" he said to no one in particular.

"A man takes what he gets," the boy replied.

I glanced at Lars. "The deer wasn't even running. Just walked right past the kid, not fifteen *feet* away. And him probably fanning the fire with his hat at the time.

"It's like Thad said," Lars replied, "they're following him around."

The boy grinned, then sobered. "One shoulder's pretty bad shot up. He's laying on it, but ..." His voice trailed off at my sudden grunt.

"You mean you shot him in the shoulder?" I said. "At only fifteen feet, you shot a deer in the shoulder?"

Lars' face broke into a huge grin and he began to chuckle. The boy snickered. Then Lars erupted and the boy started to laugh. "Go ahead and tell him!" Lars said, clasping his stomach. "Go ahead and tell him he should have shot it in the neck." ■

Chapter 28

Freezer-Filling Techniques

There was a maze of fresh elk tracks cutting the snow. *I'm getting close!* I'd spotted several bulls moving from this brush field at daylight, feeding toward the nearby forest, and it'd taken hours to climb after them. I neared the limit of my endurance. Then I heard something: "Click-clickety-click."

I paused in thigh-deep snow to catch my breath and clear sweat from a steaming face. It came again: "Click-click-clickety-click."

Bull elk fighting in late November? It can't be! I decided a bull must be sparring with a mountain-ash bush.

The bulls were there when I parted dense spruce limbs to peer between. Stark branches of a mountain ash, leaves long departed, thrust up beyond; but the bulls ignored the ash, concentrating only on each other as they thrust and parried, thrust and parried.

"Clickety-click-clickety-clickety-click."

Each bull was big. Let's see, one-two-three-four-five ... hold still, dang you! I became so mesmerized by what was taking place that I forgot that they were only jousting, while I was hunting. Neither bull put any heft into his strokes; each was as deft as a fencer, twisting their antlers, turning them, thrusting, and parrying.

I forgot my rifle, forgot everything but the moment—

and moved from behind my spruce to see better. Until he bolted off to one side, I'd not spotted the spike bull that also must have been enthralled by the sparring match. The spike, in turn, frightened two more bulls behind him, and the ensuing bedlam short-circuited my once-in-a-lifetime chance to watch a bull elk fencing duel.

After quiet settled, I stared stupidly at the rifle I cradled, then grinned at the irony and settled back in the snow to mentally reconstruct what I'd seen.

Years later, I attended a horn-rattling demonstration by a renowned Midwestern whitetail-deer expert. Like most of his audience, I sat entranced as he worked his two shed deer antlers to show us how to rattle in whitetail bucks. "Click-clickety-clickety-click. Click-click-clickety-click."

My mind turned backward; I crouched on a mountainside amid deep snow, peering between the prickly branches of a small spruce. "Click-clickety-click."

To me, it wasn't a man jamming simulated whitetail antlers together, visibly careful to keep his thumbs out of the way—"Click-clickety-click"—but two massive bull elk that had paused on their way from feeding grounds to bedding area to test the skills of a rival. "Click-clickety-click." Those bulls had attracted an audience—not only me, but other bulls, like kids in a schoolyard viewing a contest between equals.

I snapped back to the present when the whitetail expert made his pitch to sell sets of his simulated, guaranteed, never-break, fake antlers to anyone in the audience who wished to become phenomenally successful at rattling in monster bucks. But I only listened to the guy for a moment, then was gone again to a snow-covered mountain and graceful fencers, and stark mountain ash beyond.

I've wondered ever since—long after writing numerous newspaper columns and magazine articles about the many similarities between elk and whitetail deer—would horn rattling work on elk?

I never tried it, but I'm nevertheless convinced it would. What's even more intriguing, as evidenced by my experience, it just might work outside the rut.

A limb cracked, then another and another. "Run!" I hissed at my hunter.

Mike wheeled, his eyes wide.

"Run!" I hissed again.

His rifle came to the ready and he took two steps to the rear before I caught him. "Not that way!" I pointed to the sound of crackling limbs and swishing underbrush. "That way!"

Mike followed where I pointed. The noise was diminishing by then. He collapsed on a log and said, "What in hell are you talking about?"

> A limb cracked, then another and another. "Run!" I hissed at my hunter.

A forest hush descended. "Never mind," I said. "They're gone."

"What's gone?" he asked, at last tilting his rifle muzzle to the ground.

"The elk."

He leaped to his feet, swinging the muzzle back to the ready. "Where? When?"

"Up ahead. A few moments ago. Didn't you hear the noise?"

"Yeah. Was it elk making that racket?"

"Sure was. They'd heard us, or seen us, or more likely smelled us. So they headed out. In a case like that, you have one chance to get a crack at 'em. Charge ahead as fast as you can. Didn't you hear me tell you to run?"

His pencil-thin mustache trembled. "You're damn right I did. But I didn't know what you meant. Hell, I thought it might be a grizzly bear charging up behind! Or a bull moose coming from the front! Or a mountain lion crouched off to the side! I'm not a mind reader, you know."

When I quit laughing, I apologized for not explaining the strategy beforehand.

Mike collapsed back to his log, dug in a shirt pocket for a cigarette, and said, "So tell me now."

I shrugged from my daypack and settled alongside my

friend. "When a hunter is slipping through the woods in elk country and the brush starts breaking up front or off to one side, rocks rolling, limbs snapping, he can just about bet the farm it's a herd of elk taking off. Deer, now, they won't make any noise after their first jump of surprise. Bear? Maybe. But there'll only be one animal and the noise won't come from but one spot. Elk are different. You have to learn to think like them, realize you're dealing with a herd mentality, a herd animal. And besides making herd noises, elk aren't as sure-footed as deer. Bigger animals. Clumsier. They'll pop an occasional limb as they feed or walk, roll an occasional stone, but only occasionally. When a whole hillside erupts, or an entire forested ridgetop—that means only one thing: the herd knows you're there and they're getting out of Dodge."

> Sometimes it'll take a few seconds for the surprised animals to figure out what spooked their buddies.

The hunter nodded, then his forehead wrinkled. "What's the running after them supposed to do?"

"There's only one chance of getting a shot when a herd heads for the exit—and that's to run as fast as you can toward them. Lots of times one, two, or even three elk will take off while others stand and look after 'em in surprise. You damn sure need to know the pause is only momentary—sometimes it'll take a few seconds for the surprised animals to figure out what spooked their buddies."

The hunter nodded. "And that pause is when a man can dash closer."

"The *only* time. You have maybe ten seconds before the rest of those elk figure out what's going on. That's the reason the noise you just heard went on so long—all of them didn't locate their danger at once, so they charged out piecemeal."

Mike grinned. "You scared the hell out of me when you told me to run."

One of the more difficult questions I had to field from prospective elk hunters was, "What's your percentage?" At first it embarrassed me because ours was not a 100-percent success-rate outfitting service. In fact, it wasn't even 50 percent. The problem of *accepting* that we weren't to have the kind of percentages advertised by a few of our contemporaries, was mine. For the most part, our hunters seemed more practical in their expectations.

Some, as it turned out, cared more for the kind of adventures I led than whether they took home an elk. Others wished to visit spectacular country with a group of friends or family. Blown opportunities, inexplicable misses, buck fever all played a part.

It came to me early on that, though we hunted excellent elk territory and screened our hunters to exclude those who expected something for nothing, it was easier for *me* to get me on a bull elk than it was for me to get *you* on one.

So finally I began answering the 'What's your percentage?' question by asking a question: "Why don't you ask how many of our guests return?"

Or, I might ask, "How about asking how many of our guests had a *chance* to take home an elk?"

As might be expected from someone hanging out his shingle as a guide for multiple *decades*, I saw many lost opportunities. Some resulted from mechanical failure, some from human error. In order to psychologically survive, an outfitter must become philosophical about blown chances—even to the point of becoming a counselor and Father Confessor to my young guides.

"Don't worry about percentages, Rob," I would say. "The only thing we should worry about is *execution*—that we do *our* job correctly. If a plan is made and followed

This was not a blown opportunity. At least my friend Lyle was tickled.

through as planned, and nothing results, that's the luck of the hunt. But if a chance is lost because we didn't execute our part properly, then we should kick ourselves before someone else takes a crack."

The philosophical trick worked well enough that I stayed in outfitting and guiding for twenty-one years. But during all of those years, missed chances by our hunters were legion, and I never really did get over them.

"What's wrong with this gun, Roland?" he cried, near tears.

After a time, I quit trying to combat human error; elk have a way of doing that to a man—like the fine young hunter who stood mouth agape while the first elk he'd ever seen (a magnificent bull) ambled across a meadow at high noon. But the mechanical failures were something else.

Perhaps the most prevalent mechanical failures my hunters encountered was rifle-scope malfunction (most often fogging, or beads of moisture or snow on the receiver lens) or chamber, and firing-pin freeze-up during bitter weather.

"But this scope is guaranteed," one hunter protested after discovering his scope's vacuum seals weren't up to wet snow falling from trees. The manufacturer's guarantee didn't include compensation for the bull elk the man missed because his scope was fogged.

Some hunters used "flop-over" scopes, others mounted their scopes with "see-under" open sights as alternatives. Neither, in my experience, proved reliable—the flop-over because of instability; the see-under because the high mount placed the scope in an unnatural shooting alignment.

Rifle freeze-up was, of course, a constant late-season problem, and sometimes it occurred even during early season if the temperature plummeted. One such day happened in mid-october, while we were hunting out of our high-country camp. It was a turn-up-the-coat-collar morning with the temperature hovering a couple of degrees above zero.

Our trail snaked its way up a grass-covered, south-facing

hillside. The little glacier-sculpted valley that we skirted seemed an artist's rendition of wild pastoral beauty— scattered copses of trees amid lush high meadows. Our saddlehorses were as eager as we were to be out on a day like this.

We spotted a large herd of elk drifting along the forest fringe above, several hundred yards away. We tied our horses and crept within range. Charlie rested his rifle on a boulder, sighting on a huge bull that paused to gaze out over his domain. I glanced again at him. He still crouched, sighting up the hill.

There was a second large bull in the band, so I thought maybe my hunter was trying to make up his mind which of the two to take. *Damn it, Charlie,* I thought, *you'd better make up your mind pretty quick.*

Then I heard the Alabamian

This is rifle freeze-up weather.

mutter, "Aw, crap! It's a dud." Charlie wriggled into a better position to work his magnum's bolt. There was still time for a good shot if he hurried. The man pulled on the bolt, then yanked. He jerked the rifle from its perch, cradling it before him, straining to work the mechanism. "What's wrong with this gun, Roland?" he cried, near tears.

I knew right away what was wrong. The evening before, Charlie had taken the rifle into our heated cooktent for a thorough cleaning. No doubt it collected moisture from condensation with the changing temperatures. Now the bolt and firing pin were frozen. I'd had it happen to me years before, under different conditions. There was only one answer: the rifle had to be thawed enough to free the ice.

It's best never to get into such predicaments, but that's easier said than done. Climbing in and out of a warm car;

a day's hunt leading you into different moisture and temperature conditions; too much gun oil—all sorts of eventualities can lead to a stiff or iced-up weapon at a critical moment. How do you prevent it?

Most experienced cold-weather elk hunters in my part of the northern Rockies keep their weapons only lightly oiled, then wipe them clean *before* venturing out on the day's hunt. They try to keep their weapons out of warm, damp environments, too, avoiding condensation and consequent re-freezing. In our hunting camps, when we're not afield, we stacked the rifles in an unheated feed tent.

We've sometimes even pulled a rifle's bolt and laid it near a hot stove to bake all moisture from firing pin and action. And we've done the same with entire pump and automatic rifles. Afterward, we cooled them slowly and wiped them down often. If a lubricant is necessary, powdered

> Up where I headed—where the three bulls were—snow lay so deep they wallowed and plowed as they fed.

graphite is recommended—and then only sparingly.

Alas, Charlie didn't manage to thaw the firing pin in time to get the bull of his dreams. As a matter of fact, we wound up building a small fire, stripping his weapon, wiping each part down, eating lunch, and ambling up the mountain after elk that were already well on their way to Seattle.

What can you do if you discover your firing pin is frozen and a herd of elk is within shooting range? I know one solution that has worked more than once for me.

Patches of snow lay about the vehicle as I slammed its door, slung a daypack, and snatched up my rifle. Up where I headed—where the three bulls were—snow lay so deep they wallowed and plowed as they fed on the shoot ends of protruding brush.

After one more glance at the mountain, I pulled a stocking cap over my ears, turned up the wool coat collar, and trudged into the forest. I was soon drenched from rain and melting snow cascading from trees.

An hour later, quarter-sized snowflakes fell as I wriggled through a stand of doghair lodgepole pines. Wet snow clung to the trees. Squeezing through them was like bulling my way through a gaunt-let: bump one and it unloaded. I drew my collar tighter, then wiped snow from my old Springfield's barrel and action. On occasion, I'd pause to blow ice and snow from the peep sight and wipe the front bead clean.

Oh, God, no! A dud!

Up, up I trudged, growing ever more miserable, the promise of a trophy bull luring me on. Up to where the snow was drier and a light breeze whipped it from the trees. Up to where the temperature was frigid and I had to alternate gloved hands in coat pockets to keep them from freezing. Only the brisk, heat-generating climb kept me thawed enough to drive on. Up, up, until I burst from the lodgepole into the very brush field where I'd first spotted the bulls; where powder snow lay thigh-deep and gale winds gusted its surface to white-outs.

On up, now moving crablike, sidling with my back to the wind, crouching behind occasional "wolf" trees for brief shelter from the driven snow. Until at last I found the sought-after elk tracks, nearly covered by drifting powder. Now following them, ghosting along in the howling gale, until suddenly a huge bull lifted from his bed only sixty yards higher up the mountain!

I settled back into snow, throwing off the Springfield's safety, and aimed ever so carefully—the uncontrollable shaking of moments ago in temporary abeyance from an adrenaline rush—and sque-e-ezed the trigger.

Click.

Oh, God, no! A dud! I jerked at the bolt to throw in a fresh round, but it wouldn't budge. *Frozen!* The lower-elevation rain, then wet snow falling from trees, and now the freezing cold and keening wind—what could I do? With no alternative, I brought the rifle to my mouth and began blowing on the action.

Meanwhile the bull peered down, trying to unravel a gusting-snow mystery. As he twisted his head from side to side, still clearly puzzled, I panted on my rifle, willing the action to thaw. No one—not even in the heat of passion—could have panted more.

The bull had enough. He swung out to the side and plowed off, quartering away to my left through the snow. I really yanked on the bolt, and it broke free, spinning the chambered cartridge away. I flung off my daypack and lay behind it, using the pack as a steady rest for the rifle.

The rest is history. The elk rack hangs above my desk—a lesson about how, when the unforeseen happens—you improvise, brother, improvise.

Some experienced cold-weather hunters carry their rifle bolt wrapped in a dry cloth until they begin their day's actual hunt. I led two such time-tested elk hunters up a steep mountain trail a-horseback. We'd begun our ride before daylight, on our way to a series of high, distant meadows. Ten inches of powder snow lay on the ground, and the temperature hovered near zero. One man removed the bolt from his Model 70 Winchester and slipped it into the pocket of his wool coat in order to keep the firing pin moisture-free and unfrozen.

The bull had eyes only for me and my first horse.

We rode into a small sidehill meadow just as full daylight blossomed. A solitary bull stared at us, grass stems sticking from his mouth. He was a bare fifty yards away.

It was "Katie-bar-the-door" as I reined in my pony and pointed. Bud, carrying his rifle's bolt in his pocket, sat helpless atop his horse while his companion, Poke, tumbled from the saddle and ran around his pony, intending to jerk his weapon from its scabbard. The horse, alarmed at the man's frenzy, danced away while Poke muttered obscenities and danced with the steed.

The bull watched for a few seconds; long enough to satisfy himself that we weren't others of his kind. Then he decamped, disappearing into nearby trees just as the frantic hunter jerked his rifle free.

After our disappointment dimmed, we rode farther up the mountain pursuing our wapiti-Valhalla-dream. While heading up-mountain, I reconstructed the recent missed chance in my mind, wondering what we might have done different. Obviously, the outcome would have prospered had Poke slipped his rifle from its scabbard *before* dismounting. But there was something else. What?

Education is, of course, an ongoing thing, and it was another year before further pieces to the puzzle fell into place.

These antlers hang above my desk today. T₁ story is of a long stalk amid wet, cold snow. It included wind, blizzard white-outs, and a rifle freeze-up. The story really is how, amidst the unexpected, you improvise, brother! Improvise!

I led a set of hunters through a huge open basin. There was a skiff of snow. We spied two bucks running out ahead. I spurred my horse and waved to the hunters, hoping to top out on a ridge just behind the bucks.

I never saw the five-point elk feeding amid small firs only twenty-five yards to the left. Neither did the first hunter. But the last rider spotted him and he'd already slipped his rifle from its scabbard when we began our dash.

The bull had eyes only for me and my first horse. He never saw the tail rider, rifle cradled in his arms, roll from his pony. The man worked his bolt, threw off the safety, aimed, and fired.

With that incident, everything fell into place, and I began instructing guides and hunters about a new procedure to employ when we rode—or hiked—past standing elk. The first rider or hiker (the guide) *must* keep moving when curious elk or deer are encountered. So should every other rider until they've slipped their rifles from the saddle scabbards. They should then step from their horses, chamber a round, shoot, butcher, and celebrate.

As fortune had it, we were able to try the revolutionary method just a few weeks after its development. Again, I was in the lead with a couple of hunters following. We rode from a thick lodgepole forest into a hillside meadow. Eighty yards up the hill, a six-point bull grazed.

I kept my horse moving. As instructed, the hunter behind me slipped his rifle from its scabbard and rolled from his horse on the side away from the elk, thinking that his pony would continue to follow me and allow him a shooting lane. Instead, as a well-trained mountain horse should always do, Blondie stopped. Burt slapped her on the butt to get her to move, but she simply tucked her tail and stood there, ears back. Burt finally scrambled around his horse and downed the bull who still stood rooted, watching me.

With that incident, the final piece of puzzle fell into place: dismount on the side nearest the elk (our horses were all trained to do either).

To reiterate: a) the first hiker or rider must keep moving; b) the second hunter should remove his weapon from its scabbard before dismounting; c) the hunter should dismount from the side nearest the bull.

It's a great technique that proved successful many times over the years. ■

Chapter 29

Work Starts When Shooting Stops

There was no way the old man was going to take no for an answer. Way he figured it, I owed him. And maybe I did, what with me marrying his daughter, and her still wearing bobbysocks in high school. Then, too, I owed him for taking me along, after his baby and I married, when he went chasing after eastern Oregon mule deer. But the old boy was getting along toward the tail end of his life when he wanted me to take him elk hunting. And while the Oregon supermarket butcher was still in good health for his age, there was no way he was listening when I told him how tough northern Rockies elk hunting could be amid the northern Rockies.

Jane and I had moved to Montana only a few years before. The string of big bulls I took during those first Treasure State years must have made an impression on my father-in-law, because he'd never let on that he wanted to go elk hunting when I was bringing Oregon bulls to his butcher shop.

Out in Montana, I suppose he thought, Roland has horses. And some of the pictures he shows were of beautiful alpine meadows full of deer and elk. So the old boy must have got it in his head that Montana elk hunting by horseback wasn't as tough as busting through Oregon rain forests on hands and knees, and he started a campaign that

I wound up having to buy into: taking my father-in-law elk hunting. The key to his winning the argument was when he sent me the canceled check to Montana's Fish & Game Department for a non-resident hunting license.

After I threw in the towel, the *real* pressure started to build. "I been telling everybody at work," he'd say over the phone, "how I'm going out to Montana and how my son-in-law is going to get me an elk."

> "Anybody as successful at elk hunting as you've been won't have no trouble finding me a bull."

It made no difference how much I tried to explain to him that at best, elk hunting is chancey. "Sam, what you don't realize when I'm bringing big bulls in every year is that I'm hunting for *five weeks*. You're only coming to Montana for one week."

"Nine days."

"Nine days. And dang it, I'm thirty years old; you're over twice that. I climb mountains all the time; you spend your days in front of a cutting block, standing on concrete floors."

"I'm coming to Montana and get me an elk," he'd say. "And don't you forget it."

I took a couple of loads of horsefeed to an isolated basin a week ahead of our scheduled hunt, setting up camp in the process. The weather was hot and dry that September of 1967, and the danger of forest fire was so high the traditional September 15 opening date for Bob Marshall hunting was delayed. Finally it rained. Hunting season opened. Sam showed up on our doorstep like a friendly puppy dog with his tongue hanging out.

I tried to prepare my father-in-law for probable disappointment. "The weather has been so hot and dry, chances are the elk won't be in their normal places. Hunting might be tough."

He patted me on the shoulder. "Don't you worry, son, I only want one. Anybody as successful at elk hunting as you've been won't have no trouble finding me a bull."

I raised an eyebrow at Jane, so she stepped in: "Dad, what you need to realize is that he spends a lot more time hunting elk than you'll have."

"Don't make no difference. I told everybody at the supermarket that I'll be bringing home elk steaks for them. That's how it's going to be and that's that."

I'd chosen our campsite well, alongside a tiny coldwater creek, with plenty of grass for the ponies in nearby meadows. Fish were easy to catch, grouse flew into trees around camp, even deer seemed curious. But there were no elk. Not even tracks. And what was more to the point, none bugled, even from a distance.

We hunted hard, the old man dutifully dogging my every step. I bugled out my guts upon approaching every likely looking hollow or covert, to no avail. Finally I took to placing Sam on strategic ridges so I could make larger circles at a high lope, trying to cut some sign and discover where the creatures were hiding. At last the old man wore out, begging for a rest a couple of days before we were to return home.

I left camp at daylight, alone, heading on a long-abandoned trail to a densely forested mountain. Midafternoon found me struggling up a narrow creek bottom into a tiny isolated basin. Suddenly an elk crashed out ahead, clattering away through near-impenetrable brush. I had no chance to see him. But here was hope. *At last, we've found them!*

At last, we've found them!

We hadn't, though. By the sign, it looked as if one single bull had homesteaded here most of the summer. It was my bad luck that I'd blundered into the animal before crossing his tracks. But it wasn't just the best elk show we'd found, it was the only one. Unfortunately, the hike to this little basin was too long and strenuous for my father-in-law. So it seemed we were back to square one. And we had but one day left to hunt.

The moon was full—like it would swallow our entire little valley—when we turned in for the night without yet plotting a workable strategy for our last hunting day.

I was the first to awaken. *What was that?* Sam stirred in the sleeping bag nearby. Then the distant whistle came again—a far-off bull elk bugling in the full moon. I climbed from my bag and pushed the tent flap aside. The hands on my watch read 10:15, showing as plainly in the moonlight as if it was midday.

The bull bugled again, this time nearer. I moved outside, standing in my underwear, trying to pinpoint his location. Horse bells tinkled from up-canyon. The bull bugled once again—he was really on-the-peck and he was coming down the abandoned trail I'd climbed the day before! Probably the bull I'd jumped from his tiny basin. Did my spooking him awaken him to the fact that he was missing the rut? Was he just now setting out to find other elk?

I shushed him and stood barefooted on the frosty ground, mesmerized.

Sam stuck his head out the tent flap. "Is that an elk?"

I shushed him and stood barefooted on the frosty ground, mesmerized. The bull bugled again and again, coming nearer with each call. Now we could hear the deep coughing grunts that never carried as far as the whistle with which he began.

Sam slipped through the tent flap to stand beside me.

I looked at the time: 11:45. Then it was midnight. Then 12:15. By now the bull was so near we retreated inside the tent for fear we'd frighten him as he honed in on the valley where our camp lay.

Sam bent over to whisper into my ear: "You whistle once and he'll come running into our meadow. There's enough light for me to shoot."

I grinned and patted the old man on the shoulder. There was enough light for him to see the shake of my head, so he slipped back inside his bag for warmth.

Incredibly, the bull came nearer. And nearer. Then he hit the main trail and moved off up-canyon, still bugling. His was a deep-throated roar, one of the angriest-sounding I'd ever heard. Then I heard horse bells jangling, and the bull abruptly quit bugling.

The next morning found us on the move at first light. We headed up-canyon, following the bull. Though discernible tracks in the dry soil were infrequent, I did manage to make out that he forked off on a game trail, clambering up to a ridgetop that spread west of our camp.

Then we lost him.

We ate lunch on the ridgetop, and I said we might as well drop back down to camp and start getting things ready for our departure the following day. Just before we headed into a basin we'd not realized existed, I bugled one last time.

There was a reply from far below!

"I knew we'd get him," the old man said.

Again, I shushed him and we began our stalk. Sam kept looking at me, obviously wanting me to bugle again. But by his call, the elk who'd answered was a small "raghorn" and unlikely to commit to coming for battle with another, and I felt we should get right on top of him before trying again.

At last we reached a tiny clearing with a reasonably open shooting lane. I placed Sam by a log where he'd have a rest when shooting down the hill, then sat down behind and bugled long and angrily, ending with a series of grunts.

I'd not finished when an angry roar came from our immediate right. There was a screen of small firs there, only fifty feet away. The right-hand bull took us by surprise and Sam's legs tangled as he turned on his perch to peer in that direction.

The bull burst from the trees, eyes maddened and ready to do battle.

I gulped. Sam was still scrambling. The bull stopped. I actually saw the red fading from his eyes. There would be only another moment or two before the animal crashed away! I raised my rifle, threw off the safety.

There would be only another moment or two before the animal crashed away!

Then Sam's .300 Savage roared and the bull crashed to the ground.

"Told you we'd get him," the old man said.

We talked it over and decided I should go for our pack-horses while Sam butchered the bull. I was dubious, but he pshawed my hesitation aside: "I'm a butcher, boy. I know all about this kind of thing. He'll be done by the time you get back."

Personal Essentials

During the years I guided others, I furnished a what-to-bring list. It suggests no more than the bare essentials and certainly does not reflect the more advanced developments in today's outdoor-recreation equipment. But these items get you by:

Recommended Personal Gear and Clothing Lists

Fall Hunts

flashlight and extra batteries
camera and adequate film
rifle and ammo
adequate sleeping bag
foam pad or air mattress
leather boots and rubber pacs
tennis shoes for camp wear
extra socks—wool and cotton
two sets of lightweight underwear
one set heavy underwear
extra shirts—wool and flannel
extra trousers—denims or khaki
one pair wool pants
handkerchiefs
light and heavy gloves
personal toilet articles
binoculars
raingear
wool cap
moleskin

Summer Trips

Trade your rifle for a fishing rod, add necessary fishing equipment, drop the wool and your rubber pacs, throw out the heavy gloves and trade your wool cap for a wide-brimmed hat and your heavy coat for a lighter one and you're all set.

I was back in a couple of hours. The elk still lay where he'd dropped. The entrails were removed, but my father-in-law had yet to begin skinning, let alone quartering. Sweat streamed from the old boy's head. He was down to his undershirt and it clung soggily to his back.

He stood as I rode into the tiny clearing. "I always had a block and tackle before. And a place to raise 'em in the air. Tell the truth, I ain't never seen nothing so big."

I grinned, tied our ponies to saplings, and began skinning.

It was while skinning that we discovered a significant thing: though the skin was only superficially scratched, one of the bull's hindquarters was badly bloodshot. Here's my analysis:

The big bull that had passed our camp in the moonlight found the elk herd he sought, wresting the harem from this bull like brushing away a pesky fly. Unable to compete with the powerful new arrival, Sam's bull had nevertheless been on the peck and charged out to do mad battle with yet another newcomer.

At least it's a scenario that seems not only plausible, but reasonable.

Elk hunting differs from pursuing deer. And nowhere is that difference more apparent than when the shooting stops and the work starts. In a nutshell, you'd better be prepared.

I have a friend and his son who hunted behind a series

of locked gates on private forest land that's open to hunting but accessible only on foot or by horseback. My friend and his son lucked into a herd of elk, and the son took a spike bull.

"I've never seen anything so big," my friend said when he showed up at my home, hat in hand, wondering if he could borrow my horses to pack out the bull.

Because they were unprepared, the bull lay alongside a timber-company road overnight. The tag they'd placed on the bull either was removed by someone else or blew away in the wind. A game warden chanced along, thought the bull had been abandoned, and picked it up. When my friend returned to pick up his elk with my horses, the animal was gone. Naturally, the guy was lower than a busted flush when he returned my ponies, sans the spike bull.

As luck would have it, my friend found what had happened to the bull, was able to prove they'd tagged the animal, and got it back. But there's a lesson here: my friend

My Own Personal Camp Checkoff List

Though not all-inclusive, it served us well for decades:

Camp supplies
tent(s)—always canvas duck in cold weather
tent stakes (sometimes we cut our own from native material)
stove jack for stovepipe
stove and stovepipe
two-burner Coleman
axe, shovel, water bucket
pliers, hammer, nails
cooking utensils
dishes
table cloth (we usually built a table from native materials)
dish towels, towel, wash cloth, dish rag
clothespins (good for hanging many things)
garbage and recycle bags (grains sacks will double well)
two lanterns
white gas
large container for heating water
dishpan and rinse pan
extra matches and pitch (fat wood)
bailing wire
enough bulk plastic to cover tent in really foul weather
aluminum cots or foam sleeping pads
ground cloth
candles
flashlights (we used the headlamp type)
extra flashlight batteries

Kitchen staples included:
salt and pepper
hand soap and dish soap, scratcher pad
can opener
coffee, sugar, powdered milk
powdered soup
crackers
cocoa mix
a couple of dehydrated meals for emergencies
paper towels, toilet paper
first-aid kit

had no game bags, no packboards with which to pack the animal to his pickup, no axe or saw to quarter the creature. In short, he was unprepared.

"It was the first elk we'd ever seen close up," he said. "I had no idea what to do or where to turn."

"So what do you plan to do in the future?" I asked.

"Go prepared," he replied.

Other essential equipment carried in my daypack included:

Spare gloves
A stocking cap in case a storm front moved in while I was afield
A pair of nylon slip-on leggings
A down vest
Waterproof matches
A small piece of "fatwood" for ease in starting a fire
Backup food in case of an emergency.

Optional equipment might be:

A flashlight
A space blanket
And a compass

If I didn't have immediate access to horses, I always carried a packboard while hunting elk. Within the board's packsack was:

A meatsaw
Four game bags—one for each quarter
A plastic sack for the liver and heart
Some nylon cord
A small block and tackle
An extra knife
A whetstone
And a small medical kit for the inevitable finger nicks one gets when butchering an elk under less than ideal conditions.

With the opportunity to hunt elk goes responsibility to the animal—an obligation to care for it swiftly and competently. ■

Chapter 30

Maintaining Perspective

Mastering the nuances of elk hunting requires a trenchant sense of humor. Maybe it won't directly help you to put rib steaks in the round pan but you'll find it indispensable in surviving the caprices of elk and elk country.

During all the years I guided hunters into the northern Rockies, I led only two bowhunters. Rifle season traditionally began in the Bob Marshall Wilderness area we hunted on the 15th of September. With archery season beginning the weekend after Labor Day, there was too little time to squeeze in a bowhunt. But Labor Day fell early during one particular year, and I put together a six-day hunt for two swell young bowhunters from Waterloo, Iowa. Like Leo Durocher said, nice guys finish last.

The weather for the ride in couldn't have been better—sunny and warm—and we made the twenty-seven miles in good time, arriving at camp while it was still daylight. Our party consisted of the two hunters, my wife Jane as cook, and me as packer, wrangler, flunky, guide.

We were out the next morning before first light, and our mood was one of anticipation and confidence. Up one side of the valley we traipsed, with me bugling my guts out without a single answer. We worked out a side drainage after lunch, then doubled back to hunt a series of high meadows. We never heard even so much as a distant peep.

The next morning brought a driving rain on the tent canvas. By the way the three menfolk were dragging, nobody really wanted to go out in the downpour. But finally, after enough coffee was downed that we had to go outside to empty bladders anyway, we decided we might just as well work a creek drainage behind camp.

"I'm ready to go back to camp," one of the lads said.

The rain pounded down so hard water rattled through the trees like God pouring it from a celestial barrel through a divine sieve. Raingear was useless. Moisture rose from our sweating bodies to meet the penetrating downpour. Water dripped from my nose and chin, trickled down the small of my back, ran down arms and legs.

I tried bugling in the downpour, but privately expected little result—I've never had success calling elk in the rain. Even in the unlikely event that one answered, he would have had to be right on top of us or we would never hear him amid the rattle of rain.

I kept a wary eye on my two hunters, watching closely for any body language that might indicate slackening enthusiasm. None was apparent.

The temperature was falling. The rain turned cold. It began spitting snow mixed with rain.

Finally we passed a giant spruce tree with a spot of dry ground near its bole. Dead branches lay scattered about. I'd had enough. Intending to recuperate while we dried and warmed, I started to say I was going to build a fire. But I only got as far as "To hell with it, I'm going to ..." when one of them blurted, "Me, too. Let's go back to camp."

The next morning, we awakened to sixteen inches of heavy, wet snow. Ordinarily, I'd think the first heavy snow of the season would provide an excellent time to hit for the high country where there was a good chance to spot elk on the move. But that's mostly long-distance shooting, not the type safari suitable for bowhunting.

Midday found us standing miserably in a high pass, several miles from camp, snow to our thighs, wind whistling about—and we hadn't yet crossed one single elk track.

"I'm ready to go back to camp," one of the lads said.

Our rotten luck held through the next day; then it was time to go home. Our trail out began as a steep one, over a high pass and down a mountainside covered with an ancient spruce forest; down to a gloomy, brush-filled creek bottom full of muddy bogs and fallen trees. In short, this hell-hole was good elk country, and I still had hopes I could get one of my hunters a crack at a bull on the way back to civilization. So I bugled several times from the back of my saddlehorse as our string snaked down the mountain and along the muddy bottoms. Still not a peep.

I bugled one last time just before we entered the worst bog on the trail—a swamp with water and mud to the horse's knees for a hundred yards. Buck splashed into the swamp. The rest followed. We'd traveled but a few feet when a bull opened up with

both a multi-toned bugle and deep coughing grunt from the creek bottom to our left.

It was not a good day for bowhunters.

My first reaction was to consider leaping from my horse—but into swamp water to the crotch? There was no room between the felled and standing trees to turn our horses. No, we must continue on until we reached the other side, then set the hunters up in proper position and try to call the bull in. I urged Buck ahead.

Halfway through the swamp came an ear-splitting roar of an angry bull, nearer now, followed by another bugle just before we exited the swamp. The last was so close it was palpable.

It never occurred to me that our hunters, riding with five packhorses between them and me, didn't realize what was taking place. Jane, directly behind the hunters, knew,

292 • The Phantom Ghost of Harriet Lou

but she also knew how imperative it was to stay quiet.

It was just after the animal's last roar, as Buck clambered from the swamp, when one of the hunters said over his shoulder to Jane, "I don't know why Roland keeps blowing that horn—there ain't no elk in this country."

By the time he finished saying it, there weren't.

Marcus Cheek on Needle Falls Overlook glassing hillside where we spotted the same number of elk on the same date, in consecutive years.

Bob may have been out of his element. He'd hunted whitetails in Maine for a number of years, but had always reached his hunting country by boat, railroad, or automobile. His first—and only—time with me brought one of those rare glimpses proffered by the gods and certain to be swept away upon the slightest hesitation on the part of those favored.

We were only a couple of miles from hunting camp, traveling from a high pass down into a lovely valley of sweeping meadows and scattered copses. Bob had begun the ride ten hours before, full of gaiety. With every step of his horse into the Rockies, the man's good humor diminished, and now his eyes seemed glazed and it looked as though his mouth wasn't much more than a thin line slashed with a razor blade.

We paused to rest the ponies at the grade's bottom. Bob sat woodenly on his horse. I pitied the poor guy. Only a short distance more.

Then came shouts from up the hill, where other riders from our party were yet descending. An empty saddlehorse stampeded through the packstring, his rider running on foot behind, waving frantically. I reined Buck to cut the horse off and hold him for the hunter who'd allowed him to get away.

Just then, elk exploded from a stand of small firs to our left, only a hundred yards distant. They dashed across the trail, fleeing up an open mountainside to the right. Elk after elk streamed from the copse. Several were bulls.

Bob still sat his horse, showing no interest at all in this once-in-a-lifetime spectacle. "Bob!" I screamed. "Elk! Get off your horse. Elk!"

> "Bob!" I screamed. "Elk! Get off your horse. Elk!"

It had been hours since the man had said a word. Now he swung his head my way and asked, "How much farther is it to camp?"

When elk captured my spirit, they got an exclusive, and an infatuation for the great creatures tended to the toxic extreme with this farm boy turned ridge-runner. In the course of a lifetime spent stalking the wapiti, I've visited a significant share of God's most finely crafted places. During that lifetime of admiration and pursuit, many strange things have occurred—surprises, coincidences, mountain-top highs and sinkhole lows. One such high occurred during consecutive years, on exactly the same date, almost to the minute.

Jane and I conducted what we called a "Spring Explorer Trip" during the peak of wildflower season, which occurs at our latitude and mountain elevation around the tail end of June. During several of those years, we concentrated on a search for a rare orchid. It was June 30, 1980, when we led retired school librarian Doris Forkin and attractive Pennsylvanian Elene Hitz up the White River, near the geographic center of the Bob Marshall Wilderness. At a viewpoint overlooking Needle Falls, we tied our ponies to trees, dug lunches from saddlebags, and squatted on rocks to eat and admire the view.

Jane spotted the elk right away. They were across the valley, grazing at about our level on the distant grass-covered mountain.

"Ooh, there's a lot of them," Doris said.

We took turns gazing at the elk through my ten-power

Zeiss; Jane took the longest. When she handed back the binoculars, she said, "Fifty-five. There are fifty-five elk over there."

Elene asked if there were any bulls.

"Pretty far to see antlers on small bulls," I said. "They've only recently begun to develop. No big bulls that I could see."

"I saw horns sprouting on two or three," Jane added.

A year later to the day, we led another small group to the same spot above Needle Falls at lunchtime. The first thing I saw when I stepped to the overlook was elk feeding along the same distant mountainside where they'd fed on the same day the year before. I lifted my binoculars and began counting. After awhile, my voice rose a couple of octaves: "... fifty, fifty-one, fifty-*two, fifty-three, fifty-four—Godalmighty! Fifty-five elk!*

"Isn't that something!" I said, turning to one of our guests who couldn't possibly have any idea of the enormity of the coincidence.

"I saw over five-hundred one time in Jackson Hole," he said, "and they were a lot closer than these."

When the bull's throaty challenge wafted to our cliff top, both hunters stared first below, then at me. "I see him," I said, peering through binoculars. "Holy gosh, the hillside's covered with elk!"

"Where?"

> "Holy gosh, the hillside's covered with elk!"

"See that patch of alpine larch—the light green trees? Just down at about six o'clock. There's an uprooted tree ..."

"I see him!

"My God," the second hunter muttered.

"There's another bull above him!" the first hunter cried.

By then I'd counted three more bulls—all mature, with sizable racks. Moments later, we discovered numerous smaller bulls around the herd's fringe. The animals called constant challenges back and forth as we shrugged from our daypacks, dug out lunches, and found comfortable perches from which to watch. My hunters and I sat atop the Chinese Wall. That huge herd of elk, below and to the east, was in the Sun River Game Preserve.

Many folks do not know that much of the eastern portion of the Bob Marshall Wilderness is a wildlife sanctuary, off-limits to hunting. The Sun River Game Preserve—a little over 200,000 acres—was established in 1912 by an act of the Montana Legislature. The legislature's plan was for the sanctuary to provide a reservoir of wapiti that would repopulate nearby lands where the animals had been decimated by years of uncontrolled market hunting.

Pennsylvania dairy farmer Foster Hilliard and guide Scott Taylor take a break from hunting to peer into Sun River Game Preserve from crest of the Chinese Wall.

That incident along the Chinese Wall wasn't the only time I've perched on the boundary of the Sun River Game Preserve during hunting season and watched herds of elk mill about within their refuge. For those decades when I served as a Bob Marshall guide and outfitter, both my early-season and late-season camps were located within an easy ride of the preserve boundary. Many times I'd sat on the Continental Divide and drooled, thinking of the elk-hunting Valhalla that lay to the east, below my feet. Eventually the drooling turned to an obsession—and a scheme.

Finally, after my wife and I sold our outfitting business, an extensive fall packtrip into that Sun River Game Preserve became a reality. We planned to "hunt" a huge land where no one had fired a weapon in 80 years—think of it! We wouldn't be firing a weapon either, but we would be hunting elk all the same.

Four couples were in on the planning—all friends of long standing. We packed into the region in mid-August to choose a campsite with adequate horsefeed and a central location affording access to a variety of trails and terrains. Then we returned in early September. We chose a campsite well within the 1988 Gates Park burn. Recollecting old-timers' tales of the Bob Marshall's elk-hunting heyday, which came within a few years of the mammoth fires of 1919, 1927, and 1929, I was interested in how quickly elk would begin utilizing the burned-over land.

A snug camp amid the Gates Park Burn.

Our very first night in camp, a gravel-throated bull approached to offer his entire repertoire of intimidation and challenge, and my expectations appeared fulfilled. Then nasty weather set in and though we strayed occasionally from camp, our quarry stayed sheltered in their hiding places. And we may as well have remained in ours.

In subsequent days, we found a few rubs—none in the burn. Does that mean rutting bulls and cows in estrus search for green forests? Given the plethora of elk sign in virtually every bit of the burn I traveled, the wapiti used the rapidly revegetating country. But we learned that, for the most part, they abandoned it during the rut. We did spot a few scattered animals, mostly from a distance. There was one small bunch at a trailside wallow, along the edge of the burn, and a member of our party spotted one granddaddy bull, a second satellite bull, and three cows at another wallow. And I jumped a five-point still in its bed, and a spike and a cow at a natural mineral lick. But concentrations like I've observed from the Preserve boundary during my outfitting years? No.

Did we have fun?

Yes, even though there were no guns in our party. To some of our group, however, the burn appeared stark. My wife Jane was repelled by its ugliness. Another of our party considered all the burned trees "a waste" and regretted there wasn't "some way they could be removed for its economic value."

One member of our group claimed he "never even saw the burned trees," while, for my own part, I viewed only the grass that provided the most abundant horsefeed my ponies have ever experienced.

How can anyone claim to go hunting at a time and in a place where they cannot shoot an animal? How can they claim to hunt without a gun?

Perhaps if you don't already know the answer to that question, there's no adequate response. All I can say is that hunting has always been a very important part of my life and will remain so.

The thrill of the stalk—the chase; watching, studying

Leo Hargrave holds his pony as packs are lashed on for a return to civilizaton. As you may note, there's no shortage of wood in a fire's aftermath.

magnificent wild animals; the camaraderie of friends in a hunting camp; frosty mornings and crisp, clear nights; the whistling challenge of a big bull elk; all are immensely important to me. Am I to give them up simply because I don't know whether I'll shoot another animal? Don't be ridiculous!

Besides, we saw no one for nine days—except for a friendly forest ranger and his dog, who wondered what the heck we were doing. There was no shortage of easily accessed dry wood. Grass tickled our horses' bellies everywhere they stepped, and in some places reared above their backs. Trout fishing was superb, and so was their eating. And we never had to endure the sweat and pain of skinning, quartering, and packing out a tough and stringy old bull.

If you twist my arm, I'll admit that I may have experienced the world's greatest elk hunt. ■

Horses graze amid lush meadow grass springing up in years following the 1988 Gates Park Wildfire.

Chapter 31

Choosing Between Ego and Elk

"Where is it?" the hunter asked, his mouth silently shaping the words. I pointed to a small copse of alpine firs two hundred yards up the hill and a little to the right. The man peered for several long moments where I'd gestured, then shrugged as if to say, "I can't see anything."

Well, neither can I—now. But something had moved there while we labored up the mountain. It was as if an animal had stood from its bed amid the dense trees. A *big* animal. And isn't there just a hint of a motionless outline, even yet. An elk? I thought so. A bull?

I cautiously raised my binoculars, then lowered them and wiped the eyepieces clean. The hunter thrust his rifle muzzle forward between our screening small firs and peered through his scope. He shook his head. I lifted my glasses and again studied the copse. When I broke off the visual search, my hunter stared at me as if he expected an answer.

Minutes ticked by. A half-hour. The hunter fidgeted, staring my way from time to time. Still we waited. The near-zero temperature crept beneath our layered winter clothing. An hour passed. I could tell the hunter was growing restless, even angry. He stood suddenly from his crouch.

"I came to hunt. Let's hunt!"

A magnificent bull exploded from his hiding place, and with three or four mighty bounds, disappeared behind another line of trees. I didn't even have time to raise my binoculars. The hunter could only stare in open-mouthed amazement.

"We might not be so close to a bull elk again, my friend," I murmured.

The man's mouth pinched and he kicked a rock in disgust.

No human can outwait a wild animal. The patience just isn't there. We're all the time in a hurry. Either we're hurrying to get to our hunting grounds before folks from the next camp, or we're hurrying back so as not to miss supper or cocktail hour. If the creatures we hunt aren't up one canyon, then we've convinced ourselves they're in another and we hurry to get to that place.

Nope, we humans are seldom happy with where we are. Unless, possibly, we're at home with our feet propped before a crackling fireplace blaze. Elk and deer, on the other hand, are already in their living room and they're quite content to spend their idle time in any one place.

That bull had not seen us until my companion stood. Neither had he heard us until the man spoke aloud. There was no wind, so he'd not scented us. But by some sixth sense, he could *feel* something amiss. Yet what? Ever alert, he'd prepared for flight, then did nothing while he patiently waited for another danger sign.

No cocktails awaited him; he was enamored with no weekly TV soap. His mealtimes weren't ordered by a clock and his bedtime could as likely be now as then. He was, in fact, at home where he stood.

And I thought we could outwait *him*?

In this book, I've focused on animals and humans in interaction, I think I've been diligent in illustrating the wapiti's strength and intelligence and have factually represented benefits the creature gleans from herd adaptation. Too, there's been considerable focus on our own rudimentary skills amid elk living rooms, demonstrating how some of our preconceived notions can lead to the ridiculous in pursuit of North America's most challenging quarry.

But if I've properly accomplished my goals, I've also shared a few tips on wapiti weaknesses and human strengths that can aid a hunter to better understanding, and thus more success afield.

And every hunter wearing a suit of the confounded stuff makes so much noise he may as well be accompanied by a marching band.

There can be no doubt that we were under a fig leaf when God imparted crucial senses, response mechanisms, and understanding of the natural world about us. But He did give us a better brain for reasoning, year-around breeding capacity, and a set of hands that allow us to fashion tools. In fact, those God-dispensed assets are such that—unless we're also equipped with soul enough to care—threaten all too many other creatures with extinction.

Fortunately, God instilled two great levelers within us beings purported to be made in His own image: the weaknesses of vanity and a need for comfort. One is unknown to wildlife; the other of little consequence to them.

A raincoat made of the material known as Gore-Tex is tied behind my saddle's cantle. It's the best raincoat I've ever owned. Unlike previous ponchos, slickers, and jackets, this one actually sheds water while allowing body moisture to escape. I also have a pair of easy-donning leggings made of the same stuff. They'll roll up in a small package that can be tucked into saddlebags or daypack.

The way I once figured, this is the best material to come along since Joseph's coat. Now I'm not so sure.

I saw the product for the first time twenty years ago. An Eastern hunter passed through our camp wearing the new synthetic, and he swore by its weatherproof properties. Soon, there were others wearing Gore-Tex as the product's popularity mushroomed. By the time I retired from outfitting, it was common during fall to see hunters wearing full suits of the material. These days, there are rainproof outer jackets with zip-out down liners. There are coveralls, bib overalls, and bulky two-layered trousers. Even boots are made of it. So are gloves, caps, and hats.

> Raincoats should be worn in a downpour, yes. But on a crisp, cold, sky-blue morning?

And every hunter wearing a suit of the confounded stuff makes so much noise he may as well be accompanied by a marching band. Swish-swish, swish-swish. If the hunter's not swishing as he brushes tree limbs, he's swish-swishing his pants cuffs as he walks. I ground my teeth a lot when I guided hunters so equipped. It was, however, a trend that stayed. And elk hunting was never the same again.

One example was when I led a hunter clad in the synthetic garments up a ridge. By the sign, we were near a herd of elk. They fed, meandering under the canopy of an ancient spruce forest. The wind was in our favor and I guessed the creatures had no idea we approached. My hunter swish-swished along, oblivious to any problem. Finally I paused and whispered, "Henry, do you have anything on under those noisy britches?"

Clearly puzzled, he nodded. "Yeah, my underwear. Why?"

We approached only a little farther when our quarry crashed away, sounding a stampede. Henry said they must have heard me grinding my teeth.

As a result of all the noisy clothing development, we wound up not taking as many elk as we once did. Our problem was not that there were less elk. Neither was it necessarily because we had better hunters in the good old days. Instead, I wonder if it wasn't because of the technological revolution that took place in field-support material.

Raincoats should be worn in a downpour, yes. But on a crisp, cold, sky-blue morning? Whatever happened to the hunter of yesteryear who wore wool trousers and jacket? He made little noise as he slipped through the brush.

True, wool soaks up moisture and gets a bit heavy. But a

man stays warm even when wet. And above all, wool is quiet.

To some folks, though, being wet is out of fashion. Henry told me he didn't give a damn what I thought of his hunting ensemble. "Listen, Roland," he said, "it's the first outfit I've ever owned where I'm both warm and dry. And I'll be warm and dry whether I kill an elk or not."

One of my great misconceptions prior to beginning as a guide was that I doubted whether I would enjoy being around people who could both afford to pay for my services and needed someone like me to lead them to adventure—rich S.O.B.'s from metropolitan America. Almost without exception, that was a fool's idea. As a matter of fact, many of the people Jane and I led to wilderness adventure are among our fondest friends today. Careful analysis of our guests would have disclosed that a majority of hunters and anglers and hikers and riders demonstrated considerable outdoors savvy. Some even proved to be more woods-wise than their guides.

Occasionally, though, we stumbled across one who lacked a fundamental grasp of what life is about. Two such cases were when I stared into a rifle scope from the wrong direction. It's a chilling feeling.

Once I paused in a small meadow while making a drive. While catching my breath, I lifted binoculars to scan the ridgetop above. The first thing I saw was one of my hunters sitting on a boulder with his rifle pointed in my direction!

In the second or so that I froze, the man's rifle swung away into a wide arc, and I realized the guy was using his rifle scope as an observation glass to view surrounding terrain. When I reached him, I asked about binoculars.

"Naw," he said. "Never carry 'em. Just use the rifle scope."

"Uh-huh," I said, "mind if I look at your gun?" He was proud of its custom make and handed it over willingly.

When I had it firmly in hand, I said, "How would you like it if I pointed it at your head?"

"Huh?"

"Would you care if I pointed this rifle at you?"

"Are you crazy? That thing is loaded! Didn't your daddy teach you better than that?"

I stared at him until his brow wrinkled, then handed the weapon back. "Isn't that what you just did to me a few minutes ago—pointed that very same gun at me?"

His face flushed. "Hey, I was just glassing with that darned scope ..."

"Oh?" I cut in. "It'd be all right if I pointed it at your belly button as long as I looked through the scope while doing so?"

The other time I discovered someone staring at me through crosshairs was in an Oregon rainforest. Back in those days I had hunted elk only a couple of years and, being young and eager, lunged up one hill to plunge down another, sweeping through undergrowth with abandon, seeking more to outrun than to outwit. Hot on fresh elk tracks, I broke from a rhododendron thicket to confront a plaid-jacketed man holding a rifle trained in my direction! I yelped and threw myself sideways.

> I broke from a rhododendron thicket to confront a plaid-jacketed man holding a rifle trained in my direction!

The man laughed and lowered his weapon. I clambered to my feet while unfavorably analyzing his ancestry.

My daddy *did* teach me not to point a gun toward anything I didn't plant to shoot. Anytime.

If a hunter wishes to scan a far-off hillside, he or she should bring along binoculars or a spotting scope.

If a hunter spots something moving through forest or underbrush, *positive* identification should be made without the aid of a rifle scope.

If a hunter hears something coming his way on a game trail or through the brush, he should get ready, but not line his weapon until *positive* identification is made on what's creating the noise.

A rifle scope is a wonderful tool if used properly. But it's not for all purposes.

When hanging my shingle out as a guide, I accepted certain responsibilities that come with the territory. Those responsibilities included an obligation to take and train individuals who may not have had as much outdoors experience. Some of those individuals came from different cultures, different racial backgrounds, different regions, and different religions. Regardless of their background and experience, I considered it my *job* to instill in those folks the kind of outdoors acumen and ethic that I'd be proud to serve again and again.

But whereas that was my responsibility as a guide, you are under no such obligation in your own pursuit of personal adventure. Because my avocation was my occupation, I had to work with what I got. You can select your companions beforehand. Still, sometimes even that selection process turns into a crapshoot. That's why you should consider these points I once wrote in a newspaper column:

Novices tend to measure success by numbers or size of fish in the creel, pheasants in the bag, or heads on the wall. Top outdoor folk, on the other hand, learned long ago that mastery comes not from bag limits or creel counts, but from comfortable camps and cheery fires, priceless sunsets, admirable vistas, summits scaled, and trails followed.

Real outdoors folks also know there is another ingredient that can make or break any camping adventure, no matter how green the meadow, abundant the firewood, or scenic the mountains. And that ingredient is the other folks in their party. Yet some hunters spend more time assembling their gear than choosing their companions.

On the other hand, problems arising between tent mates may not stem from the other guy—it might be you. There are a few behavioral rules that might not be impor-

> **Novices tend to measure success by numbers or size of fish in the creel, pheasants in the bag, or heads on the wall.**

tant to your country-club set, but violating them is intolerable to discriminating folks visiting the big lonesome. They're worth listing:

Roland and Jane cutting camp wood.

Share the work. Nothing takes the blush off friendships as quickly as when one of your group considers himself above performing an honest share of the chores. There are no aristocrats around happy camps, no scullery maids or ladyships, barons or butlers.

One member of your party might be an expert at packing horses, another at cooking over an open campfire. But that doesn't mean they want to do it all the time or, if they do, that you shouldn't scrounge wood, carry water, or wash dishes.

Don't whine. So the weather hasn't been the best. Perhaps trails are muddy or dusty or long or steep. Maybe bugs are bad, fishing spotty, or bulls not bugling.

So what? Complaining about it isn't going to change things one iota. In fact, it'll make the situation worse for everyone else. Nobody likes being around a whiner. My favorite camping companions are those folks who are unfailingly cheerful no matter how rugged the day or dire the circumstances.

Stow the ego. Chances are you're the only person who cares how wonderful you are. Fun experiences are made of shared adventure. So you caught bigger fish down on the Firehole, or ran more exciting whitewater on the Salmon or Colorado. Who cares?

If the other folks sharing your present adventure felt a need to brag, you might be mortified to discover they floated the Blue Nile in skin kayaks and caught yellowfin tuna off Acapulco on a flyrod.

Share expenses equally. Sharing expenses is as important as sharing camp chores. If you think you'll come out ahead by someone else paying extra, think again. It's our capitalistic system at work—the person who pays the lion's share controls the trip.

Hey, it's fair!

No boss. Remember? Outdoor adventure is an egalitarian experience. No peerage, no potentates. Share the work, share the expenses. How then can anyone be the boss? The folks in your party may have to do what they're told around the house or on the job. But by the Gods, nobody yet lived who has the right to always tell another what to do around a hunting camp.

Have a meeting of the minds over the game plan and everyone has a stake in the outcome. Pick your partners, then share.

It's a formula for marriage, too.

It was late in the afternoon of the final day of hunting season. Sweat trickled from beneath the man's cap and coursed around the contour of an ear. He shifted the rifle from one shoulder to the other and snatched off his cap, tramping stubbornly on through blowing, drifting snow.

The man had been plodding like this since before daylight, climbing mountains, hiking windblown ridges, traversing canyons, trying to unravel a confusion of fading elk tracks in fast-covering snow. He was on his way back to the road when he decided to climb one last forested knob. He'd never been there before, but had glassed it from afar and knew it to be full of rock ledges and fallen timber—perhaps a dangerous place to hunt alone.

He'd taken many fine bulls in prior years. He'd been so successful, in fact, that his enthusiasm for the chase had dimmed until these last few days. Then came Thanksgiving and the late-season count-down. Three days left. Better go get his elk or spoil a good record.

He'd found elk sign easily enough amid these rugged

Our early-season hunting camp. Note the nylon corral on left.

hills, and he became caught up in the chase. But try as he might, he was unable to unravel the old tracks into fresh ones. Now it was the last day of hunting season and time running out. But what's that? Fresh tracks in the snow! Easy does it.

The man cradled his rifle familiarly, his eyes probing the immediate forest, his senses acute. He brought out a match, struck it and held it aloft. The tiniest of breezes snuffed the blaze, and a thin trail of smoke blew quartering from the right. Good. These tracks lead into the wind.

The man moved warily ahead. Another set of tracks. And another. Holy cow, a big herd. He glanced at his watch. A quarter to four. Another half-hour to forty-five minutes of daylight is all that's left. He weighed a hunter's natural instinct for caution against the limited time. The fresh tracks were so plain he could follow them at a run. And he did. The snow muffled the noise of his passage, even at the rapid pace.

He was on the cow before he saw her. She barked a warning and fled from his rush. Another cow peeled off from the left, followed closely by her calf. Instinct said to slow down, but experience told him to bolt forward into the herd before others identified the danger.

A spike bull stared at him, twigs protruding from its mouth. Another cow, and another. The man leaped a downed tree in his headlong rush, darted around a big spruce. Another cow. A small bull. Vague shapes separated from the darkening forest and scattered before him like quail from a fox. Another cow. Horns on that one—no, not big enough.

Then it was over.

Quiet fell in the forest then, except for the thud, thud, thud of the man's heart, and his labored breathing. The elk were gone. No big bulls.

You beat me this year, the man thought. *But next year ...*

It was as he'd foretold. The man was eager to hunt the following season and began another string of enviable successes. But he didn't forget lessons learned: how too much triumph can blunt desire; how his hunting image was a thing of his own making, to please himself. And he wondered about things he saw during that memorable last day: why were the elk on that particular mountain at that particular time? Was it food or security? What was the spike eating when he dashed past? Why did that single mountain thrust up by itself, away from surrounding peaks?

In subsequent years, the man's desire to shoot ebbed again, but his memory of nature's mysteries became a pulsing thing. He continued to hunt, but the urge to shoot had lost its urgency. Instead, awareness of outdoors wonders throbbed. Today the man is convinced he's a better woods-man, with a more complete understanding of his environment.

Yes, he's even a better hunter. But it's probable his marksmanship is no longer laudable.

That man is me.

Today I don't give a tiddledee damn if I shoot another elk. But I still love to hunt; still love to puzzle out where a bedded herd might be; love to stalk them and dash into their midst to case the bunch while they're still confused about what in hell is going on.

Now read the next chapter. It's another case history of a hunter who opted to take his shooting casually. ∎

Chapter 32

Great Heart and a Mile of Guts

Rufus Gehris first showed up on my doorstep with his buddy, Ted Modlens, in mid-October, 1974. They *said* they were ready to tackle the twenty-seven-mile ride into our elk camp, but privately I wondered if these two old duffers could cut the mustard. It's probably well that I didn't know the half.

Ted, the elder, surprised me. He was an accomplished horseman, in fine physical condition, with a zest for life and appreciation for all God's natural wonders. Rufus had the same zest and appreciation in spades. But he had nothing else.

The ride to camp was grueling for Rufus, though throughout the journey I never guessed how sapping it was, for the man hid his agony well. But Ted knew. When at last we pulled into camp, Ted helped his friend from his horse, Blondie, then helped him to a spot where he sprawled out of our way beneath a tree, and carried water for the sick man from the creek. Later, I discovered the water was to wash down nitroglycerin pills.

As it turned out, a weak heart was but one of the many maladies besetting Rufus: open-heart surgery the summer preceding, high blood pressure, missing ribs, blood cancer—you name it, he had it. But, God, did the man have a way of worming his heartwarming self into your mind.

Rufus rebounded quickly, but guiding for him the way we normally would for one of our guests was out of the question. A day's hunt for Rufus might be to take him by horseback out to some high point a mile or so from camp, then let him sit and admire God's craft for as long as he wished before ambling back to camp at his own pace.

One evening, Rufus was outside the tent talking to guide Kenny Averill while inside, Ted and I discussed the world's most pressing problems. "You know, Ted," I said, "Rufus is everything we'd like to see in a guest, mentally and psychologically. Physically, I wish he was hunting somewhere else."

I don't think you have any right to dictate how a man may die."

Ted told me not to worry; that he had hunted with Rufus for twenty-five years. "I've watched him get out of a hospital bed and go hunting," he said.

"That's all well and good, but I just don't want to have to pack someone out face-down over a saddle."

Ted's face actually reddened, lighting up his snow-white moustache. But when he spoke, his voice was so low I had to lean forward to catch it. "Again, I've hunted with Rufus for twenty-five years. I know that if he died tomorrow, he'd die doing exactly the thing he'd most like to do. And I don't think you have any right to dictate how a man may die."

My head fell so that I stared at a knot on our table planks. Then I looked up to meet Ted's angered glare. "You're right," I murmured.

Rufus returned the following year with another friend. The weather was some different in 1975. Snow began piling. One storm drove us into our tents for two days, then cleared. We rode out at daylight the next morning. The snow was sixteen inches deep and clinging to the trees. Rufus thought the country shrouded in snow the most beautiful thing he'd ever laid eyes on.

We weren't the only creatures moving that day; elk were on the move, too. We spotted a big band in a large open basin—really several bands feeding hurriedly on their way to winter range. I was guiding and thought it possible to get both Rufus and Pete up to elk by pushing our horses hard through the snow.

"No," Rufus said. "I'll just ride Blondie on up the trail to the pass and watch you and Pete on your stalk."

For two hours, the man stood in the snow, leaning across Blondie's back, watching through binoculars as Pete and I wound our way through a partially open, snow-laden basin, trying to overhaul a band of migrating elk. During that time, Rufus witnessed something few other hunters will ever take the time to see—a stalk from beginning to end; watched at some distance on a huge and stunning panoramic screen created by God and full of His actors.

He watched as Pete and I passed within seventy-five yards of one big bull that fed quietly, screened from us by a bend in the creek. A large bull and several cows drifted by within a hundred yards of Rufus, but he declined the opportunity because he didn't want to interfere with the hunt in progress a half-mile away.

Finally, Pete and I caught up with a bull and my hunter took it. What we didn't know, however, was that another occupied that hillside, hidden from us by the small and scattered alpine firs and lodgepole pines. Until Pete downed his one, Rufus wasn't sure which bull we were after.

Rufus came again in 1976, this time with another friend. I was standing in our driveway with my best welcoming grin when Jane brought them from the airport. But my smile turned to alarm when Rufus climbed in agony from the car and hobbled over to shake hands.

He explained that he'd fallen from a ladder at his shoe factory the day before they were to leave for their hunt and "kind of" hurt his leg and tailbone. But he was quick to add that he could make it to camp again, if we would take him.

I asked if he had been to a doctor?

"Heck no, Roland. He would've told me not to come."

So I asked if he'd like to see one of our local doctors.

"Heck no, Roland, he'd just tell me not to go."

So we went again to hunting camp. Rufus and I started a day behind the rest of our party, then took the journey slowly, for the man's suffering was intense. We laid over at the halfway point for Rufus to rest, and wound up two days behind the others. When at last we reached camp, Rufus' partner had already taken a huge mule-deer buck and a dandy mountain goat.

The following day was another great one for his partner, taking a six-point bull elk while Rufus rested in camp, unable to hunt. Another day passed. And another. The man's leg began swelling and growing more painful. I wanted to go for help, but he shook off the suggestion. At last, after supper one evening, Rufus and I were outside the tent watching the sunset. I told him I must ride out and send in a helicopter. He said he'd rather try to ride out. I told him he'd never make it. I explained there'd be few places to land a chopper if we got too far into the deep forest and he could go no farther.

I laid a hand on the man's shoulder. "Rufus, if we don't get more immediate help for that leg, you may never get to see the Bob Marshall again."

The light faded. At last, in the gathering gloom, he said, "It's so ... so beautiful."

I left camp long before daylight, riding Buck. The air-ambulance team had the injured man in a hospital by one o'clock in the afternoon. Rufus called Jane as soon as he could, and wouldn't answer any of her alarmed questions until he first told her of his partner's astounding luck.

Rufus was in the Kalispell Regional Hospital for a week after his aborted 1976 hunt. He walked with crutches until Christmas, then with a cane until hunting season, 1977, when he threw away his cane and rode to hunting camp.

It was surprising to find the man as able as ever. Rufus turned down a small four-point bull early in the hunt, and we guides privately thought the man would never kill an elk because elk were his reason for coming. Then Rufus shot our biggest bull of the season.

It all happened so fast! I'll always wonder if Rufus would've pulled the trigger had his guide not become excited at sight of the big bull and talked him into it.

Rufus was unusually meditative for days after, and I wondered if he agonized over whether he could still find reason for his annual pilgrimage. Then he brightened visibly and said, "Roland, next year I think I'll try for a big mule-deer buck."

The highlight of this particular hunt was when we met

the very Kalispell doctors who'd flown helicopter med-evac the year before. They were heading up-trail for a hunting trip of their own when they encountered Rufus, riding our party's point on Blondie.

"My God," one of the doctors cried, "it's that crazy Dutchman! What are you doing here?"

Rufus grinned, shook hands all around, then pointed to our pack-string, just rounding a trail bend, his elk's massive antlers riding atop one of the loads.

Rufus' health was precarious in 1978 and I grew more alarmed than ever. The long trip took its toll, and he had to stop only a mile from camp to rest. I laid him out on the ground and brought water. He told me which saddlebag his nitroglycerin capsules were in and asked me to bring them. He lay in agony, his face ashen, until finally that racing heart slowed. At last, his color returned and he said he thought he could make it. I helped him to his feet and onto Blondie, then led his horse the rest of the way to camp.

Rufus Gehris with bull his guide talked him into taking.

The trip took so much out of Rufus that he didn't function well throughout the hunt, popping nitros on several occasions. One day I asked why he punished himself like this on a fall hunting trip, where we ride long distances and can run into tough weather. I suggested that he consider a summer trip where we can be more casual in our daily movements and the odds of good weather are better.

"No, Roland," he said after mulling over the suggestion. "There's something about getting together with a group of men for a hunting trip that I don't think I could find in a summer trip—the camaraderie, the hunt."

After the problems Rufus had experienced the previous year, I decided to take two days with him going in. While the rest of the party went on to our high camp, Rufus and I spent the first night halfway. The next day, we took a different trail, one that climbed a mountain, then followed a high ridge for several miles. Rufus made it fine with the two shorter days of riding and was, in fact, like a kid in a candy store when he traveled new trails and saw new country.

One day, he and Robert West, with guide Rich Mattson, were single-filing up a trail in an open basin when a bull loomed from a copse of trees. Rufus never moved from his horse. Instead, his voice rose an octave as he shouted, "Robert! There's the bull you've wanted!"

It was a fitting hunt for Rufus in 1980. He was joined by his old-time Maine hunting companions, Ted Modlens and Bob Auten. But he didn't have it easy, despite making the trip to camp in stages. He did get to witness another exciting day, however, like the one in '75 when he watched Pete and me stalk Pete's elk on horseback.

Rufus and guide Kenny Averill watched from afar as a mammoth bull walked away in disdain while other members of our party tried desperately to clamber within range. And Rufus held center stage as he recounted the spectacle that evening at the supper table.

As always, at the conclusion of his 1980 hunt, Rufus rescheduled for the following year. Ted Modlens called in late March and said Rufus was in the hospital and wasn't doing well. I called Alma Gehris to ask about her husband a day or so later. She was hopeful; he seemed to be improving, and they thought he might once again pull through.

Alma said Rufus had told her she probably should "call Roland and tell him that he'd certainly like to go back to hunting camp one more year, but he doubted if it was in the cards."

"Rufus is still scheduled to hunt with us this fall," I said. "But we'll talk about it later, when he's out of the hospital and feeling better."

Ted called again on April 1. Rufus' great heart had failed him at last. "He rebounded so many times," his old friend said, "it's hard to believe he didn't make it this last time."

I hung the phone ... and my head. Tears tumbled. There were memories. ■

Chapter 33

Passing the Torch

She wore a somber, perhaps severe, dark suit. Silver-streaked hair was pulled back into a bun—just what I'd expect in a literary agent's secretary. The lady knocked discreetly on the oak paneled door, opened it, and ushered me into the inner sanctum.

"Hey!" he shouted, rising from his desk. "It's about time you visited our town."

Town? Forty-two minutes by fast-transit commuter train from the Connecticut line to downtown Manhattan and nothing but town all the way. I shook Rollie's hand, then the hand of the editor I'd traveled from a land of shining mountains to the Atlantic Ocean to meet. The editor met my eye—something no one in the commuter car had done.

"How was the ride in?" Rollie asked, taking my coat. "You stayed out at Larchmont, right?"

"With old friends. The ride in? I've been in wild-horse stampedes that weren't as scary. Likely I'd still be standing on a station platform if I hadn't had lots of coaching from our friends."

It was the truth. Rene drove me to the Larchmont Station, ran interference with a cheeky ticket agent, then led me to the best place to stand for entry into the rapid transit. After that, the decisions were no longer mine.

The train was jammed, and I wound up packed against a door with a face not six inches from mine. It was not an unpretty face, topped as it was by shiny, shoulder-length black hair shaped in a pageboy cut. Big liquid brown eyes took up a bunch of that oval, as did high cheekbones that were maybe flushed from her rush to commute. The face ended with a dainty chin that was in perfectly curved proportion to an intelligently wide forehead. And did I forget to mention the tasteful shade of pink lipstick and the faint aroma of Chanel? I've seen faces on thoroughbred mares that weren't as pretty as the one riding nose to nose with me on the train from Larchmont Station.

> **During the entire forty-minute ride, I never managed to catch the eye of one single person—not one! So this is New York.**

Yeah, sure, I know I'm old and ugly and too stove-up to attract attention from a bag lady combing through supermarket garbage. But it did hurt that the cute young thing never once looked my way—I didn't think I was *that* ugly. So I studied the well-dressed black couple standing not three feet away—he with a briefcase, she clutching his arm. The man's eyes burned a hole through a point just over my head, and she stared at the floor without so much as a twinge of expression. A bespectacled blond man in a three-piece suit studiously eyed the same spot on a folded newspaper's financial page all the way into Grand Central Station. During the entire forty-minute ride, I never managed to catch the eye of one single person—not one! So this is New York.

"Rollie," I said, "why won't anybody in this 'town,' as you call it, look me in the eye."

The agent frowned, then pushed the button on his intercom to say, "Doris, coffee, please." He waved me to a chair. "Won't look you in the eye? What do you mean?"

The editor cut in, "He must be talking about that story in the *Times* about not looking someone in the eye because by doing so, you acknowledge their presence and they'll feel threatened."

Rollie chuckled. "Must be some psychiatrist working on

a government grant. No doubt his research concluded that by looking somebody in the eye you court a switchblade in the ribs."

Just then, Doris bustled in carrying a tray loaded with what I took to be real china cups and saucers and a silver coffee pot. As she poured, I recollected how some researchers say the same thing about grizzly bears—dasn't look 'em in the eye for fear they'll take it as a threat and move to eliminate it.

"It's not that way in Montana, is it?" Rollie said, holding a cup and saucer my way. "Cream? Sugar?"

I shook my head. "In Montana, somebody don't look a man in the eye, chances are good they've just lifted your wallet, been kicked out of a convent, or they're from the government and they're here to help you."

Both men laughed, so I added, "I kept my hand on my wallet all the way into 'town'." They laughed again.

Rollie turned serious. "Eddie has a schedule to meet. You did bring a tie?"

I fingered my string tie. "I'm wearing it."

Rollie and Eddie exchanged glances. "Not right for Enrico's. You'd never make it past the door without a New York tie."

So we went instead to a dingy joint off 53rd. The light was so lousy poor Eddie couldn't see any of the sample photos I'd lugged from Montana. Wasn't enough room on the cramped table to lay anything out anyway. As it turns out, big-time book publishing is still mystifying, even after having lunch with a Simon & Schuster acquisitions editor. Leastways no contract was offered. Back at his office, Rollie waved away my concern.

"All he wanted was to get a feel for you and a free lunch out of me. Believe what I say, my man, they don't go this far unless they're serious. Take it from Rollie Damascus, the sale is on."

I glanced at my watch.

"How long will you be in town?" the agent asked.

I shrugged. "How long will it take me to get to Grand Central Station? My friends told me to catch the 3:38."

320 • The Phantom Ghost of Harriet Lou

> **"So go? I'm talking elk hunting."**

"You got lots of time. But before you go, there's something I want to talk to you about."

"What's that?"

"I want to go hunting."

"So, go."

"So go? I'm talking elk hunting."

I stared out the window, knowing where this was going. "You don't have to ask my permission."

"So you'll take me."

"Dammit, Rollie, I'm not outfitting any more. You know that."

"I still want you to take me. Hey, I sell your books, remember? I've read every page of every book. We talk on the phone at least once a month. The way I see it, I want to go with the guy who wrote the book."

I pushed up from my chair and walked to the window. "I'm too old to guide me, let alone somebody else."

Rollie had the upper hand and was agent enough to know it. He leaned back in his chair and clasped hands behind his neck. "I'm fifteen years younger than you, old man, and I'd give an arm and a leg to have your health. You take your grandson hunting every year. So what would it hurt if I tag along?"

I studied the man, this time with a different eye. Deskbound, easy-living, at least thirty pounds overweight, a tendency to sweat a lot. He tries to climb my mountains, the damnfool will be a hot candidate for a heart attack. But before I could play my best card, the sonofabitch trumped it.

"This is serious stuff, man. Eddie wants to go, too. What could be better than having your agent and the guy you're working on for a sweet book contract in a hunting camp for a few days?"

Rollie saw me hesitate, then double-trumped. "Besides, you owe me."

I sighed. "You'd ought to be the best agent money can buy, because you're a first-class bastard."

He smiled. "There's not many first-class ratings left. I'm glad you appreciate it."

Lars and Thad and the boy all sensed how important this hunting trip was, and they pitched in to make it a really great negotiating environment. Thad and Lars, of course, had lots of experience wrangling dudes in the old days, so they knew where and when to give me a boost—like leaving us alone when we wanted to be alone; like giving a little extra to make sure the tents were tight and comfortable, the woodpile plentiful, the atmosphere cordial. Lars took over my usual cooking chores, while Thad and the boy took care of the ponies. I handled all the guiding, because that was the way both Rollie and I wanted it.

> **"You'd ought to be the best agent money can buy, because you're a first-class bastard."**

The weather started out mild for November, then followed with a series of light, dry snowfalls—perfect for tracking. Trouble was, the elk proved to be no respecters of our need to punctuate nighttime discussions of contracts, plot mechanics, dialogue adjustments, and storylines with their daytime presence.

In addition to that problem, though Rollie's spirit was willing, his flesh proved as weak as I expected, and Eddie was so overwhelmed by the big lonesome that he hardly dared to leave his horse. I did get 'em both into a band of mule deer while bluebird weather still held in the high country, and we crossed elk tracks at the end of the Kettle Mountain trail. But neither of my New Yorkers had the will or the physique to return to that long trail, so we contented ourselves with riding out each morning, checking for tracks along the main trails, then returning to camp in time to catch the sun passing over the yardarm.

For their part, Lars, Thad, and the boy stayed well out of our way. Thad nailed a five-point bull down in a valley-bottom spruce thicket on day five, but the boy, hard as he hunted, kept coming up zero. I knew why—he hunted mostly with Lars, and they spent the bulk of their time wandering the high country—just what I would've done if

I was able to hunt with the lad.

Still, the fact that the boy seemed no longer driven to hunt elk troubled me, so one evening I asked him, "How come you're spending so much time up in the high lonesome, boy? I thought you came to hunt elk."

There was a faint smile and he shrugged. "I don't know, Grandpa. I guess I'm just coming to where you was all along. Elk shooting isn't as important as elk hunting."

> **"Elk shooting isn't as important as elk hunting."**

I turned owlie. One day Rollie and I coasted along a low grass-covered ridge, making a half-hearted drive for Eddie. We paused to eat a candy bar. Rollie said, "Something's bothering you? The contract's almost in the bag. Don't blow it now."

Clouds scudded fitfully across the tops of far-off peaks. Off in the distance, Grayback Mountain loomed, its cowhorn daring the lowering weather to come nearer. I glanced at my agent-friend. "You know, Rollie, I could care less about the book contract. You take care of it however you want."

He stared at Grayback. "Do I understand?"

"Probably not. I'm doing what I want to do for the rest of my life. Books? Yeah, they're important. Money? Yeah, I need some. But *this*—this is what's important. This and the boy. Now you tell me—do you understand what I'm saying?"

He fell silent. At last he said, "I'm trying."

It was on our way back to camp when we crossed the fresh set of elk tracks. The animal had climbed from the creek bottom to the east, crossed the trail, wandered while feeding through some grass-covered openings, then headed back whence he'd come. I looked for the sun, couldn't see it and consulted my watch.

"A half-hour of daylight left. We'll ride slow on our way back to camp. I want Eddie right behind. You boys keep a sharp eye out down in the bottom. Maybe this bull—and bull it is—will still be out feeding where we'll get a look at him."

We didn't. But the next day's plan was made for us.

Daylight found us patrolling that same stretch of trail.

There were more tracks in places that had none the day before. The bull had again crossed Military Creek to feed on the open meadows above the trail, then returned to cross the creek, probably to bed down.

My hunters caught the fever, but when I suggested crossing the icy creek, they took a look at the obstacle and opted to patrol farther up-canyon.

The next day was more of the same: the elk leaving his refuge to feed on our side, then returning to his day bed before first light. I pleaded with my hunters, but the editor and agent weren't up to crossing the creek to hunt the other side, even when I suggested we might be able to cross on horseback.

"Look, I've been over there before. There's a sloping bench covered with second-growth timber. It's good elk country. We'll have to hunt it on foot after we get across, but at least it's a chance."

"You know, Rollie, I could care less about the book contract. You take care of it however you want.

Eddie shook his head, so I suggested that we leave him to patrol the trail on foot. That way he could watch the bottom while I took the agent across to work out the bench. Rollie stared at the creek and Eddie in turn, then decided New Yorkers ought to stick together. "You guys do know we're going back to civilization tomorrow?" I said.

Eddie nodded. Rollie said, "It's been a good hunt. We both got our bucks. Don't worry about it."

The boy came in from Angel Basin with a lame horse. Apparently his little bay had jammed a stick into the back of his right rear leg. Lars and Thad pulled the stick and washed out the wound with water. At camp they doused it with iodine from our first-aid kit, but the pony was done for the season.

So was Lars—the rancher had cows to feed and saddles to build. Thad still hoped for a buck, so he planned to go out with us and bring back the ponies needed to pull camp. Meanwhile, the boy would stay to tend camp and do a little roaming for a bull elk on his own. Hunting season was due to end the following Sunday.

I left my old saddlehorse for the boy. "You'll need something to replace your bay. Buck's the best thing on four legs. And I can ride a packhorse on the way out."

"There's a bull working the bench across Military Creek."

"Cheyenne is good," the boy said.

Just before we pulled out of camp, I took the lad aside. "There's a bull working the bench across Military Creek. I believe he's holed up on the south end."

"How would you hunt him, Grandpa?"

"Depends on the wind. But if it was blowing up-canyon like it usually is, I'd hike to the upper end, cross the creek, and work my way down the bench until I cut tracks, then follow them. If I didn't cut tracks first, I'd approach the lower end of the bench real careful. There's a deep draw coming in from Chair Ridge, and the forest on the north bank is open enough for reasonable shooting for several hundred yards."

"Maybe I'll try it."

"Luck," I said, swinging into the saddle.

"Ride careful," he said.

I saw Rollie and Eddie off at the airport on Thursday morning. Rollie flashed a thumbs-up signal on his way through the metal detector.

Back home, I tried to catch up on correspondence, but still suffered from wilderness lag. I'd missed another year to hunt with my grandson, and his grandmother said I was accepting it none too graceful-like. So I shut down the computer, picked up a book, and read the same page a half-dozen times before throwing it across the room.

Then I donned a coat and felt-lined boots and went out to mend fence—God knows they needed it. At least that kept me busy until dark. When I came in, there was an envelope lying on the kitchen table with my name on it. When I opened the it, the card read, "Happy Anniversary From Your Loving Wife." So I surprised her by bringing out the orchid I'd never forgotten to give her on our anniversary for over forty years.

Then we went out for dinner and as much dancing as a stumblefooted old ex-outfitter could stand. The night sort of slipped away.

Friday was more of the boredom I'd found on Thursday. I expected the guys to hunt through Sunday, then pull camp and head home the next day. The boy's grandmother was cleaning up the kitchen after supper when she stuck her head around the door and said, "The guys are back."

"What guys?" I said.

> **Rollie flashed a thumbs-up signal on his way through the metal detector.**

"What guys do you think?" she replied. "Your grandson. They're pulling in now."

"That's impossible!" I shrugged into a coat and tramped outside. When I turned on the porchlight, I muttered, "Well, well, look what the cats drug home."

It was a big elk rack—no doubt about it. And it was lashed to the top of the load, like they were unusual proud. Thad climbed from the cab of the truck first, followed by the boy.

"Hmm," I said to the boy's grandma, "we brought Thad's bull home with us. This can only mean ..."

They were throwing tie-down ropes from the canvas covering their load. The boy lifted the elk rack down. "Nice bull," I said. "Who got it?"

He looked at me, eyes dancing.

I counted. The rack was seven on one side, six on the other. "Where'd you get it?"

"Later," he grunted, lifting down a heavy pack. "After we get unloaded."

Horses whinnied from the pasture, answered by horses from the trailer. When we turned them loose, they farted and rolled and galloped around the corral snorting and blowing like always when they come home. Buck stopped circling to sniff his buddies and trotted over to nuzzle me. I scratched an ear.

The canvas-covered packs still had snow and ice clinging to them, making the frozen manties and ropes hard to handle. It took a couple of hours to unwrap them all, then hang the meat and stow the gear that needed no drying. We draped the canvas manties and tents and drenched horse pads over fence rails to dry.

At last, the boy and I sat down on the porch steps. Thad joined us. "Okay, let's hear it. When did you get it?"

"He was right where you said he'd be, Grandpa," the boy said.

Thad barked. "He had it all packed to camp when I got back to camp on Wednesday."

Thad barked. "He had it all packed to camp when I got back to camp on Wednesday."

"And you got it the same day we rode out?"

"Yep. I left right after you did. Hiked to where the canyon squeezes down and the trail crosses the creek—you know where it is."

I nodded.

"Well, it's a little tough getting onto the upper end of that bench from there, but"—he broke into a smile—"I'm tough."

"Hurry up with this story, boy," Thad said. "I want to see your grandpa's reaction and I'm getting cold."

I waved toward the house. "Go on inside, Thad. There's a fire in the fireplace and unless I miss my guess, a hot buttered rum a-waiting."

Instead, the man turned up his coat collar.

"Well," the boy said, "I worked out that bench and didn't hit a track until the lower end—just like you said. Then there were a bunch of 'em. Looked like they came from the same animal, some old, some fresh. I moved to the ravine you told me about and worked up the north side of it. I was within seventy-five yards when he came up out of his bed."

"Good."

"He started to run, and I grunted like you told me sometimes worked, and he stopped cold and looked at me."

"How many shots?"

"One."

"Where'd you hit him?"

"I anchored him. I'm past getting cute."

I ran a hand over the antlers. "Pretty big elk, must've been. And you skinned and quartered him by yourself? Thad said you had it to camp when he got back. That couldn't have been easy, was it?"

"Nope. I hiked back with the horns and liver and heart, saddled Buck ..."

"With a riding saddle?"

"Didn't have nothin' else. Then I went back and loaded the front quarters."

"What'll they go—maybe a hundred each?"

Thad said, "We weighed a hind before we hung it in the garage. Weighed a hundred and twelve."

I shook my head. "Good-sized bull. I don't see how you got it up on a riding saddle alone."

The boy shook his head. "I'm not sure how, either. Especially the last load, because I was wearing out. But gosh, Gramps, I only knew I just had to do it, because my grandpa would."

> "But gosh, Gramps, I only knew I just had to do it, because my grandpa would."

I reached out to lay a hand across his shoulder. Thad said, "When I rode in, he had a lantern hanging in a tree, standing by them horns, with his arms folded. 'Looks like you got him,' I said. And he said, 'Yep. I'm ready to go home now.'"

I squeezed the boy's shoulder. "Well, boy, you've done everything I've done."

He shifted on his perch as I continued.

"You've taken a seven-by-six and that's the biggest I ever took. You've butchered and packed in a hell of a bull all by yourself. And I, too, have done that."

He turned in interest.

"You've even packed in a big bull on a riding saddle, just like I had to do a time or two. And you did it on Buck— my old saddlehorse—who's been such a partner for so long. But you haven't done one thing I've done."

His brow wrinkled. "What's that?"

"You haven't yet lived to see your grandson do it." ■

Our son, Marc, with seven-point bull he took at eighteen. Note boxes of packaged meat—good winter's chewing.

Afterword

It was while following this book's trail that I came to realize just how much the Rocky Mountain Elk Foundation has meant to the American wapiti. In existence for little more than a decade, RMEF has been single-minded in pursuit of habitat to benefit elk, no matter where they exist. Across international boundaries, amid suburbia or wilderness, near tidewater or on mountaintop, in the East or in the West, I usually discovered that RMEF biologists, fund-raisers, counselors, or administrators had been there before.

The American wapiti might have made it without the organization dedicated to their benefit. But if I were an elk, I'd like to have the Rocky Mountain Elk Foundation co-signing my notes, too. ■

Resources

Chapter 9

Elk of North America, compiled and edited by Jack Ward
Thomas and Dale E. Toweill; Stackpole Books, 1982.

The Elk of North America, Olaus Murie; Stackpole Books,
1951. "Elk Speciation: Genetics or Environment" / Bugle,
Fall/1990. "An Evolutionary Primer-History of the American
Wapiti" / Bugle, Winter/1990.

The Journals of Lewis and Clark.

Chapter 14

"Kansas City, Here I come" / *Montana Outdoors*, May/June,
1991.

"Sweetgrass Hills Elk Monitoring Project"—1991; Gary Olson.

Wapiti, Journal of the Rocky Mountain Elk Foundation, Winter, 1992.

Selected news reports.

Key interviews: Gary Olson, biologist-Montana Department of
Fish Wildlife & Parks; Jim Pyland, Kansas City Metro Services Coordinator, Missouri Department of Conservation.

Chapter 24

Oregon Big Game Regulations, 1998.

Chapter 25

Status of Elk in North America, 1975-1995, compiled by Dwight Bunnell; produced by The Rocky Mountain Elk Foundation.

"Elk Management in a Nutshell," "Gateways to Good Hunting" / *Idaho Wildlife*, Fall, 1989.

"Idaho Is Elk Country" / *Idaho Wildlife*, Winter, 1993.

"Bull Talk" / *Montana Outdoors*, Nov/Dec, 1992.

Oregon Big Game Regulations, 1998.

Key telephone interviews: Scott Stouder, journalist, Corvallis, Oregon. Craig Ely, N.E. Region Assistant Wildlife Supervisor, Oregon Dept. of Fish & Wildlife. Harvey Nyberg, Region I Wildlife Manager, Montana Dept. of Fish, Wildlife & Parks. Larry Green, Colorado Division of Wildlife Manager, Glenwood Springs.

Chapter 26

Jackson Hole Elk (produced by the Rocky Mountain Elk Foundation), Bruce Smith.

History and Management of the National Elk Refuge (pamphlet), John Wilbrecht and Russell Robbins, NER. Edited/updated by James Griffin, NER, Dec., 1995.

Theodore Roosevelt Memorial Ranch Elk Study / Gary Olson, Les Marcum, Thomas Baumeister; Montana Dept. of Fish, Wildlife & Parks; University of Montana, School of Forestry (1994)

Lewis & Clark National Forest Record of Decision, Oil & Gas Leasing, August, 1997

Selected newspaper accounts:

Index

Want More of Roland?

Roland's writings can also be found weekly in his syndicated column *Wild Trails and Tall Tales*. Here are a few samplings from his hundreds of articles.

Cornice Watching
April 2, 1997

Under the wrong conditions, most folks would consider the activity a yawner. But when you catch circumstances just right, my wife and I consider cornice watching to be an exciting way to spend an afternoon.

Uh, come again? Cornice watching. Hit it right—as the cornices are breaking off and falling and triggering avalanches—and you can predictably witness an exciting, unfolding page of the powers of nature at work.

First off, it must be a warm (ideally sunny) day. The aspect must be right, snow levels just so, cornices in place, and your personal safety assured. When it comes to cornice watching, one can be as avant-garde as one wishes. Jane and I have sat in lawn chairs, sipping cocktails while observing the annual phenomenon of falling cornices.

We first discovered the thrill of this most unusual activity while visiting Glacier Park's St Mary's area in early May. We were ostensibly there to observe elk. It was mid-afternoon of one of those rare, warm, sunny spring days when one could see for two lifetimes. We coasted into a roadside pullout at the edge of a sagebrush/bunchgrass meadow where dozens of elk grazed. In order to better see, we clambered from our vehicle, binoculars in hand. Suddenly there was a loud snap, followed by what we took to be rolling thunder.

Jane's already oversized Irish eyes were the size of dinner plates as I turned to search the skies for the thunder source. Then I shrugged and lifted binoculars to study the elk. They had not seemed to notice the clap or the thunder.

Another report came, again followed by rolling thunder. "What's going on?" I muttered, again turning to search the sky.

"It's an avalanche!" Jane said. "See? Across the way, running down the slope of that tallest mountain."

I looked where she pointed. The evidence of a fresh avalanche was there right enough, but it had stopped running by the time I located it. Then there was another report and we both searched to the right of Jane's first avalanche, catching the beginning of yet another avalanche.

"It's the cornices!" I shouted. "They're breaking and falling, triggering avalanches."

Another loud report, followed by yet another rumble came from the far left of the ridge we watched.

Jane lifted the hatchback on our car and pulled out a lawnchair. I grinned and followed her example, going one better by setting out the ice chest. "Lunchtime," I said.

A relentless sun beat upon our south-facing ridge as we sat glassing in shirtsleeved leisure, betting we could pick the next drift to fall. Those great snow ledges were originally formed via gale force winds winging out of the frozen north, blowing across the ridgetop and depositing drifting snow in great overhanging cornices. Now, as winter loosed its icy hand, we had ringside seats.

On another year, we skied up Josephine Lake at Many Glacier while cornices fell from a ridge to our right. But the day wasn't sunny and warm—not the best weather for leisurely observation. ■

One Last Time
July 4, 1997

It would be impossible for love to flourish more between man and horse. He was a buckskin, standing 15-1 hands high and weighing an even 1,200-pounds. I was still in the blush of young manhood, uncertain about what was possible, let along do-able. Buck came to me as a six-year-old, unbroken. His taming proved marginal. And only my obtuse stubbornness made the accomplishment possible.

How it happened we became inseparable friends was probably as much surprise to the black-maned pony as to me. But it's indisputable that we had a great 26-year run—the big buckskin and the man who loved him with passion.

I tried to retire the old horse late in life. It wasn't because he'd lost his endurance or agility or willingness, but because he was 26 years old. For his part, the aging buckskin wanted nothing of it. If I started the stock truck in the spring, here came Buck loping in from the pasture. If I dropped the tailgate and began loading other horses, here was Buck trying to crowd into his old up-front place.

Disgusted after a time, I took the big horse, at age 28, for one last wilderness adventure. Though I walked leading him much of that week, I was amazed at the buckskin's performance. Just as of old, Buck led the packstring at a steady four-miles-per-hour. Just as of old, Buck was, each morning, near camp waiting for his oats when I rolled from my sleeping bag. Just as of old, Buck stood easily for the saddle, swelled with the cinch and allowed me to "surprise" him by yanking it three inches tighter a couple of minutes later. There could be no doubt, the old horse was his old self. And he seemed to accept, at last, that he must stay home while he friends left for adventure.

Buck died at 32. He may have died of a broken heart because he could no longer do the things he once did—I don't know.

The reason for this tale is I'm now where Buck was and that jolt of insight has given me pause to think. At age 62 I'm no longer pretending I can do all things I once did. Or can I?

Oh pshaw, Roland! You can't climb a mountain as fast as you once did. True, but can I not still climb any given mountain, given the time and inclination?

Thirty years ago, I first poked my nose into a high, wild basin. The trail there was grueling, exhausting to man and beast. But it was the exact spot for which I'd spent decades in search; it was lonesome, surrounding views gorgeous, sweet water burbled from a rock cliff, horse feed plentiful, and the country filled with wild game. I went back each year until I began outfitting.

I've not been back to that wild place in 25 years. But as I grow long in the tooth, I lean more toward Buck's philosophy of wanting to at least try to do some of the things I once did. That such earlier adventures were more often inspired by ignorance than spirit doesn't mean one last attempt to recapture those halcyon days might not be stimulated by spirit alone this time around.

Buck! Oh, Buck! If only you were here to join me one last time. What's that you ask? What then if he was? That's easy. If we were to make it to my favorite spot, then we'd consider trying it one more "last" time. ■

Order form for Roland Cheek's Books

See list of books on reverse side

Telephone orders: 1-800-821-6784. *Visa, MasterCard or Discover only.*

Visit our website: www.rolandcheek.com

Postal orders: Skyline Publishing
P.O. Box 1118 • Columbia Falls, MT 59912
Telephone: (406) 892-5560   Fax (406) 892-1922

Please send the following books:
(I understand I may return any Skyline Publishing book for a full refund—no questions asked.)

Title	Qty.	Cost Ea.	Total
_____	_____	$ _____	$_____
_____	_____	$ _____	$_____
_____	_____	$ _____	$_____
		Total Order:	$_____

Ship to: Name_____

            Address_____

            City_____ State_____Zip_____

            Daytime phone number (_____)_____-_____

Payment: ☐ Check or Money Order

            Credit card: ☐ Visa ☐ MasterCard ☐ Discover

Card nunber_____

Name on card_____Exp. date___/___

Signature:_____

Other Books by Roland Cheek

Non-fiction

Chocolate Legs 320 pgs. 5-1/2 x 8-1/2 $19.95 (postpaid)
An investigative journey into the controversial life and death of the best-known bad-news bears in the world. by Roland Cheek

My Best Work is Done at the Office 320 pgs. 5-1/2 x 8-1/2 $19.95 (postpaid)
The perfect bathroom book of humorous light reading and inspiration to demonstrate that we should never take ourselves or our lives too seriously. by Roland Cheek

Dance on the Wild Side 352 pgs. 5-1/2 x 8-1/2 $19.95 (postpaid)
A memoir of two people in love who, against all odds, struggle to live the life they wish. A book for others who also dream.   by Roland and Jane Cheek

The Phantom Ghost of Harriet Lou 352 pgs. 5-1/2 x 8-1/2 $19.95 (postpaid)
Discovery techniques with insight into the habits and habitats of one of North America's most charismatic creatures; a guide to understanding that God made elk to lead we humans into some of His finest places.   by Roland Cheek

Learning To Talk Bear 320 pgs. 5-1/2 x 8-1/2 $19.95 (postpaid)
An important book for anyone wishing to understand what makes bears tick. Humorous high adventure and spine-tingling suspense, seasoned with understanding through a lifetime of walking where the bear walk. by Roland Cheek

Montana's Bob Marshall Wilderness   80 pgs. 9 x 12 (coffee table size) $15.95 hard-cover, $10.95 softcover (postpaid) *97 full-color photos, over 10,000 words of where-to, how-to text about America's favorite wilderness.* by Roland Cheek

Fiction

Echoes of Vengeance 256 pgs. 5-1/2 x 8-1/2 $14.95 (postpaid)
The first in a series of six historical novels tracing the life of Jethro Spring, a young mixed-blood fugitive fleeing for his life from revenge exacted upon his parents' murderer. by Roland Cheek

Bloody Merchant's War 288 pgs. 5-1/2 x 8-1/2 $14.95 (postpaid)
The second in a series of six historical novels tracing the life of Jethro Spring, a young mixed-blood fugitive fleeing for his life from revenge exacted upon his parents' murderer. by Roland Cheek

Turn page for order form